THE LORD
of DEATH

THE LORD
of DEATH

Eliot Pattison

Copyright © 2009 by Eliot Pattison

Published by
Soho Press, Inc.
853 Broadway
New York, NY 10003

Library of Congress Cataloging-in-Publication Data

Pattison, Eliot.
The lord of death / Eliot Pattison.
p. cm.
ISBN 978-1-56947-579-9 (alk. paper)
1. Shan, Tao Yun (Fictitious character)—Fiction. 2. Ex-police
officers—Fiction. 3. Politicians—Crimes against—China—Fiction.
4. Assassination—Fiction. 5. Fathers and sons—Fiction.
6. Prisoners—Fiction. 7. Tibet (China)—Fiction.
I. Title.

PS3566.A82497L67 2009
813'.54—dc22
2009005421

10 9 8 7 6 5 4 3 2 1

This book is dedicated to the people of Tibet.

Chapter One

No one ever died on Mount Chomolungma, the sherpas always told Shan Tao Yun when he was sent to retrieve a body. A man might freeze so hard his fingers would snap like kindling, his bones might be shattered in a thousand-foot fall, but the mother goddess mountain—Everest to Westerners—captured their spirits, keeping them alive and within her grip for her own purpose. They weren't exactly alive, but they weren't dead in the traditional sense, an old sherpa had warned him, as if Shan should expect the corpse he conveyed to be summoned back up the mountain at any time. More than one of Shan's new friends in the climbing camps insisted that in the winds blowing from the summit they sometimes heard the voices of those who had died years earlier. Shan glanced at the snow-capped peak as he soberly tightened the rope fastening his canvas-wrapped burden to the pack mule, lightly resting his hand for a moment on the roundness that was the dead man's shoulder. This one had been a friend. If Shan heard the voice of Tenzin Nuru on the wind he would recognize it.

He had taken several steps down the trail when the lead rope jerked him backward. The old mule, his steady companion on such treks, refused to move. Shan studied the high, windblown landscape warily, trusting completely in the animal's instincts. The Tibetans always gave him the same mule, a graceful long-legged creature, whose bright intelligent eyes followed Shan attentively as he recited ancient Chinese poems during their descents with the dead. Its ears were back now, its head cocked.

He heard the sound of hooves on the loose gravel a moment before a small horse, saddled but riderless, burst over the low rise ahead of them. Rock and roll music blared from a battered tape player suspended on a string from the pommel; an old bolt action rifle dragged in the dirt, hanging on a broken strap. Shan's heart sank, then he leapt for the reins to stop the horse and grabbed the gun, deftly popping out the magazine and tossing it into the rocks. He glanced quickly about for a side trail to flee down. Then, finding none, tossed his coat over his cargo, calmed the horse by stroking its neck, and shut off the music.

A moment later a man in a tattered gray uniform trotted over the rise, panting, spitting a quick curse as he recognized Shan. He paused and straightened his tunic, awkwardly accepted the rifle from Shan, then turned the weapon around and aimed it at Shan. "In the name of the People's Republic I arrest you," the man said in a weary voice.

Shan stroked the horse's neck. "On what charges today, Constable Jin?"

The constable, a Tibetan in his mid-thirties who had assumed a Chinese name when he'd put on the Chinese uniform, eyed the mule's cargo uncertainly. "Murder?" he offered in a hopeful tone. Jin Bodai did not work for the dreaded Public Security Bureau but for the county, as a law enforcement functionary whose main job consisted of checking on permits and writing up traffic violations.

Shan watched patiently as Jin tucked his carbine under one arm then untied the outer rope on the mule's bundle, exposing Tenzin's head. The constable lifted the head by the hair, bent closer to study it, then dropped it, and looked back at Shan with a quizzical expression.

"Any doctor," Shan explained in a steady voice, "even those in Tingri county, would tell you this man died at least two days ago. A dozen people could testify I was with them two days ago, in town, working at the warehouse."

Jin, more peeved than ever, jabbed the gun toward Shan again. "Still," he ventured, "a man without his papers, an illegal carrying a corpse. It would be enough to get me off this damned mountain at least."

"You lost your ammunition, Constable." Hardly a week went by when the two of them did not spar, but more than once Shan had rescued Jin by preparing paperwork needed for China's vast law enforcement bureaucracy.

Jin opened the bolt of the gun, saw the hole where the magazine should have been then cursed again, in the tone of a crestfallen child. "A piece of junk, like everything else they give me," he groused. The gun, like his uniform and nearly everything else used by his small office in Shogo town, was a hand-me-down from the Public Security Bureau.

"Illegal transportation of a corpse might work," Shan suggested. "Even unlicensed disposal of the dead."

The constable brightened. "I arrest you for illegal transport of a corpse."

"But not this day," Shan continued in a fatigued voice. The mule nudged him, as if reminding him of their task. "Not this corpse."

Jin sighed, lowering the rifle. "Why not?"

Shan pulled a bottle of water from one of the packs, poured some into his cupped hand for the mule to drink. "Because this sherpa is from Nepal. Take us in and you'll have to call Public Security, who will begin asking how a foreigner got across the border in your district without papers. A dead foreigner. Then there's a whole other set of paperwork for international shipment of bodies. You'll spend a week filling out papers, and you won't have me to help if I am behind bars."

Jin winced.

"Then," Shan said, "you'll spend the rest of the season dealing with all those who complain about how bad it is for business to suddenly have policemen flooding the Westerners' climbing camps."

The constable worked his tongue in his cheek. "Better than chasing this damned nag up and down the mountains."

The mule gave Shan another impatient nudge. It seemed to be

remembering, as Shan did, that they still had miles to go before turning the body over to villagers from Tumkot, where Tenzin's kin waited for his body. "Then you won't do it," Shan said with a tinge of shame, "because if you hold me up any longer I will not return to work on time and in this county the man I work for is the senior Tibetan member of the Party."

The constable sagged. He extracted a crumpled pack of cigarettes, lit one as he settled onto a flat rock then studied Shan with a suspicious air. "There's a name for people like you on the other side of the ranges," he observed as he exhaled a column of smoke. "Untouchables. Disposers of the dead and other garbage. The lowest caste of a low society. You're Chinese. You're educated. Why do you let them do this to you?"

"I prefer to think of it as a sacred trust." Shan extracted two apples from a pouch on the mule's harness, offered one to the horse, the other to his mule. As he did so he studied the equipment hanging from Jin's saddle, noting for the first time the heavy ammunition belt tied around rain gear at the back of the saddle, beside the portable radio Jin usually left switched off in the field. "What particular war did you come up here to fight, Constable?"

Jin frowned. "I left headquarters to check out a report of stolen climbing equipment. Ropes and harnesses taken from the base camp two days ago."

"But?"

"I was stopped by a Public Security lieutenant with a truck-load of troops. A security alert has been declared, he announced. Minister Wu, head of tourism, is traveling up the road to the base camp today. So the lieutenant changed my orders."

"They didn't give you all that ammunition because of tourists."

Jin inhaled deeply on his cigarette, studying Shan, no doubt weighing how much he needed Shan to navigate the bureaucracy. He shrugged. "Since the road was going to be closed they decided to do a fidelity raid, at Sarma gompa, one of the little monasteries up the valley. Just one bus, with an escort of knobs," he explained, using the common slang for soldiers of the Public Security Bureau.

Shan fought a shudder. After destroying nearly every monastery in the region decades earlier, Beijing had allowed a few of the surviving gompas to operate under the close supervision of the Bureau of Religious Affairs. One of the many tools that Religious Affairs used to keep the Tibetan monks closely leashed was forcing them to sign loyalty oaths to Beijing. Individual monks who refused lost their robes. But when entire groups refused to sign, it was considered an act of organized resistance to the government. They would be given one final chance to sign, then rounded up for imprisonment in Tibet's gulag. Shan closed his eyes a moment, fighting a flood of wrenching memories from his own years of imprisonment in one of those camps.

After a moment he scanned the slopes above them. They were empty. There had been families with small herds of sheep and yaks when he had passed through on the way to the Chomolungma base camp the day before. After fifty years of living with the Chinese army, many Tibetans seemed to be able to sense soldiers from miles away.

"I don't understand why they do it," Jin said in a more conversational tone. "How many does it make this season?"

Shan turned and saw that the constable was gazing at the body on the mule. "This will be three I've taken down." Although trucks and utility vehicles could make it to base camp, Tumkot, the village that provided most of the porters, was very traditional. It had no monks, but it had an astrologer who often played that role, and she had told the villagers the deities wanted them to keep their dead out of Chinese trucks. Later, for reasons Shan still did not understand, she had foretold that he was the one who would convey the bodies. "They say the mother mountain is angry this year."

"Angry?" Jin smirked, streaming two jets of smoke out his nostrils. "I'd say she's become a bitch with a feud against the world."

He gestured toward the dead man. "Damned fools. They must have a death wish going up there. Acting like they're gods, thinking they have the right to be at the top of the planet."

Shan laid his hand on the back of the dead man. He had not known the other dead sherpas he retrieved from Everest and had only briefly worked with the ever-cheerful Tenzin, but he had developed a strange affinity for all of them. The old Tibetans would say their ghosts were befriending him. "They just carry the bags of those who would be gods," Shan quietly corrected, "so they can feed their families." His gaze drifted down the trail as the mule nudged him again. "How soon are they coming?" he asked. Not far below, the trail passed within fifty yards of the road. He could ill afford to be stopped by Public Security with an unexplained body.

The constable's expression hardened at Shan's reference to the knobs. He tossed his cigarette into the rocks with a peeved glance, as if Shan had ruined its enjoyment, then rose to mount the horse. "Soon enough," he complained.

"Don't play music when you ride," Shan suggested as the policeman awkwardly tried to mount with the rifle over his shoulder. "It frightens the horse. And don't always stay on his back. Tibetans walk beside their horses half the time, speaking with them."

Jin sneered at Shan and reached for the power switch on his tape player.

"It's a long walk home," Shan observed. The constable frowned again but did not touch the switch. He straightened, dug his heels into the horse and disappeared at a slow, stiff trot.

Twenty minutes later Shan stood in the shadow of a boulder and watched the cloud of dust that marked the passage of the bus, his gut tightening. He too had developed an instinct about Public Security. He found himself leaning forward, the way the small mountain animals did when they were about to leap away from an approaching predator. Forcing himself to keep watching as the cloud passed a tower of rock a quarter mile away, he glanced down as he realized his hand had clamped around his wrist, over his prison registration tattoo. He picked up the lead rope for the mule and had begun to slowly retreat when he felt an odd shaking at his feet, like a small earthquake. Then came a screech of metal, the sound of a tire bursting, followed by angry shouts, the flat crack of a pistol, and the frantic blowing of a whistle. He glanced at the mule, which had begun to graze on a clump of grass, then leaped down the trail toward the road.

Moments later he crouched at an outcropping, gazing down on a scene of chaos. A small military bus, designed to hold perhaps twenty prisoners, was wedged sideways in the narrow road, jammed between rock ledges on either side. The windshield was smashed. The front right wheel was flat, the bumper and fender above it crumpled where they had struck a column of rock that had fallen across the road. Other rocks from the apparent avalanche had smashed against the side of the bus, knocking in two of the wire-bound windows. A young Public Security soldier, probably the driver of the bus, sat against a rock, dazed, his head bleeding from where it had smashed the windshield. Only one other knob could be seen, racing into the rocks at the far side of the road, desperately sounding his whistle. The monks who had been imprisoned on the bus were escaping, except for one old man in a red robe who was bent over the injured driver.

Shan slid down the ledge and onto the road. The driver was losing consciousness, and the lama had torn a strip from his robe to tie around the soldier's bleeding head.

The old lama cocked his head as Shan approached. Shan did not know the man, but he knew well from his years in prison the weary smile and the calm, unafraid countenance. "You have done what you can do for him," Shan said to the lama, his words urgent. "Please go." He knew what the lama meant to do, and it filled Shan with dread. "By stepping off that bus, you escaped. It won't matter if they find you ten feet or ten miles away. I will tend him," he said, kneeling by the unconscious soldier. "You have no idea what they will do to you. Go to your friends, they need you more," he said as the lama lowered himself into the meditation position. "The soldiers will—" the lama cut off Shan's words by lifting a hand in a familiar gesture, an invitation to join in a mantra. Memories flashed through Shan's mind, of monks in his former prison beaten senseless with batons and pipes, of old Tibetans kicked in the jaw until their teeth fell out, of lamas gazing serenely as their executioners aimed pistols at their skulls. The lama offered a small, wise nod, then began a low, murmuring mantra aimed at the injured soldier, an invocation of the Medicine Buddha.

"*Lha gyal lo,*" Shan offered in a tight voice as he retreated. *Victory to the gods.*

A patch of maroon flashed among the rocks fifty yards away. He sprinted toward it, finding three monks hiding, trembling with fear. "Away from the road!" he shouted, gesturing them toward the maze of outcroppings on the slope above. The soldiers would return at any moment. They would have batons and electric cattle prods with which to deliver stunning blows. He grabbed the wrist of the first monk he reached, a young Tibetan with a jagged scar on his chin, whose eyes flashed defiance as he jerked his arm away. "These are prison guards, they will not stray far from the road," Shan explained. "But they will call in border commandos in helicopters. Get to the high valleys," he urged. "Get out of your robes. You can't go back to your gompa. Stay with the shepherds, stay in the caves."

"We've done nothing wrong," the young monk protested. "Rinpoche is correct," he said, using the term for revered teacher as he nodded toward the old lama sitting by the road. "There is just a misunderstanding."

"There is no misunderstanding. You're bound for years in a Public Security prison." The other monks grabbed up the loose ends of their robes and began running up the slope.

The young monk took several hesitant steps toward the lama who was tending to the soldier. "I cannot leave him."

"They won't keep you together," Shan said to his back. "Go to him now and all it does is guarantee you will spend the next five years in a Chinese prison. They'll crush your prayer boxes, burn your robe."

The monk turned, anguish on his face. "I have heard of a Chinese who was a prisoner himself, who helps our people now. How are you called?"

"You don't want to know my name, and I don't want to know yours. Go." Shan insisted, pointing up the slope.

"But Rinpoche—"

Shan looked back to the lama, his heart rising in his throat. "The old ones in prison just consider themselves on a long hermitage. The best thing you can do for him is to flee, save yourself so you can keep being a monk. Spare him the pain of knowing he cost you your freedom."

The monk mouthed a silent prayer toward the lama, touched his empty wrist where his beads had been before the knobs tore them away, then sprinted up the slope.

Metallic whistles screeched from farther down the road, followed by sharp commands and a long anguished moan. Shan, fighting the panic rising within, surveyed the scene, spotting arcs of color among the debris of rocks on the slope above. A thick red climbing rope, a sling of black and yellow rope. He had found the stolen climbing equipment. Something rattled by his foot and he bent to retrieve a steel snaplink carabiner used with climbing ropes. He was looking up at the debris again, trying to decipher how the ropes had been used, when three loud cracks erupted from the ridge above him. Gunshots. He ran.

There would be wounded monks, he told himself, there would be furious knobs. As he ran he made a mental note of what he had on him that he might turn into bandages. But when he emerged onto the small, flat plain at the top of the ridge it was not monks he saw but a traffic accident. A large dark gray sedan had veered off the narrow road. He reached the car gasping, leaning on the fender by the open driver's door to catch his breath, realizing the car had not hit anything, had been pulled onto the shoulder by a grove of short, gnarled juniper trees. Watching for soldiers, he walked warily around the car and froze.

The two women leaning against boulders appeared at first to be having a quiet conversation, the middle-aged Chinese woman in a white silk blouse gazing inquisitively at the younger woman with close-cropped blond hair, her hands on her belly as if she had indigestion. But the older woman's hands were covered with blood. Shan knelt, his fingers on her neck, finding no pulse. She was dead, though her flesh was still warm.

The blond woman gazed toward the horizon with a lifeless expression. But then he saw the fingers of one hand move, trembling, as if gesturing for him. She had been shot twice, in the chest. Blood stained her red nylon windbreaker and the pale blue shirt underneath, blood bubbled at one corner of her mouth. His heart wrenched as she turned to him, her eyes confused and pleading. He sat beside her, put an arm around her shoulder, wiping away a bloodstain on her temple.

"Stay still," he whispered in Chinese, then repeated himself in English, stroking her crown. *Run!* a frantic voice inside shouted. He had to flee, had to help the monks if he could. But he could not leave the dying woman.

"Who did this?" he whispered.

The woman's lips opened and shut. "The raven," she whispered in English, and her hand found his, gripping hard as she looked back at the sky. Not the sky, Shan realized, not a bird, but the tall, fierce mountain to the south. She was gazing at Everest. She glanced at him with an apologetic, lopsided grin. "Is it me . . ." she began in the thinnest of voices, then more blood flowed out of her mouth, choking her words. She raised her hand, touching the blood at her mouth, smearing it on her cheek as she coughed.

"Help will come," he said, his own voice hoarse now. "You will be fine." When the soldiers came he would ask them to run back to the bus, where there would be a first-aid kit and a radio to call an ambulance.

Her weak grin returned, as if she had caught him in a joke, then she lowered her head onto his shoulder like an old friend resting a moment. With what seemed to be great effort she raised her free hand and touched an ornate box that hung from her neck, pulled out from under her shirt. A *gau*, a traditional Tibetan prayer box. She pushed it toward him, as if to show him, then her hand fell away. He stroked the dirty blond hair on her crown and whispered more words of comfort as the strength ebbed from the hand that held his and her frail, labored breathing gradually ceased.

He watched as if from a distance as his hand kept stroking her head, her lifeless eyes still aimed at the mother mountain, hearing his voice whispering desolate, useless assurance as he pushed the gau back inside her shirt. Too late he saw the shadow beside him, too late he noticed the gray uniformed leg at his side. The electric prod touched his hand, his neck, his spine, and he watched from an even greater distance as his body convulsed, pulling the dead Westerner on top of him, her blood smearing onto his face and chest. Then something slammed into his skull and he knew no more.

Chapter Two

WITH HIS ONE good eye Shan watched the dead prisoner's hand twitch, disturbing the flies that fed on its oozing wound. He had seen this before, the reflex of a laboratory frog, in those who had recently died after torture from electric shock. The sinewy fingers kept grabbing at thin air, as if frantically seeking the rainbow rope that pulled good Buddhists to heaven. With a stab of pain he raised his head from his pallet high enough to follow the dead arm, in search of its owner. Then a deep, shuddering moan escaped his throat. It was his own.

With agonizing effort he pushed himself upright against the painted cinder-block wall, ignoring the numbness in his legs, exploring his blind eye with his fingers to confirm it was only swollen shut. The pain that erupted as he lifted his head was like none he had known for years. His head swirled as he tried to study his cell, noticing pools of fresh blood and vomit on the concrete floor below a filthy porcelain sink. The last thing he saw as he slid down the wall, losing consciousness again, was a faded political poster on the wall outside the cell, an image of workers with radiant smiles over the caption REJOICE IN THE WORK OF THE PEOPLE.

When he woke again it was night, the only light a single dim bulb hanging in the middle of the corridor of cells, over a metal table with a blackboard easel beside it. He rose onto unsteady legs by pushing against the wall and took a step forward. The cell floor heaved upward and his knees collapsed. Again he struggled to his feet and took another step, using the lessons of his Tibetan teachers to fight the agony of each movement, until at last he crumpled onto the floor in a front corner. He gripped the bars of the door to pull himself into the light to examine the work of his captors. His left arm was mottled with blood, the skin scraped away in several places. His lips were bloody and swollen, several upper teeth loose and bleeding. The prisoner instincts that had lurked within him ever since leaving the gulag took over, taking inventory of the instruments used on him. A baton to his jaw and shoulders. A club covered with coarse sandpaper to his arm, which lifted patches of skin wherever it touched, a favorite of rural garrisons. Steel boot toes to his shins. Boot heels on the top of his feet. He closed his eyes, collecting himself, then explored the inside of his cheek with his tongue. There was no lingering taste, no metallic tinge. They had not begun to use chemicals on him.

He pulled his legs under him, in the meditation position, clenching his teeth against the pain, and stared at a little oblong window with wire-reinforced glass near the top of the back wall. Stars made their transit across the window. He dipped his finger into the nearest pool of blood and drew a circle on the wall, then a circle within a circle, then patterns within the circles. As he worked on the mandala, his mind clearing, the hairs on his neck began to rise. He turned to see the glow of a cigarette from an open cell at the end of the dark corridor. Someone was sitting on a cot, watching him.

Shan twisted, grabbed another bar, and with an effort that sent stabs of pain through his shoulders pulled himself around to squarely face the corridor. He stared back at the moving ember of the man who watched, until a new tide of pain surged within, lighting a fire at the back of his head that left him writhing on the floor. He faded in and out of consciousness, his mind churning with memories and visions, his body rioting in pain, leaving him unable to discern what was real and what was not. The bodies of the escaped monks were stacked like firewood, with a knob officer pouring gas on them. His father, the professor, recited Shakespeare in short, gasping syllables as he was tortured with burning sticks. Shan stood at the summit of Mount Chomolungma with Tenzin and the blond woman, then the wind seized them and threw all three into a shaft where they floated with the bodies of dead climbers.

He became aware of dim light filtering through the small window. Hours had passed. He was lying on the floor again, sprawled in his own filth. A man paced along the front of the cell, his black officer's boots glistening as they passed a pool of sunlight. The man paused, spoke to someone. A moment later someone threw a bucket of frigid water over Shan.

He did not react. Someone cursed. Someone murmured new orders. A metal door opened and shut, then opened and shut again. Shan watched through a fog of pain as the officer began emptying a plastic bottle into the bucket.

With the first acrid sting of the odor Shan struggled upward, clenching his jaw in agony, pushing himself forward, reaching for the bars. He knew from experience that some knobs liked to throw ammonia on prisoners.

"Risen from your nap at last," the officer observed in a slow, refined voice with an accent that sent a chill down Shan's back. He had been trained in Beijing, probably was from one of the anonymous disposal units that cleaned up embarrassments for the Party elite. New foreboding rose within him. Why would such a man be sent to deal with Shan?

Shan gripped the bars, his eyes drifting in and out of focus. Blood trickled down one leg. He could not take a deep breath without wincing from the pain. He closed his eyes, centering himself a moment, then fixed the officer with a steady gaze. "I need some tea," he declared in a hoarse voice.

Though the officer's eyes were still in shadow Shan could not miss his bloodless grin. He turned with quick, whispered orders and a jailer hastened down the corridor.

No one spoke again until Shan was ushered to the metal table in the center of the corridor and chained to a chair, a mug of tea in front of him. He held the mug to his nose before drinking, letting the steam burn away the cloud inside his head, then drained nearly half the near-scalding liquid in one gulp.

"My name is Major Cao," the officer announced as he filled

another mug from a tea thermos. "We will be working together to resolve things."

"Traditionally," Shan said in a ragged voice as the officer settled into a chair across from him, "interrogation begins before the torture. It might be—" he searched for a word— "counterproductive to incapacitate a prisoner before seeing if he is going to cooperate."

"You misunderstand," Cao replied. "What they did to you was just a going-away present. Every Public Security officer in this district, every soldier of that detail, has been reassigned because of what you did. Most to desert outposts where they won't be heard of for years. They felt an urge to express their true feelings to you before they left."

Shan watched in chilled silence as the officer opened a tattered, stained yellow file on the table with familiar characters inscribed boldly across the front. The man was a master of his craft. It would not have been difficult to ascertain Shan's identity from the prison registration number tattooed on his arm, but he had thought his file had been buried so deep no one would ever find it. With a new, desperate realization he looked up. "What day is it?" It would have taken at least forty-eight hours to retrieve the file from distant Lhadrung.

Cao ignored him. "Reads like one of those operas written for the Party," the officer observed dryly as he leafed through the file. "Tragic misjudgments lead a reliable cadre down an antisocial path, at each stage sinking him deeper among the criminal element until, in a last gasp of self-hate, he commits an assassination. His subconscious longing to be executed finally finds voice." He spoke looking toward the empty cells as if to an audience before turning to Shan. "If the Party doesn't decide to muzzle it your execution will make headlines all over China."

Shan clenched his abdomen, resisting the threats in Cao's words, finally piercing the chaos of pain and fear that welled within. "She was an official then? The one shot in the belly?"

"His rage was so blind it affected his memory," the officer continued toward the cells before turning back to Shan. "You destroyed a paragon of society, severed the head of Beijing's favored monument. You, Comrade Shan, assassinated the Minister of Tourism."

Shan stared into the shadows, a new kind of pain surging through his body. Images returned, of the dead Chinese woman, of the blond woman who had died in his arms, her final mysterious words sounding like a question to the mountain. Finally he gestured to his mug and Cao refilled it with another icy grin. "What day is it?" Shan asked again, in a voice that quivered. "Is it Thursday yet?"

Major Cao produced a pencil and a blank sheet of paper from a drawer in the table and carefully drew seven blocks joined together, crossed off the first two, and shoved it across to Shan. "For the rest of your life this is all the calendar you will ever need," he declared.

A wave of nausea swept over Shan. He bent over the steam of his mug again, closing his eyes. "A crime so important will require a real investigation," he said when he looked up, fighting to keep his voice steady. "Forensic work."

"You were found clutching one of your victims, soaked in blood. You had the name of the minister's hotel in your pocket." With new fear Shan's hand shot toward his now empty pocket. He had forgotten the paper, could not afford to have Cao know why he had it. "The only other evidence we need," Cao said, with a gesture toward the file, "is the pathetic story of your life."

For the first time Shan gazed into the officer's eyes. "No," he said, his voice steadier now. "Otherwise they would not have sent for you."

Cao sighed, as if already fatigued from his work. "A hundred million. That's what the climbing trade is worth in one year. Beijing asked us to be certain it wasn't Tibetan separatists or something else that might threaten this vital segment of the economy. An abundance of caution, you might say."

"So it's not about murder, it's about foreign exchange."

The major stared at Shan as though for the first time, with cool curiosity. "As you are well aware, Inspector Shan, we prefer the subjects of our executions to be conscious, so they can express their remorse in their final moments. But you can be strapped to a chair and still recite your sins. Do you know how many bones and nerves there are in the feet and ankles?"

Shan fixed Cao with a level gaze as he considered the man's words. "Beijing asked you. So you're not from Beijing. That means Lhasa. Provincial headquarters."

Cao's eyes flared. Shan had hit a nerve.

"When you were unconscious, you shouted out a name, again and again. Ko. Who is this Ko? Should we be seeking a coconspirator?"

Shan's gut tightened into a knot. He feigned another spasm of pain to hide his reaction to the name. "A political parable might be enough to explain things to the public, Major. But in the end, in the final secret discussions about the death of a state minister, the State Council will expect proof. Forensic work. You seem to shy away from the topic."

Cao lifted a another mug from beside the tea thermos, squeezing it so hard Shan thought it might shatter.

"I was only there by coincidence. I saw the minister's wounds. She died of a shot at point-blank range," Shan said. "I had no gunpowder residue on my hands. Did you even bother to check?"

"I arrived twenty-four hours after your arrest. Other officers were responsible for the initial fieldwork."

"The ones lost in the desert now," Shan observed.

"I believe some were also sent to oil platforms in the China Sea. The twenty-first century equivalent of Mongolia."

"Sort of like Lhasa," Shan observed, "for an ambitious Public Security officer."

A ligament in Cao's neck tightened as he stared at Shan. "Some of our country's greatest security challenges are in Tibet. I am honored to serve the motherland wherever she sends me."

It was, Shan knew, the code, and tone, of a man who had suffered disappointments in his career. "Did you at least search the rocks?"

"For what?"

"The murder weapon. The murderer obviously knew that Public Security had closed the road and was focused on that bus of monks. He apparently even knew it meant that Public Security had decided the minister didn't need her usual security detail. He knew he could get close to her as long as he avoided that bus. He also knew he could not afford to be found with the gun."

"What are you admitting?"

"I am admitting how incompetent Public Security has been. The pistol is in the rocks there, probably no more than two or three hundred feet away."

"In twenty-four hours you will be begging to show us where it is."

Shan returned Cao's stare without expression. "Public Security interrogation is such an inexact science, Major. What you might have in twenty-four hours is either a dead prisoner with no confession or the murder weapon, fresh enough that the elements haven't damaged its evidentiary value."

Cao closed the file and covered it with a fist. "Who the hell are you, Shan?"

"I am the sour seed that Public Security always spits out," Shan said in an earnest voice.

Cao lifted a new folder from the table. "A leading local Party cadre has submitted a petition. He reminds us that the bureau operates a hospital for the criminally insane not far from here. A famous hospital, at least in Public Security circles. The spa, we call it in Lhasa."

"The yeti factory," Shan murmured. "The Tibetans call it the yeti factory."

"No doubt because the spa is producing superhumans."

"Because inmates sometimes escape and are found wandering

aimlessly in the mountains, usually naked, in the snow, with the mental faculties of a large ape."

Cao's thin lips did not move but his eyes lit with amusement. "This cadre suggests we owe a duty to the people to cure you before we shoot you, so you can explain to the inhabitants of this county why you shamed them so. I called him in. I asked him what proof he has of your insanity. He said every conversation with you is proof enough."

So the real torture had begun. Cao undoubtedly had the authority to send him to the knobs' experimental medical units. Shan had spent time in one before being dumped into the Tibetan gulag over five years earlier. Any sane man who knew about them would rather take a bullet in the skull than be sent to such a place.

Cao rose and circled the table. He was older than Shan had thought at first, and had a gutter of scar tissue along the top of one hand that could only have been made by a bullet.

"Surely, comrade," the major stated, "since the day you left Beijing in chains, you must have expected that your life would ultimately be claimed by the government."

Shan stared into his empty cup. "I remember an old uncle telling me I would end my days writing poetry at some mountain retreat, surrounded by singing birds."

Something low and guttural escaped Cao's throat. It might have been a laugh. "I have read and reread your background. Especially your early career, when you grew famous for sending high officials to jail for corruption. I even spoke to some of your former colleagues. I begin to understand you. Your defining characteristic is completeness. You must have all the loose ends connected. For you, justice has little to do with judges and courts. Your justice must be absolute, must be cathartic. You must have redemption. It is what I offer you now. Help me avoid calling in the team that waits outside. Make a clean end of it."

Cao paused, then stepped to the blackboard, tossing a piece of chalk from hand to hand for a moment before quickly writing. "I always enjoy the Japanese verses," he declared. "Simple, absolute words." He stepped to the side for Shan to see.

Confession to release the heart, bullet to release the soul, Cao had written. Then *Blood spatters on small birds.*

"I will take you to the mountains, Shan," Cao offered in a near whisper. "I will find a place with songbirds."

Shan read Cao's strange haiku several times before responding. "Major," he said at last, "you strike me as vastly overeducated for your job."

Cao glared at Shan then spun about and disappeared into the shadows. Shan did not look, just listened as the door opened and shut, twice. Guards appeared, unlocking his chains, escorting him to an interrogation room in another hallway off the cell corridor, chaining him to another metal chair. Moments later three men appeared, all wearing white laboratory coats, the oldest one carrying a doctor's bag. He extracted his instruments slowly, fastidiously laying them in a line on the table. A small stainless-steel hammer. Four dental probes of various sizes. Two pairs of pliers. Several long, very thin, stainless steel needles. Short lengths of latex hose. A tooth extractor.

As they stood staring at him in the odd silent prelude with which such sessions always commenced, Shan grabbed one of the oversized needles. The three men stiffened, stepping back as Shan wielded it like a knife, leaning forward in his chair, swinging the treacherous-looking needle toward them until the chain on his wrist tightened and halted the movement. "Not to disappoint you," he declared, "but I am no virgin." With a single swift motion he buried the needle halfway into the bicep of his left arm.

One of the technicians gasped and threw his hand to his mouth as if about to lose the contents of his stomach; the other's face drained of color. The doctor smiled.

* * *

SHAN DOUBTED THAT in all the history of the world anyone had organized the administration of misery and fear as efficiently as Beijing's Public Security Bureau. The knobs had manuals, charts, entire six month training programs on what they termed physical interrogation. Like all mature sciences, it had its own jargon. Shan, in the hands of a master, had been given what the knobs called a ranging exam, a quick application of each of the primary tools, to gauge which he seemed to be most responsive to. As he had learned from the lamas with whom he had been imprisoned, he had gone to another place, had removed himself from his self. *Let it be a storm that rages outside*, a lama had once told him, *over which you have no control. Stay on the inside, where the storm cannot reach.*

He lay on the cell floor where they had thrown him afterward, unaware of anything except the pain that rose and ebbed, gradually becoming curious about the strange white pebble clutched in one hand, until he finally remembered. The knobs, becoming frustrated when he had responded only with silence, had rushed the rest of the session, knowing they would need Cao with them before they began in earnest, reacting only with disgust when, as they had lifted him from the chair, he had vomited onto the table, sending them reeling backward so that they did not notice him palm the tooth they had extracted.

He spat out blood then, steadying his shaking hand, stuffed the tooth back into the socket with a hard shove to seat it. His years in prison had taught him that a tooth so recently removed had a good chance of reattaching to the jaw. Stretching the fingers of his left hand, he rubbed the place where he had punctured his arm. The knobs had not recognized the trick taught to him by an old prisoner years earlier. If you were careful, and lucky enough, you would not only put your interrogators off their pace, you could also achieve a crude acupuncture, blocking the nerves from the left hand, a favorite target of interrogators, who preferred to keep the right one intact for penning confessions.

He crawled to the pallet by the back wall and collapsed on it, losing consciousness. When he awoke again night had fallen. He struggled into the meditation position and stared into the dark. Bits of his life outside again mingled with nightmarish visions. The serene faces of the two old Tibetans he loved like family, whom, for their own safety, he had left months earlier in the mountains east of Lhasa. The screams of other prisoners coming from behind closed interrogation room doors. Again and again, he ventured toward a chamber in his mind whose door had come ajar during his interrogation, not daring to look inside for fear of what he might see. But then a new storm of pain erupted, the door swung open and he could not stop the nightmare, seeing in his mind's eye his son Ko, gulag prisoner Shan Ko, lying in his bed at the yeti factory, being tortured by the same team that had worked on Shan.

IN THE MORNING a slip of paper lay on the stool beside his pallet. It was a notification on a printed form. Unless directed otherwise by a signed statement, witnessed by a magistrate, a prisoner's organs would be harvested for medical purposes immediately after execution. Not a prisoner, he saw, *the* prisoner. The form was made out in his name.

HE DID NOT acknowledge the team when they arrived, he just stared at the symbolic circle, the mandala he had drawn on the wall with his blood. The day before he had had the strength to make a show of resistance. Today it was all he could do not to cry out in pain as they pulled him to his feet. He tried to withdraw, to remove himself from the prisoner who shuffled down the corridor, raging at the voice inside that kept recounting to him the dozen ways a clever prisoner could bring about his own death during interrogation. His body reacted involuntarily, wretching in dry, shuddering heaves as the doctor opened his bag.

He fell into a strange torpor, unaware of the activity around him, roused only by a new, shooting pain in his right arm. His gaze followed the needle in his vein toward the hose that led to an intravenous feed. A technician was injecting something into a valve in the tube. With effort he focused on the bottle of clear liquid the man left on the table. He would know in a moment, from the taste in his mouth, whether it was one of the knobs' truth serums or one of the solutions designed to set the muscles on fire. He gazed at the bottle numbly, not comprehending at first as a soothing warmth oozed through his limbs. Then abruptly he was fully awake, searching the resentful faces of the team for an explanation. They were giving him a painkiller and a bottle of glucose. They were silently bandaging his wounds.

Ten minutes later the team was gone, the glucose tube still in his arm, nothing left on the table but a steaming mug of tea. Shan had barely taken his first sip when Cao materialized out of the shadows.

"I understand there are hundreds of miles of wilderness above here," the major observed in a sour voice.

Shan's answer came out in a hoarse croak. "Thousands."

"Good. Get lost in them." There was a cold vehemence in the major's words. "If I ever see you again I will find a meat cleaver and a plane, and I will drop pieces of you over the mountains as you watch."

Shan silently sipped his tea, calculating the ways Cao could be setting a trap for him, then recalled the gap of hours when the team should have been working on him. "You found the pistol," he concluded.

Cao answered by stepping to his side, jerking the glucose needle from his arm and pointing to the door.

* * *

SHAN STOOD BLINKING in the briliant morning sun as the door slammed shut behind him. Shogo town was still waking up. A small flock of sheep wandered along the cracked pavement of the street. A group of shiny sport utility vehicles sped by filled with tourists bound for the Himalayas after a side trip to see the center of commerce at the top of the world. Somewhere someone burned incense, an offering to the gods for the new day. He had taken two stumbling steps before he noticed the well-dressed Tibetan sitting at a table outside the tea shop across the street. He paused as two army trucks, packed with border commandos, sped past in a cloud of dust. Then he limped across the road.

Tsipon, the leading businessman in Shogo, preeminent local member of the Party, was the only man in the town who ever wore a tie. In his suit and white shirt he looked as if he were attending a business meeting.

"I am grateful that you tried to get me transferred to the hospital," Shan offered as he dropped into the chair beside him.

"It's the climbing season, damn it. I can't afford to lose another worker. The fool knobs don't have a clue about economics."

Another man appeared, holding three mugs of black tea, which he placed on the table, sliding one toward Shan, before settling into a third chair. He was tall and athletic looking, his skin bearing the weathered patina of one who spent long days in the high altitudes. With his black hair Shan might have taken him for a Tibetan waiter at first glance. Except that his features were Western and his clothes and boots would have cost a year's income for the average Tibetan.

"Look at him," the man groused in English to Tsipon. "He's in no shape. The deal's off."

Shan glanced back at Tsipon, who stared at him expectantly. Apparently they were at a business meeting after all.

Tsipon offered a sly smile, then motioned to a woman standing inside the open door. She leaned over him, listening as he whispered, then hurried away.

"What day is it?" Shan asked in Tibetan.

"I'm sorry. It's Saturday."

Shan shut his eyes. For a moment he lost his grip on his pain, every synapse seeming to scream in agony.

"The region leading to the climbing trails on the Nepal side of the mountains has been sealed off by the Nepali military," Tsipon said, switching to English. "Problems with the rebels who want to take over Katmandu. No Westerners are allowed to climb the south slope this season. Mr. Yates here has three groups of climbers already signed on for the season, expecting to be taken to the summit in the next six weeks. He needs to put them up the north face instead."

As the stranger drank his tea, Shan saw the discolored flesh on two of his fingers, one of them missing its top joint, the mark of frostbite at high altitudes.

"Impossible," Shan said. "You know it is impossible." Putting an expedition on the slopes meant weeks of planning, permits, surveying advance campsites, staging supplies.

The stranger pushed a small stack of napkins toward Shan, motioning to a wet spot of crimson on the table. Blood was dripping from the bandage on Shan's temple.

"Damn it Shan," Tsipon snapped, switching to Tibetan, "this American is fat with cash. His company has three expeditions already paid for. Do you have any idea how much money that means? He is going to charge them another twenty percent for coming to China, which I'm to get a quarter of."

As Shan pressed a napkin to his head the woman reappeared, setting a plate of steaming *momo*, Tibetan dumplings, in front of him. His free hand seemed to act of its own accord, darting out, stuffing one into his mouth.

"I need sherpas," Tsipon said, "mountain porters, mules, and horses. New camps have to be laid out, supplies staged, new safety lines rigged."

Shan glanced back and forth from one man to the other. "Just go up to the villages," he said as he gulped down another momo.

"Enough cash can work miracles." He was suddenly ravenous, and recalled he had eaten only a few mouthfuls of cold rice during the past three days.

"Not this time," Tsipon explained. "There is a complication. The sherpas blame me. I blame you."

Shan glanced at the American, who sipped at his tea with a confused, self-conscious expression, obviously not understanding their Tibetan words but not missing the tension between the two. "For what?"

"That sherpa you were carrying. Tenzin. He was well liked, came from a big family living on both sides of the border, famous for having reached the summit as a teenager years ago. They want his body."

The momo in Shan's hand stopped in midair. "Surely someone found the mule. It wouldn't wander far."

"No. Nothing."

"I don't understand."

"Let me spell it out," Tsipon said, still in Tibetan. "This fool American and his partner are offering the best opportunity I've ever had, the best this town has ever had. You agreed to work for me because I could get you into the yeti factory to see that worthless son of yours."

Shan's head snapped up, strangely fearful over the mention of his son, even more alarmed that someone might overhear and guess the secret that had brought him to the region. A wild hope had nurtured him through the dreadful hours in the jail and many dark nights before, a dream, a fantasy, that somehow he would not only reach his son in the knobs' secret hospital, but discover some means to get him out, at least back to the gulag camps in Lhadrung where Shan and his friends could help him.

"I agreed to hire you because of your magic at fixing problems with those old-fashioned ones, up in the mountains."

Shan stared at his momo, shaking his head from side to side. "You were supposed to get me in. I've waited two months."

"That was Thursday, when you were going to join me on an official Party delegation to inspect the place. You missed your date."

The desolation that gripped Shan was so overpowering he had to brace himself with a hand on the table. "Then when's the next one?" he asked in a hollow voice.

"Find me that dead sherpa," Tsipon said in a matter-of-fact voice, "or forget about seeing your son."

Shan stared at Tsipon in disbelief. He hadn't been released from captivity. Tsipon and the knobs had just found a new form of torture.

He gradually became aware that more napkins were being pushed toward him by Yates. Blood was dripping onto his dumplings. He pushed away his plate, nauseated, and with great effort rose. He swayed, took a single faltering step, and collapsed to the ground unconscious.

HE WAS NOT aware of being moved, only of the pain coursing through his body then, later, of dim lights in the blackness, and more nightmares. The pain rose in tides, ebbing and surging, making it impossible to focus, to try to make sense of the events that had occurred since he'd left Tenzin's body on the mountain. Faces from his past in Beijing mocked him. Visions of Ko being tortured intensified, mingled with questioning, lifeless faces: of the blond woman on the mountain asking why she had to die, of Tenzin asking why Shan had abandoned him in the hour he needed him the most. When Shan woke, in the blackness, a single thought sustained him. Tsipon did not understand. Shan had another way to reach his son. He simply had to reach the new hotel at the base of the mountain, and he could leave Tsipon and Cao and the murders behind. Before he passed out again he heard himself call out for Ko, pleading with him to survive, to endure the tortures of the clinic.

At last there was only the goddess. Floating in the darkness, she gazed at him with strained tolerance, reproach in her eyes, reminding him there were fugitive monks in the mountains, frightened monks who needed his help.

Each time he woke he became more aware of his surroundings. Tea and noodles appeared beside his pallet, and when he consumed them they were magically replenished, waiting for him beside a flickering candle each time he regained consciousness. Then, finally, suddenly, he was awake, able to sit up.

He discovered that his dark chamber had been made by hanging heavy black felt blankets around his pallet, supported by climbing ropes. At each side of his makeshift closet sat an upturned wooden crate. On another upturned crate to his left was a stack of gauze topped by a roll of medical tape and an envelope of antibiotic powder. To his right was a small figurine of the Tibetan protectress deity Tara. Flanking the Tara were two brown smoldering sticks stuck in a plank, a familiar mantra scrawled on a scrap of paper between them. He recognized the odor of aloe. Someone had been tending him with bandages and pills. Someone else had been treating him with healing incense and an invocation of the Medicine Buddha.

Shan slowly rose, stretching, rubbing the stiffness out of his limbs. Then he probed the blankets until he found an opening, and staggered out into a familiar maze of stone and old beams. The stable that he had adopted two months before as his living quarters, abandoned decades earlier, was at the mouth of the wide gully that served as the dump for Shogo town. Though it was shunned by the townspeople, though Tsipon had offered him quarters in the rear of his warehouse, Shan had been drawn to the place. It was old and decaying, but as he aged he found himself more and more comfortable with the old and decaying, particularly the old and decaying of Tibet. He had seen the heavy hand-hewn posts and beams rising out of the rubble, as solid as they had been when erected centuries earlier. He had also seen under the rear piles of rubble something else that had been the real reason he had set up his meager household there. He hobbled to the makeshift workbench, threw off the dusty canvas that covered it, and confirmed that nothing had been touched. Spread over the planks were a score of ancient carved printing blocks, used for printing *peche*, the traditional Tibetan books of prayer. His spare hours at the stable were spent restoring the long rectangular blocks retrieved from the rubble, fitting and gluing together pieces that had been split apart, scraping away the dirt and dried manure that filled the carved characters and ritual images. He lifted the block he had last worked on and without conscious effort began scraping away its grime.

It had become a nightly ritual, the thing that brought him so close to his old friends Gendun and Lokesh that he sometimes sensed them at his side, a better restorative than any salve or pill.

Shan finished the rosewood peche plate, a page of the heart sutra with images of birds carved along the borders, and put it in a sack he kept in the shadows; he would take the best of the peche boards back to Lhadrung, so they would be safe with his friends in their secret hermitage. He had begun another block, clearing it with a brush he had made with hairs from the old mule's mane, when a thought began to nag him, growing until he set the brush down and stared into the shadows. Not once had anyone mentioned the dead Westerner. The murder of a state minister might be big news in Beijing but the murder of a Westerner in the shadow of Everest would draw global headlines.

The open, pleading face of the blond woman who had died in his arms kept leaping into his consciousness, the foreigner who, impossibly, had been traveling alone with the minister. *Is it me?* she had asked, as if she had been uncertain who was dying.

"They say there is still a gompa in the mountains that uses these things," an uneasy voice suddenly declared behind him.

Shan spun about to see a tall Tibetan in sunglasses silhouetted in the doorway, looking at the peche plates.

"With a printing press I mean, the last in the region."

Shan felt a rush of joy at the unexpected news. "Do you know where?" He had a sudden vision of himself carrying a bundle of the plates to the gompa, could almost see the joy of the old lamas when they saw what he had brought them.

Kypo shrugged. "In the mountains. We have to go. Tsipon said the moment you could stand I was to bring you." Tsipon's lead manager for expedition support was always a man of few words.

Shan rose from his stool. "Thank you, Kypo, for my—" he gestured to the stall that had been concealed with blankets—"my hospital room."

"Tsipon said to put you in one of the storerooms in the warehouse, or that cottage behind the warehouse. I said you would want to be here, with your—" Kypo glanced at the workbench—"things."

Shan had not hidden his work on the blocks from Kypo, but the Tibetan never once had asked about them, or seemed remotely interested. "He said make sure you were somewhere dark and warm."

"You brought the food and things?"

"I brought the food and bandages," Kypo replied pointedly, and stepped into the sunlight.

Minutes later Shan walked through the open garage door at the side of the largest building in town, emblazoned with a sign for the Himalayan Supply Company. Workers were carrying boxes, loading trucks bound for the Chomolungma base camp. Tsipon, standing with a clipboard in the entry to a storeroom lined with shelves, gestured Shan through the door. Shan found himself glancing around the room, where he had conducted inventory a week earlier. The shelves then had been overflowing with cartons containing oxygen cylinders, flashlight batteries, pitons, harnesses, heavy ropes coiled over long pegs. Now half the supplies were gone.

Tsipon tossed Shan an apple. "If you cost me this contract, Shan, you and I are done," he growled. "And if I say goodbye,

it's not just goodbye to your son, it's goodbye to the Himalayas."
Everything in Tsipon's life was a negotiation. He had to be sure
Shan knew that without his protection Shan would be picked up
and detained for having no residency papers.

"You should have wakened me," Shan said. "I should have been
in the mountains already."

Tsipon shook his head. "There were troops all over the mountains searching for those damned escaped monks. If some officer
in the mountain commandos found you, without registration
papers, how long do you think you'd last? And the shape you were
in, you probably would have crawled off to some cave and died
just to spite me."

Shan took a bite of the apple. "Who else came to the stable?"
he asked. He knew Tsipon, one of the most worldly Tibetans he
had ever known, was not capable of making the little altar or writing the mantra.

Tsipon ignored the question. He stepped to the shelves,
reached into a carton and tossed out clothing, kicking it toward
Shan. "I've promised the American a dozen experienced porters
next week. I went to Tumkot village yesterday," he said, referring
to the mountain village that supplied most of the porters and
guides used by the foreign climbing parties. "I offered double
wages. They practically threw me out. Their damned fortuneteller
er has them all worked up, telling them the signs say the mountain
must be appeased, that the mountain had claimed Tenzin first and
needed him back. They demand the body. I promised them you
would get it for them."

"When?"

Tsipon stuck his head out the door long enough to chide a
Tibetan woman who had dropped a box of fuel canisters. "We
have maybe three days, no more," he snapped, and gestured Shan
out the door into the cavernous main chamber of the warehouse.
After locking the storeroom behind him, Tsipon lowered himself
onto a crate and lit a cigarette.

"Have the foreigners arrived yet?"

"You met that Yates."

"I mean officials. From some embassy, over the other dead woman."

Tsipon cast a puzzled glance at him, blew a stream of smoke toward the ceiling. "They must have hit your head pretty hard. There was no dead foreigner."

The announcement silenced Shan for a moment. He closed his eyes, again fighting his confused swirl of memories from the day of the murders. "What was the bargain you struck with Major Cao?" he asked at last.

The Tibetan blew two streams of smoke from his nostrils. "Bargain?"

"What was your accommodation with Public Security?" Shan pressed. "If I wasn't his prime suspect, I was the closest thing he had to a witness. He would have at least held me for having no papers."

"For this kind of case he needs to paint a very complete picture. He seems to want nothing more to do with you, though he knows you were on the fringe of the scene he is painting. I am to watch you and report back to him," Tsipon admitted. "He might try to have you followed, though once in the mountains that should not be a problem for one of your capabilities."

"Why would he still think I am involved?"

"Because of the paper in your pocket with the telephone number of our new hotel, where the minister stayed."

Shan lowered himself onto one of the crates. Cao had never asked about the paper, but of course he would not have forgotten it.

"I can go to Lhasa," Tsipon added in a speculative tone, "and come back with a bus full of workers. More Tibetans are being put out of work every day. That new train to Lhasa brings a hundred Chinese immigrants a day, each one poised to take a Tibetan's job." Tsipon fixed Shan with a meaningful stare.

It was a threat. Tsipon would prefer to use seasoned mountain tribesmen but he could always sweep up two dozen desperate Tibetans in one of the cities who would leap at the chance of earning wages. Such men would be hopelessly unprepared for dealing with the dangers of the upper slopes. Some, perhaps a fourth or more, would die. It wasn't simply that Tsipon would blame him, but that he would also send Shan to retrieve the bodies.

"Why did you have that paper with the hotel number?" Tsipon demanded, anger abruptly entering his voice.

"There's a chance," Shan said, not sure why his voice had grown hoarse, "that I can get my son out of the yeti factory, get him back to the prison in Lhadrung County where he came from, with lamas and monks, where he will stand a chance of surviving. He's going to die if he stays where he is."

"That doesn't explain the paper."

"Someone I know from Lhadrung is staying there for the conference—the colonel who administers Lhadrung county, who is responsible for the prison camp where Ko came from."

An odd expression appeared on Tsipon's face, a mixture of confusion and glee. "His name?"

"Tan. Colonel Tan. He's the only real chance I have for saving my son."

The laugh that erupted from Tsipon's throat grew so deep he had to hold his belly.

"I don't understand."

"Tan is the one. He's not in the hotel, he's in Cao's jail. Colonel Tan is the one who murdered Minister Wu."

Chapter Three

THEY SAILED IN a smoking junk over the mountains. Jomo, the mechanic who accompanied Shan from Tsipon's compound, believed in the reincarnation of machines. The ancient, sputtering Jiefang cargo truck he was now teaching Shan to drive had, the wiry Tibetan insisted, centuries earlier been a junk in the emperor's battle fleet. Half its forward gears were missing, its rear window was gone, and its seat had so many gaps in the vinyl they had to sit on burlap sacks. Shan did not ask what kind of wretched life the ship had led to justify such a rebirth.

On the opposite side of Shan, Kypo gazed out the window with a dour expression. Tsipon had sent Jomo to show Shan how to drive the battered blue truck, but Kypo, Shan suspected, was there to watch over Shan.

"Soldiers like ants crawling over the rocks," Jomo explained when Shan asked about the day of the killing. "More soldiers than anyone has seen in years. Border commandos, knobs, military police. Everyone ran into holes, some so deep they probably are still buried."

"There were monks," Shan reminded him, "from a monastery in one of the side valleys."

Jomo was silent so long Shan did not think he had heard. "It was like old times," the Tibetan said in a tight voice. "Hunting red robes like they were wild game. The soldiers were angry, they had rifles with scopes like they use when they see people in the high border passes. One monk was brought back dead."

Shan found he could not speak for a long time. "Did any . . . did they find all the others?" he finally asked.

"Who knows? The government won't even officially say they raided the gompa in the first place. Once," Jomo added after a moment, with a gesture to the high peaks, "there were hermits living in hidden caves above here."

The decrepit truck groaned and shuddered as Shan took over the wheel to climb the next slope, the gears slipping, the engine backfiring with each shift. He began to think of it not so much as a truck as a conveyance to some peculiar new form of hell. He couldn't save his son without saving Colonel Tan, a man he reviled, a man who had overseen Shan's prison camp, where so many old lamas had died.

THE CRIME SCENE had been reincarnated as a dump site. Tire tracks and boot prints crisscrossed the clearing. Cigarette butts were scattered everywhere. Empty water bottles had been tossed on the side of the road. Candy wrappers and crumpled cigarette packs had been trapped by the wind under stones. There was no trace of where the bodies, the blood, or the car had been.

Shan crouched at the edge of the clearing, trying to recall the terrible few minutes he had spent here, his gaze settling on the two rocks where the women had been leaning. He rose, then knelt by the rocks, sifting the oddly sandy soil in his fingers before surveying the murder scene in his mind again. There had been blood near the car, and shallow ruts scraped in the soil ending at their heels. The women had been dragged from beside the car and propped up. Before fleeing the killer had arranged them against the rocks, as if to make them comfortable. The Western woman had gazed at Everest with longing as she died.

"You're supposed to be getting Tenzin's body back," Kypo declared from over his shoulder. "I could have told you it wasn't here."

Shan turned to meet the Tibetan's challenging stare.

"In the village people won't talk with me," Kypo said. "They blame me, because I helped persuade them that you should be the corpse carrier. It was a sacred trust, they say, and you broke it."

The words hit Shan hard. It was true. He had failed the sturdy, honest people of Tumkot village, had failed Tenzin himself. Of all the mysteries before him, the one he would have no time to address was why the old astrologer of the village had, after the first fatality of the season, abruptly declared that Shan was to be the carrier of corpses that year.

"If Tenzin cannot be found," Shan ventured, "it must mean the villagers tried to search for him after I was arrested."

"Up the trail, down the trail, along every side trail for a radius of two miles or more."

"Not the road."

"Not the road," Kypo confirmed. The trails belonged to the Tibetans, the road to the government. "After a few hours there were too many uniforms on the mountain to continue."

"The body was lost during the confusion here," Shan explained in a patient tone. "Because of what happened here."

The lean, athletic Tibetan, something of a local hero for having twice ascended Chomolungma, winced. "They raked it," he announced. The sullen expression behind his sunglasses had not changed.

"Raked it?"

"It's the road the tourists come up. All that blood was bad for business. They brought in a load of dirt and raked it." Kypo turned and paced once around the small clearing, then wandered around the high outcropping that concealed it from the road below.

Shan stared in disbelief at the fresh soil at his feet. Once an investigation had been turned into a melodrama scripted for the Party, nothing could be relied upon. Even here, all he could do was grab at shadows. The knobs had buried the crime scene.

He shook his head then stepped to the rocks where he had found the women and with his heel dug two outlines, the shapes of the bodies as he had seen them. When he looked up the mechanic was standing in the middle of the raked dirt, gazing fearfully at the outlines. It was as if Shan had brought back the dead.

"Who did it, Jomo?" he asked. "Who was the killer?"

The Tibetan cast a longing glance toward the truck, as if thinking of bolting. "I never thought it was you," he offered.

For a moment Shan considered the mechanic, who was such a wizard at coaxing life back into old engines that he was in demand at every garage in town. "What does your father say?" he asked, seeing the expected wince. Jomo's father, the tavern keeper who was more often drunk than not, often professed publicly that he hated his son, had even named his son the Tibetan word for princess. But Jomo, well into his forties, had kept the name, and dutifully cared for his father, the town jester, often conveying him home at night in a wheelbarrow.

Jomo looked up apologetically. His father, Gyalo, occupied the rundown house closest to Shan's stable, and more than once had entertained himself by throwing empty beer bottles at Shan's door. "Some men in the tavern said they should drag you out of the jail and give you what you deserve, because killing the minister was going to ruin the season for everyone. My father said we pay taxes so Public Security could have bullets, and he wanted his money's worth." Jomo shrugged and looked away. "He was drunk." Several times Shan had found Jomo in the dawn outside his door, sweeping up shards of glass. Suddenly Shan realized that if it had not been Tsipon or Kypo who had made the little altar by his pallet there was only one other possibility.

"I didn't thank you, Jomo, for the prayers when I was injured, for summoning the Medicine Buddha."

The mechanic glanced up nervously, not at Shan but toward the road, as if worried Kypo might have heard. "There aren't any good doctors in town," he muttered.

"What do they say in the market about the killing?" Shan asked. In such a place, in such a case, Public Security would have operatives, disguised as merchants or even truck drivers, not just to pay for secrets but to plant rumors.

"Someone from away. A private grudge. The minister was a great hero in Beijing. Someone said she was fighting corruption back in the capital and paid with her life when she was about to expose it."

Not particularly original, Shan thought, but effective enough for one of the morality tales that always accompanied assassinations.

"It's not the killing most talk about," Jomo added in a conspiratorial tone. "It's the monks in hiding, who refused to kowtow to Beijing. People who haven't flown them for years are stringing up new prayer flags." He stopped, grimacing as if frightened of his own words, then turned back to the truck and busied himself examining the tires.

Shan planted himself on a low rock where he could study the outlines of the bodies and the terrain. He had come from below that day, from the wrecked bus beyond the rise in the road, around the large outcropping that had obscured the car. The killer had done his work after the bus had been stopped, out of sight of the knob guards below. Out of sight, yet close enough for the pistol discharges to be masked by the firing of the knobs' own guns. Monks had been wounded and beaten; one had later been killed. The thought chilled Shan to the bone. If the killings had been timed to coincide with the ambush on the bus, it meant the killer had used the monks, had played with their lives to accomplish his own crime. But the ambush below seemed to have been planned so the monks could get away, not merely as a diversion. It did not seem possible that a person who would take such risks to free monks would also fire bullets into two defenseless women.

He paced along the clearing, spotting Kypo leaning against a boulder at the side of the road, cleaning his sunglasses, staring at Jomo, his face drawn tight. One of the mysteries of Tsipon's company was why these two men, Tsipon's two trusted deputies, did not like each other, barely spoke to each other, seemed to go out of their way to avoid each other. Certainly the two men could not be more different in personality—Jomo the nervous, efficient mechanic always flitting about the garage and warehouse, Kypo the silent, contemplative climber and guide, always hiding behind sunglasses who, Tsipon insisted, knew the upper slopes of the Himalayas better than any man in China. But there was something else, Shan sensed, a wedge between them that neither seemed interested in removing.

As Kypo turned and moved down the road, Shan followed, pausing to study the scattered shell casings from knob rifles and the four large DANGER! NO STOPPING! signs that had been leaned against rocks at the eastern side of the road. Public Security might have balked at putting up crime scene tape, for fear of its effects on tourists, but had still made it clear the site was off limits. He halted at the stump of rock where the column had broken away to block the bus, seeing now the chisel marks along the side opposite the roadway. He lay on a small ledge behind the stump, exploring the shadow at its base with an outstretched hand, pulling up first one heavy wooden wedge, then two more before scrambling up the rock debris to lift the end of a red rope trapped under large boulders. It was as thick as his thumb, the heavy nylon rope brought in by Westerners for their expeditions. Kernmantle, they called it in English, the term for braided nylon filaments encased in an outer woven shell. This one had been ruined, crushed by boulders.

He tried in vain to recreate in his mind the pattern of ropes he had seen that day on the rocks, then spotted another remnant of red rope still wrapped around the broken column of rock that had stopped the bus, now pushed along the edge of the road. The rope had been used to ease the column forward as the wedges were inserted. But it made no sense. The strength of several men would have been required to topple the rock, but they would have been conspicuous to anyone coming up the road.

Kypo sat at the edge of the road examining a section of the red rope that he had cut away from the debris. It was, they both knew, some of the rope included in the inventory they had done a week earlier.

"How do I set up an avalanche to trigger when a bus passes?" he asked the Tibetan.

Kypo considered the terrain a moment. "These rocks get rearranged all the time," he said, as if the mountain itself had willed their release. "It wouldn't take much persuasion." He pointed to the slope above the road. "Undermine a few of the biggest boulders until they begin to roll, then brace them. Chip away the support of the column so that when it is hit by the boulders it snaps."

Shan realized the rope had not been used to pull the column down, but to stabilize the loose rocks above. "How would I know how far to chip into the base of the column?"

Kypo shrugged. "Luck, I guess," he said with an uneasy glance toward Shan. They both knew it had taken consummate skill with chisel and wedge to loosen the column just enough to be toppled by a rolling boulder at the right moment.

"But the timing of the avalanche wasn't just luck."

Kypo adjusted his glasses, his gaze shifting back and forth from the road to the slope. "If you knew how to work with ropes and harnesses, you could fashion a tether, like a cradle, and roll the stones into it, putting pressure on it so the stones would roll away when the tether was released." He pointed to another large out-cropping that shadowed the slope. "I would do it behind there, so no one in a vehicle coming up from the valley could see me. Stay in the shadow, release the ropes, and run away into the maze of rocks above."

"It might take only one person to trigger such a rockslide, but more than one to rig it."

Kypo shrugged again. "Two, four, ten, who cares? When the wind blows your house down, you don't care about how many clouds were pushing it."

It was a particularly Tibetan perspective. Violence was like a storm, seizing both those committing it and their victims. It was a waste of time to try to explain, it was only necessary to burrow into a safe place and let it blow itself out.

"How many people in the base camp knew about the bus?"

"No one. It was a Public Security secret. Why?"

"Because someone planned all this very carefully. Stole the ropes and rigged the avalanche in advance. The ropes were taken from the base camp days ago, and the camp is full of people who know how to rig ropes. How long do you think it will be before Public Security realizes that?"

The words seemed to hit Kypo like a blow. His face darkened. He whipped the section of rope in his hand against a rock. His livelihood, and that of his entire village, depended on the base camp, and Public Security could easily shut it down if it suspected the camp was connected to the murders.

Shan paced along the rocks that had tumbled down the slope to block the bus, now pushed to the side of the road. Halfway along the row he paused. At first he thought the faint pattern was a trick of the light. Then he knelt and studied the marks, seeing more, one on each of the large rocks. Someone had lightly chalked an ancient Tibetan mantra, an invocation of a protector demon, on the rocks facing the road. It had been done after the stones had been bulldozed to the shoulder. He stood and looked at the warning signs and bullet casings on the opposite side of the road. The opposing teams had squared off, facing each other.

He watched Kypo climb back up the road and followed, finding him staring at the killing ground with a hollow expression as Jomo, leaning against the truck, nervously watched him.

"There are people already leaving for the season," Kypo stated, his gaze fixed on the outline of the bodies Shan had drawn in the soil. "Good porters, the seasoned ones who know the mountain, will be hard to find."

"Because the traditional ones respect the mountain deity," Shan ventured.

Kypo nodded. "Violence like this could anger the mountain for months. Every team last week had to turn back from the summit because of storms."

"There are always storms."

"Not like these. One of them had ice needles, like little knives.

Two sherpas came back with bloody faces, their parkas ripped to shreds. She's furious, more than anyone can remember," Kypo declared, and walked around the truck to climb in.

Shan knelt again, studying the contour of the ground. Where they had not dumped the fresh soil the knobs had raked the ground clean, but he perceived the bare suggestion of a disturbance, a subtle mound with cracks at the top, as if the mountain were pushing something out, rejecting something. He bent and with his fingers probed the loosened dirt, quickly extracting three dirty pieces of black plastic and metal. He experimented with the pieces a moment, fitting them this way and that, until he had constructed most of what had been a cell phone. Someone had smashed it before burying it. He gazed at it in confusion. The only wireless phones that worked in the region were the larger satellite phones. Such a phone would have been useless. Why would someone—the murderer?—think it so dangerous it had to be destroyed?

He rose and showed the fragments to Jomo, holding them together so they were clearly recognizable. "What was this phone in its prior life?" he queried absently.

Jomo's expression became very serious. He took the pieces, turning them over in his palm, then looked up. "A prayer wheel," he declared.

The words filled Shan with a strange, unexpected sadness, and he spoke no more as they climbed back into the truck.

THE HIMALAYAS WERE the great planetary train wreck. Here, at the high spine of the world Shan now gazed over, was where tectonic plates constantly crashed and ground, here the Eurasian plate was clawing its way over the Indian subcontinent. As he paced along a high knoll, waiting as Jomo scanned the slopes with binoculars, Shan watched a huge slab of ice and snow slough off the side of the nearest mountain, taking house-sized boulders with it. Here was a place where worlds were constantly changing, and Shan had a gnawing sense that he was caught up in one of the seismic shifts that would alter the region forever.

After leaving Kypo at Rongphu gompa, the monastery nearest the base camp, Shan had directed Jomo to cruise slowly along the high mountain roads, pausing frequently to scan the slopes.

"There!" Jomo now called, pointing to a white spot on the adjoining slope before handing Shan the glasses. He studied the familiar white land cruiser that was parked on a steep dirt track near a shepherd's house, then motioned Jomo back into the truck. They reached the weather-beaten structure just as Constable Jin emerged around a corner.

Looking as if he had bitten into something sour, the constable passed Shan and circled the truck once before speaking. "You can hear this old crate two miles away. You're going to put the sheep off their grazing."

"It was the only one in Tsipon's fleet he could spare."

"Bullshit," Jin said, eyeing Jomo, who still sat inside, nervously gripping the wheel. "It's his way of trying to bell his dog. He knows he can't entirely trust you."

An adolescent boy, his face smeared with soot, peered around the corner of the house, wide-eyed, clearly fearful of Jin. The constable often let it be known that he carried enough authority to put any Tibetan away for a year, without a judge's order, on what in China was called administrative detention.

"Is Colonel Tan still in the town jail?" Shan asked.

"He's not going anywhere. That cell will be the last room he ever sees."

"I need to talk with him."

Jin's raucous laugh shook a flight of sparrows from a nearby bush.

Shan did not alter his steady gaze.

Jin turned away, lighting a cigarette as he surveyed the slopes. "Those monks could be a hundred miles away by now. Religious

Affairs thinks I can just knock on a few doors and they will run out, begging me to put manacles on them."

Shan glanced back at the shepherd boy, considering Jin's words. A woman was pulling the boy backward now, tears staining the soot on her face. "Your assignment is for Religious Affairs? Not Cao? Not Public Security?"

"The Bureau of Religious Affairs has jurisdiction over monks. After all the protests last year, the policy is for Public Security to keep a low profile with monks and lamas, especially in this area, so they loan men to the bureau and put them in neckties. And Religious Affairs is taking this personally. The fire, then the ambush. Someone betrayed them, someone shamed them."

"What fire?"

"Two days before the murders, in town. The Religious Affairs office was nearly burned down. Officially they say it was an accident. But the unofficial version is different. They found something in the fire, a statue of an old protector god that didn't belong there, sitting in the ashes, unharmed. Like the god had decided to take revenge after all these years."

Shan's mind raced. Since the last season of protests in Tibet the government had grown unpredictable in reacting to anything that might hint of political unrest. More than ever, Public Security worked in the shadows. It would have worked especially hard to assure no one suspected an overt act against Religious Affairs. "What kind of deity?" he asked.

Jin grimaced, as if Shan were trying to trap him. Displaying such knowledge in some circles would show dangerous reactionary leanings. "The mother protector, Tara. Not like at the killings."

Shan went very still. "There was a deity at the murder scene?"

Jin frowned. He clearly had not intended to divulge so much. "On a high, flat rock a hundred feet away, found the next day, looking at the crime scene. The head of a bull, holding a rope and sword," he explained.

"You mean Yama the Lord of Death."

As if to change the subject, Jin reached into his pocket and produced a heavy steel carabiner, the snaplink model favored by climbers on the upper slopes. "They think I can find a trail of these that will lead me to the traitor."

"A trail of snaplinks?"

"Someone handed these out to shepherds and farmers in the upper valleys, like favors or souvenirs. They must have been stolen, like those ropes that were used in the ambush." As he spoke, the handheld radio in his vehicle crackled to life with a report that the town of old Tingri, forty miles away, had been searched with no sign of the fugitives. Jin muttered a curse, then reached in and shut off the radio. He hated being accountable to anyone else when he was outside the office.

The woman appeared on the slope above the house, frantically running with the boy toward their pastures. "Did they have one of the snaplinks?"

Jin shrugged. "You know these hill people. They won't talk to anyone in a uniform. I said I'm coming back tomorrow to shoot ten sheep if they don't tell me where I can find those monks."

"But you won't."

The constable shrugged again. "I am fond of mutton."

"They'll spend the day moving all their sheep. Come back tomorrow and you'll find no trace of the sheep or the shepherds. And shepherds don't go anywhere close to the base camp, there's no grass that high up. You need to look in town or in the base camp itself."

"I don't get paid to concoct theories. Someone's coming from Lhasa for that. A real wheelsmasher. He'll start with the other small gompas, assuming monks help each other."

Shan's mouth went dry. A wheelsmasher was one of the senior zealots from the Bureau of Religious Affairs, notorious for crushing old prayer wheels under their boots. A wheelsmasher team had come through the month before, removing all public statues of Buddha. "I need to see Tan," he said again, more urgently.

"We used to have a captain from Shanghai who kept a pack of those big Tibetan mastiffs, the ones they say are incarnations of failed monks. He would cruise along the roads and shoot a stray one, then skin it and feed it to his pack. He could never stop laughing when he watched, telling everyone it was the story of modern Tibet. Dog eat dog. That's what you are to those who are running the jail now. Fresh meat. It's not the county's jail anymore. It belongs to Public Security until this is over."

"They have to eat. They have to have their toilets cleaned."

"Meaning what?"

"Meaning they still rely on your office to assure the dirty chores get done."

Jin's silence was all the confirmation Shan needed. "Just get me in with the cleaning crew. Today. This evening."

Jin studied Shan with a new, appraising gaze. "If I don't find those monks soon," he offered in a tentative tone, "Religious Affairs will have me on my hands and knees looking under every pile of yak dung."

Shan clenched his jaw, gazed for a long moment at the snowy peak above them. "I will share what I learn about the ambush. You share what you know about the killings. But I will not help you find the monks."

"Not good enough. This is my one chance at a victory big enough to get me out of this damned county." The week before, Jin had stopped Shan on the road and asked him to look over his application for a transfer to one of the cities in the east. More than once he had dreamily spoken of living in Hong Kong, or even Bangkok.

"I can help with your relocation," Shan stated flatly. "I can do it today."

Jin's face tightened. "What the hell are you talking about?"

"I've been to the desert in Xinjiang," Shan observed, referring to the vast province north of Tibet, a favorite dumping ground for disfavored government workers. "The sand is always blowing.

It gets in your nostrils, in your mouth, in your clothes, in your rice. In the summer it can be hot enough to boil tea. Once I saw a man's eyeballs roll up into his head and he dropped dead from the heat. In the winter people who stop to sleep in their cars are usually found frozen to death. After a month there you will think this is paradise."

Jin fidgeted with the pistol on his belt.

"I will go back to town now," Shan said. "I will find Major Cao and give him a signed witness statement that you were near the crime scene, right there when those monks escaped."

Shan watched for a reaction, confident in his assessment of Jin.

"You don't know that."

"You heard the guns and you went to investigate. But as soon as you saw all the knobs, you fled. An armed officer on a horse could have rounded up those monks, and maybe the murderer as well. Religious Affairs and Public Security will fight over the right to interrogate and then punish you. Every other law enforcement officer known to have been there has already been shipped to the desert, or worse. How long before you're breathing sand into your lungs? A week? Three days? I don't think they even gave the others time to pack."

"Cao will eat you alive if he finds you with his prisoner."

"Me? Men like Cao have tried more than once." Shan studied Jin's anxious face, then shrugged and turned back to Jomo, waiting in the truck. "Don't forget the sunscreen," he called out. "You'll need barrels of the stuff where you're going."

AN HOUR LATER Jomo eased the truck to a stop by the curb in the center of Shogo town, shaking Shan from the slumber that had overtaken him on the long descent from the high ranges.

"Wait five minutes," the Tibetan instructed as he climbed out. "Then I'll take you back to the stable."

Shan watched the mechanic uneasily as he disappeared behind the door of the familiar two-story building, then climbed out to stretch his legs, pacing past the signs that advertised Tsingtao beer and karaoke, stepping to the corner where he could see the squat gray complex that housed the jail. In his mind's eye, before turning back and entering the tavern, he constructed where Tan's cell would be.

Gyalo's inn was the most popular place in town after working hours, filled not only with townspeople but also the truck drivers who used Shogo as an overnight rest stop on the route to Nepal. Cigarette smoke hung heavy in the dimly lit room, laced with the smell of unwashed bodies and the raw onions that patrons chewed on like apples between swigs of pungent sorghum whiskey.

The customers hooted and whistled as a wiry old man in a red robe danced along the top of the bar, waving the robe provocatively. Jomo had come to see his father but he just stood in the shadows, staring in shame at the floor. Drunken customers were tossing coins at his father. The robe he wore, covered with bumper stickers, souvenir button pins and sewn patches meant for army uniforms, was intended for a Buddhist monk. Jomo's father, the town jester and keeper of the tavern, had been a member of Shogo's monastery before it was leveled decades earlier.

Shan followed Jomo into the shadows, though a moment too late.

"Demons!" Gyalo cried jubilantly as he pointed at them, his voice slurred from drink. "Fresh demons have arrived!" With astonishing speed he picked up an empty beer bottle and threw it at Shan. It would have hit him squarely in the head had he not sidestepped. The crowd went wild, raucously cheering at the new show.

"We should go," Jomo muttered, not lifting his gaze from the floor. He looked as if he were about to weep. "I'll come back when he's sober."

As they began to move toward the door, Gyalo pranced across two tables to alight on a heavy wooden chair mounted on an ornate altar salvaged from a temple destroyed years earlier. On the back of the chair a T-shirt was stretched, with the image of a woman making love to a skeleton dressed as a pirate. On the wall to the left, an image of Buddha as a rock star had been painted, on the right was another Buddha on a motorcycle, a cigarette dangling from his lips. Beneath it was a large bronze deity in the meditation position, an antiquity, its hands pocked where cigarettes had been extinguished, its lap now an ashtray.

Hands reached out and grabbed Shan and Jomo, pulling them toward the altar. Shan struggled at first, knowing what was to happen, but it was futile to resist. He let himself be manhandled into a standing position next to Jomo, beneath Gyalo.

"Gulag prisoner!" Gyalo shouted, lifting his cup to salute Shan. "We worship at your feet!" He drank, then lowered his voice to a stage whisper, addressing the crowd. "He never speaks of what crime he committed to be condemned to Tibet. Mass murder maybe? Drug lord? Raped the Chairman's sister?" Shan did not resist as the old Tibetan, not for the first time, lifted Shan's arm and rolled down his sleeve to display Shan's tattoo for all to see. "Marked by the gods!" he cried, and poured the remaining contents of his cup over the tattoo as if to anoint it.

Jomo spat a curse at his father, grabbed Shan's arm, and pulled him from Gyalo's reach. His father sneered at Jomo, then broke into loud, howling, wheezing laughter that quickly spread through the room. "*Pum phat!*" Gyalo shouted at their backs. They were old words, used as an emphasis at the end of certain prayers.

"Why do you let him do that?" Jomo demanded as they stepped outside.

"He's just trying to sell more drinks."

"He's trying to get rid of you. He knows that the more people who know you are a convict the less safe you are."

Shan studied Jomo's face, which had become tormented at Gyalo's mention of rape. His father had been a young lama, had taken his vows of celibacy, when the town monastery had been destroyed. For some reason, he had been singled out for a special punishment used to break monks and build a new breed for Tibet. A female Chinese soldier had been ordered to become pregnant by him. Jomo had never known his mother, only that she had been one of the Chinese invaders and had forced Gyalo to surrender his robe by giving him a son.

"Why did you go in there?" Shan asked as Jomo coaxed the aged truck to life.

"He left me a note this morning. He said he urgently needed to know everything about those murders."

THE CLEANING CREW assigned to the constable's office performed its chores after the supper hour, entering in the dark through the rear door under a guard detail that Jin had decided to supervise. Shan kept his head low, half concealed by a mop. Fighting a terrible, nearly paralyzing fear, he worked his mop toward the metal door that marked the corridor of holding cells, sliding the bucket forward with his foot. The heavy door was locked when he reached it. Suddenly an arm extended past his shoulder with a key. Constable Jin blocked Shan's passage as the door swung open, gesturing forward a gray haired woman, clutching two empty plastic buckets, who advanced with a businesslike air. The constable stood guard at the door, glaring at Shan as he went through the motions of cleaning a row of benches along the adjacent wall. Moments later the woman reappeared, expressionless, her buckets now filled with stained rags, splinters of wood, and other debris from the interrogation rooms. Jin held the door for Shan, escorted him to the cell at the end of the corridor and opened it.

"If he takes one step outside this cell," Jin hissed, "I will shoot you both."

The cell, still reeking of blood, vomit, and ammonia, had changed little since Shan left it. The blood soaked pallet had been replaced, the stains scrubbed from the floor, replaced by new ones, the piles of rags had been tossed against the back wall. Only one of the filthy piles was Colonel Tan of the People's Liberation Army, the dreaded tyrant of Lhadrung County.

Shan turned and confronted Jin with a silent, expectant gaze.

"Fuck your mother," Jin spat, then spun about and retreated to the door at the far end of the corridor.

Tan, either unconscious or sleeping, was slumped against the wall, his body convulsing every few moments— the aftereffect, Shan well knew, of electroshock. Shan did his best to clean the filthy tin cup at the sink, filled it from a bucket of water and bent to Tan. When he touched the colonel's shoulder, Tan reacted as if he had been struck, jerking away with a groan, his upper body slowly falling toward the floor, lacking the strength to right itself.

Shan cradled Tan's head against his leg and dripped water over his split, bloodied lips. After a moment the colonel reacted with another groan. His eyelids fluttered, struggling to open, then he gave up and lost consciousness. Shan dripped water over his head. Then with a wet rag he wiped the blood from Tan's face, tied another rag over an oozing wound on his temple, and inspected the bloody ends of his fingers. Shan thought of running to the interrogation room for a medical kit but realized the knobs would raise unwelcome questions when they discovered their prisoner in bandages. Tan's feet were bare, badly bruised. Beating the soles of the feet was a trademark of older interrogators, used widely by the gangs of Red Guards who had terrorized the country a generation earlier. The fingers of Tan's left hand twitched; on his forearm Shan found the telltale marks of two electrode clamps.

He found himself murmuring the *mani* mantra, the prayer for the Compassionate Buddha, as the lamas in his prison had done when they first cleaned his own interrogation wounds, years earlier. Tan's eyelids fluttered again and stayed open this time, eyes still unseeing. Shan held the cup to his lips and he drank.

After draining the cup, Tan breathed deeply, rolled his head toward Shan, and recoiled in horror, jerking himself upright, lashing out with a hand to slap Shan's cheek with surprising force.

"*You!*" he snarled, and mustered enough strength to kick at Shan, flailing the air with his feet, until he collapsed against the wall again with an agonized groan. He seemed to regard Shan's presence as a new form of torture.

"The old lamas taught me a trick," Shan said in a low, steady voice, "for when the pain gets unbearable. Hold your breath as long as you can and count. When you breathe again, start over. Just focus on breathing and counting."

"You have no right!" Tan spat. His voice was hoarse but its fury was unmistakable. His face narrowed in confusion. "How could you possibly know? How could you possibly be here?"

"Have you forgotten this is where the medical prison is you transferred my son? I assumed you did it to get rid of me, knowing I would follow."

A battle raged behind Tan's black pupils. The animal the knobs had reduced him to fought with something else, the brooding, conscious thing that had been pushed deep inside. His eyes glazed then brightened, then glazed again before a hard, familiar gleam returned to them. "I sign papers for the transfer of dozens of recalcitrant prisoners. I can't be expected to remember every parasite who transits through my county."

It was a lie, they both knew, for Shan and Ko had presented persistent headaches to Tan in Lhadrung. "You use the present tense. I admire your optimism." Shan rose and filled the cup again. As he extended it Tan knocked the cup away with a violent sweep of his arm.

"If they knew who you were, Shan, you'd be in the next cell. Get out or I'll tell them."

Shan silently retrieved the cup, filled it again and set it on the stool just beyond Tan's reach.

"I was there, Colonel, minutes after the murderer left. They found me soaked with one of the victims' blood. For a few days I was their favorite solution. Then I told them how to find the gun."

Tan's eyes flared. For a moment it seemed he was summoning the strength to leap at Shan. He was ten years older but he was all sinew and bone.

"They have only just begun on you," Shan explained. "You know how it works. They are rewriting the script so they will know exactly what song they need you to sing. Tomorrow or the next day you'll start seeing new faces, new devices, probably a doctor or two from the prison clinic. It's what we used to call a half-moon case."

Tan spat out blood, then with a finger probed the teeth of his upper jaw. "Half moon?"

"A case of vital political implications. It is too inconvenient to have it linger. Worse, it is politically embarrassing. Beijing will insist it be closed in two weeks. And one is already gone."

"I don't want your damned help. Go find one of your Tibetan beggars to coddle."

"I predict a closed trial. Then they will take you to somewhere private, maybe just the cellar of this building, though I rather expect it will be somewhere remote up in the mountains. You will face a small group of senior Party members, probably a general or two. An officer young enough to be your grandson will sneer at you a moment, then slowly draw his pistol and put a bullet between your eyes.

"By the end of the month there will be a new colonel in your office in Lhadrung. All those photos of you on maneuvers, commanding brigades of tanks and missile batteries, presiding over National Day celebrations at town hall— they will take them and burn them. I recall you kept personal journals of your illustrious career. Toilet paper is in short supply. They will probably take your journals to the prisoners' latrines. The last evidence of your existence on earth will be wiped on the backside of a starving Tibetan monk."

"Get out!" Tan spat. A thin rivulet of blood spilled down his chin.

Shan looked up at the window high on the back wall, noticing for the first time the crimson splotches on the reinforced glass, then glanced at Tan's bloody fingertips. The colonel, incredibly, had been climbing up, trying to break the window. "When they stop the torture," Shan continued in a matter-of-fact tone, "that's when you know it's over. They will give you two days to heal, to be cleaned up. When the barber comes, you're a dead man for certain. They want you to be able to stand up straight, clean and trimmed, ready for final inspection, before they eliminate you and everything you ever touched."

The light faded from Tan's eyes. His gaze shifted past Shan and settled on Constable Jin at the end of the corridor. "So you bribed a guard so you could gloat?" Tan muttered. "Maybe take a picture to share with your Tibetan friends in Lhadrung?"

"I came because you are innocent."

Tan's eyes turned back toward Shan, though his stony expression did not change. "You don't know that."

"Colonel, if you had murdered a minister of the State Council you wouldn't have run, wouldn't have tossed away your gun. You would have sat there and waited and berated the arresting officer for his dirty boots."

With obvious effort Tan pushed himself up against the wall, high enough to grab the cup of water from the stool and gulped it down. His hand began twitching again. He seized it with his other hand, squeezing until the knuckles were white. "I'm not one of your pathetic lamas. I don't want your pity. I don't want the help of the likes of you."

"When was your gun stolen? At the hotel? Have they asked you about the Western woman? Have Western investigators arrived?"

Tan pushed against the wall harder, until he could stand. He staggered a moment then straightened, the ramrod-stiff soldier again. He pulled off the rag Shan had tied around his head and threw it at Shan's chest. He took a single step forward, raised a battered, bloody hand, and with a powerful blow hit Shan on the chest so hard he was slammed against the bars of the cell door.

"Guard!" Tan shouted toward Jin. "This lunatic has breached security! Get him out! He endangers your murderer!"

Jin led Shan out of the building with a victorious gleam in his eye, leaving him alone on a corner under one of the town's few streetlights. Shan sat on the curb and stared at the fresh stain on his shirt. Tan's blood.

Gradually he became aware of someone hovering near the edge of the pool of light. It was a teenage Tibetan, wearing one of the red T-shirts Tsipon gave to his porters, his features tight with fear. It seemed to take all of Shan's strength to gesture him forward.

"It's Tenzin!" the porter exclaimed in a terrified whisper. "Kypo said to find you. Tenzin's ghost was seen in the village, doing the work of Yama the Lord of Death."

Chapter Four

THE ARRIVAL OF one of Tsipon's trucks in one of the high villages was usually a cause for celebration. Shan had often watched as children climbed over the visiting trucks while Kypo negotiated for porters and guides, exclaiming as candy and fruit were handed out by Tsipon or Kypo, the matrons of the village just as excited over handouts of household wares. But as Shan eased the old truck toward the edge of Tumkot village, he might as well have been Public Security. In the hills above, a flock of long-haired sheep was being hurried into the maze of rocks at the foot of the high escarpment that curled around to the south. Children were being pulled into the stone and timber houses, several women even jerked closed the shutters of their houses as if one of the violent Himalayan storms had arrived.

Tumkot was not the largest of the hill villages, nor was it the closest to Shogo town. But here the mountain tribesmen were most skilled at high altitude climbing, here the inhabitants were most traditional, here was the one village where people still openly spoke of life before the Chinese arrived. More than once Shan had found time on his village errands for Tsipon to sit in the shadows unnoticed, taking joy in watching the villagers in their simple daily routines, cheerfully hauling water from the well, singing old songs as they carded wool, hauling night soil on their backs in large *dogo* baskets braced with head traps.

He parked the old Jiefang in the shadow of a stable, its engine still sputtering after he switched off the ignition, then walked slowly along the highest of the streets, looking down on rooftops that were nearly covered with peas and turnips drying for winter stews. He proceeded to the far end of the village, climbed down a flight of stone stairs, cupped from centuries of use, onto the main street, then ventured into the small central square surrounding the hand pump of the village well.

A young girl struggled to fill a battered wooden bucket, the long, heavy pump handle nearly lifting her off her feet on the upward strokes. She gasped in surprise as Shan, reaching from behind her, clasped his hand around the handle and began pumping. Casting a nervous glance up the street, she offered him a shy smile then sat on the granite step beside the bucket.

"Only half," she whispered. "It's all I can carry. And don't go out of the square. Mother says it is dangerous out of the square."

Shan recognized the house the girl looked toward, not because its appearance was much different from the other squat two-story structures adjoining it, but from the colorful coils of climbing ropes arrayed on pegs in its front wall. "But you and I," he said, filling the bucket, "are going to the same place."

The girl placed her hand on the bucket handle as Shan carried it out of the square.

"What dangers does your mother speak of?" Shan asked as they walked past the first of the shuttered houses.

The girl looked up with wide eyes. "Gods are disappearing," she declared in a solemn tone. "That angry ghost is vengeful. Messengers of the Lord of Death have come," she said, and pointed to a pole with a crosspiece like a mast that held prayer flags, one of the highest points in the village. Two crows, traditional emissaries to Yama, sat on the wooden crosspiece.

As they passed the next house, a man opened a door, saw Shan and slammed it shut. Since Shan wore a broad-rimmed Tibetan hat low on his head, he and the girl might have been taken for a niece and her uncle out on an afternoon chore. But months earlier, on Shan's first visit to the village, Tsipon had decided to share what the Tibetans would have called the essential truth about his new employee, to avoid wrong impressions, he explained. The villagers didn't resent Shan as a Chinese, they merely feared him as a gulag prisoner without papers, an illegal. He was another of the phantoms condemned to roam the sacred mountains.

A bright-eyed handsome woman smelling of cardamom appeared inside the doorway as the girl gleefully called out, her smile fading as she saw Shan. Taking the bucket, she spoke low and fast to her daughter, who skipped out the rear door toward a white goat grazing in the rear courtyard, then turned toward the steep ladder stair that led to the second-floor living quarters. "Kypo!" the woman called in a peevish tone.

Tsipon's manager appeared on the stair a moment later, pulling a sweater over his shoulders. He offered Shan an expectant nod, muttered something to the woman, and gestured Shan up the stair. Kypo seemed to have no time to observe the usual formality of waiting for tea to be served before taking up the subject of their meeting. "She'll bring tea," he started, as if to acknowledge the custom, then leaned forward as soon as Shan joined him at a red-painted table by the front window. "There's been nothing like this since the invasion," he said, an odd desperation in his voice. "The younger men are furious. Some got drunk last night and tried to convince people to go raid the Westerners' base camp and destroy their equipment and supplies to end all climbing for the season. The older ones point to the crows and the empty altars and say Yama has withdrawn his protection of the village after all these centuries. Since before memory, Yama has been the special deity of Tumkot. People say it is why we have survived with so little interference from the government."

"Empty altars?"

"Nearly every family in the village has always had a little statue of Uncle Shinje," Kypo said, using another name of the Lord of Death. "They are disappearing. Since the day Tenzin died they have been disappearing. People say it is Tenzin. An old woman said she saw him floating along the street at midnight, with a star following his head."

A shiver ran down Shan's spine. "I don't understand. The killings had nothing to do with the village." While Shan knew many of the local tribesmen were increasingly frustrated with the outsiders—who paid huge sums of money to the Chinese government for the right to climb their sacred mountain—they also owed their livelihoods to the climbers.

"They say the mountain goddess has a claim on Tenzin, that she must have him back." Kypo looked up with pleading in his eyes. "We need him back. We need him on a pyre at the burning place above town. They want to say the necessary words to him and release his ashes back to the mother mountain. We need," Kypo added with a twist of pain in his voice, "proof that he is still dead." He looked down, avoiding his wife's gaze as she brought two mugs of buttered tea, then scurried away with a jingling of her silver necklaces.

Shan sipped his tea uneasily, as worried about the hint of fear in the sturdy Tibetan's face as about his strange words. A brawny man wearing a sheepskin vest, the village smith, appeared on the stairs from below, casting a frown at Shan before slipping off his shoes and disappearing into a bedchamber. Shan had almost forgotten. Some of the mountain tribes still practiced polyandry. Kypo was married to the demure woman who had served them tea. But so was his cousin.

"I carried his body down from the heights, Kypo."

"How long have you lived in Tibet, Shan?"

"Soon it will be seven years."

"Then you should know better. Death is not so straight-forward among our people. Chomolungma took him, people say, but then he was stolen from her. Now the deities fight over him. Yesterday," the Tibetan added in a lower voice, "people went to my mother to ask about you."

Shan's mug stopped in midair at the mention of the stern, forceful woman. The villagers weren't going to her because she was Kypo's mother but because she was the village astrologer, the closest they had to a monk.

"Me?"

"They asked her to throw her *Mo* dice about you again," Kypo said, referring to the bone dice with Tibetan syllables inscribed on each face that were used by fotunetellers. "They were looking for a way to punish the corpse carrier for failing in his duty."

"And what did the dice say?"

Kypo shook his head. "She won't be forced into consulting the fates. She says it makes them angry. Instead I reminded them about you and the dead," he said with a self-conscious glance at Shan.

"About me and the dead?"

"I'm sorry. Once I was on the trail when you were coming down with a body. I didn't know what to do. I hid. You were reciting old poems."

"You told them I scared you?"

"I told them," Kypo explained, "that you know how to speak with the dead."

Out of the corner of his eye Shan saw Kypo's wife lingering at the edge of the hallway. "And what did they do?"

"Some went home. My mother told the rest we had brought this on ourselves, for ignoring the old ways. She sent them to their altars to recite mantras."

Shan drank his tea, desperately trying to understand what was happening in the village. "Has Public Security come?"

"So far only some bully from Religious Affairs, late yesterday. The fox, people are calling him already, because he wears a fox-fur hat." Kypo's face tightened. "He had four men with him, plus Constable Jin. They searched for the escaped monks in every house, made sure everyone knew they would be imprisoned if they lifted a finger to help the monks. There were problems."

"Problems?"

"The monks weren't here, of course, but that wheelsmasher wasn't convinced we were telling him everything. He tried to change the minds of some of the older villagers, put them in chairs in the square like a *tamzing*." Kypo sighed. "He tried for a couple of hours, then went away."

Shan fought a shudder. Tamzing was a term from a painful past, the name for the public struggle sessions when the Red Guard had tried, figuratively and literally, to beat correct political thought into wayward citizens.

"What do they say in the village about the trap set for that bus?"

"Nothing. The only thing we know for certain is that it was set by someone who doesn't understand what the knobs are capable of doing to us."

"Those monks must have been from local farms and villages," Shan suggested. Like in the old days, he almost added. Once, Tibetan families had always sent their oldest son to the local monastery. "That's where they would search first."

"Funny thing," Kypo replied. "The government doesn't know who they were, don't have any names for those monks. The only files the knobs had about those monks were on that bus. They disappeared in the confusion."

"How would you know that?"

"There aren't many qualified mechanics in these mountains. Jomo sometimes gets asked to help at the government garage, where they towed the bus. Tsipon sent me to pick him up when he was finished. I asked to see inside the bus. Those prison buses have a little lock box bolted under the dashboard for records being transported with the prisoners. This one had been pried open."

Shan felt a stir of excitement. With the records gone, the missing monks had a real chance of freedom. "Why did you ask him to look?"

"Like you said," Kypo replied in a taut voice, "the monks had families."

Shan looked up in surprise, with a surge of fear. Was Kypo saying he had meant to steal the files himself? The offense would have guaranteed him years in prison had he been caught. "If things don't go well in Cao's investigation, Kypo, he will have to cover himself with a politically foolproof explanation."

"I don't understand."

"He will say that the ambush and the assassination were one and the same act, that it would have taken many people to coordinate, that what happened that day was an act of organized rebellion by the mountain people. He will have martial law declared, call in hundreds of troops—"

A frightened gasp, a shattering of pottery interrupted Shan. Kypo's wife, listening in the shadows, had dropped the dishes she'd held. Shan did not complete his sentence, did not mention that the very existence of a village like Tumkot would stick in the craw of any military commander trying to subdue the region.

"And have you decided what to say when the knobs finally come to ask you about the ropes?" Shan continued.

Kypo feigned a look of confusion then, as if to hide his true reaction, rubbed his eye. He was one of the only Tibetans Shan knew who wore contact lenses.

"It's only Religious Affairs for now because Public Security is obsessed with the assassination. But they can't ignore the coincidence much longer."

"Coincidence?"

"Between the ambush on the bus and the murder of Minister Wu."

Kypo buried his head in his hands a moment. "Cao already came to the warehouse, asking about the stolen equipment."

Shan pressed his hand over his arm. The patch on his bicep where the knobs had connected the electrodes had begun to quiver. "What did he ask?"

"Not much. I explained we are a climbing support company owned by the leading Tibetan in the local Party organization. We have strict inventory controls. The rope had been ours, yes, but was ordered by a foreign expedition, put on a truck going up to the base camp, and delivered days before the killing."

"What expedition?"

"The Americans. Yates and that woman who works with him."

Shan's head shot up. "What woman?"

"I don't really know her. Ross is her name, a famous female climber apparently. His climb boss, Yates calls her."

Shan drank his tea in silence, trying again to piece together the puzzle of the Western woman who had died in his arms. No one had mentioned her disappearance. If she was Yates's partner, why hadn't he reported her missing? "Where is this woman now?"

Kypo shrugged. "Sometimes she sleeps in the bungalow behind the depot, sometimes at the base camp. But usually she's out climbing. She's a relentless climber."

"Surely Cao inquired about the day of the killing?" Shan asked.

Kypo rose and stepped to the rear window, gazing into the yard where the girl played with the goat. He absently kneaded a patch of discolored skin on the back of his hand, a remnant of frostbite. "Technically most of our work is done under license from the Ministry of Tourism, which also contracts with us for special projects. He already knew the minister had accounted for all of us that day."

Shan moved to his side before speaking again. "What are you saying?"

"Minister Wu called it an exhibition. We had ropes set up to demonstrate rappelling and other techniques. She wanted a full mobilization, as she called it, a demonstration to her important visitors of all the resources available to support increased utilization. That's how people from Beijing speak of the mountain. Utilization rates of equipment. Base loading of camps. Capacity of the slopes. She gave a speech at Tsiipon's new guest house when she arrived, for a gathering of local businessmen. She accused us of wasting the people's resources, urged us to work harder. You know the speech. All of us Tibetan children need to mind our aunts and uncles from Beijing. Afterward she handed out ballpoint pens with red flags on them."

"Where did she arrange these demonstrations?"

"A few miles up the road, near Rongphu gompa," he said, referring to the restored monastery that was the last habitation before the base camp. "That's where she was going, to inspect everything before the important visitors arrived that afternoon. Nearly everyone was up there. You know how it goes when groups come from Beijing. They use Rongphu like a bus stop. She had a film crew there and at the base camp for days before, shooting footage for a film she was going to show in Beijing. A big outdoor lunch was planned on the grounds of the monastery. It was the minister herself who ordered that section of road closed that day, so she could enjoy her mountain."

"Who would have known about the minister's orders?"

"Only every villager, farmer, and herder for twenty miles."

"But not in advance."

"Of course not in advance," Kypo agreed. "It would have been a state secret."

From the window Shan could see up the slope above the town. Boys and dogs were returning to the open pastures, tending small flocks of sheep. Women in dark wool dresses toiled in fields of barley. Above them, on a trail that led toward the high peaks was another woman, leading a donkey piled high with boughs of juniper. Juniper was the sacred wood, its smoke used to attract deities. Such large quantities would once have been regularly carried to temples and gompas. But in this region, long ago scoured of its temples, such an amount was used for another purpose.

"Did someone else die?"

Shan did not miss Kypo's wince. The Tibetan gestured toward the woman leading the donkey, now approaching a long cleft in the high rock wall above the village. "It's the village diviner," he said in a tight voice.

"You mean your mother," Shan said, trying to grasp the mix of frustration, anger, and regret in Kypo's eyes.

"The last one to see Tenzin's body was her uncle. Except,"

Kypo added in a hollow tone, "our old uncle, that friend of yours, has been murdered."

MOVING AT THE slow jog used by the mountain people to cover distances, Shan soon reached the cleft in the rock face where Kypo's mother had disappeared. He paused before stepping into the shadows to glance back at the village, still trying to make sense of Kypo's announcement. He had never heard Kypo speak of an uncle or great-uncle, could not think of an old villager who was a friend of Shan's, could not fathom why there would not be a greater disturbance in the village if one of their elders had been killed.

Emerging from the long, dark passage after fifty yards, he found himself in a small wind-beaten valley populated only by a couple dozen of sheep and, at the base of the cliff at the far side, a solitary woman unloading a donkey.

Shan had met Ama Apte, the astrologer, weeks earlier at Kypo's house when he had come to retrieve equipment that Kypo and the blacksmith had repaired. He had accepted her abrupt invitation—more like a command— to return to her house with her so she could divine his fortune by casting her pair of bone Mo dice. She was not the oldest person in the village, but she was the most respected, and the villagers spoke of her with awe. She lived, like many of the older Tibetans, in more than one world at the same time. They all endured twenty-first century Chinese Tibet, but did their best to live in a second world, the traditional Tibet that had existed prior to the Chinese occupation. And Ama Apte walked in one more world, a much older one, from the mists of early Tibet, in which sorcerers and demon gods were as alive as the long-haired sheep he now walked past.

Shan halted before he reached the woman, lowering himself into the meditation position beside a large boulder, one hand draped downward over his leg, in what Tibetan Buddhists called the earth-touching gesture. He watched her work, half expecting to be chased away. The fortuneteller had little patience for outsiders. He had known several astrologers and oracles in Tibet, nearly all of whom were intense, inwardly troubled people who, even in towns, lived their lives apart.

Ama Apte paused momentarily when she spotted him several minutes later, then touched the gau, the prayer box, that hung from her neck and continued unloading the boughs of juniper. When she finished, she slapped the donkey on its flank to send it off to graze, then she ventured out onto the valley floor to gather scraps of dried wood from the gnarled shrubs scattered across the landscape. As he watched he recalled the fortune she had told him at their first meeting. He had not asked for the divination, but she had insisted, as if she had her own secret reason. The dice had come up with the symbols *Pa Tsa*, meaning the Demon of Affliction in the charts used by astrologers. She had seemed strangely pleased, and when he asked its meaning she had said it depended on the question that was being asked. If, for example, he was worried about his inability to find inner harmony, then the dice foretold that his unrest would continue, that he would even break his own vows in search of it, that he would never find it again without doing great and painful penance. Only afterward, on his pallet that night, had he understood he had missed the entire point. Shan should have asked what question *she* had been asking about him.

The uneasiness of that day returned as he watched Ama Apte. She was like no other Tibetan woman he had known, strong yet somehow seeming as vulnerable as a child, handsome but with a face that was always lined with worry. She had the eyes of an old lama but the quickness and energy of a young woman. She had, he realized, cast the dice about Shan more than once before, for Ama Apte had been the one to declare Shan must be the carrier of corpses made by the mother mountain. He had accepted the duty without questioning her, for he knew she would have resented the query, as if he were challenging the fates.

Shan warily approached her as she worked, following her lead in stacking wood beside the green boughs. After a quarter hour he stepped over to a flat boulder, covered it with his jacket, and set upon it several walnuts and pieces of dried fruit from the pouch that hung from his belt. He made a sign of offering, then lowered his head. Moments later the woman stood over him. She silently selected seven morsels, the traditional number for offerings to the deities, and disappeared around a high outcropping thirty feet away. Quickly returning, she settled at the makeshift table opposite Shan.

"In all my life my uncle Kundu has been with me," the diviner suddenly said, with something like a sob, "except for that short time between faces. This time I will not find him again, not the way he was taken. He was not prepared for what happened. He will be an angry ghost, roaming alone, confused, battered about by the winds."

At death, traditional Tibetans believed, someone who was adequately prepared, who had the right prayers in his mind at the moment of passing, and spoken over him after death, could make a quick, peaceful progression to a new incarnation. But the souls of murder victims could wander aimlessly, without hope, even without comprehension, for years.

"There are things we can do to help," Shan suggested. "Speak to his spirit. Reconcile his death."

Ama Apte had begun to whisper an old song toward the sky, a song used by pilgrims. Shan did not think she had heard until she abruptly turned her head toward him. "How?"

"Identify his killer. Explain the circumstances of his death. It is something I have helped with before. Truth is a powerful force, in this world and the next."

"You're Chinese," she observed. It was a statement of fact, without rancor.

"I began my life in China, spent more than forty years there," Shan confessed.

A grin flickered across her face, then the diviner searched the distant clouds as if looking for explanation. "But you started a new one in Tibet, to atone for the first." She looked down at his arm, as if in afterthought. "People say you are one of those convicts."

Shan rolled up his sleeve and showed her his prisoner tattoo. "My reincarnation began at government expense."

The woman's fingers were on his arm, rubbing the numbers the way she sometimes rubbed the figures on her fortune-telling dice before casting them. She grew sober and stared intensely at the numbers as if they contained some hidden message. Two cubes of bone appeared in her palm, her Mo dice, which she tossed onto Shan's open jacket. She gazed at the dice in silence, then abruptly scooped them up, took his hand, and led him around the outcropping

Shan was prepared for many possibilities, perhaps every possibility but the one he encountered. His gaze shifted back and forth, searching the rough ground along the bottom of the cliff face, bracing himself for more tragedy. There were more spindly shrubs, a smaller pile of firewood, a pika that squealed and fled as they appeared. And a dead mule.

As if to resolve any doubt, Ama Apte sat beside the body, put the mule's head in her lap, and stroked it.

Her uncle had been murdered, Kypo had said, *a friend of yours.* Shan knelt uncertainly, studying the corpse, seeing the large hole in the mule's forehead and realizing as he saw the jagged white blaze that it was indeed a friend. It was the mule the villagers always brought for him to carry the dead down the mountain. In the cold, dry atmosphere flesh decomposed very slowly, and the mule still wore the harness Shan had used to carry Tenzin's body the day of the murders.

He gazed at the animal numbly, confounded by the strange discovery, then paced along the body as Ama Apte murmured a prayer. Finally he knelt again and stroked the mule's nose as he often had on the trail.

"I knew him," he said, struggling to find words that would

offend neither the human uncle nor the mule. "He had the surest feet I have ever seen," he offered. "He and the mountain deity had a special relationship."

Ama Apte offered a grateful nod as a tear rolled down her weathered cheek. Shan thought back on his visit to her house, near Kypo's in the village. On the ground floor, used by traditional Tibetans to shelter their livestock, there had been a sleeping pallet by the biggest stall.

"Tell me about it," Shan said after a moment.

"When he didn't come back that night I went looking in his favorite places, little meadows with sweet grass protected from the wind. He wasn't in any of them. The next afternoon I finally found him here, his packsaddle empty. The first thing in my mind was that they had taken him to this wall and executed him." She stared at the dead animal's head. Her voice had become that of a young girl. "It happened to my mother and father, not far from this very spot. Those Chinese just dragged them out of their house because they were landowners." She grew very quiet. "I don't know what happened here. I see the future, not the past. I hear that's what you do. Tell us about the past." When she finally looked up her face was like one of the haunting hollow masks Tibetans wore at religious festivals.

Strangely embarrassed by her words, Shan rose. He walked along the cliff face, considering the barren ground, the cliff above, the undisturbed soil between the trail below and the spot where the body lay.

"I spent much of his last day with him," Shan said. Increasingly it felt as if he were attending the funeral of an old friend.

"My uncle was a monk last time, one of those who kept the Yama shrine on the mountain above the village. He told me often that he would pay in the next life for letting it be destroyed," Ama Apta said. Her words were taking on the thin, ethereal quality of a lama's prayer. "When he came looking for a new place to live I said I would never let them drag him away the way they had my parents, that I would protect him, if he would take off his robe and become a shepherd with us. He agreed, because he knew someone had to watch over me and Kypo. He was with us more than twenty years. Six months after he died this young mule appeared while I was tending sheep. I offered him some barley in a bowl but the mule wouldn't touch it. He kept looking at me like he had something to say, then he followed me home. I put more grain out, in four different bowls, including an old cracked wooden one used only by my uncle. He went right to the wooden bowl and ate all the grain. I understood then. As a mule," she added after a moment, "he was always a good uncle."

It must have been Ama Apte, Shan realized, who had arranged for the mule to be used for carrying the dead. It had always been waiting with Kypo at the side of the road, without an explanation. She had been sending her sturdy uncle, the mule. Shan remembered the attentive way the mule had always listened to his poetry.

"I need to examine his body," Shan declared.

When the Tibetan woman did not reply, Shan reached into his pocket for his notepad. Ripping off a blank page, he wrote, in Tibetan. *Thou were dust and now a spirit, thou were ignorant and now wise.* It was a traditional expression of mourning. Ama Apte studied Shan as he set the prayer under a stone by the body, then she gestured him toward the animal. He removed the harness, stretched out the bent legs of the animal, then systematically ran his hands over its body, pausing over a lump here, a patch of dried blood there. Nearly a quarter hour later he wiped his hands on a tuft of grass and stood.

"This wasn't one of his favorite places," he ventured. "No water, not much grazing."

"No," Ama Apte agreed. "But here is where he must be burned. He is too big to move."

"But above," Shan suggested, "there is a place he favored." He pointed to the top of the cliff high above them, then paused a moment, surveying the nearby outcroppings. He had a vague sense of being watched.

The Tibetan woman cocked her head. "He had favorite places, with grass and sun. There was an old shrine we would visit, now lost to the world. He liked the flagpole. There's a trail from below that winds up toward a little grove of juniper and grass above. He would go with me there sometimes, in both his faces."

Shan nodded. "He was shot at the top of the wall, here—" he pulled at the animal's right front shoulder to reveal a wound that been pressed against the rock—"and he fell to the bottom of the cliff. Then someone came to put a bullet in his head with a pistol held between his eyes."

A tear rolled down Ama Apte's cheek. "How can you know that?"

"There are no hoofprints anywhere near here, except for a few from sheep. He has several broken bones, from the fall. If you look closely at his head you will see burned hairs around the wound, from the discharge of a large pistol pressed to his skull. There are prints from a heavy boot, a military boot, from someone walking close along the cliff face."

"He hated soldiers. He would have avoided soldiers," Ama Apte said in a distant voice. "But why? Why go to the trouble? What did they have to fear from him?"

"I don't know. I left him near the road the day of the assassination, carrying Tenzin, a few hours before he was shot." Shan turned and surveyed the little bowl-shaped valley defined by the ridge that curled into the massive Tumkot mountain. The trail that went upward led to a glacier that was said to be impassable. But on the other side of the mountain would be the road to the base camp. "He died because he was a witness to something." Shan looked back at the seated woman, realizing only afterwards that he had given voice to the unlikely thought that had entered his head.

But the old diviner only nodded, as if the explanation made

perfect sense to her. "Are you strong enough to find the rest of it for him, so he can move on?" she asked.

"I'm sorry?"

"The truth. The truth about my uncle will be a heavy, dangerous thing. It will not want to be found."

Shan nodded. The truth about the dead mule would also be the truth that would protect Tan, and therefore could be the truth that kept Shan's son alive. Someone, on the same day, had assassinated the minister, a Western woman, and a mule.

"But I was casting the bones last night," she declared in an apologetic tone. "And again just here. They said the same thing each time. A very strong portent. On the path of death lies more death."

Shan closed his eyes a moment then gazed at the snowcapped peaks beyond the little valley. He extended his hand to the woman to help her up as he spoke again. "We're going to need more wood."

Chapter Five

ONWARD AND ONWARD! *It was the shining light of the Party and Chairman Mao Tse-tung who gave us boundless strength and wisdom!* read the dusty banner on the wall behind Tsipon's desk. The quote was famous in the region, the fervent declaration from the journal of the first Chinese team to have ascended Chomolungma, emblazoned on tourist brochures and regional histories. On the adjoining wall was a new banner, almost as big, announcing the opening of the Snow Leopard Guesthouse, the most luxurious accommodation in the Himalayan region.

It was an hour after dawn, far too early for Tsipon to have stirred from his comfortable house on the slope above town, but with enough light cast through the windows for Shan to see without switching on a telltale bulb. He headed straight for the table under the window, where Tsipon's secretary maintained an informal archive dedicated to local mountaineering: photos of early climbers, year-by-year statistics on expeditions, annals of the Chinese Mountain Institute, and copies of the regional newspaper.

With the battering of his mind and body, his memories of the murder scene had become so blurred he could almost believe everyone's denial that any Westerner had been there. But he believed his dreams. Her face had haunted his sleep ever since that terrible day. In a nightmare the previous night, Shan had been lying broken and bleeding on a cell floor when the blood-soaked blond woman had appeared and carried Shan away from his cell, telling him in a comforting tone that the mountain was calling him for his final climb, that he shouldn't think of it as death, just a cold, windy passage to a loftier existence.

He had decided that her face, though not familiar to him,

was not altogether new. He had a sense he had seen Yates with a woman at the base camp, though he could not be certain since Public Security worked hard to discourage the support staff from mingling with the Westerners. But Kypo had confirmed that the American had a partner who was a famous climber, a woman named Ross.

He had planned to find her photo, tear it out and rush out of the office. But it took much longer than he had expected, as he futilely leafed through every newspaper from the past three months then started over, reminding himself to look for different hairstyles, different apparel, as he studied each of the many group photos. When he finally found her, her hair was much longer, shadowing part of her face, under an American style visored cap. She stood in the center of the front row of a group of two dozen, described in the caption simply as the American guest speaker at a luncheon of the local climbing industry, celebrating the launch of the season, announcing American funding of a new environmental campaign to clean litter off the upper slopes of Everest.

He ripped the page out of the paper, folded it, and stuffed it into a pocket, then resumed his search. Westerners were conspicuous and popular subjects during the season. Within five minutes he had found her again, a clearer image showing an athletic woman with a gentle, self-conscious smile shaking hands with a representative of the Ministry of Education in front of a new one-room schoolhouse donated by an American climbing club. He was scanning the second article, about to extract it, when the overhead light switched on.

Tsipon stood in the doorway, his face smoldering.

"Who is she?" Shan demanded before the Tibetan could speak. Shan held the photo in front of him, advancing toward the door.

The image of the woman seemed to jar Tsipon. He stared at it, his anger fading, as Shan repeated his question, then he pulled it from Shan's grip.

"Megan Ross, it says," Tsipon read. "Citizen of the United States."

"You knew her. You must have known her."

Tsipon glanced expectantly toward the entry to the building, then frowned. "Known her? I know her. A troublemaker. An agitator from the outside who has no notion of the delicate balance of politics in our world. Last year she started a petition demanding that Beijing send the climbing fees it collects to the mountain villages, abruptly announcing it at the climbing society banquet at the end of the season. She said every cent should be given to rebuild the temples leveled by Beijing so the mountain would be content again and stop taking so many lives. I told her if she wanted people to listen to her speak about temples she was going to have to die and come back as a Buddhist nun."

"She did die, in my arms, beside Minister Wu."

Tsipon rolled his eyes. "I read about a particular form of paranoid delusion, imagining that celebrities die in your presence. I know of a hospital near here that could deal with all that ails you," the Tibetan added with a meaningful gaze, then saw Shan's insistent expression and shrugged. "You can't possibly think the death of an American could be kept quiet."

"Cao has somehow managed to do so. Find someone who has seen her since that day. Anyone."

"She is secretive. She has people who grant her confidential favors. She doesn't like the spotlight."

"You seem to know her well. If she is alive, contact her," Shan pressed.

Tsipon glanced out the door again before taking another step inside. "I have to get along with all the foreign climbers. They are our lifeblood. Megan Ross has a list of the peaks she wants to climb. A life list she calls it. Did you know there are over twenty peaks of more than twenty thousand feet in this region alone? Lhotse, Makalu, Cho Oyu, Sishapangma. And nearly all of them officially closed to foreigners. Sometimes she goes off for a few days and when she returns another mountain is crossed off her list."

Shan considered the challenge in Tsipon's eyes. "You mean *you* help her. *You* grant her secret favors."

Tsipon shrugged. "She's American," he said, as if it explained much. "She's been coming here for years, works with that man Yates now, and has influence with all the expedition companies. She needs equipment sometimes. Nothing much. Freeze dried food. Some climbing hardware, most of which she returns. A guide who can keep secrets. Sometimes even a private truck ride in the middle of the night. She pays in dollars. Dollars are very helpful to have. Some of the sherpas from Nepal insist on being paid in dollars."

"Contact her."

Tsipon glanced at his watch. "She isn't stupid. She doesn't tell me about every trip. And no one will talk even if they know. These are illegal climbs. No permits. No fees. Some are close to military bases."

A new thought occurred to Shan. "Why would she know the minister of Tourism?" And why, he asked himself, would she have confronted the minister as she was driving up the mountain?

"You need to see a doctor for this disease of yours. She hated what the Minister was doing to the mountain. Ross said the minister acted like she owned Chomolungma. The minister was the enemy to her."

And that, Shan realized, might have been exactly why Ross had met the minister on the mountain.

Tsipon stepped to a calendar on the wall by the door, lifting a marker from a nearby bookshelf. He put crosses through the past five days. "I need the body of that sherpa. You've got one more day. You should be in the mountains."

Shan kept pressing. "How would a foreigner like Ross get past the Minister's security?"

"The road was closed. When the minister suggested she go up without an escort, no one objected. She wanted to drive herself, experience the passage up the mountain as a tourist."

"How do you know that?"

Tsipon offered a sly smile. "Because she borrowed one of the rental cars from the new guesthouse, free of charge."

"And you," Shan ventured, "have gone into the rental car business."

Tsipon smiled again. "I only have a partial interest in the guest-house. But the car agency is all mine. When I heard she wanted to drive herself, I readily offered our biggest car. The front license plate had an advertisement for the agency. Celebrity promotion."

Shan gazed with foreboding at the calendar. "How is the prisoner?"

Tsipon looked out the door one more time, then paused, look-ing down, as if deciding something. "Yesterday they brought in more specialists, from out of town. An ambulance was called to the jail last night. Forget your colonel. I need the dead sherpa. And right now," he added in a pointed tone, "I need for you to come with me."

Shan silently straightened the newspapers, considering the many ways Tsipon could be laying a trap for him, then followed.

Outside a black sedan waited, bearing the number plates for a government car from Lhasa. Beside it paced a refined Chinese man, overdressed in a black overcoat and red fox cap.

"Comrade Shan," Tsipon declared, "I don't think you have met our distinguished visitor from the capital. Comrade Director Xie of the Bureau of Religious Affairs."

Shan's mouth went bone dry. He offered a hesitant nod.

"One of our glorious rehabilitated émigrés," Xie observed in a polished voice as he reached for Shan's hand. He made it sound as if Shan had decided to migrate to Tibet for his health. "I have heard about your skills with the local population."

As Shan retreated a step Tsipon's hand closed around his arm.

"At work before dawn as usual," Tsipon declared to Xie, pull-ing Shan with him toward the car. "Two of the sharpest minds in Tibet gracing our little town at the same time. Great deeds can't be far behind." He herded Shan into the rear seat as Xie walked around and climbed in the opposite side, leaving Shan trapped between the two men as the sedan pulled away.

The Snow Leopard Guesthouse was a compact two story building of stucco and wood with a steep roof designed, Shan surmised, to conform to a Chinese concept of an alpine chalet. As the sedan pulled up to its front door the sun burst out through low-hanging clouds to the east, casting a brilliant gold light on snowcapped Chomolungma. Shan walked casually along the front of the building as Tsipon boasted to Xie about his new hotel, proudly pointing out its Western structural features and the adjacent plot they had targeted for expansion with a swimming pool. Shan reached the end of the building, looking around the corner before turning back. The old Jiefang truck was visible at the side of the hotel, two Public Security cars at the back of the parking lot.

Director Xie insisted that the driver take photos of him posing with his new friends with the mountain as a backdrop before following Tsipon inside, past the reception desk, into a private room with a table set for breakfast. The walls in the room were adorned with photographs not of the Himalayan highlands but of Beijing, with one wall bearing nothing but a large airbrushed portrait of the Great Helmsman. The buffet on the sideboard was a cosmopolitan blend of dumplings, rice porridge, pickled vegetables, red bean soup, fried bread, pastries, tea, and coffee. As Director Xie settled into a chair at the head of the table with a cup of coffee and a plate of pastries and vegetables, a solemn middle-aged woman in a dark business suit slipped into the chair at the opposite end. "Madame Zheng from Beijing," the director offered in introduction.

"It isn't often we are given an opportunity to so directly serve Beijing," Tsipon said with an uncertain glance at the woman before turning back to Xie. "Shan will be pleased to tell you all about the local gompas."

Shan's hand tightened around his cup of tea.

"The soft spots on our southern underbelly," Director Xie put in as he lifted a pickle in his chopsticks. "We have long suspected renewed criminal efforts by the Dalai Clique." Although the government never officially referred to the Dalai Lama by name, this new, more conceptual term had crept into government pronouncements, always the two words together, in the same tone used for the notorious Gang of Four.

"The gompas are small," Shan replied in a tight voice. "Harmless."

"If they were harmless my office wouldn't exist," Xie offered good-naturedly. "And once," he added, looking at Madame Zheng now, "they were much bigger, building great wealth by oppressing the peasant class."

Tsipon sampled one of the small, hard pastries. "Director Xie has a fascinating theory."

"They had jewel-mounted statues, figures made of gold accumulated over centuries," Xie announced, "the fruits of their enslavement of the masses. Are you aware, Comrade Shan, the Party has decreed that all religious artifacts belong to the state?"

"Of course." Shan felt the steady, probing gaze of Madame Zheng. Although Tsipon had stopped looking at her, apparently dismissing the silent woman as a clerk, Shan had learned to be wary of anonymous, well-dressed bureaucrats from Beijing.

"We have chronic problems with the accuracy of our inventories. I believe we will find these monks were smuggling state artifacts across the border to fund the criminal element, the splitists, in exile. Why else would they refuse to sign their loyalty oaths?"

Shan struggle to keep emotion out of his face as he studied the bureaucrat from Lhasa. Here, according to government doctrine, was one of the handful of officials to whom Tibetan Buddhists were accountable, a supreme regulator of lamas, a genuine wheelsmasher. Under the direction of officials like Xie, teams had been moving through Tibet during the past year, replacing prayer banners with slogans in praise of Mao.

Xie pushed back his dishes and began to unfold a map. "I

look forward, Comrade Shan, to working with you in apprehending our fugitives. They no doubt have conspirators in other monasteries."

Shan stopped breathing for a moment. He looked at Tsipon. The Tibetan had not planned on Shan's joining his private breakfast. He had brought him as punishment for trespassing in his office, had brought him to demonstrate again that no matter how hopeless Shan's plight might seem, Tsipon was always able to make it worse.

The Tibetan rose and poured more coffee for Xie. "I apologize," Tsipon said in a generous tone, "if I gave the impression that Shan could be spared at this particular time. The entire climbing industry depends on a handful of skilled individuals. Of course, just a few insights for now from our envoy to the mountain people could be invaluable. Comrade Shan, you should point out on the map locations of the gompas that are active."

Some might have thought it merely ironic that a Tibetan would force a Chinese to identify the location of monks targeted by Religious Affairs. But for Tsipon it wasn't about intimidating monks, it was about intimidating Shan. Any number of people, including Tsipon, could have given Xie the location of the gompas, he could even have obtained them with a quick stop at the town's library. But Tsipon meant to shove Shan into Xie's scheme.

Shan swallowed hard, extracted a pencil, and began to draw little circles on Xie's map.

"And that of the fugitives?" Xie asked. "Sarma gompa, I believe it is called."

Shan hesitated, feeling Tsipon's hard stare, and made one more mark on the map, down a dirt track a few miles off the road to Chomolungma.

Thirty minutes later, Tsipon having at last departed with Director Xie, Shan walked down the second-floor corridor of the guesthouse, attired in clean coveralls, carrying on his shoulder a canvas bag of tools borrowed from Kypo, whom he had found in the garage. As he expected, a Public Security guard sat on a chair outside the best corner room, eyeing him with idle curiosity. Tacked to the door was a sign declaring the room sealed by order of Public Security. A tray with dirty dishes lay on the floor beside the guard's chair. He was not leaving for meals. Shan was not going to get past him.

Outside, along the edge of the parking lot, he found a ladder being used to paint the balconies of the second-floor rooms.

"Those guards will shoot you if they find you inside that room," Kypo warned over his shoulder.

"I need you to switch the ladder to the adjoining balcony after I climb up, hang a bucket of paint on it. Then put it back ten minutes later."

"Not a chance. Then they'll know you had an accomplice."

Shan eyed the old truck parked beside the rental shed. "Then get in the Jiefang. Start it up if anyone in a uniform comes around the front corner. I'll hear it."

Moments later Shan had the ladder up and was over the balcony. With a prayer to the protector deities he put his hand on the sliding door. It silently slid open.

Stepping to the inside wall he lowered himself to the floor, folding his legs underneath him, moving his head from side to side as he studied the room. From left to right he saw a writing table, a trash can, then the open bathroom door, a side table with a lamp, an unmade bed with a coverlet decorated with pandas playing on clouds, a stand holding an open suitcase bearing an Italian logo, and finally a small closet with a half opened door. He pressed his hands together, his index fingers raised like a steeple, focusing himself, then repeated the process, turning his head much more slowly. On the desk the writing pad supplied by the hotel had been used; a ballpoint pen leaned against a blue three ring binder beside a clear glass ashtray bearing two cigarette butts, both with smears of dark lipstick. On the floor beside the trashcan was a sheet of paper that had been wadded then later straightened out, probably by a Public Security photographer. The bathroom rug was askew, towels tossed on the floor. The lamp on the bedtable had something of red silk, a blouse or nightgown, thrown over the shade. On the floor beneath the open suitcase was a pile of clothes.

He rose and went to the desk, lifting one of the cigarette butts to his nose. Menthols. The front of the binder bore the imprint of the Ministry of Tourism arrayed over stylized mountain peaks. Inside the cover was the agenda for the conference, followed by other meeting materials. Shan quickly leafed through the pages. Maps of tourist attractions. Lists of proposed new attractions, including a new Museum of the Yeti. An attendance list. The minister was at the top of the listed attendees, followed by several national and Tibetan officials, then over a dozen county administrators, including Colonel Tan of Lhadrung County. Next came a keynote speech by the minister, to be presented the day of her murder, titled A Ten Point Plan for Converting Himalayan China to a Global Tourist Destination.

The shelves of the closet looked like those of a department store. A new digital camera. A tiny white box into which earphones were plugged. A pair of binoculars. A new sweater from Tibetan looms. Several small boxes of jewelry. Some of the packages showed no sign of ever having been opened. The giving of tribute to high-ranking officials was one of the few ancient traditions Beijing had decided to tolerate.

Car ready at 9 a.m., said the crumpled paper on the floor, a note from the front desk. He quickly examined the clothes on the floor, then in the suitcase, finding denim jeans and running shoes along with many expensive foreign-made blouses and skirts. He eyed the red silk on the lamp by the bed. The minister had been at least as old as Shan, but she had lived young.

The drawer on the nightstand was slightly ajar. Using the tip of his finger on the bottom of the drawer he pried it open. On top of a small silk handkerchief lay an empty box of cigarettes into which a tightly rolled paper had been stuffed, its end extending from the box. Not just any paper. It was a parchment page from a Tibetan peche, one of the traditional unbound books of scripture. With a chill he extracted the page, unrolled it. It seemed to have no particular meaning, just a page extracted from the teachings of the great poet Milarepa, once a resident of the region.

Shan gazed, uncomprehending, at the parchment, turning it over, finding only spots of age on the reverse side. It was easily a century old, probably much more. He looked inside the package, finding nothing, then sniffed it. It had contained a strong, unfiltered brand, not the kind smoked by the minister. He rolled the paper again and was putting it back into its container when he saw words scrawled on the inside of the folding top. *Eight o'clock tonight*, the note said, nothing more.

He quickly checked the rest of the chamber and the bathroom finding more of the minister's expensive accoutrements, then returned to the bedside drawer. The cigarette package and page would have seemed like trash to anyone else in the hotel but the minister had placed them on a silk handkerchief and kept them by her bed. He closed the drawer then opened it one more time. The prayer rolled up like a cigarette filled him with foreboding.

Moments later he was outside, the ladder stowed away, surveying the parking lot again for watchers. Finding none, he went to the largest of the rental cars, in the rear of the cinderblock garage, a gray sedan with a yellow Public Security warning sticker on its windscreen and gray tape in a large X pattern sealing the driver's door. Before taking a step closer, Shan rummaged in the mechanic's bag and extracted a roll of similar duct tape, which he waved as he approached Kypo.

The Tibetan's face drained of color. "If they found us touching that car they would leave us attached to the battery charger all night."

"Which is why you are going to stand at the entrance to the garage and honk one of the car horns if you glimpse any uniform coming in this direction. If they ask why, it is because you are testing the rental cars." Shan hesitated a moment before turning back to the car, wondering why it was Kypo not Jomo, the mechanic, who was working on the cars that day.

He worked quickly, stripping off the tape, opening the door to examine the seat, the seat belt, the position of the adjustable steering wheel, before slipping in behind the wheel. Minister Wu had driven her own car, Tsipon had said, spurning any escort. Shan tested his own legs in reaching the foot pedals, stretching to reach them. The car had been towed there, and he could rely on the knobs to have sense enough not to tamper with the interior. But he had seen the woman, knew that the minister was shorter than Shan. Someone else, not the minister, had last driven the car.

He opened the front passenger's door, again examining the seat then, with a piece of the tape wrapped around his fingers, adhesive side outward, lightly brushed the fabric of the seat and headrest, picking up nothing but dirt and lint. He paused, glancing at Kypo at the entrance, then opened the rear door and repeated the process with new tape, quickly finding several black hairs on one side of the rear seat, then several blond hairs on the other. He stared at the hairs, the first tangible evidence that he not imagined the dead American. But he had been wrong to assume she had intruded, had been lying in wait for the minister. She had been in the car, riding up the mountain with Wu.

The rest of the vehicle offered nothing else except two cigarette butts in the rear ashtray, bearing smudges of dark lipstick. He sniffed the cigarettes. Menthol again.

"Who else was in this car just before the minister took it?" he asked as Kypo helped him tape the door again.

"No one. Tsipon said save it for her, clean it like new before she arrived. Put in some peaches."

"Peaches?"

"She was from Beijing. He read in a book somewhere about

how the imperial family always liked peaches. So Tsipon ordered a little basket of peaches from Shigatse for her."

"Were you here to present the car to the minister?"

"Not me. Tsipon wouldn't let any of us near her. She was like a visiting deity. He probably had the hotel manager do it."

Shan paced slowly around the car. "Guests can charge a car to their hotel account?"

Kypo nodded.

"How do you know if they are registered at the hotel?"

"They send a list each morning from the front desk. Guests get special rates."

"What happens to the list?"

"The hotel has only been open two weeks. No one's going to worry about filing until piles of paper cover the desk."

Two of the guest lists Shan sought were hidden under a repair manual, the third, covered with stains of grease and tea, lay beside a bulky cloth-draped object. The day of the killing, and for two days before, Minister Wu had been booked as a guest. Colonel Tan had arrived the day before the killing. Megan Ross's name appeared nowhere, though the American Yates had been a guest the night before the murders, when there had been a banquet to launch the tourism conference.

Shan studied the vehicles in the garage. "How many other cars are there?"

"These three. But Tsipon is arranging for more vehicles. He's betting big on tourism. Last week I found him looking over brochures for apartments in Macau."

"What kind of vehicles?"

"Utility vehicles mostly, for climbers and base camp organizers. When my grandfather took climbers, they walked with packs for miles, from the highway to Rongphu gompa to sit with the gods before climbing. It's no wonder so many die today."

Shan studied the Tibetan, wondering whether he meant it was the long acclimatizing trek or the worshipping that saved lives, then noticed the cloth-draped object again. He had assumed it was an engine part under repair. But now he saw a small naked foot protruding from the oil-stained cloth.

Kypo, noticing Shan's gaze, sprang into action, turning out the desk light, taking a step toward the old blue truck that waited for them, suggesting they leave. Shan gestured for him to lead and stood as if to follow, then flung off the cloth.

The bronze statue of Yama, the Lord of Death, was perhaps eight inches tall, atop a heavy base set with a ring of turquoise stones.

"Is this the secret of Tsipon's success, a god in every car?"

Kypo muttered a curse and trotted to the bench, lifting the cloth to cover the figure again. "It's nothing, just an old thing that nobody cares about."

"It's one of the stolen statues."

"Not stolen. They're wandering back now." Kypo, like many Tibetans Shan knew, tended to speak of their deities as if they were members of their households.

"You're saying the thief is bringing them back?"

"More or less. The first one that went missing was found on the doorstep of an old weaver at the edge of the village, a couple days ago. Half a dozen were taken from the village, and most have been brought back now. Found on a doorstep, in a hay manger, one inside a butter churn, one down at the flour mill."

"Sort of a Yama scavenger hunt," Shan mused. "But surely this one wasn't returned here."

"No. But I need to fix it before my mother sees it. She would call it an omen, that this happened to one of deities from the altar behind her house."

"One?"

Kypo nodded. "There was a much older, more valuable statue of Tara, the goddess, beside the Yama. But only the Yama was taken. Then last night he came back, left on the wall behind my house. He was changed like the others," Kypo added in a voice full of worry. "Her altar is special, people come there from all over the village. She might tell the villagers something through her dice that—" Kypo stopped, glancing uneasily at Shan. What was he saying about his mother's use of her astrological powers?

"What do you mean the statues were changed?"

"When an old man down the road had his statue returned, he told her something inside had been released, said no one should insult Uncle Shinje this way," Kypo said. "She was upset when he showed her. I found her in her house crying," he added, confusion entering his voice. "She is the strongest woman I know, and she was crying over someone's little god."

Shan lifted the statue, testing the weight. As with most such figures, the base was hollow, for the small slips of prayers and charms that were traditionally sealed inside when the statue was consecrated. He turned it over. In the center of the bronze plate on the bottom was a neat half-inch hole, recently drilled.

"They all come back like this," Kypo whispered in a haunted tone. "I thought I could repair it before my mother saw. Like the others, the sacred papers are left inside but the same hole is made in each. People say something inside has been incubating, waiting all these years to hatch. People say Yama is sending out worms of death."

THE TWO-LEGGED DEMON of Shogo town was communing with his gods, sitting on the altar he had built against the wall of an old shed that overlooked the trash pit. Gyalo was so drunk he did not seem to notice Shan as he lowered himself to sit before him. The former lama, perched on his altar beside a candle, swayed back and forth, gazing without focus into the darkness of the gully below, into which the remains of the old town gompa, once the largest in the county, had been bulldozed decades earlier.

At first Shan thought the low murmur arising from his lips

might be a mantra, but then Gyalo belched and he recognized it as a bawdy drinking song favored by herdsmen.

Shan had returned to his stable home and searched in his second, hidden workshop to find another Yama statue, which he now placed in the circle of light cast by the candle by the altar. "Where is the home of the Lord of Death, grandfather?"

Gyalo started, then grew very still as he gazed at the pool of light. He had, Shan suspected, thought the deity that had materialized before him was speaking. With an oddly solemn air he filled one of his little altar bowls from a white porcelain jug and tossed it in the little god's face. Gyalo had hung an old chart in his tavern the month before, doubtlessly from some long-extinct monastery school, with images, in descending order, of the hierarchy of existence, with *bodhisattvas*, living saints, at the top and something resembling a worm at the bottom. He had written his name under the worm. Devout monks strived to leap from human form to sainthood in one lifetime. Gyalo's sacred goal, he had solemnly declared that night during a drinking bout, was to leap to the bottom of the chart in one lifetime.

Shan leaned into the light and repeated his question. Gyalo looked up, carefully poured some more of his *baijui*, the foul-smelling sorghum whiskey that was the staple hard liquor of China, drank half, then tossed the rest into Shan's face. Shan, accustomed to such baptisms, wiped his cheeks and spoke in a level voice. "Nowhere in Tibet have I seen so many statues of Yama as here. There must have been a temple devoted to him."

"The army has a missile base up the road. They say it can destroy all of India in half an hour. That's our temple of death."

"A temple of Yama, Gyalo. Uncle Shinje's retreat."

"I once dug out twenty fresh skulls after an explosion on Tumkot mountain. I have learned to eat flesh three times a week. I saw a cat eating a butterfly today. Everything in the shadow of the mother mountain is dedicated to the Lord of Death." Gyalo turned the jug upside down, draining its last few drops into his bowl. "To the glorious chairman of the glorious republic," he toasted with the raised cup. "You Chinese have taught us what life is really about."

"When the Yama statues started disappearing, people started dying."

"What kind of people?"

"A Chinese, an American, a Nepali."

Gyalo shrugged, as if it were to be expected.

"A Tibetan was murdered too, near Tumkot village."

Gyalo's head slowly shifted upward, from the jug to Shan.

"Perhaps you knew Ama Apte's uncle." Shan did not miss the way Gyalo shuddered at the mention of the astrologer. "He took a bullet between the eyes."

Gyalo suddenly grew very sober. "Two legs or four?" he asked in a hoarse whisper.

"Four."

The news disturbed the tavern keeper, as if he had known, and feared, the mule. "It's something of a habit in that family," he said dismissively. But Shan saw the worried glance he shot over his shoulder, into the night, toward Tumkot. "No one should worry about that one. He knows how to throw off a face." But Gyalo *was* worried. Of all the people who had died, of all the hardships that had come to the town, and his life, the only thing Shan had ever seen worry him was a dead mule.

"No," Shan said quietly, "Ama Apte and I burned juniper and spoke to him. He is a hungry ghost. He will be in pain, unable to move on, until he reconciles his death, which means understanding the other deaths."

Shan recalled Jomo's report that Gyalo wanted to know about the murders.

Gyalo leaned forward, exposing a steel incisor, so close Shan could smell his rancid breath. "What do you know of dead people?"

"Most of my friends," Shan explained, "and all my family but one are dead people."

Gyalo's laughter came so abruptly it seemed he had exploded. Bits of rice and sputum shot onto Shan's shirt. But as quickly as it came it was gone, replaced by more worry, as Gyalo searched the shadows, his gaze lingering for a moment on the door to the shed behind him. Shan had seen inside that door only once, had glimpsed stacks of old tools and rusted artifacts.

"Why would the town's living demon be scared of a dead mule's ghost?" Shan asked.

"You don't know ghosts like I do," Gyalo said in a near whisper. "Make light of him and you make light of Yama."

"I am going to stop him," Shan declared.

"Yama?"

"Yes."

Gyalo's grin returned. His drunken cackle was like that of an old rooster. "The Lord of Death never loses. I will look forward to his victory. I will carry your body to the next valley where there are some old *ragyapa*, and personally help to cut up your flesh for the birds."

"Of all the people in town, you are the only one I can rely on, because I know your hate is genuine, and it is like a pure thing between us. An old lama taught me that only pure things are real. You will not contaminate it with a lie."

Gyalo cast a crooked smile at Shan. "You are such a joy to hate, I admit it. A Chinese demon sent to torment me. The perfect neighbor."

"But this time you have a problem, Rinpoche," Shan said, using the term for revered teacher. "You can hate the gods or you can hate me. People say the old gods have let loose the worms of death. I am going to fight the gods. That makes us allies."

Gyalo belched. "If it's you versus the worms I'll chose the worms every time."

"Tell me where the old Yama temple was."

Shan had seen the light that grew on Gyalo's face before, in the eyes of demons painted on the walls of old temples. "You'll never get past the flagpole," the old Tibetan said.

Shan's brow creased in confusion. Ama Apte had spoken of a flagpole, one of the places her mule liked to visit. "Then let me try and fail," he ventured, still not grasping the warning in Gyalo's words.

"The price for that particular information has already been set," Gyalo spat. "One jug of sorghum."

Shan gazed at him a moment as he pieced together the puzzle of his words, then with a small bow rose and slipped away toward the center of town.

Half an hour later, Gyalo's information bought and paid for, he faded back into the darkness, pausing at the entrance to the rundown old farmhouse Gyalo called home. It had once been a sturdy structure, well kept for generations until abandoned when the gompa was destroyed. It was a stone's throw away from the shed and Gyalo's altar, where the former lama was now loudly singing one of his drinking songs to the ruins below.

A solitary butter lamp sputtered in one corner. The floor was littered with pots and dirt and kernels of dried cheese too hard even to interest the two stray dogs that slept on a soiled pallet in the corner. Though the tavern was one of the most successful businesses in Shogo, Gyalo still lived in poverty, because Tsipon owned the business, and the salary he paid the old Tibetan mostly went for alcohol. He glanced back in the direction of the shed where he had left Gyalo, then grabbed the ragged broom of barley straw by the door, herded the dogs outside and began sweeping. He worked quickly, refilling the *chomay*, the butter lamp by the pallet, folding the tattered blankets. He had almost finished when a peeved voice interrupted from the doorway.

"I don't know why you do this," Jomo groused. "He thinks I am the phantom who comes to clean. If he knew it was you he would write curses on the doorway, to keep you away."

Shan leaned on the broom a moment. "My experience in Tibet has taught me that helping my enemies is usually less painful than helping my friends."

"So what does that make that colonel rotting away in Cao's jail?"

Shan began sweeping the floor again, without reply.

Jomo muttered a curse then lifted the pallet for Shan to sweep under.

"Who has come to see your father recently?" Shan asked after several minutes of silent work.

"Everyone comes. He's the town mascot. He sits on that throne of his and they want to touch him for good luck, leave a cigarette or a candy bar and touch him. I used to try to stop them, tell them he was the opposite of a saint. But they act like it's some form of worship. He spits a curse at them and they treat it like a prayer. They've been starved so long they don't even know what food is."

"Someone different came," Shan said, "and brought a jug of baijiu whiskey."

"Half of those who come bring him drinks. The old goat sometimes tells them he only performs for alcohol. The drunken poet saint."

"For *chang* usually," Shan said, referring to Tibetan barley beer. "The locals can't afford a whole jug of whiskey."

An odd sadness passed over Jomo's face. Before replying he gathered up bits of debris in a rug and emptied it out the open window. "In Shigatse I was in a bar with a tiger on a chain. There's a tavern on the border, by Nepal, that has a tame monkey trained to fill glasses. My father is a tourist attraction. I'm thinking of applying for a Ministry of Tourism grant to buy him a cage."

"He has so much anger inside, Jomo, it's burned away everything else."

Gyalo's son ignored him. "Tourists come, Chinese and Westerners, usually with one of those government guides to translate for them. They give my father gifts and ask him to write a prayer in Tibetan. I overhear them sometimes. They say they will take the prayer home and frame it. I read one. It said, *I am a reincarnate demon. I hereby summon ten thousand scorpions to crawl up your ass.*"

Not for the first time Shan saw Jomo close to tears. "When was the last time someone came?"

"Yesterday someone came, alone. I saw his back as he was leaving. It was dark. All I could see was that he was tall, wearing a red wool cap and one of those windbreakers that say North Base Camp. A Tibetan or Chinese, since there was no translator. Afterward, my father was singing one of his old songs and swigging from a fresh jug."

"The flagpole in the mountains," Shan said. "Is it high enough to see from a distance?"

"Flagpole?"

"The one above Tumkot."

"Only people from Tumkot go in those hills. They're haunted. And the flagpoles in the mountain tribes have legs."

"Legs?"

"*Tarchok*," Jomo said, using the Tibetan word for flagpole. When he saw Shan's confusion he placed his hand behind his head and extended a finger upward. "Tarchok," he repeated. "They say there used to be scores in the mountains."

Shan closed his eyes for a moment, chiding himself. He had forgotten a hurried explanation from Kypo, weeks earlier, when he had seen a man walking near the village with his hair bundled into a three-inch topknot at his crown. It was a holdover from much older days, more common among the border tribes of Nepal. The topknots, and the hermits who wore them, were called *tarchoks*, flagpoles.

"No one goes near the mountain above Tumkot because of the tarchok. They say he's like a wild animal living in the ice world up there, going backward to the origins of hermits, turning into a yeti."

Shan cocked his head, not certain he had heard correctly. "A hermit becoming a yeti?"

Jomo glanced over his shoulder as if wary of being overheard. "We have had Tibet for maybe a thousand years, that was all we could hope for." He referred, Shan realized, to the period of the Tibetan Buddhist state. "Before our time, long before our time, the only mountain tribe was that of the yetis. They tried to fit into the rest of the world but eventually they gave up on people and they all became hermits."

Chapter Six

TRADITIONAL TIBETANS WOULD have called it a power place. The tiny hanging valley opened to the south toward the mother mountain, its spring and grove of junipers helping to focus spiritual energy. It had been only an hour's walk on the trail up the ridge that curled around and above Tumkot, but the ruins of the old shrine felt a world away. Shan lowered his small backpack to the ground and studied the site from the narrow trail before descending to the ruins. Below, visible in the distance, was the village. He was, he realized, at the shrine Ama Apte had mentioned, where she and her uncle had visited. He considered how the foundations of the ruined buildings were set back from the high cliff to the south, against an overhanging ledge, making the site invisible from below. The army probably had sent a bomber to destroy it, but never would have been able to locate it without local help.

There was little left but a few charred beams and piles of stone. Bits of plaster, some bearing signs of weathered paint, lay strewn about the landscape. A singled tattered prayer flag fluttered from a frayed yak-hair rope anchored to a cairn of stones. He set another stone on the cairn and positioned himself in the center of the ruins, pacing in an ever-widening circle as he tried to imagine the structure as it had been built, and how many monks had lived there. Once on Tumkot mountain, Gyalo had said, I dug out twenty fresh skulls.

The Lord of Death was indeed there, at least the shards of Yama. Shattered bits of bronze statuary and shards of ceramic lay around the clearing, heads and arms of the deity of death, mixed with those of protector demons. He shuddered as, too late, he spotted the clay torso of a tiny god under his descending boot and crushed it into a dozen pieces.

Shan found the altar in deep shadow, against the wall of the living mountain at the rear of the overhanging ledge. At the back of the little sheltered alcove were traces of paintings, now so faded as to be barely discernible. They were probably centuries old, dating to when the first emissaries of Buddhism had begun to cross the Himalayas.

Irregular slabs of rock, some scorched from fire, leaned against boulders on either side of the alcove to form makeshift walls. Along the back wall an old beam had been balanced on square stones for an altar, on which stood the surviving gods, a Compassionate Buddha in the center flanked by a score of bronze Yamas and lesser deities along with several less elegant plaster figures, crudely painted, the kind sold as souvenirs to tourists. The altar and nearly all the bronzes were encrusted with dust, each exposing an outline of naked wood underneath when he lifted it. The last Yama had scant dust on its surface, but dust underneath. It had been brought to the altar recently. None yet had holes in their base plates. He paused over a low, anomalous shadow at the back, and lit the hand light he had brought from the warehouse to investigate.

The shape was so alien that at first it did not register. Once it did he stared in mute confusion. It was a two-inch long, dirt-encrusted cross, with a small bearded figure entwined on it. With trepidation he lifted it. The back of the cross was clean, exposing tarnished silver, its shape pressed into the film of dust that had fallen from the rocks above.

He searched for the word, one he had learned from his father in their secret, illegal lessons during the reign of the Red Guard so many years earlier: *crucifix*. He stared at the image in wonder, then with even greater wonder at the deep outline it had left in the crust on the altar. It had been put there many, many years earlier, probably one of the first things deposited on the makeshift altar, never touched since. With unexpected guilt, he set the cross back exactly where it had been, pausing only to wipe the dirt from the Christ figure's eyes.

He retreated, pacing uneasily around the ruins again, wary of the precipitous drop at the edge of the cliff, then retrieved his backpack, settled onto a flat boulder, and began scanning the mountain with binoculars he had borrowed from Tsipon's depot. The shrine was on the long ridge that cradled Tumkot, curling out from the south, allowing him to look out over the sheer drop in front of him to the adjacent slopes, though still not high enough for him to be able to see the ice field that lay atop the imposing escarpment of the main mountain.

A family of goats walked single file up the far rock face, past a patch of blooming heather. A large bird of prey landed on a spine of rock over a grassy ledge. Far below, at the foot of the mountain, shepherds with dogs pressed a herd of sheep into the little hidden valley where he and Ama Apte had mourned with the dead mule. He looked back up at the top of the ridge and began systematically sweeping downward with his eyes, nursing his growing conviction that there must be a hidden trail over the top that the mule had descended, either with or closely followed by the murderer. He saw the patch of grass above where the mule had fallen, on a shelf less than a third of the way up the steep rock wall. No matter how sweet the grass, surely the affectionate old creature had not gone up from the valley after the long strenuous day, passing the village, passing the woman who so tenderly cared for him.

He watched a coasting raven, then the family of goats for a moment, comforted that the pace of natural life in the mountains continued despite the chaos below. Then he froze. The patch of heather the goats had passed was gone. He urgently searched the slope behind them, trying to follow the thread of shadow that marked their trail along the near vertical wall, then saw there were several threads, multiple trails, some leading up, some stretching along the flank of the escarpment, coursing around the ridge toward the Yama shrine.

When at last he found the speck of color it seemed to be impossibly distant from where he had first seen it. But then he realized the patch of color was running. For a frantic instant he thought that he might be watching a yeti, that the creature had seen him, was coming to attack him. Then the figure stopped and stepped onto a formation that jutted out from the wall and spread his arms. He stood there, motionless in the updraft, his red robe fluttering around him like some hovering bird, then he spun about and bounded cat-like to the next jutting rock, where he repeated the performance. The man wasn't running to Shan, he was running for joy.

Shan glanced back at the shrine, knowing he risked missing the thief if he left, then trained his glasses on the trails in front of the monk, calculating that the man was making a circuit on the ridge, out to the end of the trails then back to the massif. Shan selected a prominent ledge half a mile away where the trails converged, then he too began to run.

When the man in the red robe reached him Shan was sitting at the outer edge of the shelf of rock that marked the intersection of the two main goat paths, his legs folded under him in the meditation position, gazing out over the valley below. He did not turn, did not move except to fold his hands into a ritual gesture, the earth-touching *mudra*, as he began a quiet mantra. The man approached, so close Shan feared he might try to shove him off the cliff, then stepped to his other side, touching him tentatively with the toe of a tattered high top boot before retreating to pace back and forth behind Shan.

As his movements slowed, Shan turned and extracted two objects, offering them on his palm to the man. The leathery, weatherbeaten face that looked back at him had deep, moist eyes that softened as they saw Shan's offerings: a small cone of incense and a box of matches. Wordlessly the man lifted them from Shan's palm, lit the incense, and set it on a little black patch of soot Shan had noticed when he sat down. Incense had been used there before.

As the Tibetan sat on the opposite side of the fragrant cone, he too extracted something, not the prayer beads Shan half expected, but a *chillum*, one of the deeply curved wooden smoking pipes traditional in the mountain tribes. He lit the pipe, returning the matches to Shan with a nod of thanks.

After several puffs on the pipe, the man opened and shut his mouth, then made a low rumbling sound in his throat. It was the way of many hermits Shan had encountered in Tibet. They often had to remember how to speak with other humans.

"You made a mudra," the hermit finally said in a raspy voice. It was not an accusation but an expression of curiosity. "You spoke the mani mantra." He puffed again on his pipe. "Do you think you are heard?"

Shan looked back over the mountains. "The way I reach the Buddha," he said, "is the way the Buddha reaches me." The words had been part of his first lesson with his old lama friend Gendun.

The hermit nodded, as if Shan had passed his first test, and Shan turned and dared to examine the man tarchok as he cupped his hands around his chillum and puffed repeatedly to encourage the embers to burn in the thin air. He was a compact, sturdy man, perhaps ten years older than Shan, his robe patched in several places, his ankles naked under his heavy boots, his topknot tightly braided and doubled over, fastened with red thread.

"When I visit the shrines near Chomolungma, people who are not Tibetans come sometimes," the hermit observed. "But they always have better clothes than you," he added whimsically.

Shan could not resist a grin.

"They ask me many questions." Now that the hermit had found his voice it was slow and melodious. "Though in the end they are all asking the same thing. They want to know how to find peace." He worked on his chillum again, letting the smoke drift out of his mouth. "I tell them the only peace you find up on a mountain is the peace you bring with you."

For a moment Shan wanted to forget everything, to bask in the wisdom of the old hermit, who was so much like his friends in Lhadrung. But then the hermit spoke again.

"On this mountain, though, there is no room for strangers. Strangers just die. When the incense burns down you must leave."

Shan's throat went dry. The man was no longer speaking like a hermit, but like a sentinel, a protector demon. "My name is Shan," he said. "I seek a ghost, and one who makes ghosts."

"I am called Dakpo. I speak for the mountain. When she wakes she will shake you off like a flea."

"I am no intruder," Shan ventured. "I am the corpse carrier, named by the astrologer of Tumkot."

It sounded like a line from a fairy tale, but the words gave the hermit pause. He puffed on his pipe, studying Shan intently. "I saw you on the road burying your first corpse under rocks."

Shan looked up in surprise. On his first visit to the base camp he had stopped to remove the corpse of a dog from the road. He had given it a quick burial under a mound of stones, whispering a prayer to send the dog on its way.

"I said to myself, there is a man who appreciates death."

Shan hesitated, biting down the questions that leaped to his tongue. Dakpo had not been on the road itself, and the slope on the far side of Tumkot mountain was said to be impassable. He replayed the words in his mind. Had the hermit just told Shan why he had been selected as corpse carrier?

Shan pointed to the valley below. "There, against the wall, you can still see the soot of the pyre. When we burned her uncle, only Ama Apte and I were there but I sensed someone else close by. He was a friend of yours too. If I had not lost the corpse our mule friend would still be alive. It is a heavy debt I owe, Dakpo. To the corpse, to your old friend, to the mountain. I must be allowed to pay it."

The hermit's brow furrowed. He cast a mournful gaze toward the barely discernible smudge on the distant cliff face and puffed again on his chillum. "His name was Kundu. I knew him all my life," he said at last. "It is a rare honor, when a friend comes back the way he did."

"But he came back on four legs."

Dakpo offered a strangely sad smile, then swept his hand across the horizon. "For as far as you can see there will be none of us coming back on two legs."

It was the most remarkable statement of a remarkable conversation. Shan dared not ask what terrible sin the inhabitants of the region had committed to all be reborn as lower life forms. "Do you live in a cave, Rinpoche?" he asked instead.

The hermit's mood had darkened. He only nodded.

"Above the cliff where the mule was killed?"

He nodded again.

"I don't think he was going up the trail for grass. I think he was coming down. Did you see him?"

"He was not anywhere above," Dakpo shot back, too insistent. "There is nowhere above."

"He would not have been alone," Shan continued. "He would have been with his killer, or closely followed by his killer."

"He went to get grass. He fell. Someone shot him in an act of mercy."

"No. He was first shot above."

"You don't know that."

"I do. That wound was on the far side of his body, against the wall. His killer could not have done it after he fell."

Dakpo fell silent.

"How long have you lived in your cave, Dakpo?"

"As long as I care to remember."

"But you are from the village?"

"A long time ago."

"Then you must know the secrets that Ama Apte's uncle died for."

"What are you talking about?"

"The mule took a secret trail home. The minister's killer was on the same trail, eluding his pursuers. But I can't find the truth, can't release the soul of your friend without knowing that secret.

There are probably helpful signs on the trail, clues I could use. What is so important that it keeps you from helping him?"

"There is no such trail. And we have our own ways of dealing with death, Shan. The mountain will work it out." Dakpo stood, stowed his pipe in the pouch at his waist and without another word walked away. Shan watched a long time, watched as the patch of red against the massive stonewall grew smaller and smaller and finally disappeared, then he turned back to the shrine.

Thirty minutes later he had settled into the shadows of a small ledge from which he could watch both the path from below and the sheltered altar where the deities, both Eastern and Western, patiently waited.

Purple and gold fingers stretched out in the sky above the snowcapped western peaks. He relaxed, wondering absently if his son was watching the same sunset, constructing dragons and fish out of the clouds as Shan and his father often had done. Then, as so often happened, a whisper of reality crushed his dream. It had been his particular psychosis during his years in prison, one for which he still had found no cure. He would dream of his son Ko as a happy, innocent youth, had laid on his own dark prison bunk for hours imagining his son studying the old poets, flying kites, folding paper hats. But all the time, unknown to Shan, his son had been a criminal, a gang leader, a drug dealer, a drug user. And just as Ko had begun to transform, to heal in the hands of the prisoner lamas of Shan's own former camp, he had been transported for being a chronic disciplinary problem to the knobs' infamous prison hospital. Ko, the only person on the planet who shared blood with Shan, lingered on a slow but certain path to death. With one of the silent, wracking sobs that sometimes woke Shan from a dead sleep, he had a vision of Ko emptied out, cauterized by chemicals and electrodes.

He steadied himself, forming a calming mudra with his hands, pushing himself into the present, remembering that he too had a path to follow that might, with the slenderest reed of a chance, allow him to alter Ko's fate. His lips began to move in a silent mantra. Stars twinkled to life above the mother mountain, around which a silvery moonlit plume of wind-driven snow hung like a prayer scarf. A tide of fatigue surged through Shan's limbs. He leaned against the rock behind him.

He awoke with a terrible sense of falling, so vivid he clutched at the stone beside him, his heart pounding. Above, the stars had shifted hours to the west. And below, someone stalked the gods.

Shan rose silently to his feet. The dark figure held a flashlight near his head as he surveyed the makeshift altar. No, Shan saw as he advanced, the man had a light strapped to his head, leaving both his hands free to handle the figurines. The intruder worked quickly, hefting each little statue, shaking it, stuffing two, then three, into a bag hanging from his shoulder. A light on his head. What had the old woman in the village seen? A ghost with a star over its head. Shan rose and stealthily descended into the ruins.

He felt the pressure of the ceramic shard under his boot an instant too late to prevent it from snapping. Twenty feet away, the thief spun about at the crunching sound, instantly switching off the light, crouching so that he was just another low, dark shadow among the moonlit rocks.

"I just want to speak with you!" Shan called out in Chinese, then Tibetan, as he took another step forward. A ball of shadow exploded from under the overhanging ledge, colliding with Shan, knocking him off his feet before bounding down the path.

Shan was up in an instant, in frantic pursuit, stumbling on the loose gravel, running with his arm slightly extended to warn him of the outcroppings hidden in shadow, then sprinting forward as he spotted the thief in a patch of moonlight a hundred feet ahead of him.

He sensed the fist a moment before it connected, just as he rounded a column of rock. It would have pounded his eye but he twisted so it bounced off his ear, feeling like someone had taken a mallet to his head. As he fell he swung wildly, grabbing a booted foot, jerking his assailant off his feet but inviting a kick that sent an explosion of pain into his ribs. He rolled, thinking he had knocked the man down, then realized it was not the man's body he clutched but the nylon bag of figurines.

The two men began a treacherous tug of war. Shan suddenly sensed that they were at the cliff's edge, with a thousand feet of void less than a yard away. He reached for his flashlight and hammered with it on the man's knuckles until it was wrestled from Shan's grip and tossed away. The bag caught on a rock and began to rip. The ancient figures tumbled out, rolling on the ground. The man gasped, losing interest in Shan as he desperately reached for them, grabbing the last one just as Shan's own fingers closed around it. It was one of the very old bronze Yamas, its jeweled eyes lit with moonlight. Shan jerked it onto his shoulder, the intruder wrenched it back. The deity seemed to watch their struggle in disappointment.

Shan found a handhold on a boulder and heaved backward. The Yama broke out of the man's grip but the force of Shan's effort sent the statue tumbling backward, out of Shan's hand. A choked cry left the thief's throat as the bronze disappeared over the cliff. Then a boot slammed into Shan's chest, and he lurched backward, sprawling on the ground, gasping for air as he clutched at his heart. When he could breathe again he saw the shadowy figure running in another pool of moonlight a hundred yards below.

Shan crawled to the edge of the cliff and looked down, overcome with desolation. He hadn't just lost the thief. He had killed a god.

Shan stayed bent, his head touching the ground, at first because it relieved the pain in his chest and then because of his shame. When at last he rose it was not to stumble downhill but toward the altar, gathering a small bundle of dried grass which he lit to examine the thief's work. The intruder had started at the end opposite the crucifix, had been stopped by Shan before he reached the Buddha in the center of the altar. But five of the bronze Yamas, the largest ones, were gone.

As his makeshift torch sputtered and died he glanced at the stars and the shadow-black trail. It was only a few hours until dawn. He gathered more wood and lit a fire a few feet in front of the altar, then retrieved his blanket and pack, withdrawing the pouch of food he had brought. Ignoring his hunger pangs, he emptied all his food onto the altar and divided it into seven portions and distributed them along the front of the altar, adding a smoldering, fragrant juniper twig to each offering. He murmured prayers of apology then placed another smoldering twig by the crucifix. It was as out of place as a fish in a tree but it seemed the most significant discovery he had yet made.

ALTHOUGH IT WAS only an hour after sunrise when Shan reached her house, Ama Apte was not at home. He settled against the frame of the doorless front entry, pushing to one side the copper pot of milk someone had left beside a worn butter churn, then shifted to pull his shirt away from the blood matted on his ribs. The only thing he knew for certain about the thief was what he wore on his feet. Where the stranger had kicked him his skin had been torn and bruised in the clear pattern of a cleated climbing boot. Pulling his hat low over his face, he watched the villagers go by for several minutes, glancing at the women who sat at several doorways working their own churns before exploring the chamber that comprised the first floor of the astrologer's house. A pallet with a folded blanket still lay on the packed earth by a stall, as if she waited for her mule in the night. Two buckets, one of water and one of fresh grain, stood by the pallet. Ama Apte was conducting the traditional Bardo death rites for the lost mule, during which food and drink were left for the departed.

At a small bench by the solitary window at the rear, squares of yellow cloth lay under a spool of red thread beside the sheets of handmade paper on which fortunes were recorded. He opened the door of a small wooden cabinet above the bench, finding more spools of thread and old nibbed pens with a bottle of ink. On the inside of the door, yellowed tape held a photo of a young Dalai Lama on a horse, with armed men escorting him. Leaning on the back of the cabinet was a tattered book of Mo divination tables and several worn pairs of the astrologer's dice.

His gaze drifted back to the photo. Though they were considered contraband and were regularly burned by the Bureau of Religious Affairs, images of the Dalai Lama were secretly kept by many, probably most, Tibetans. But he had never seen one like this. He studied it closely, swinging the door into the sunlight, considering the teenaged countenance of the reincarnate leader, the fur-capped soldiers with old British Enfield rifles. All the faces were tired and travel worn. One soldier could be seen on a slope in the distance, watching the trail behind them. He suspected it had been taken during the Dalai Lama's secret flight across the border, while the Chinese army had been trying to kill him by shelling his living compound in Lhasa.

He returned to the entryway, watched the women at their chores, then bent and poured the milk into the fortuneteller's churn and began to work the plunger. It was a daily ritual performed for centuries by millions of Tibetans, still very much part of life for nomads and remote villagers.

When Ama Apte finally arrived, leading a goat, she offered neither complaint nor greeting, but uttered a grunt of satisfaction as she lifted the lid to the churn and saw that the morning chore was almost complete. Dropping in a palmful of salt from a small crock near the door, she disappeared into a neighbor's house and returned moments later with a steaming kettle, two tin cups, and one of the tall, narrow churns used for mixing buttered tea. Whether he was invited or not Shan was a guest and she would serve him buttered tea.

She did not speak as she prepared the tea, nor as she arranged two low milking stools just inside the house and finally handed him his steaming cup, straightening her colorful apron before sitting down.

"What happened here?" Shan asked. "I mean before, when the Yama temple was still used. Were there priests from far away?" He knew no Tibetan word for missionaries.

"People used to say we were the most faraway of any place in all the world," the woman replied. "We were proud of that. The Himalayas protected us. What I remember most of all was the peacefulness. Villagers sang songs at the well. There was a village loom where everyone worked on rugs to sell to the caravans that came across from Nepal. Monks were always in the square, prayerflags on every house. "

"From the Yama temple?"

"They say before that temple there was another, to earth deities and the mountain spirits. Before that, the gods played there."

"I was thinking more of the past century."

"In 1924 Westerners began driving nails into our mountain," Ama Apte declared, her voice growing distant as she referred to the first expedition to climb Everest.

Shan sipped his tea in silence. "Kypo said his grandfather took climbers up. You knew some early climbers?"

"None of us called it climbing. Monks had gone up the mountains for centuries, not to reach new heights but to visit the gods. We called it paying homage, or said we were going to speak with the goddess. The Westerners mostly climb her because she happens to be a few feet taller than other mountains. Put a pole on the peak and they would climb that too."

Shan struggled to understand, not what she was saying but what she was not saying. He replayed her words in his mind several times, then abruptly understood the question he had to ask. "Climbers come to the village sometimes, to talk with Kypo, mostly the expedition leaders. You give them blessings."

"Do I look like a monk?"

"Forgive me. You provide them with propitious dates and words to say at the top. I've seen the climbers carry charms in little yellow bags sewn shut with red thread."

When she did not reply Shan pressed on. "Did Megan Ross first come to you last year or was it earlier?"

The astrologer went very still.

"I read she was working with Tibetans and sherpas to spread the word that the mountain was sacred," Shan explained. "She was working with someone to learn the old ways of going up mountains."

Ama Apte began to stroke the back of the goat.

"Did she learn to drink your buttered tea?" he tried, hoping to get her to admit she at least knew the American.

"She carried a little bottle of mint extract," Ama Apte said in a strained voice. "With a few drops of that Megan said she could swallow the strongest Tibetan tea."

"Surely she couldn't speak Tibetan."

"She spoke some Chinese."

"Why would she go see the minister? She could never have expected to persuade Wu to stop the climbing tours."

"You will have to ask her yourself."

Shan watched the woman carefully as he spoke. "Megan Ross is dead."

Ama Apte cocked her head at Shan. There was no grief in her eyes, no surprise. "She plays tricks, that American girl. She goes places the government doesn't want her to, so she lets stories be spread to divert their interest. She may seem dead to you. She would pretend to be dead if it helped preserve one of her secrets."

"She isn't on one of her secret climbs. I found her, Ama Apte. Shot twice, lying beside the murdered minister. She died in my arms."

It was not grief that came now but anger. "No," Ama Apte said in a simmering voice.

"I was a good friend of your uncle's," he ventured. "You and I said prayers for him. When speaking of the dead the truth must be spoken."

"She is not dead," Ama Apte insisted. "I would know it."

"Are you saying that as her friend," Shan said, "or as her fortuneteller?"

The Tibetan woman turned back to the goat. "She is on some high peak, laughing into the wind. And Tenzin will not be found until he is ready. The dead of the mountain will keep coming back if they have unfinished business," she declared to the animal. "That has always been the way of the mountain."

Reality is nothing but a shared perception, a lama had once told him. It didn't seem to matter that Shan had been stained with the blood of the dead woman, for the reality that everyone perceived was that she had not died. Shan had never encountered a murder where the dead kept moving, where the dead were still players in events even after they stopped breathing.

"Tell me how you met her," he said softly.

"It was up high," she said after a long silence. "Two years ago. There are secret places, little shrines only my people know about, shrines where words must be spoken every spring. I was hiding because some climbers were passing close by. I waited a long time before I emerged, but there she was, waiting for me at the shrine. She asked me why I was afraid of climbers."

"Afraid?"

"I told her I wasn't afraid of who they were, but of what they did. I told her that if the shrines were ignored, more and more climbers would die. I said dead foreigners were accumulating all over the upper slopes, with no one to pray for them, no one to help them make the passage to the next life. She helped me clean up the shrine, and when she saw that the prayer flags were old and tattered she said she would give me money for some new ones. I explained it wasn't money that made flags valuable, that these scraps of cloth were holy for having sent out a million prayers, one with each flutter. It was only when she helped me tighten the line and straighten the flags that she really understood. Half the line was empty."

"Because foreigners had been taking the flags for souvenirs."

Ama Apte nodded. "She asked Kypo about me, not knowing then that I was his mother, and she found me here the next week, to tell me she arranged for the climbing groups to delete that particular trail from their route maps. That's when she began asking me how Tibetans went up the mountains in the old days."

"Did you know she was trying to meet with the minister?"

"She comes every week or two during the climbing season. Last time she told me she was going to attend the conference at that new hotel. She said they needed what she called a dose of reality, as if she would give it to them like a pill."

"You mean she was going to stop the minister from doing something?"

The fortuneteller decided to change the subject. "Have you found the answer for my mule?" she asked abruptly. "If he is not settled, things could go badly," she added, as if she were now telling the fortunes of ghosts.

"To find your uncle's killer," Shan explained, "I need to know more about your way to the mother goddess. When I needed to carry bodies, Kypo always met me with the mule below Rongphu gompa, on the trail that parallels the road from the base camp. The mule knew the trail instinctively."

"He walked it for over eighty years, in both his lives."

"But that is a trail that winds down toward the highway. The way from the village to that trail is cut off by the steepness of Tumkot mountain and the glacier on top of the mountain. But Kypo and the mule seemed to know a way across."

"Ridiculous. We go around, on a trail that circuits the base of the high ridge."

"To go around to the road means walking at least fifteen miles. To go over the top would be no more than five."

"Fifteen miles is a morning stroll for one of us."

"But suppose there was a secret trail," Shan suggested. "Your mule would know it as the way home, would lead anyone to it who cared to follow, because he would make fresh tracks that would highlight the trail. If the murderer also used such a secret trail to do his work he would want the mule dead."

"There were many cars and trucks going up and down the road that day after the killing. So many army trucks they had no room for an ambulance," she said in a pointed tone.

"But there was an injured man," Shan observed. "That bus driver."

Ama Apte cast him a disappointed glance. Shan thought again of the photo of the young Dalai Lama with soldiers. It hadn't been ripped from a book or newspaper. It had been an original photograph. Every time he peeled one layer of the woman's secrets he found one more.

"I thought you were going to tell me how that Chinese colonel killed my uncle, like the minister."

"I came to find out the truth."

"It's a strange way you have with the truth."

"I'm sorry?"

"You act as though someone from Tumkot was the killer."

"Your uncle was shot less than a mile from here. Maybe he was scared away by the bullets, and was coming home."

"My uncle knew bullets. He would have told me, and told Tenzin."

"Tenzin?" he asked with rising foreboding. "Tenzin was dead."

"I thought you would better understand the dead here," she said in a tone that sent chills down Shan's spine.

"Is that why I am the corpse carrier? Dakpo saw what I did with a dog and the two of you assumed I knew the dead?"

Ama Apte fixed him with a sober stare. "Dakpo spoke with me, yes. But I had to meet you first. Right away, I saw it in your eyes. You are one of those the dead speak through. The threads of your life become entwined with the dead you touch."

It took a long time for Shan to respond. "But Tenzin was dead," he tried once more.

"I told you. The mountain needed him again, so Tenzin rose up and rode my mule away."

Ama Apte cut off any response from Shan with a challenging gaze, then reached into the sleeve of her dress and extracted her Mo dice. Oblivious to Shan now, she closed her eyes, her lips moving in the short mantra that evoked the wisdom of the Mo, then tossed the dice onto the packed earth. She studied them a moment, then scooped them up and turned to Shan with an apologetic expression. "Only sorrow can come of it," she declared, then stood, straightening her apron, signaling that her hospitality had been exhausted. Shan watched as she climbed the ladder stair to the upper story. Again she had told him the answer, but she had not told him the question.

Chapter Seven

THE SHOGO TOWN infirmary was mostly an aid station used more often than not for tourists who needed relief from an attack of altitude sickness or mending of sprains and minor broken bones after tumbling off a rock. It was a small, shabby affair, housed in a rundown former army barracks at the edge of town, its only remotely new adornments the bright metal sign on the door marked EMERGENCY in Chinese, English, German and Japanese and a banner reading EMBRACE POLITICAL STABILITY, a favorite of Party sloganeers since the 2008 uprisings. After watching the street behind him in the mirror for nearly a minute, Shan parked the old blue truck at the curb, then climbed the crumbling concrete steps and took a tentative step inside.

At a reception counter a plump woman sat on a stool, her head cradled on her folded arms, fast asleep. Beside her on the counter were racks of faded brochures in half a dozen languages about the symptoms and treatment of altitude sickness. Behind her were wooden shelves with more than a score of small oxygen bottles fitted with breathing masks, under a sign that proclaimed the bottles to be the property of Tingri County. Past the counter were two cots with folded blankets, for those who had to take their oxygen lying down. Beyond them a single wooden door with peeling red paint was flanked by glossy posters advertising the Chinese International Travel Service. Shan went to the door, glanced at the sleeping woman as she emitted a loud snore, and pushed it open.

Only one of the six beds in the dusty, poorly lit chamber was occupied. At first, from the patient's strange jerking motions, Shan suspected the young Chinese man lying on it, knees folded up, had suffered some sort of nerve damage. But by the time he reached the bed he could see the little black box in the man's hands, could hear the dim pinging noises as he feverishly worked the buttons. Shan studied him in silence a moment, taking in the bandage on his crown, the short line of incisions on his temple, then noticed the uniform hanging on a peg by the bed.

Not until Shan had pulled a stool close to the bed and sat down did the patient take notice. His fingers stopped in midair. The color drained from his face. The game box dropped onto his blanket.

Shan gestured to the bandage on his head. "There seems to be no permanent damage."

The soldier took a long time to find his tongue. "I didn't . . . " he stammered. "I wasn't . . ."

"There was a lot of confusion that day," Shan suggested.

The young Chinese straightened up against the metal head-board, nervously examining Shan, noticeably relaxing as he saw his worn pants, his tattered hiking boots.

"I'm not an officer, Sergeant," Shan assured him. "Is it sergeant?"

"Corporal."

Shan nodded. "All the officers from that day are gone, Corporal, disappeared deep into China." He poured the soldier a glass of water from a pitcher on his bedstand. "It's why no one has missed you yet. There are a lot of distractions right now. The new officers must assume you were reassigned too. All the ones who would know for sure are gone."

"I wrote a note to my lieutenant but it came back saying he was gone," the corporal ventured uneasily. "I'll be back by payday."

"I have no doubt," Shan said. "And until then, who could deny that you needed some protracted sick leave?"

The soldier drained the glass. "I still get headaches. I have cuts in my scalp. The bandages need changing."

"Your first bandage was from a lama's robe. Do you remember?"

The soldier slowly nodded. "The old fool. He could have run, could have saved himself five years of misery. But he settled down beside me like some old yak. When I came to my senses and stood he didn't even notice, just kept up that chant of his."

"Before you stood, did you see anything?"

"My vision came and went. People were running. The guards ran down the road, shooting pistols. Something ran in and out of the bus."

"You mean somebody."

"A yeti," the soldier offered in a tentative voice.

Shan leaned closer. "You saw a yeti jump into the bus?"

The corporal shrugged. "In the barracks some of the old sergeants say yetis throw stones at our trucks when they drive in the mountains. When things go missing at the barracks the men say a yeti took them, kind of a joke. Whatever it was moved fast, without fear of our guns. My vision was blurred. I saw something dark, the size of a man. I thought I smelled spices for a moment, and heard tiny bells." He shrugged again. "They say strange things happen with concussions."

Someone, Shan reminded himself, had taken the files from the prison bus, someone wise enough to know the files represented the primary connection the government had to the monks, someone brave—or foolhardy—enough to chance being shot by a guard.

"And then," Shan asked, "after the lama tended your wounds you went up the road? Not to go search for the others in your squad?"

"That's where they all were by then, around the bodies, shouting, calling on radios, all frantic, scared to death. They weren't worried about the monks anymore. They barely noticed when I got there so I sat against a rock and watched. I was still bleeding. I was fading in and out of consciousness."

"What did you see of the dead?"

The soldier shrugged. "Two corpses. Bloody down the front, propped against the rocks."

"You're sure it was two?"

"Of course it was two. I saw them. The lieutenant was on the radio, shouting that there were two dead people. Both women."

Shan took a deep, relieved breath. At last someone else shared his perception of reality. "How do you know?"

"One was that minister. We had seen her the day before at a rally. The lieutenant started looking for identity papers on the other. Someone said it was one of those men from the climbing conference."

Shan recalled Megan's Ross's closed-cropped hair, the blood on her sturdy, weathered face. It was a simple human reaction, that he had often had to fight early in his career. No one liked to look into dead, bloody faces.

"What happened?"

"The lieutenant opened the jacket, searched the pockets, found nothing, became frantic, and pulled open the shirt. He cried out and jerked backward like he had been bitten by a snake. The body had *breasts*."

"Then what?"

"There was another problem, a man lying on the ground by the road. A tough bastard, he kept trying to get up. They used those electric sticks on him. I passed out."

Involuntarily Shan's hand grasped his own upper arm, which still twitched from the many sticks that had touched him that day, and the days after. He had not remembered resisting the knobs, but he had no doubt who was the bastard the soldier spoke about.

"I remember watching the lieutenant open the trunk of the car and pull out a quart of oil. He used it to outline the bodies."

Shan's head snapped up. "He what?"

"Those other fools didn't know anything about investigations. He understood. I watch murder shows too. First thing you do, he told the soldiers, you mark where the bodies were found. Usually they use chalk or white tape or something. But he couldn't find anything else to use."

Shan nodded solemnly. "Excellent. And then you looked for evidence?"

The soldier frowned. "Who are you exactly? I don't know if—"

"I am someone who so far has no particular reason to report your whereabouts to the garrison. It would be a shame to disturb your hard-earned vacation."

The corporal swallowed hard. "I kept passing out, in and out of consciousness. I remember seeing that someone had closed the shirt and jacket of the younger corpse, and someone had pulled a blue cap low over her head. Someone was shouting to the lieutenant, pointing to a man standing on the road above at that sharp switchback curve, a hundred yards away. He had gotten out of his car and was looking down. When I came to again, the lieutenant was there, arguing with another officer, pointing at the man on the ground, who was covered in blood. Then my head exploded in pain and I blacked out again, for a long time. Next thing I knew, I was in a car bringing me here. The lieutenant had flagged it down, and ordered it to transport me here since all available military transport was being used to bring in teams to search for those damned monks. I passed out again. I woke up here. A doctor came in the next day, on his rounds out of Shigatse."

"The bodies. What were they saying about them? Who carried them away?"

The young Chinese gazed thoughtfully at a stain on the opposite wall. "My memories jump around, like those movies where the camera keeps changing. There was an army truck. People were eating peaches. The bodies were on planks being lifted into the truck, the minister and the one in the blue cap. They have a place they keep bodies on ice at the spa in the mountains. The last thing I remember is the lieutenant sitting with his head in his hands, looking like his world had ended. That new officer was kicking dirt over the blood, saying all foreigners had to be kept away. Then he lit the oil that showed where the bodies were."

"He burned it?"

The soldier nodded slowly. His eyelids seemed to be getting heavy, his head was sinking deeper into his pillow. "He had his own chant, like that old monk. Except he kept saying *Ta ma de, ta ma de, ta ma de.*" *Damn, damn, damn.* "I remember seeing the shapes of the bodies in flames. It was as if he were cremating their spirits."

Shan watched as the corporal slept, replaying their conversation. There had been a witness, in the distance, who had seen two bodies. The knobs had carried away two corpses. But on the slope that particular day, at that particular hour, there had been three dead bodies.

THE GOVERNMENT OF the People's Republic often boasted of its achievements in bridging the gaps between disparate peoples, and discovering ways to push old traditions into the cause of modern socialism. Here, in this high, hidden corner of Tibet, at the gate of the People's Institute for the Treatment of Criminal Disorders, the knobs' infamous yeti factory, Shan encountered proof of this miracle. Half a dozen solemn Tibetans, four men and two women, slipped on frayed and faded laboratory coats, on the backs of which large black X's had been marked. Two young knob guards nervously watched, hands on their rifles, as if expecting to be attacked. The six were ragyapa, fleshcutters, the peculiar, often shunned breed who traditionally disposed of bodies by cutting them up and feeding them to vultures. Public Security had reincarnated them for the twenty-first century, had reversed the polarity of their existence, had decided to supply them pieces of bodies out of which to make something whole. This particular clan of ragyapa was assigned to removal of infectious waste and body parts from the knobs' special clinic.

Shan pulled his hat low, turned his face away as he donned

one of the coats, not daring to look back toward the entry road, half expecting Tsipon to appear and pull him away from the gate-house.

"By my count you have less than a day left. I need those por-ters," the Tibetan had growled when Shan found him in his office late the day before.

"I know where the body is." Shan had then produced a ragged sheet of paper from his pocket then scribbled something and handed it to the Tibetan.

Tsipon's face sagged as he read Shan's words. "You have suf-fered a complete mental breakdown. I hear it is common among former prisoners."

"And I hear you want to buy an apartment in Macau. You won't be able to afford a broom closet without those American dollars."

Tsipon frowned. "My little bird Kypo sings too much," he snapped, then stood, lit a cigarette, and gazed out his window. "I promised you I'd get you inside the spa. If I grant your request, this is it. Your one and only chance inside. I'm done bending rules for you. You can go in for that damned colonel now or for your son later."

Shan had expected it would be the bargain Tsipon offered, but now, hearing the words, something inside frantically urged him to reject it. He spoke looking down at his feet. "They go in before dawn, every other day."

"How do you know?"

"I've seen them," Shan said. He was not about to tell Tsipon that at least once a week he found a way to steal onto the remote ridge by the yeti factory and watch, praying for a glimpse of his son at a window or exercising on the grounds.

"If you are discovered," Tsipon declared in a tentative tone, "I won't even return the call when Public Security tries to reach me."

"If they arrest me there," Shan rejoined, "they won't bother to make any calls."

The thought seemed to encourage Tsipon. He waved the paper toward Shan. "These people you want to use for cover," he added with a perverse grin, "they are like animals. They even scare the knobs."

SHAN HAD INDEED been counting on the guards' discomfort with the fleshcutters. The soldiers who handed out the lab coats seemed not nearly as interested in screening the workers as quickly getting rid of the shabbily dressed, low-caste Tibetans.

Moments later they were inside, retrieving stainless steel buckets and two large laundry tubs on wheels from a janitor's closet before disappearing down a dimly lit corridor.

The Tibetans did their accustomed chore with silent determination, moving from one surgical room to another, emptying several sacks of bloody towels into one of the laundry tubs, then tossing in stained cloth bundles from canisters marked CONTAMINATED before looking to Shan with an air of anticipation. He had known several ragyapa before. They were people of few words and fewer fears. He had met them before dawn to explain his goal that morning, and had listened and agreed to their rules about touching even the smallest of mortal remains. Unknown to the knobs, the ragyapa did not burn the body parts as they were instructed to do, but took them to consecrated grounds for dispersal to the birds. Touching the dead was not taboo to them; it was a sacred duty.

The oldest of the men now took the lead, walking down a corridor marked *Kitchens*. A woman in a nurse's uniform saw them and scurried away. A janitor with a broom muttered an oath, then ducked into an unlit room. Many in modern Tibet regarded the fleshcutters with disdain but others knew them to be special emissaries of the Lord of Death.

Four of the party took up positions at each of the kitchen entry doors as the others watched Shan enter the large walk-in refrigeration unit at the back of the room. He moved toward the heavy racks at the rear. Slabs of beef and pork. Boxes of fresh vegetables beside dressed chickens. Like sailors on submarines, the staff at such remote sites were well fed and well paid to offset the hardship.

He studied the pipes that carried the coolant, noting how they disappeared through the side wall, then spoke in low, urgent tones to his companions. Soon kitchen staff would arrive to begin fixing the morning meal. A minute later they stood at a set of double swinging doors in a short corridor behind the kitchen, secured not by locks but by a single small sign. *Morgue*, it said, in Chinese. Shan left two of the men at the entrance to the corridor, then gestured for the others with the empty laundry tub to follow, pushed open the door and trotted to the heavy metal door at the back of the chamber, an identical match to that in the kitchen. Turning on the light switch by the entry, he stepped inside.

There were four bodies under sheets in the huge refrigerator, laid out on long metal shelves that lined the walls. Shan hesitated a moment, knowing that two of the bodies must be inmates, then saw the red tags extending from the two bodies laid out at the rear wall, a warning not to tamper with Public Security evidence. One body was obviously female. He pulled the sheet from the face of the second.

Even though he had come expecting to find Tenzin, his gut still wrenched at the sight. The compact, swarthy Nepali was much grayer than when Shan had wrapped him in canvas the week before but he was still recognizable as the steadfast sherpa Shan had known at the base camp.

He whispered a greeting to his friend then stared at him awkwardly, thinking perhaps there were other words that should be said. "I'm sorry," he muttered, and had extended his hand to untie the red tag when a hand grabbed his elbow. The old ragyapa whispered a reverent greeting to the dead man then pulled Shan back. Shan was about to protest when the Tibetan lifted Shan's hands, palms upward. He placed his own fingertips on Shan's palms as if passing something very fragile to him, then spoke words that were so fast and low Shan could not understand. The man nodded solemnly and motioned for Shan to continue. Shan pointed to the cardboard box under the shelf, which contained familiar clothes, but as one of the Tibetans lifted it away he reached out and extracted a blue wool cap, the cap the driver said had been pulled low on dead American's head after she had died. He tossed it back into the box, turned to remove the sheet and froze. Tenzin had been shot.

He quickly bent over the two near-perfect circles in his chest, examining the flesh around them. They were positioned roughly where the wounds on Megan Ross had been, but the flesh had never been stained with blood. It was part of the disguise the knobs had given him. Witnesses from afar had seen two bodies; closer ones had seen two victims dead of gunshots, one with a blue cap on. Just as they had placed the cap on Tenzin, they had also put two bullet holes in his chest after his body had been switched for that of Megan Ross. He leaned over the holes once more, gauging the size with a fingertip. They were large, huge, compared to the holes made by the 9 millimeter bullets of most Chinese pistols.

Shan realized no one was moving behind him. He turned to see the ragyapa standing, staring at him. He motioned them forward.

The ragyapa worked with their usual silent efficiency, lifting Tenzin's body to the floor, rolling him in a sheet taken from a stack by the door before dropping him into the large tub on wheels and covering it with the cardboard box of clothing and bloodstained refuse. As they began to wheel it away Shan stopped them and uncovered the box, pulling away an envelope taped to one of its flaps, marked Evidence. Inside was a Public Security form confirming that the contents had been removed from Unnamed Accomplice, and two heavy bullets. He closed it and left it on one of the rear shelves. Unnamed Accomplice. Tenzin had had quite a career since dying.

Shan stared uneasily at the two dead prisoners hidden by the sheets, then forced himself toward them. It seemed to take all his strength to lift the sheets and glance at each of the faces. Having confirmed that neither was his son, he stepped back, gasping. He did not realize he had been holding his breath.

Shan touched the shoulder of one of the ragyapa and the two of them lifted the nearest dead prisoner onto the shelf where Tenzin had lain. Shan fastened the red tag to the dead man, covered him with the sheet, then gestured for the Tibetans to move back into the corridor before he lifted the sheet covering Minister Wu's upper torso. The bullet holes in her abdomen were puckered at the edges, the flesh stained, but the holes were much smaller than those in Tenzin. She had been an athletic woman but, he saw as he studied her hands and the little lines in her face, considerably older than he had thought. On the back of one hand someone had written her name in ink as if fearing she might be misplaced. On her shoulder someone had written something else. No, he saw as he bent over the mark, it was a tattoo. A hammer and a lightning bolt, crossed like an X.

The ragyapa waited for him in the kitchen, nervously glancing at their rolling carts, apparently heaped high with anatomical waste. He offered a nod, then gestured them toward the exit. An instant later the sound of running feet rose from a distant corridor.

"Guards!" he called to the Tibetans, who stared at him expectantly, not frightened but like steady soldiers awaiting orders. He turned, his mind racing. The lights. He had risked turning on the lights in the kitchen and the corridor beyond because they were not visible from the guard station at the entrance to the hospital. But he had forgotten the chance of patrols around the grounds. Shan cast about desperately then tossed a small bag of oranges onto the cart, covering it with a single layer of towels. "They will think you came to the kitchen to pilfer some food," he explained.

"Let them find this bag. They will have no appetite for digging farther into the cart. And they will certainly have no appetite for firing you since there is no one to replace you."

"But if they check the morgue before we leave . . . ," one of the women protested, her voice cracking with the fear of one who understood the ways of Public Security.

"Go!" Shan ordered. "I will make it safe." He watched as they hurried away, knowing the woman was right. If the guards suspected foul play they might search the morgue, and if they discovered a body missing, they would radio for the ragyapa to be detained at the gatehouse. He sprinted back to the morgue. He entered it in the dark, finding his way by touch, retrieved a sheet and climbed onto the shelf form which they had removed the prisoner's body, contorting his own as he tried again and again to cover himself with the sheet, finishing only seconds before he heard angry voices approaching. Static from radio sets cut through the silence. From somewhere came a bell that, he suspected, signaled the beginning of the workday.

He began to shiver. A dozen thoughts swirled in his head. He was alone with his fears, unprotected, with no way out now. In such a place he might be considered a financial windfall, a man without a name for whom they would never have to account. If done right, in correct sequence, at least four vital organs, all highly valuable in China's underground organ market, could be harvested before he died. They would simply lock the door and turn down the thermostat to assure he was nearly frozen, to incapacitate him. Disparate, wild thoughts pounced on him. They would discover the ragyapa were part of his conspiracy and send them all to the experimentation labs. They would lock the door, leave him to freeze solid and drop him off a cliff so he would shatter into a thousand pieces. They would make a mistake and bury him alive with the others.

He clenched his jaw, concentrating, remembering how the lamas had taught him that someone in the right meditation state could generate inward heat. This was nothing compared to what he had endured at some of the higher elevations the winter before. He conjured up memories of sitting with lamas in cold meditation cells carved out of living rock, tried to imagine he was with them again, listening to their soothing mantras.

When the guards entered the cooler—was it five or fifty minutes later?—they were quick and angry and vituperative. Shan heard at least three different voices and sensed through the sheet the beams of three different flashlights. Someone cursed the locusts, a favorite epithet for Tibetans because of their droning mantras. Someone else groused that they were going to miss breakfast. Then the heavy metal door clanged shut.

Panic seized Shan again as his sheet began to slide off him and his numbed hands could not move fast enough to stop the inertia. His last frantic effort caused his body to roll so hard he could not stop the inertia. He watched, his wits chilled, his reactions numbed, as his body fell off the shelf, striking the floor with a loud thud.

He lay there, torpid, wondering at the strange disconnect between his brain and body. The pain he had begun to feel in his extremities was gone. He was relaxed for once, feeling an unfamiliar, languid lightheadedness. He marveled at the impossible length of time it took to bend his fingers after consciously willing them to be bent, and recalled a training manual Tsipon had loaned him the day he had been hired, with a passage about frostbite. After losing just two degrees of temperature the body began shutting down blood flow to the limbs to conserve vital organs. A strange croaking sound rose from his throat, his best attempt at a laugh. Right now his most vital organs were his fingers.

A grunt of protest came from somewhere, as if from one of the dead, and he was up on his knees, then standing, staggering, before he realized he himself had made the sound. Holding the shelves for support, swaying, he turned and aimed himself for the door.

Moments later, free of the cold, he collapsed into the darkest corner of the empty outer chamber of the morgue, hugging his knees to his chest, contracting and relaxing his muscles. As his circulation mounted, so too did a grim realization. The fact that no alarms had sounded, no squad had returned to the morgue refrigerator, meant that the ragyapa had successfully left the facility. The villagers would at least have Tenzin's body. The Americans could climb. Megan Ross would somehow know he had not forgotten her. But the time he had lost meant the workday had begun in earnest. It would be virtually impossible to leave the building undetected.

After ten minutes he rose, the intense aching in his joints making him nauseous for a moment. He stood before the double swinging doors. To the left lay the hall to the kitchen, busy with staff entering and leaving the adjoining cafeteria. To the right was the heart of the complex, with signs pointing the way to *Labs* and *Containment Halls One through Eight*. To the left he knew he would find more guards. To the right, for now, he saw only orderlies and nurses. He straightened his fingers, making sure he could freely move them again, then began stripping off his clothes.

There are parts of every life that never die, that you keep reliving, whether you choose to or not. It wasn't fear of being caught as an intruder that now gripped Shan as he wandered down the hall in his tattered gray underwear, it was the old terror that sometimes erupted with a heart stopping gasp in the middle of the night, banishing sleep for hours, the memory of what these doctors could do, and once had done, to him.

He gazed into the middle distance, without focusing, without reacting, when an orderly snapped at him, still shuffling forward when someone else shouted that another damned fool had wandered away from his treatment.

"You! Monkey!" someone barked behind him. "What's your damned unit?"

Shan, not looking up, stopped, pushed some spittle out of his mouth and let it roll down his chin onto the floor.

The man cursed again, then grabbed him roughly by the arm and pulled him into a small cubicle that served as a nurses' station. He unlocked a cabinet and extracted a rack of preloaded syringes, setting it by a computer screen before impatiently seizing Shan's arm and typing the number of Shan's tattoo into a glowing box at the top of the screen.

He had entered all but the last two digits when Shan snatched a syringe and jammed it into the man's thigh, slamming down the plunger. For one brief instant the orderly began to rise, began to protest, then his legs and voice collapsed. For good measure, Shan injected another syringe into the man's bicep and he sank back, unconscious.

Shan worked fast, first deleting the number typed on the screen, then pulling the man's blue uniform off and donning it himself. Slipping the man's security card lanyard from his neck and draping it over his own, he quickly hid the limp form under the desk, stuffed another of the syringes into his pocket, then scanned the papers beside the computer screen. The list he was looking for was tacked to the wall beside it. He was only looking for a name, he told himself, and then he would leave, for every minute he lingered increased the likelihood of his capture. But the tide of emotion when he found the name was so sudden, so overpowering, it almost brought him to his knees. Shan Ko, it said, Hall Five. His son was alive.

Five minutes later he stood outside the door of the room marked for his son, a locked ward with six beds. Shan glanced up and down the empty corridor and looked down at his shaking hand. He closed his eyes a moment to calm himself then slid the card through the electric lock mechanism and pushed open the door.

The room reeked of urine and vomit. The first two inmates lay comatose on their metal frame beds, their skulls shaved and wrapped in bandages. Two others, older men, stared blankly at walls, another sat against the wall between two beds drawing with a pencil on a pad of paper, surrounded by sheets torn from the pad, all covered with precise penciled triangles, hundreds of triangles. The last inmate was tied to a corroded metal armchair facing the small, dirty window. Shan's heart raced as he approached the chair and looked past the ragged, tangled hair. His son was alive, his son was intact. And completely oblivious to Shan and everything else in the chamber.

Ko stared, unfocused, toward a snowcapped peak on the horizon.

Shan tried to speak his son's name but could summon only a hoarse moan. He put his hand on Ko's arm. His son did not react, did not even blink. He began to untie the tethers, latex tubes knotted at his wrists and ankles, then reconsidered and only loosened them. Lowering himself onto one knee in front of the chair, he saw for the first time the fresh bruise that ran the length of Ko's jaw, the work of a baton to the face, and two broken fingers crudely bound with duct tape, a tongue dispenser used as a splint. He rolled up Ko's sleeve. The skin inside his right elbow was perforated with syringe holes. A long ugly line along his forearm showed where one of his veins had collapsed. His chin was caked with dried salvia and grime. Shan wiped it clean and stroked his son's cheek.

"It's your father," he whispered after scrubbing a tear from his own cheek. "I am here." Words were useless, words were ridiculous. He found himself examining Ko's body again, finding more bruises, old and new, checking his pulse, his fingernails and toenails. It could be worse, he told himself. If he had to be tied, Ko must still have use of his arms and legs, must still have some dim spark left that flared up from time to time. He found a plastic crate in a corner and sat on it beside his son, draping Ko's limp fingers over his own hand, looking out with him through the smudged window to the same distant peak. Images flashed in his head of Ko as a laughing infant. This wasn't how he had imagined it would be when he had strolled with his baby son through Bei Hai Park in Beijing.

He fought to stay in the moment, pushing away the world,

but an incessant voice inside kept shouting that the alarms would sound at any moment, that he would never be able to help Ko if he was captured and tethered to another chair. There was a bus, he had been told, a shuttle bus that took workers through the gate, into town. He had to find the bus and board it using the stolen identity badge, before they discovered its true owner.

Shan rose and checked the empty bed beside Ko, finding another plastic crate under it with his son's possessions. A worn denim prisoner uniform. A comb. A stick of plastic with a few bristles at one end, the remains of a toothbrush. A pencil. A red book of the sainted Chairman's teachings, issued by the prison system, with several pages ripped out. In the pocket of the pants was another pencil, its end built into a bulge with layers of tape and paper. Shan recognized the device. It was used by diehard prisoners to vomit up drugs.

He rinsed out a tin cup at the small metal sink in the corner, filled with water, and held it to Ko's lips. His son did not react at first but when Shan tipped it, letting some of the moisture spill onto his lips, Ko reflexively swallowed and drank half the cup. His eyes wandered, still unfocused, but did not find Shan.

"I have had a pleasant visit in the mountains," Shan heard himself say in a whisper. "There is a place I will show you, with waterfalls and butterflies. You will come stay with me in my cottage in the hills by that snow-topped mountain you look at. Little birds fly in my window." At first he wasn't entirely sure why he lied, then he realized it was simply because he couldn't bear to tell the truth.

"From the Red East rises the sun," Ko suddenly said in a wooden voice. "There appears our Mao tse-tung." He rocked back and forth. His fingers began to tremble. He repeated the words, putting them to a feeble melody. He was singing the Party's favorite anthem, *The East is Red*.

Shan shuddered then gently placed two fingers on his son's lips to silence him and bent closer to his ear. "Living water needs living fire to boil," he whispered. "Lean over the fishing rock and dip the clear, deep current." The words of the ancient poet Su tung-po came out uninvited, but he did not cease speaking them when he recognized them, a thousand-year-old poem that was one of his father's favorites:

Store the spring moon in a big gourd, return it to the jar
Frothy water, simmering, whirls bits of tea
Pour it and hear the sound of wind in pines.

His son's eyes blinked and he turned in the direction of the sound. For a moment Shan thought he might have seen a flicker of recognition in Ko's eyes, then his son looked away, staring in confusion at Shan's hand, entwined with his own. Shan repeated the poem again, all of it this time. Ko cocked his head toward the sky and a vacant grin crossed his face.

One of the many old lamas Shan had known in his gulag camp had, like Shan, been a rare survivor of such a knob medical facility. They had spoken about it once, on a frigid winter night as they watched the stars. Shan had confessed that he could not explain how he had survived, could not even find words to explain how he had felt, only that when he was released he had been amazed to find only sixty days, and not ten years, had passed.

"Those soldier doctors had no feeling for the truth of what they do," the lama had explained. "They think they can destroy you by breaking your body. It isn't like that."

Shan had always known better than to ask questions of such men. He had stayed silent, pointing out a shooting star.

"There are many levels of hell," the lama went on. "They don't exist to test your body or mind but to test your soul. I realized that the doctors were but smiths at the forge who push the iron into the furnace, then pound it with hammers. The only thing of any importance is going on inside the iron. You drift in and out of consciousness. You live in dreams and nightmares all day and night, in the furnace, under the hammer. What brings you back are the moments when you wake and find a little shard of reality. That's what keeps you anchored to the real world, so you don't entirely drift away. A monk with me had a hummingbird feather, another a tiny piece of sacred wood. I had a small turquoise pebble my mother had given me as a boy. I kept it in my mouth for days at a time."

When the alarm finally came it was not a claxon in the hallway but a chicken from the beds. One of the sleeping men had awakened, was pointing at Shan and crowing like a rooster.

Shan was on the man in an instant, injecting the syringe into his thigh, apologizing as he did so, straightening his blankets as the man slumped back into his pillow. When he looked back, Ko was staring at the horizon again. Shan stroked his cheek for a moment, took a step toward the door then paused. He moved quickly to the window and wiped a pane with his sleeve, so Ko could see the mountains more clearly, then lifted one of the sheets of paper covered with triangles and grabbed the pencil from his son's crate. On the reverse of the paper he quickly wrote the ancient poem then, before slipping out into the hall, he left it in the pocket of Ko's shirt. Something inside Ko had heard, he was certain, and Shan was leaving him a little shard of reality.

Chapter Eight

AFTER FIVE FALLS you die. The warning about fatigue in climbing ropes had been the first of the many warnings he had received during his first visit to the base camp. Kypo had offered no greeting before tossing the length of rope Shan now held. He had simply appeared as Shan sipped his morning tea by his front door and thrown the rope at him with a resentful expression. One end of the rope had been cut; the other, stretched and frayed, had been snapped by a heavy load. The thick kernmantle ropes took amazing abuse on the high summits, but they were retired to serve as base camp laundry lines after taking the stress of five falls.

"I was at the first advance camp yesterday," Kypo explained. "I asked a porter why this piece of junk was there. He said he thought he should keep it because it was Tenzin's rope, the one he was using when he died."

"But he would never—"

"Right," Kypo interrupted. They both knew a seasoned sherpa would have checked his rope before climbing. "Tenzin was just setting a practice wall, for customers to use while acclimatizing for the final climb."

Shan looked at the crushed, frayed end of the rope. He recalled Tenzin yelling at a porter for stepping on a rope in camp. A careless step could press mineral particles into the rope, which would gradually cut the fibers.

"We don't know where this has been for certain. I wasn't there when it was cut off him."

"No," Shan agreed. "I thought he was free climbing and slipped." Tenzin had been renowned for his unassisted climbs up sheer rock faces.

"It looked like he was just taking some equipment to the bottom of the wall, a quick up and down." Kypo was silent a moment, clearly disturbed by the thought that his friend Tenzin, who had climbed the summit with him, had died from such an obvious mistake. "It was written that the mountain would call him," he murmured. It sounded like he had been speaking with his mother.

"The rope came from the Americans' supplies," Shan observed. "It's their advance camp."

"Tsipon wanted Tenzin and me to take the Americans on the final leg to the top. I told Tsipon I would think about it."

Shan considered the edge of emotion in the Tibetan's voice. "You don't trust Yates?"

"He plays with the truth. I was in Tsipon's office when Yates first came in to speak about moving his spring climbs from Nepal to here. Tsipon said Yates should come with him to apply for the permits the next day, since foreigners always get sent to the front of the line. Yates declined, saying he had to go to Shigatse on business. But the next day I saw him in the opposite direction of Shigatse, standing in a field of barley."

Shan cocked his head, not sure he had heard correctly. "Standing in a field doing what?"

"All by himself, tramping down some poor farmer's crop, tearing apart an old cairn in the center, the bastard."

"He lied?"

"He lied, then paid the farmer twenty dollars when the man discovered what he'd done. Told him to keep quiet about it."

"But you spoke with the farmer," Shan surmised.

"When I passed on my return. The farmer said Yates had gotten out of his car and kept looking at the sky, as if expecting something to come down and meet him."

"He must have had a satellite phone and was trying to get reception."

"No. Everyone here knows what those big phones look like, because every other foreigner has one."

"And the farmer spoke with you, after taking money to keep quiet."

"In Tibet, comrade, keeping something secret means keeping it quiet from the Chinese."

A loud horn from the road broke the silence that followed. They looked up to see Jomo with his beloved old blue truck, his battle junk. Kypo faded into the shadows.

By the time Shan reached the truck the wiry mechanic was standing at the curb, gazing at Shan with an apologetic expression.

"Tsipon says Director Xie needs you. I am supposed to take you to him and help you."

Shan pushed back the dark thing within him that rose at the mention of the wheelsmasher's name. "Help me?" As Shan spoke, several Tibetans appeared from an alley on the opposite side of the street and began climbing into the cargo bay of the truck.

"The engine is unpredictable. He doesn't want you stranded," Jomo said plaintively, then gestured toward the half dozen Tibetans settling into the bay. "They heard we were going up the mountain."

"Are we? Going up the mountain?"

"Xie is up there," Jomo replied. He climbed in and with a loud cough and a cloud of smoke the old truck began to move.

It was not unusual for trucks to give rides to Tibetans, who seldom had their own vehicles, but when Jomo halted for four anxious older women near the truck stop where the road to Chomolungma left the highway, Shan turned to the mechanic. "Don't you think I should know at least as much as they do?"

"What they know is that Religious Affairs is in the mountains," Jomo replied in a tight voice, leaning forward as if needing all his concentration to negotiate the winding curves.

"Then tell me this," Shan tried. "What happened between Ama Apte and your father? What prevents him from going into the mountains?"

"Before my time," Jomo shot back.

"They avoid each other."

"They hate each other. If my father sees me speaking with Kypo, he berates me and throws things at me like when I was a little boy. He calls her the false prophet, says everything she does is a lie, says all of Tumkot hangs on the thread of a lie."

"Surely, Jomo, you have wondered what that lie is."

"Before my time," Jomo replied again, and would say no more.

Shan studied the Tibetan, doing some rough calculations. Jomo's time would have begun, he decided, sometime in the late 1960s.

DIRECTOR XIE HAD his fox-fur hat pulled low against the chill wind as he waited for them at a crossroads that connected to one of the valleys defined by the long, high ridges that jutted out from the Himalayas.

"Excellent!" Xie exclaimed to Shan. "You brought laborers! Such foresight!"

Shan nodded uncertainly, then with rising foreboding complied with Xie's gesture and climbed into the back of his government sedan.

He did not recognize their destination until they were within half a mile of it. The only other time he had seen Sarma gompa, the small monastery, had been weeks earlier, from the ridge above when he had been hiking on a pilgrim's path. The compound of centuries-old stone and timber buildings nestled against a high, flat rock face. Sheltered to the west by tall junipers and rhododendron, it had seemed a serene oasis in the dry, windblown valley.

"We are closing in, comrade," Xie declared. "This is the landscape of our victory," he added with the tone of a field commander, and was rewarded with a vigorous nod from the young deputy who sat in the front seat.

Shan glanced from the bureaucrat to the gompa. What landscape? What victory? Then Xie answered his unspoken questions with an announcement that sent a shudder down his back.

"That Cao has not even found this place," Xie said with a conspiratorial gleam. He was competing with the Public Security Bureau.

"Major Cao," Shan ventured, "seems overly rigid."

Xie laughed. He was enjoying his field trip immensely. "A dinosaur. Pretending he can deal with an assassination without severing the root it grew out of."

Shan's confusion over Xie's intention disappeared as they pulled to a stop by the gompa, renowned in the region for its ancient murals. The faces of the Tibetans who climbed out of the truck told him everything. Some scrubbed tears from their faces, others clenched prayer beads or gaus with white knuckles. Jomo tried to scurry away as he climbed out of the cab, but Shan stepped in front of him. The mechanic slowly turned his guilt-stricken face up to Shan. He often worked at the town garage. He would have known when the dump truck, now parked near the trees, had been dispatched, would have known it was pulling a trailer carrying a compact bulldozer. Sarma was the gompa of the fugitive monks.

One of the Tibetan women uttered an anguished cry when the bulldozer roared to life, another clutched her breast as if she had been stabbed. Men in white shirts appeared by the buildings, Xie's deputies from Lhasa. Several of the Tibetans Jomo had brought from town settled on a knoll by the front gate, folding their legs under them, pulling out their prayer beads.

The sound of the machine plowing through the gate and into the brittle old wood of the temple at the front of the gompa nearly brought Shan to his knees. Shards of painted plaster flew into the air. Splinters of wood popped and cracked over the metallic clinking of the treads as the bulldozer cut a swath from one wall to the next. The wide eye of a god that dropped onto the cage of the operator seemed to take on new expressions—shocked, then terrified—before slipping away to be crushed. The end of an old altar became trapped under one end of the blade and was dragged along until shattering into a dozen pieces. Suddenly the machine emerged from the building, massive holes now in opposite sides of the structure. The bulldozer pivoted on one tread and slammed into one of the standing corners. The building staggered, swayed violently, then collapsed. Two of Xie's deputies clapped. Jomo fell against the front of the truck, his head buried in his arms.

Shan fought the temptation to race to the machine and seize the key from the ignition, to stand in front of the blade. But nothing he did would change the fate of the serene little gompa, which had withstood storm and strife for so many centuries, sheltered so many prayers, only to be annihilated at the whim of a bureaucrat. Eventually, through his numbness, he realized that half the Tibetans had disappeared. He recalled that the pilgrim path rose up the ridge from the shadows of the trees, past the painted rock face in the rear courtyard. Slowly, inconspicuously, he paced along the front of the compound, seeing movement in the shadows of the trail. There were storerooms in the back, the last place the bulldozer would reach. Some of the Tibetans had come to save what treasures they could.

He returned to Xie's side and pointed to a building with a fierce demon painted on its wall at the corner farthest from the storerooms, out of sight of the trail. "The *gonkhang*," Shan explained, choking his guilt. "The protector chapel should be next."

Shan watched in silence as Xie gleefully directed the bulldozer into the sturdy little building, saw the demon crumble, the lathe and plaster of the wall burst apart, an odd wooden frame with wooden screw mounts shatter as the blade hit it. The rumble of the machine drowned out the sob that escaped Shan's throat. He felt his knees giving way, and braced himself against Xie's sedan. It had not been a protector chapel, it had been a *barkhang*, a traditional printing press. There had been one old printing press left in the region, Kypo had told him, one place where the reverently carved rosewood sutras could still be used. Shan shut his eyes as dozens of ancient printing plates, each a unique treasure, fell from shelves and were crushed under the tread of the bulldozer.

Xie's fox-covered head bobbed up and down enthusiastically as he watched the destruction, and he called out to one of his deputies before gesturing for Shan to follow him past his limousine. Several chests had been removed from inside, and were lined up by the dump truck.

"You are the expert," Xie said as he opened the first of the chests.

"I don't understand."

"The cults. The factions. The separate cadres within the church. We will need to inventory everything here for our warehouses. Bur first I need you to tell me what they say about the links between the monks of this compound and others nearby."

So Xie did know something about the Tibetans he regulated. There were several sects of Tibetan Buddhism and affiliated gompas supported each other. The director opened the second trunk, which was loaded with ritual implements. "We have people who know the names of all these artifacts," he boasted.

Shan slowly walked along the chest, lifting some of the implements as he identified them. "*Purba*," he said, as he raised a ritual dagger, then "a *dorje*, a *drilbu*, a *kangling*, a *damaru*," indicating a scepter, a bell, a bone trumpet, a skull drum. He looked up to meet Xie's impatient gaze. "This gompa was one of a kind," he lied. "It is not affiliated with others here, only some in Nepal and India." He looked back over the chests, all of which Xie had now opened. Most were only half full. The slow moving dump truck and its heavy load must have been dispatched the day before. The Tibetans in the surrounding hills would have understood. They had already salvaged many of the treasures.

"Still," Xie observed, "a lost sheep looks for any flock it can find."

"But the others," Shan ventured, his voice growing strangely hoarse, "have signed loyalty oaths." Only one gompa had been targeted for a raid.

"True."

"Then your mission is successful. You have dealt in a permanent way with those who would not sign." He gestured to the chests. "You have added artifacts worth several thousand to the government coffers."

"Still," Xie said, "this region seems so—" he searched for a word—"fertile."

Another shudder moved down Shan's spine.

A deputy jogged up with a small radio unit and handed it to Xie, who stepped out of earshot to speak into it. He handed it back to the assistant then offered a pointed grin to Shan. "Foreigners. Always causing complications."

"You mean that American Yates?"

"Him? No. He is away, they say, up high scouting advance climbing camps." The announcement caused Shan to glance up toward the summit that loomed large on the horizon. He had stayed away from the base camp because of the American. "We can't search the base camp the way we would like. The foreigners have everything out of context; they don't understand our family matters."

"You mean they might misinterpret the government putting a bullet in a monk."

Suspicion rose in Xie's eyes. "Comrade, my office is responsible for the whole family of Buddhists in Tibet. It does not serve our policies for monks to be shot. The government strives to make them patriots, not martyrs."

"What are you saying?"

"That fleeing monk wasn't killed by Public Security. They found his body on the trail."

The purba in Shan's hand slid out of his grip, dropping back into the chest. He stared at Xie in disbelief. "Cao knows this?"

"Of course. It is why I was brought in."

Shan considered Xie's words. "You mean you are giving cover to Cao." Xie's presence assured that everyone assumed the monk was killed for defying the Bureau of Religious Affairs. Otherwise Cao would have another murder to account for, complicating his case against Tan.

"We are all soldiers in the service of the motherland," Xie replied, then turned away as another deputy handed him a radio.

Shan retreated, back to Jomo. He quickly spoke to the Tibetan, then eased into the cab of the blue truck.

ENTERING THE BASE camp below the North Col of Everest was like entering a war zone. Stacks of materiel for doing battle with the mountain lay under tarps fastened with rocks and ropes, each labeled with a trekking company name. Clusters of tents were scattered across the rocky landscape—some elaborate, brightly colored nylon structures, others, from less well-endowed expeditions, affairs of tattered canvas. Porters—the ammunition carriers of the annual spring war—scurried about under heavy loads, weaving in and out of small groups of climbers. The foreigners could instantly be identified as new recruits or veterans. The haggard veterans, back from the oxygen-starved, frigid upper slopes, looked as if they had come from weeks of artillery barrage. Sometimes stretchers would move among them, urgently being carried to waiting trucks. Kypo had made sure Shan knew the statistics before he ventured to his first advance camp weeks earlier. Nearly two percent of all those who ascended Everest died. One in twenty of those over sixty died. It was too dangerous to bring down those who died on the upper slopes, so they were left as grisly, contorted monuments slowly being mummified by the dry, cold wind. Others, the walking wounded, came back with injuries that would mark them for life. Two weeks earlier Shan had seen a man writhing in agony on a stretcher, half his face dead from frostbite.

Completing the battlefield effect were the many foreign flags that fluttered near the groups of tents. On a low, gravelly knoll between two rutted tracks a familiar figure in a uniform sat in a folding chair, as if expecting to direct traffic. Except Constable Jin was fast asleep.

Shan did not bother to search for the striped red, white, and blue flag before hoisting a crate to his shoulder for cover. He aimed for the most populous of the encampments.

With a businesslike air he entered the largest tent in the base camp, an expansive pyramidal structure used as a supply depot. Confirming that he was alone, he set down the crate and studied the chamber. To his right was a tall wooden tool chest with folding chairs around it, a makeshift table. Small nails had been driven into the wooden tent posts near the table, from which hung lanyards with compasses, whistles on chains, several open padlocks, and a small net bag filled with hard candy. In the far left corner, taking up at least a fourth of the space inside, was a huge square stack of supplies in cardboard cartons. Opposite was a little alcove, separated from the rest of the tent by felt blankets hung from climbing ropes. Shan glanced behind him, then slipped through the curtain of blankets.

A piece of heavy canvas covered the gravel and sand underfoot. A folding chair sat between a metal cot and a folding camp table, which was covered with papers. He sifted through them quickly. Lists of climbers, schedules for future expeditions, weather reports for the summit and the Bay of Bengal, correspondence between Yates and the Ministry of Tourism on the payment of climbing fees, inventories of equipment.

He moved to the cot, searched the bedding, then pulled out a heavy foot locker that was under the bed. Secured with a large padlock, it bore the legend *Nath. Yates* in large black letters on its top. Behind it were three pairs of boots, a plastic bin of pitons and a nylon climbing harness. On an upended wooden crate at the other end of the bed lay several personal items. A plastic bag of toiletries. A bottle of Diamox tablets, for altitude sickness. A small basket holding dozens of small denomination coins from several countries, with a deck of well-worn playing cards. He sifted through a pile of clothing thrown on the canvas rug, scanned the chamber once more, then found himself gazing again at the padlocked trunk. The padlocks by the main entry had been almost identical to the one before him. The wooden tool box there might hold one of the heavy bolt cutters sometimes used for slicing through the thickest climbing ropes. He moved back to the entry then, as voices were raised outside, slid open the front tent flap to survey the camp. Four weary figures in parkas were descending the trail from above, three Tibetans and Nathan Yates. Shan watched as the American was hailed by a bearded man near a tent flying a German flag, who gestured for Yates to join him. Shan lingered long enough to confirm that Yates was moving toward the German, then darted to the languid form of Constable Jin, still sprawled in the lounge chair.

Jin jerked upright as Shan touched his arm. "You know the American Yates?" Shan asked.

"Buys me a beer whenever he's in town." Jin studied Shan uncertainly. "So you're back to work then?"

"What do you mean?"

"There's nothing more you can do about the murders. You forced his hand. Cao called my office to arrange for Colonel Tan to be transported to a jail outside the county. He says he wants him safe from tampering while he completes his file."

Shan clenched his jaw. With Tan out of his reach he had little hope of finding the truth or helping Ko. "I am going inside," he said, pointing to the Americans' depot tent. "If Yates enters and I do not come out in five minutes, you must come inside, with your gun ready."

Jin looked up with a hopeful expression. "Is he going to attack you?"

"Five minutes," Shan repeated, then slipped back towards the tent. With relief, he discovered bolt cutters in the tool chest and was about to dart back to the Yates' sleeping quarters with them when he noticed two unfamiliar objects at the bottom of the chest, a long flexible black tube and a black oval box the size of his hand. The box had an eyepiece at one end. He held it to his eye, saw nothing, then noticed a battery compartment. He found a small sliding switch, pushed it, and an intense light spilled out the end opposite the eyepiece. The hole emitting the light was threaded. He studied the tube and found it was filled with a clear plastic material, with one end threaded. He screwed the tube into the box, looking into the eyepiece, then switched on the light again and gazed through the eyepiece. A pebble at the end of the tube leapt into view, brilliantly lit by the optic cable. With a thrill of discovery he experimented, bending the tube, seeing pebbles, the back of his boot, the back of his head, the inside of an empty beer bottle on the table.

He carried both the optical instrument and the bolt cutters with him into the sleeping quarters, pausing for a moment to study the huge block of cartons again. He tapped several cartons as he returned to Yates's quarters. Several on the top tier seemed to be empty.

Moments later he had cut off the padlock on the American's trunk and tossed it behind the bed before bending over to examine its contents. Several pairs of thermal socks and underwear, in original packages. Two large boxes of matches. A small, sophisticated stove with several canisters of fuel. An envelope containing several black-and-white photos curling with age, of an athletic looking man in a uniform, posing by a large airplane with four propeller engines, then on a horse, then with a dozen other soldiers in a group in front of a barracks.

He shut the trunk, locked it with the spare padlock, and studied the area again, certain he had missed something, looking under the upended crate, lifting the cot, studying the aluminum bed frame. The hollow metal legs had rubber caps at the bottom. He popped off two caps to no avail but as the third twisted away a rolled paper slipped out. It held nothing but six rows of numbers. They could have been international dialing numerals. They could have been bank account numbers. Shan extracted a scrap of paper from his pocket and hastily transcribed the digits. He returned the rolled paper to the bed frame and was about to leave when he noticed something in the shadows behind one of the heavy tent poles, suspended from a small nail. It was a silver gau, a Tibetan prayer amulet. He lifted it with reverence, and not a little awe, for he could immediately see that it was exquisitely worked, from the intricate brass hinge that allowed it to be opened for insertion of blessings to the rows of sacred images engraved on the top and bottom. He lingered over it, moved as always by the centuries old artifacts of the Buddhists.

"When I first came to China years ago," a simmering voice said to his back, "I had a ballpoint pen that I left behind in a hotel room in Shanghai. Two days later in Beijing, my escort gave it back to me. Later I got him drunk and asked him about it. He explained that half the people who work for the government actually do the work of the government, the other half watch the first half and every foreigner who enters the country."

Shan, the gau still in his palm, slowly sank onto the bed.

Yates pulled off the wool cap he wore. "So what kind of spy are you? Animal, mineral, or vegetable?"

"I don't understand."

"Do you spy for the Party, some economic enterprise, or just the police?"

Shan extended the gau. "Do you have any idea how rare this is, how old it is? Did you steal this too?"

"I'm no thief."

"Show me your knuckles."

Yates, confused, began to lift his hand, then glanced at it and hid it behind his back. But not before Shan had glimpsed its scratches and abrasions.

"You son of a bitch, Shan!" the American spat. "It was you up there last night."

Shan dropped the gau into Yates's hand. "Some of the older Tibetans say that with the right prayers inside such an amulet, the one who holds it is incapable of lying."

"I asked people about you," Yates snapped. "You're one of those prisoners, one of the gulag outcasts with nothing to lose. Tsipon should have told me."

Shan picked up the strange optical instrument, aiming it like a gun at the American. "I've got you. Theft of cultural antiquities is a serious charge. The constable will be overjoyed when I present you to him. Having a constable indebted to you is what every outcast dreams of."

Yates bent the black tube downward, away from his chest.

"I've never seen one of these," Shan said.

"It's called a borescope," the American explained in a sullen voice. Shan did not resist as Yates pulled the instrument from his fingers. "There's a cult of climbers obsessed with finding evidence of expeditions from decades ago. A lot of people died then, disappeared without a trace. Some think they stuffed messages into cracks in the rocks, to avoid having them blown away. With this they can see inside the cracks." Yates unscrewed the tube from the body of the instrument, putting the pieces on his bed. "The constable will be more inclined to believe me when I say I caught you stealing my things. What's the word of an unreformed criminal against that of a valued American entrepreneur? Foreign currency buys instant respectability in this country."

"Did you kill them, Yates?"

The American seemed to grow very weary. He settled onto the cot. "Kill them? You mean Minister Wu."

"I mean Minister Wu and Megan Ross."

Yates gazed at Shan without expression. "Minister Wu was killed by some deranged army officer. Megan Ross is away, back in a few days."

Most people were scared of ghosts because they were dead but Shan was becoming scared of this one because she would not stay dead. "Everyone keeps saying Ross is alive, but no one can say where she is. Did you help her get away, did you take her to one of her secret mountains?"

"People are deported for such things. She says she won't expose anyone else to that risk. Being banned from the Chinese Himalayas would be a deep personal tragedy for a serious climber."

"Almost as tragic as being murdered in the Himalayas. Was she a competitor? Is that why she had to die? Didn't want to share your piece of the Himalayan enterprise?"

"I told you. She is away on a climb. And she's not a competitor, she's a partner. She has a contract to help me with my expeditions this year, arranging the routes, handling the bookkeeping for the money going into China. She's famous in climbing circles. She knows China better than I do."

Shan gave an exaggerated shrug and gestured to the amulet, still in Yates's hand. "I guess we have proved the gau doesn't work on foreigners. Or maybe it's lost its power after all these centuries."

"Your boss is going to be very unhappy when he finds out I won't be doing business with him."

"But we found that missing body. Porters from the village are already arriving."

"I was thinking more about whether I want to work with you."

"The better question," Shan rejoined, "is whether they will want to work with someone who steals from them, then insults them."

"What are you talking about?"

"Taking the deities is bad enough. But giving them back damaged, that's demeaning."

The ember that had been smoldering in the American's eyes was about to ignite. He pointed to the entry. "Get out!"

"I found the instrument you use to spy inside the statutes. Now all I need is a high-power drill. Where's your workshop?"

Shan paused, suddenly remembering the structure of cartons in the outer tent. He stood and backed away, ready to dodge the fist that Yates seemed about to throw at him. "I understand how the government handles these matters, Mr. Yates. Write a confession about the thefts and the murders. I'll hold it for a day, long enough for you to drive across to Nepal."

The American's fury seemed to paralyze him as Shan slipped out between the blankets. He darted to the carton structure and began shoving the outer cartons away, quickly revealing a narrow passageway between the stacked boxes.

"No!" came a frightened gasp from behind him. Yates leaped at Shan, arms outstretched to grab him just as, from the corner of his eye, Shan saw movement at the entry.

"Shan!" Constable Jin stepped inside the tent. "Where are you, you bastard?"

Shan pushed forward, reaching a small, dark chamber in the center of the block of boxes as Yates seized him by shoulder, desperately trying to pull him away.

"Shan!" Jin called again. The constable began walking toward the boxes.

Three Tibetan men in tattered, soiled robes looked up at Shan with terrified expressions. Yates was hiding the fugitive monks.

Chapter Nine

SHAN SPUN ABOUT and rammed his shoulder against Yates, shoving him out of the passage, lashing out sideways with his arms to collapse the entry to the hidden chamber before pushing the confused American, toward the constable. Yates stumbled, landing in a pile of long limbs and ragged hair at Jin's feet.

"This foreigner," Shan declared, with a furtive glance toward the cartons to make certain they gave no evidence of the hollow inside, "is a smuggler." He hovered over Yates, as if to prevent his escape. "I have discovered that he brought several crates of food into our country and declared them as climbing equipment that would be reexported after the season. Evading the payment of customs fees is a crime against the People's Republic."

Jin seemed a bit frightened, glancing uneasily from Shan to Yates. Then he rose to the occasion as Shan began carrying full boxes from the front of the stack and dropping them at his feet. A case of powdered chocolate. A case of energy bars. A case of oatmeal.

"A serious crime," Jin affirmed with a new air of authority as, with a tentative finger, he pushed open the top flap of a carton. "Smugglers go to prison in our country. If you are lucky, Mr. Yates, you will only be fined and denied future entry."

"We can wait until we return to town to contact the Ministry of Tourism," Shan stated in a sober tone.

"Tourism?" Jin asked uncertainly.

"At least three climbing expeditions will have to be cancelled," Shan added. "But I know that won't stop you from doing the right thing, Constable. And of course there's the notification to Public Security."

Jin's face clouded. "I am fully familiar with procedures," he interjected. The constable glanced nervously out the entry, toward the main track of the camp, where his truck was parked. Shan brought another box to the pile. Dried fruit. The constable took a step outside, surveyed the compound and returned, his chest inflated. "Perhaps I may be able to handle this administratively," he suggested in an inviting tone. "But the contraband must be confiscated," he declared. "You understand it is my duty, Mr. Yates."

Yates settled into one of the folding chairs, looking duly contrite. "How am I going to feed my customers?" he asked, finally taking his cue.

"You should have thought about that when you first decided to cheat the People's Republic," Jin chided.

Yates slumped over, hanging his head.

Jin victoriously escorted Shan as he carried the cartons to the constable's vehicle, then offered a conspiratorial grin as he climbed inside.

Shan watched the dust plume as the truck disappeared down the barren valley toward Rongphu gompa, then turned back to the supply tent to see Yates at its entrance, shouting at a Tibetan woman in a black dress who was walking briskly away from a red tent a hundred feet away.

"You! Hey!" Yates yelled, taking several steps toward the woman as she raised one of the baskets used by the porters to her shoulder, then halted to look back at the small tent. "It's Megan's tent," he explained as Shan reached his side, then broke away to follow the figure in the black dress.

The woman did not turn but, seeming to sense her pursuer, lowered her head, hastening toward the maze of tents that marked the center of the makeshift international village. Yates shot across a low pile of gravel to intercept her, reaching the head of the path she hurried down, blocking it, waiting with crossed arms to confront her.

When she stopped ten feet from the American and raised her oddly fierce countenance Shan almost called out Ama Apte's name, but the words died away as he saw the strange flood of emotion on the astrologer's face. Her face went blank for a moment as she looked at Yates, then contorted in confusion, even fear, before shifting into a small, worried grin. The American wavered, as if intimidated by the woman's intense emotion, and said nothing more as she pressed her hands together in a traditional leave-taking gesture, then, with a remarkable burst of speed broke off to the right, over another mound of gravel, and disappeared into the throng of porters.

"What the hell was that about?" Yates asked as he returned to Shan. "She was in Megan's tent."

"You haven't met Ama Apte?"

"The astrologer? Never did." He looked back toward Megan Ross's tent, as if thinking of investigating further, then shrugged. "She and Megan are friends," he added, then motioned Shan back into the supply tent.

He followed the American back into the entry to the hiding place, which Yates had already rebuilt. The fugitive monks gazed fearfully at Shan as he knelt in front of them, studying each in turn, looking for injuries. Each clutched his gau tightly, with whitened knuckles, and each of the gaus, Shan saw, was an ornate box with intricate lotus blossoms worked in silver. He recognized the young one with the scar on his chin who had lingered by the bus with the old lama.

"I mean no harm," Shan said in Tibetan. "Hiding among foreigners was very clever," he offered. "The sherpas helped you?"

The monks' only answer was to look toward Yates.

"The only risks I want the sherpas to take is above twenty thousand feet, juggling oxygen containers for my wheezing customers," the American stated in a flat voice.

Shan looked back and forth from the monks to Yates. "My God," he said in an astonished whisper, "you speak Tibetan."

"You keep stealing one secret after another from me," the American replied, a trace of resentment in his voice.

Shan could count on one hand the number of Westerners he had met who had taken the trouble to learn Tibetan. He replayed in his mind his prior encounters with the American. "Tsipon doesn't know," he concluded. Shan reminded himself of the conversation in which Tsipon had switched from Tibetan to slander the American.

"He and I do fine in Chinese. No need to complicate our relationship."

A dozen questions leaped to mind but a movement at his side caused him to turn away. The monks were folding and tying the sleeping bags they had sat on, as if preparing for travel, glancing nervously at the strange Chinese in their midst as they worked. He raised his hand, palm open. "There is no need to leave. I only have some questions about what happened after you went up the slope that day."

The youngest monk paused, lifting the solitary candle closer to Shan's face. "You're the one!" he exclaimed, then turned and whispered urgently to his companions..

"The one?" Yates asked suspiciously.

"He was there," the young monk explained. "Just after the rocks hit the bus. He made me understand we had to flee. He pointed out the safe way to go. Without him we would have been taken by those soldiers again."

Shan glimpsed the confusion on the American's face before leaning forward toward the monks, taking the candle, and holding it close to each of them in turn. They were bruised and scratched, their robes in tatters. A hollow desolation had begun to settle on their faces. It was an expression he knew all too well. The three Tibetans had probably spent their entire lives since boyhood in their remote, sheltered gompa. It was entirely possible they had never seen a gun, had never been inside a motor vehicle, that the only outsiders they had ever experienced had been the occasional bureaucrats from the Bureau of Religious Affairs who had tried to tame them for Beijing, until they had been herded at gunpoint into a prison bus.

Now here they were, hidden by an American, surrounded by cartons of strange supplies in a camp of Western climbers bundled in gaudy nylon and down, raucously speaking half a dozen languages. They had been stripped of their prayer beads, stripped of the peaceful, prayerful existence they had carried on in the high ranges, cast out into an alien world.

Shan bent, silently lifted a large, flat pebble from the ground, then turned to Yates and extracted the felt-tip pen extending from the American's shirt pocket. He quickly wrote on the stone and handed it to the young monk.

"A mani stone!" Yates exclaimed.

Shan had written a mantra on the stone, the mani prayer to the Compassionate Buddha that could be found on stones of all sizes, all over Tibet, left at shrines, stacked in walls leading along pilgrims' paths. He held the pen up in silent query toward Yates, who offered a nod, then handed it to the young monk, who enthusiastically began scooping more pebbles from the ground.

"I had a mule that day with a dead man on it," Shan stated after the monk had made two more stones. "Did you see it?"

The monk nodded. "There was a mule on the trail we cut across above the road. It was wandering up the mountain, eating grass along the way."

"Was its burden intact?"

"With its burden," the monk replied with a nod. As he made another prayer stone his brow wrinkled. "Later, when we had climbed for an hour, I looked down and saw it like a little toy creature far below. A toy horse was coming up behind it with a toy man chasing the horse. But the man stopped when he reached the mule."

"What happened?" Shan asked.

"We kept climbing, faster than before. Some of the soldiers had begun shooting into the rocks, as if we were wild game." One of the two older monks leaned toward the novice, whispering. "We must find our friends, the other members of our gompa," the novice announced.

Shan and Yates exchanged an uneasy glance.

"Ten of you were on that bus," Shan said. "Six of the others have been recaptured. Another was killed."

Small moans of despair came from the monks. They clutched their gaus again.

"The old one, at the side of the road?" the young monk asked, his voice cracking.

"They took him away. He'll be in a prison somewhere by now, far from here."

The novice sank back against the wall of cartons. One of the other monks, the oldest, placed a hand on the young one's shoulder. "We will begin anew at our gompa, when things have quieted down," the monk offered in a consoling tone, then explained to Shan and Yates. "We are in a line of caretakers who have kept the old shrines there for more than four hundred years. The books Sarma gompa makes have been used all over Tibet for centuries."

Shan's mouth opened but he had no words. "Your gompa," He stated at last, his voice gone hoarse, "has passed on." He could not bear to meet the puzzled gazes of the three monks.

"Passed on?" asked the oldest.

"The government went back with machinery," was all Shan could say.

The silence was that of a death rite. Yates cursed. Another anguished cry escaped the throat of the youngest monk, and he squeezed one of his new mani stones until his knuckles were white. With trembling hands, one of the older monks formed a mudra, an invocation of the protector goddess.

Yates stared intensely at the ground, his eyes filled with pain. Shan could see in his eyes that, like Shan, he felt a share of the guilt for the gompa's destruction.

"That old Buddha," the older monk said at last. "Does he still live?"

Shan recalled the painting on the rock face at the rear of the gompa. "The last time I saw, he was untouched."

The monk nodded gratefully and spoke in a serene tone. "Now he will be able to see the mother mountain without any obstruction."

The American's face flooded with emotion. He looked at Shan with a mournful, pleading expression.

"I need buttons," Shan said to him in English.

"Buttons?"

"I need three hundred twenty-four buttons. And some of the thread used to repair canvas tents."

Yates stood warily, shaking his head but gesturing Shan to lead the way out of the chamber. They searched together in the big chest of tools, then in several smaller plastic chests that contained miscellaneous supplies. When they found the heavy thread but no buttons, Shan asked for washers, but they could only find two dozen, all in the tool chest. He studied the stack of cartons, then pointed to one near the top.

"You want rolls of candy?" the American asked incredulously.

"And a tin plate," Shan said.

When he returned to the hidden chamber, Yates a step behind, Shan carried the spool of heavy thread and twenty rolls of candy rings. He broke three rolls open, dumping their contents onto the plate. The oldest monk, understanding immediately, reached out with a grin and started tying a red candy circle to one end of the thread.

"*Malas*," Shan explained to Yates. "They need to have prayer beads. One hundred eight to the string. In my prison," he added, "the old Tibetans sometimes made them out of fingernail cuttings."

They left the monks, working on their makeshift malas, Yates leading Shan in silence back to his makeshift quarters. The American lit his little stove, produced two metal mugs, two black tea bags, and brewed each of them a cup of tea before speaking.

"What the hell do you want, Shan?"

"An innocent man is being held for those murders. I mean to find the truth."

"That man Tan is a colonel in the army, head of some gulag county, one of those that goes around destroying monasteries. They say dozens of monks have died in his prison. No one would call a man like that innocent."

"I mean to find the truth," Shan repeated.

"And you want me to help free a monster like that? Not likely. You were a prisoner yourself once they say."

"I was his prisoner."

"My God. Then why would you want him freed?"

Perhaps it was the soothing warmth of the tea, or just his exhaustion, that caught him off guard. The words were out of his mouth as if of their own accord. "My son is in the Public Security mental hospital twenty miles from here. The only chance he has of survival is for me to get him out of there, get him transferred back to the camp he came from. It was my old prison. There I could see that he was looked after. Colonel Tan is in charge of the prison."

"Christ!" Yates stared into his mug. "China!" he groaned, as if it explained everything, shaking his head back and forth. The American searched Shan's face for a moment, drank deeply, then gazed back toward the hiding place inside the cartons. "Those monks have to be saved," he declared.

"Those monks have to be saved," Shan repeated. He decided not to push Yates into telling him how the monks arrived at his depot.

"Fine. I won't tell the knobs you helped the monks escape, you won't tell about me helping them. So finish your tea and get out of here. You depress me. You and I have an understanding, Shan, that's enough."

"No, we don't. The people in the valley will be very upset with you, with all American climbers, when I tell them that you have been stealing their Yamas. The Lord of Death is tough enough on them without someone deliberately affronting him."

"I don't think you'll tell them. I saw what you did with those monks in there. You're not like that."

"You weren't listening. My son is going to die if I don't get Tan out of jail. You think I am going to be upset about embarrassing some American?"

"You act as if the murders are connected to someone at the base camp, even connected to me. They are not. You are not going to solve the killings here."

"It's not the murders I'm looking to solve right now. It's the mystery of the ambushed bus. The mystery of how that equipment got there, how someone expert in rigging rope set it up."

The American said nothing. He drained his mug and stood.

"Likewise not connected to the murders."

"It doesn't matter if you know they are not. The government believes they are."

"What the hell are you talking about?"

"At the scene of the murders they found a statue of Yama."

Yates seemed to stop breathing for a moment. His brow creased with worry. "I had nothing to do with the murders."

"Director Xie has begun investigating the monks and those who might help them. The Bureau of Religious Affairs office in Shogo was burned down and a figure of Tara left in the ashes. Even he can see such an obvious pattern. He will soon discover that the other old Yamas are being stolen, then he will convince himself that whoever stole the Yamas committed the murders. When Cao finds out, they will try to pick up the trail of the missing Yamas, interrogating all those innocent people in Tumkot, probably run fingerprint tests on those figures that were returned. In a few days they will declare that whoever stole the Yamas was Tan's partner in the assassination."

"The statues I collect are only of Yama."

"A subtlety that will likely be lost on Xie, and certainly on Public Security."

Yates's face drained of color. "Are you saying someone is trying to make it look like it was me, to frame me?"

"I don't know. Maybe they want to cast suspicion on traditional Tibetans. But once they find the trail of the stolen Yamas . . ." Shan didn't finish the sentence. "Foreigners engaged in crime aren't always deported. Some disappear into the gulag, though I have never heard of one lasting more than a year or two. If I were you I'd get in my car and not stop driving until I was in Nepal."

Yates turned his head, back toward the hidden monks. "Those monks have to be saved," he repeated in a hollow voice.

"Cao and Xie don't have to wait for fingerprints. They will have discovered by now that a ministry film team was here for two days before the Minister's visit, collecting background footage. Cao will isolate every frame that contains your red and black ropes, and every person who touched those ropes."

"We have lots of rope. We are always moving it around, measuring lengths, testing it, cutting out frayed sections. So what if they catch me on film with those ropes?"

"You miss my point. For the knobs, a foreigner is an obstacle, something they just have to work around. They will look for every Tibetan who touched that rope. They will call in Constable Jin and Tsipon, and probably other leading citizens, to connect names to faces. They already have squads out, looking in public places in town." Shan shrugged. "Tibetan porters faced with Cao know he has the power to send them away for a year, on his signature alone. They will talk, they will remember you driving away with the ropes in your truck, they may even be persuaded to state they saw you on the rocks setting up that ambush on the bus."

"Damn your eyes!" Yates muttered as he dropped onto his cot. "It wasn't like that. . . ." He sank his head into his hands, his elbows on his knees. Shan lit the stove and began preparing two more cups of tea.

It had been a perfect confluence of events, Megan Ross had told Yates. The hotel opening, the conference, the visit of the minister with reporters and cameramen. Ross, Yates explained, had repeatedly asked to meet with the minister in Beijing and been rebuffed. "She told me I would have special impact, as the owner of the new trekking company coming to the Chinese side of the mountain, representing a victory for the minster's policies, that if I told Wu I would bring a three or four new American expeditions a year the Ministry would agree to Megan's Himalayan Compact. So she wanted me to be there, waiting."

"Waiting?"

"There is a bend along the edge of a cliff that overlooks pastures and buckwheat fields below, the mountains in the background. Really beautiful, untouched by the centuries, a perfect example of what Megan's compact seeks to preserve. She insisted that was the place to intercept the minister's car. We would wait there, pretending to have a flat tire, blocking the road. The minister would have to stop. We would meet, she would learn who we were, and about the important opportunity we represented."

"Megan was to be with you?"

"That was the plan. But Megan has never been big on keeping to plans."

"But surely she expected the minister to have an escort. The closing of the road was a Public Security secret until that morning."

"Megan knew. She never said how. She said they would stop all traffic from below but they wouldn't think about the foreigners who might already be above, and those few of us who were around were invited to the minister's big picnic reception closer to the base camp."

"So you rigged the rock slide to block it, after the minister's car went through."

"No. I just helped her identify the place, a bend in the road with loose rocks above. That was it. She said the rest was too risky for me to be involved. Too many people depend on me as the head of the expedition company."

"You never wondered where she was that day?"

"No. The night before she called from town, asking if she could use the room reserved for our company at the new hotel, said she would meet me the next day."

"But she never called, never showed up."

Yates shrugged. "Megan is impulsive. She's behind on her life-list for climbs. She figures she has ten more good years of climbing, and she has thirty peaks left on her list. If she found a secret way to get to one of her mountains she would have jumped at it, and would know that I would understand. She always keeps a pack of climbing equipment ready. I left her in town at Tsipon's little bungalow, where she keeps the pack."

"Then how did she get to the hotel?"

"She never went to the hotel. She went climbing. She'll be back any day now."

"She's not coming back, Yates. She died with the minister."

Yates gave Shan a sour look. "What's your game? She is alive. Why would you say otherwise?"

"She died in my arms."

"It's a nasty kind of game to play with me, Shan. She didn't die. I had a message. A porter gave it to me that afternoon. A chance at one of her mountains came up. She said she'd be back in a few days."

Shan leaned forward with new interest. "What porter? Was the message in her own writing?"

"Nothing was written. He told me and was off. I don't know many of the porters by name." Yates shrugged. "Megan's been coming here for years. She knows most of them." He fixed Shan with a challenging gaze. "It wasn't her. I saw them put two bodies in an army truck. Neither was her."

"You saw *what*?"

"I told you. I was waiting above. But after a while I got in the car and drove downhill. At a switchback I got out, a couple hundred yards above the minister's sedan, close enough to see two bodies. I didn't have my binoculars but I could see well enough. They were Chinese, or Tibetans. No blond American."

"They put a wool cap on her. From a distance you wouldn't have seen her hair. Then they switched her body for that of the dead sherpa."

"You're going to look like a fool when she comes walking in for a cup of tea."

"What else did you see?"

"Enough soldiers to start a small war, scattering over the slopes. An army truck that took the bodies away. That was all. Later, I saw that she hadn't even used my suggestions for triggering the rock slide."

"You mean you went back there, afterwards?"

"The knobs had cleaned everything up. They'd left a few markers and some tape. It's the only road in to the base camp, they couldn't keep it closed for long. I stopped, started climbing the slope up to the ropes. A knob sergeant tried to stop me and I explained they were my ropes, stolen from my depot. He let me go under escort, on the condition that I didn't disturb anything. I didn't have to touch a thing to see that she had not used the configuration I had sketched for her."

"What do you mean?"

"What I sketched involved putting a log on the road to act as the release for the rock slide. A heavy vehicle hits the log, tied to a rope, and triggers the slide from above. She changed it, made it simpler. Except with her version someone had to be there to release it."

Shan considered Yates's explanation. "For the first week or so," he began at last, "Cao was considering whether to ignore the rockslide, pretend the bus just had an accident, since adding an act of sabotage against Public Security might complicate his case too much. He's a man used to quick, easy kills. But now he's thinking this could be the one case he's been waiting for, that with this case he can fire a shot that will be heard all the way to the Politburo itself. If he succeeds he'll be a colonel in a month's time, feted as a hero of the people in Beijing. A medal, a banquet with senior Party members, maybe a new job as secret investigator for the Party bosses. So he's decided to raise the stakes. Which means whoever triggered that ambush had better find a new planet to live on."

"There was something else, which they didn't find at first. On a rock near where the avalanche was released there was an old sickle."

"A sickle?"

"A reaping hook, for cutting grain. I climbed up to where the rocks slid from. It was jammed in a crack in a rock, deliberately left there. It had words etched on the blade, and what looked like the image of a range of mountains. I was thinking about hiding it when that sergeant came up to check on me and saw it. He took it down to his vehicle."

Shan had seen such a blade, a stack of such blades, in the shed where old Gyalo kept his artifacts.

"Later I asked one of the older porters about it at base camp. It scared him, scared him a lot, not the blade but the writing I described. He said I should not speak of such a thing, that we should all pray the Chinese do not know what it is."

"What were the words?"

"I don't read Tibetan. I asked him what he thought it said, from my description. He knew, I could tell, but he wouldn't say."

"You keep telling me about other people," Shan said after a moment. "I haven't heard the truth about you. I haven't yet heard why I shouldn't warn the Tibetans that an American is raiding their shrines."

Yates rose, paced back and forth, paused to study Shan, then paced again. "My father," he finally said, "died somewhere near here, when I was three years old. He was a scientist, studied the anthropology of religions, was trying to piece together evidence of the various emigrations of the Buddhists across the Himalayas from India."

"By chopping up religious statues?"

"By taking metallurgical samples of the metals used. You can date the statues that way, but you can also establish where the metal came from. The exact mixture of alloys is like a fingerprint."

It did not have the ring of truth, Shan sensed, but it was a step in the direction of the truth. "And now you are continuing his work?"

"Right. I want to conclude his research. Maybe get something published, in both our names. I never really knew him. Doing this brings me closer to him than ever before."

Shan touched the tool on the bed beside him. "So you do use this instrument, this borescope?"

"Sure. Sometimes its helps show the thickness of the metal, and internal structure of the casting, which also can be like a fingerprint."

"You could have asked to borrow the statues, even asked a Chinese university to help."

"How long have you lived in Tibet, Shan? An American working with Tibetans on a project that shows how Tibetan culture came from over the mountains and not from China? They would deport me in a second, and do much worse to any Tibetan who helped me."

That much, Shan knew, was the absolute truth. But Yates had done nothing to close the biggest hole in his story: Why, if he was studying the metal of religious statues, was he only taking those of the Lord of Death?

Shan stood. It was late in the day. He still had a long drive back to Shogo. Yates followed him into the pool of sunlight by the entry, the worry on his face proof enough that he had finally grasped Shan's point. He and Megan Ross had unleashed a chain of events that were endangering every Tibetan in the shadow of the mountains.

"When she comes back," Yates said, "Megan will know how to patch things up. She'll know where to take the monks."

"She's not coming back," Shan said.

"Nonsense. I told you. I saw the bodies. No Megan."

"She died in my arms," Shan tried again.

Yates shook his head in disagreement, then turned his back on Shan.

"'The raven,' she said at first, then 'is it me?'" Shan told him.

The American froze for a moment, but did not look back before disappearing into the shadows.

Chapter Ten

HE STOPPED THE truck at the crossroads where Xie had waited that morning, looking in the dusk for signs of the director's watchers. The local people would descend on the ruins after Xie and his men departed. There would be prayer stones to retrieve. Even smashed prayer wheels would still be considered sacred. The Tibetans would know that the government tended to return to such sites, with excavators, to remove every stone, to scour the site to bare earth and salt it so nothing would grow. But that would be in the daytime, and in Tibet, everywhere but the cities, the night belonged to the Tibetans. He waited for five minutes, seeking signs of watchers, then turned onto the valley road.

The weathered, compact structures of the gompa were gone. Three thick stone walls alone remained standing, their soot-stained murals exposed to the elements. Everything else was leveled, reduced to a rubble of stone, plaster, and wood. Chairs and tables lay in splinters, smashed not only by the bulldozer but by what looked like sledgehammers. Shreds of old *tangka* paintings trapped in the rocks fluttered in the wind. There was no sign of any Tibetans. Then he paused, seeing why no one was salvaging anything. In the shadow of the trees at the far side he could see the low, dark shape of the director's sedan.

He wandered into the rubble without conscious thought, numbed again by the devastation, vaguely aware of a rhythmic, metallic rumble, the sound of an engine straining, revving then ebbing. He walked past a patch of whitewashed stones that marked where the old *chorten* shrine had stood, passing a futile moment searching for the bronze or wooden box with relics that would have been secreted inside. Then he stepped toward the sound of the engine, past the three standing walls that had been too thick to topple, to the rock face that defined the back of the compound.

The small bulldozer had been aimed at the Buddha painted on the rock face. Driverless, its engine was on, but something in its drive gears had broken so that it was pushing forward several inches, hitting the rock face, revving and falling back, repeating the process over and over. With new foreboding, Shan looked about the compound for any sign of the driver, then approached the machine, intending to switch off the ignition. Two steps away he froze. The levers that controlled the steering had been fastened in place, tied with old *khatas*, white prayer scarves. As he reached for the ignition a splash of color by the blade caught his eye. He looked at the scrap of red fur with a vague sense of recognition, not seeing the blood and fragments of expensive overcoat until he was inches away. He staggered, bracing himself against the rock wall, fighting a spasm of nausea. Caught between the rock and the heavy metal blade was a different, bloody rubble, the remains of Director Xie of the Bureau of Religious Affairs.

He did not know how long he stood against the wall, gripped by horror, but eventually he turned and switched off the ignition, using his knuckles on the key so as not to leave prints. He covered what was left of Xie's head with a scrap of tangka. The Radiant Light of Pure Reality, said a prayer on the scrap, from the beginning of the Bardo death ritual. The words stopped him. Xie might have been a wheelsmasher, might have come to the county to enhance his reputation at the expense of the Tibetans, but no one deserved such a fate. "Recognize the radiant light that is your death," he murmured, continuing the rite, "recognize that your consciousness is without birth or death."

He searched the grounds in the dusk, trying to understand how Xie could possibly have let himself be alone with his killer, half expecting to find the bodies of one or more of his deputies. But there were no other bodies. As darkness fell he found a hand lantern in his truck and searched Xie's car, finding nothing but a box of ritual tools that he removed to the hidden trail at the rear of the gompa. Then he methodically paced along the packed earth. It was crisscrossed with tire and boot tracks, probably of more than two dozen different people and half a dozen vehicles. He wandered a few paces up the pilgrim trail, where he knew many Tibetans had traveled that day. If they had seen anything they would be burrowing deep into the hills by now.

Shan did not hear the approaching vehicle until it was too late to hide. It came rolling into the compound with its lights out, coasting the last hundred feet with its engine off. He switched off his own light and took refuge in the deeper shadow of one of the standing walls.

"*Lao* Shan?" came a nervous voice from the dark, a respectful call in Chinese, as lanterns were lit from the road. Shan stepped toward them to find a small pickup truck overflowing with Tibetans, most of them porters from the base camp. In the back of the truck were shovels and a wheelbarrow.

They would not be dissuaded from their salvage efforts, not by Shan's warnings, not by being shown the grisly remains in front of the bulldozer. These were men who had been hardened by the mountains, who were no strangers to death, and their reverence for the objects that might be buried in the rubble overcame all fear. This was how they preserved their faith.

"Quickly," Shan urged at last, "let us move the trucks so the headlights light the rubble. If you have canvas, cover the murals. Those walls may yet survive." Giving up all hope of finding evidence of Xie's killer, he worked with them for an hour, uncovering many more ritual implements, intact robes, even some costumes used in religious festivals. Some were tied into larger bundles and set on pack frames that several men carried up the moonlit trail. Others were piled on the trucks.

They were sorting through the rubble, retrieving every stone inscribed with prayer, when the man left to watch the road whistled. The lights were extinguished and they watched with rising fear as a single headlight wound its way up the road. The Tibetan on the battered motorcycle had barely dismounted when he was told the news of Xie's murder.

"The death demons are out this night," the newcomer said in a hollow voice. "In the mountains. In the town. It will mean the end of us."

"The town?" Shan asked.

"The knobs attacked Gyalo. When they finished they threw him in the gully with all the other ghosts."

Nearly an hour later Shan climbed off the back of the motorcycle a block from Gyalo's compound. The shutters of every house on the street were closed, every gate and door shut fast. Shogo town was bracing for a storm.

The storm had already struck at the old farmhouse of the drunken lama. Half the contents of the household were strewn about the courtyard. The house itself had been attacked. Something heavy, a sledgehammer perhaps, had slammed into the plastered walls, the window sashes, the door. The brittle plaster had shattered and fallen, some hanging loose on the horsehair that had been mixed with it in another century. The windows were nothing but splinters of wood and shards of glass. The door dangled on its bottom hinge. Inside, the two wooden chests that Gyalo had kept his clothes in had been reduced to fragments of painted wood, their contents scattered across the stone flags of the floor. The acrid scent of sorghum whiskey hung in the air from a jug smashed against the wall.

He retreated slowly, watching the street for any movement, then approached the shed at the edge of the dump pit. He had nearly reached the decrepit little structure when the sound of voices caused him to dart into the shadows behind it. He edged along the walls until he could glimpse the speakers.

Kypo and Jomo stood at the lip of the low cliff where trucks dumped their loads of garbage, studying the shadows below, speaking in low, worried tones as the odor of decay wafted up from the pit. Shan glanced inside the shed before approaching the two men. The inside walls were bare, the packed earth floor empty. The artifacts Gyalo had secretly hoarded there were gone.

The two men greeted him with silent nods, and the three stood wordlessly, staring into the shadows below.

It was Jomo who finally broke the silence. "It's how you destroy infestations of insects, my father used to say," Gyalo's son said in a mournful voice. "First dig into the heart of the colony. Destroy them by the thousands at the heart, collapse every chamber they live in. Expect it to take a long time because you will find colonies hidden in the most unexpected places. But eventually there will be only a few left, surviving alone, and when you find them smash them hard, leaving only little greasy stains on the floor."

"We have to get him out," Shan interjected. "We can't just. . . ."

"They beat him before they threw him over the side," Jomo said in a desolate voice. "Hard to tell, though, how many of the broken bones and cuts were from the beating, and how many from the rocks they threw him on." He glanced at Shan with a grim expression. "Being drunk probably saved him, kept his muscles relaxed, kept him from fighting back, from trying to move and making his injuries worse."

"He still lives?" Shan's question came out in a hoarse whisper. "Where?"

"He lives for now," replied Jomo. "Gone from town. Where no one will ever expect him to be," he added with a glance at Kypo.

Shan looked back at the shed, noticing for the first time the three bulging burlap sacks near the gully's edge. Jomo seemed about to block Shan as he stepped toward the sacks, but Kypo restrained him with a hand on his arm.

The first of the sacks was stuffed with prayer wheels, all of which were damaged, some crushed nearly flat, like tin cans being sent to a dump. The second ritual implements, many bent and disfigured. The third held old barley hooks, many of the sickle-like blades corroded and pitted. Shan rubbed his fingertips over the blade of one, then extended it into the moonlight. He could barely make out the crude outlines of mountains, Tibetan script scrawled underneath, too dim to read. "What are these marks?" he asked. "Why do they scare everyone?"

"What does it matter now?" Jomo shot back. He was growing more nervous, casting worried glances toward the street. "If Public Security comes back it will just infuriate them more to find these."

"Because it could be why he was attacked," Shan quickly explained what he had learned about the barley hook at the bus ambush.

"It doesn't matter," Gyalo's son replied, lifting the sack with the hooks. "We just know it won't happen again." He began to swing it, to throw it deep into the darkness below.

Shan touched his arm. "No. I have a better place."

"There is no better place," the Tibetan said in a bitter tone.

"For your father's sake. He wanted them preserved."

"So I should trust you?" Jomo snapped. "It was your kind who did this to him."

Shan did not reply but hoisted one of the bags to his shoulder and turned to the short trail to the stable.

At first the two Tibetans did not want to enter the old stable at the mouth of the gully. They had climbed down the trail in silence, each carrying one of the heavy sacks over his shoulder but Kypo and Jomo set theirs down at the door when Shan stepped inside to light a lamp. Though they had both been there before, it had never been at night.

"They say this place is haunted," Kypo said hesitantly. "They never did recover all the bodies from the old gompa."

"One thing I can tell you for certain, Kypo," Shan said as he began to drag the sacks inside. "All the dead are on our side."

Kypo muttered something that sounded like a prayer and picked up one of the sacks, followed by Jomo. Shan lifted his lamp and led them past the stall with his sleeping pallet, through the decrepit stable into the adjoining storage room, its roof hanging by only a few beams, roof tiles littering the ground where they had fallen through. He handed the lamp to a confused Kypo, then knelt, running his fingers through the layer of loose earth on the floor until he found what he was looking for, the buried edge of a canvas sheet. He gripped one edge of the sheet, hands on two corners, and slowly flipped it, exposing a hatch of wooden planks bound with heavy iron straps, a recessed iron ring near one edge.

A gasp of surprise escaped Jomo's throat. Kypo silently bent to help Shan lift the hatch. "The gompa was here for centuries," Shan explained, "giving them lots of time to construct tunnels and secret escape routes and passages to secret shrines." He carried the lamp down the steep stone steps, set it on the workbench built along the wall, then reached up to help the Tibetans lower the sacks into the chamber.

"Ai yi!" Kypo exclaimed as he stepped down the stairs. The demons painted on the facing wall centuries earlier were still vivid enough even through the layers of soot to have their intended effect.

"They thought they had pushed all of the gompa into the gully," Shan explained as he lit another lamp. "This was just an old stable, and the bulldozers couldn't get down the steep slope to touch it. The stable was used as a granary when the army had a garrison here, then abandoned when they moved on. I wouldn't have even known about this chamber if I hadn't dropped a piece of firewood on the floor one night and heard the hollow sound of the hatch."

Shan held the lamp near the wall, exposing a savage head with horns and fangs. "Like many of the old gompas, its first chambers were underground, built into the wall of the gully. This was a *gonkhang,* a chapel for protector demons. They often built them in hidden places, using them only for special rituals or for testing the fortitude of novices."

When he turned Gyalo's son had the second sack in his hand and was staring at the workbench, which held artifacts in various states of repair. "You're digging these up," he said in a spiteful voice. "Every Tibetan for fifty miles is scared to go into the gully so you just go in and help yourself." He lifted a figure of a deity mounted on a tiger. "These make a big profit on the international market, I hear." He lifted one of the sacks over his shoulder as if to take it back outside. "You must think us such fools, bringing you more inventory to get rich on. You Chinese always want to just have your way with us!" He took a step toward the stairs, then paused, looking at Kypo, who was stroking the head of the Buddha Shan had been working on when he was not cleaning the printing blocks in the stable above.

"These things don't belong to Western collectors, just as they don't belong to the government," Shan declared. "They belong to the reverent." He lifted one of the bags from the floor and stuffed it onto one of the storage shelves carved out of the living rock at the back of the chamber. Kypo watched him without expression, then placed his hand on the bag Jomo had thrown over his shoulder.

"You're a fool to trust him," Jomo spat, but did not resist when Kypo took the bag from him.

"What he is doing he could be arrested for," Kypo observed. "The restoration and distribution of such artifacts is regulated by the Bureau of Religious Affairs."

"So what?" Jomo shot back, "he is already a criminal, already an illegal."

Kypo stuffed the bag beside the first one then turned to Gyalo's son with an impatient frown. "So now he has shown us his secret. He has put himself at risk of arrest in order to save the old things."

Jomo's protests began to fade away as he examined the work Shan had been doing. When they finished stowing the sacks, Kypo stood in front of a dirt encrusted painting of a ferocious deity with a horse head. "There could have been other hiding places," he said. "Why show us this one?"

"Because it is the best of the hiding places I know. I don't want it forgotten for another fifty years."

"You sound like you are going away."

Shan too gazed for a moment at the deity before replying. "I am always going away," he replied. It was, he had realized years earlier, the only way he could survive, by not lingering anywhere too long, by living on the fringes, out of sight of the government.

Kypo reached into one of the sacks and pulled out a corroded sickle. "It is a symbol from the war," he explained as he pointed to the marks on the blade. "The resistance didn't have many weapons. They used farm tools when they had to. The army of Tibetan fighters had a name. Four Rivers, Six Ranges, it was called. The soldiers liked to scratch the name on their weapons. Some of the units had modern weapons but still carried the blades as symbols, like badges of honor." He looked at the deity on the wall. "It's just a sickle. Tools are in short supply. It was a just a blade they used to cut the ropes. Finding it at the ambush doesn't signify anything," he said to the horse-headed god on the wall, as if trying to convince it.

But it did signify something, Shan knew, and it was why the porter had been frightened when Yates described it. The sign on the sickle had been used by resistance fighters decades earlier, and the ambush on the Public Security bus had been an act of resistance.

HALF AN HOUR later, as Shan walked along the street outside Gyalo's compound, weighing his growing suspicion that it could not have been Public Security who attacked Gyalo, a familiar red vehicle rolled to a halt beside him. Nathan Yates stepped out, wearing a haunted expression, and blocked Shan's path.

"It was poetry," the American declared in a hollow voice. "She carried a book of Buddhist poetry in her pack and would read it by candlelight up on the mountainside, because it is a Buddhist mountain. She would write out the poems sometimes and hide them under stones. It was one of her favorites, a death poem by a Japanese poet." As he looked up toward the stars his voice dropped to a whisper. "Is it me the raven calls," he recited, "from the world of shades this frosty morning?"

"She died well," Shan said softly, realizing that Yates's acknowledgment of her death was releasing his grief. But the American did not express his sorrow in silence. Shan leaned against the car and listened as Yates quietly spoke of climbing with Megan Ross, of mountains they had conquered together, of the great spirit that welled up within her when, in her phrase for reaching a summit, she touched the sky.

"Porters came in with the news of the murder at the gompa," Yates finally announced, in a louder voice. He gestured Shan toward the front seat of the car.

"There's nothing I can do," Shan said, glancing toward the mountain road. He prayed that the Tibetans he had left at Sarma had taken his advice and stayed no more than another thirty minutes before leaving with their artifacts and returning the truck to Tsipon's compound.

"If I don't get my expeditions staffed they will pull my permits."

Shan paused, trying to connect the American's words.

"Those porters who returned when Tenzin's body was found are disappearing, back to the village. No one will speak with me. If it was just about money I could go to Tsipon. They know Public Security will swarm over the slopes when they learn of Director Xie."

"You should go to Tsipon in any event." Shan began to back away.

"Not for this. One of the remaining sherpas says everyone is gathering in the village square, asking for the astrologer to read the signs. I saw Kypo speeding away, back toward the village. They are bringing things to use as weapons. They say what Tenzin is doing shows how angry the mountain is."

A chill ran down Shan's spine. "Tenzin is dead."

"A villager came into my tent before he left. It scared the hell out of me. He said Tenzin keeps trying to rise up to serve the mountain and someone keeps killing him."

THE SNOWCAPPED PEAKS were like silver islands, under stars as thick as pollen. Yates drove slowly up the treacherous, twisting road, slamming the brakes more than once as the small nocturnal mammals of the mountains hopped across their path. Shan began to urge the American on after one such stop when he saw that Yates was staring uneasily at the village on the slope above. Tumkot was strangely glowing, launching its own flickering stars into the night sky. A huge fire was burning in the square.

"What if it's Tenzin's funeral pyre?" Yates asked. "We're not going to be welcome."

"They wouldn't place a pyre in the town square," Shan said, though he still directed Yates to extinguish the headlights. For the last half mile he walked in front of the truck, guiding it forward with the American's hand light. They left the truck a hundred yards from the village and approached on foot, Shan guiding Yates through the dim alleys and stairs. Twice they flattened against alley walls to avoid being seen, once for two men carrying pitchforks as they marched down the main street, then for a woman who hurried by with a length of white cloth and a bucket of steaming water.

Two ghosts waited at the rear of Kypo's house, glowing in the moonlight. Neither the long-haired white goat nor the girl, who was wearing one of the white T-shirts handed out in expedition camps, uttered a sound, just watched with fearful expressions as the two men entered the back door.

Inside, beside the ground-floor stalls, Kypo stood at a make-shift table on which a body covered with a blanket lay. "Are you crazy?" he growled as they emerged from the shadows. "Do you have any idea what is going on in the square?"

"Public Security doesn't know about Xie's death yet," Shan pointed out.

"It's not about Xie, it's about the original murders. Cao has decided he needs additional witnesses. A convoy is getting ready at the garage in town, with maps for Tumkot."

Shan refrained from asking how Kypo had learned such a well-guarded secret. They both knew someone who collected secrets at town garages. Kypo and Jomo seemed to be forgetting the grudge that had stood between them for so long.

"They will seal off the roads in the morning, order every man, woman and child to assemble in the square. Anyone without papers will be arrested. But that's not why the porters refuse to work," Kypo added, pointing at the body. "That's why. They say his soul is being beaten to a pulp. Every time the goddess tries to take him he is killed again."

Shan stepped closer to the table. The incense that burned at each end traditionally was for attracting spirits. But Kypo had increased the usual measure because of the smell of decay. Though the body had been in cold storage much of the time, it had been more than a week since Shan brought it down from Chomolungma.

"I can't be responsible for what they might do if they see you touching that body," Kypo warned. "It's been cleansed." A shadow emerged out of the darker shadows. Kypo's wife came to his side, her face tight with fear.

"What do you mean he is killed again?" Shan asked.

It was Kypo's spouse who answered, her eyes flaring for a moment as Shan took another step toward the body. "Bones, heart, head," she said, her voice heavy with warning.

Another figure appeared, silhouetted in the doorway to the street. The hulking blacksmith, the second husband of the household, cursed and made a quick lunge at Shan. His fist was blocked by Kypo's raised arm.

"I was taking him on his passage," Shan declared in a level voice, "before half the people of Tumkot even knew he was dead."

The blacksmith shoved Kypo back and took another step toward Shan, his hand reaching for a hammer on his belt. "He is the one who brings them back when they die," Kypo called out. "Shan knows the words to say. He wears a gau. He was a prisoner of Major Cao," he added, struggling how best to explain Shan.

The big man's arm swung up again, but more slowly. Shan did not move as the man pushed open the top of Shan's shirt and pulled out the prayer amulet hanging from his neck. The blacksmith's face wrinkled in confusion. He did not protest when the wife of the household pulled him away, back into the shadows.

"I explained already that his bones were broken in the fall, that the holes were put in his chest by the knobs," Shan said to Kypo. "Those are the explanations for what happened to his body." But what had Kypo's wife said? Bones, heart, head.

The Tibetan just stared wordlessly at Shan, as if to say Shan did not understand.

Shan, more confused than ever, pulled the blanket back to expose the upper torso. "The body was given to me on the trail above the road to the base camp. I helped wrap him in canvas and tie him to the mule."

Two Tibetan women appeared, carrying *torma* offerings, little deities shaped out of butter. As they positioned themselves beside the body, a teenage boy appeared, anger in his eyes, holding a staff before him as if to threaten the two outsiders

"Megan!" Yates suddenly exclaimed, then quickly lowered the pack on his back, extracted his small computer and set it on a half wall along one of the stalls. A moment later its screen began to glow and he started scrolling through lists of files.

Shan eyed the gathering Tibetans behind Kypo. There were more than ten now, all watching him with intense distrust, several holding objects that could be used as weapons.

Yates, oblivious to the hostile, expanding crowd, tapped on the keys of his computer. "Megan has . . . had a special technique she used to weed out the climbers she thought wouldn't make it to the top. She kept a file in her computer of photos. On any expedition she was affiliated with she made sure everyone saw them before they climbed above base camp."

"I don't understand," Shan said.

The American gestured Shan toward the screen with a grim expression. "The dead," he said in English. "She collected the dead." Yates began to scroll through a series of macabre photographs. "According to this, Tenzin was the twenty-fifth dead climber she photographed."

With a shudder Shan recognized the sherpa. He had gone up to the advance camps himself only once, but it had been high enough to see three of the gruesome figures frozen to the mountain, slowly being covered with snow and ice. He glanced up at Yates in confusion. The image on the screen was simply Tenzin in repose, his body laid out at the base of the rock face from which he had fallen.

"I looked at it the day you took Tenzin away," Yates explained. "My gut said there was something amiss, but I couldn't find it."

It took Shan a few seconds of silent searching to find the answer. With new foreboding he pointed to Tenzin's feet.

The American sagged. "Damn it, no," he moaned in an anguished voice. "Not Tenzin." It was indeed as if Tenzin had just died again.

"What is it?" Kypo demanded over his shoulder.

"The boots," Shan explained.

"They're backward," Yates said. "His climbing boots are on the wrong feet."

"But what does it mean?" the Tibetan asked.

"It means he was murdered," Shan said. "I should have seen it," he said, anguish now in his voice. "If I had seen it I might have. . . ." His words drifted off. Done what? Shan himself felt like one more victim running before the deadly avalanche let loose the day the minister died. No, he chastised himself as he turned back toward the body, these villagers deserved the truth. He knew now the avalanche had started with Tenzin, not with the minister. "What it means," he said, "is that it was not the hand of the mountain that killed Tenzin, it was the hand of a man."

"Who here is his family?" Shan asked after a moment.

"A sister is here, with her son," Kypo said, gesturing to a woman in her forties and the teenage boy who wielded the staff. "His mother is on the other side, in Nepal."

"They must roll him over," Shan said.

"He's been cleansed," the sister protested. "Purified for his passage on."

"And what kind of passage will that be," Shan asked, "if we cannot send him with the truth? I need to turn him over. You saw something when you cleaned him, evidence of the third killing."

The woman searched the confused faces of her companions then gestured for Kypo, not Shan, to help turn the body over.

Bones, heart, head. At first everyone had thought he had died from the fall that had crushed so many bones. Then two bullets had been shot into his heart. Shan investigated the third killing of Tenzin by studying the back of his head.

Somehow murder always seemed abstract to Shan until he saw the sign of the deathblow. A dark, empty thing began gnawing inside him as he gazed at the mark at the base of the sherpa's neck, but the foreboding was quickly replaced by shame. He should have known. He had failed Tenzin, and by doing so had given room for the murderer, then the knobs, to play their games with the people of the hills.

After a moment he spoke into Kypo's ear, then waited as Kypo disappeared, the Tibetans getting more and more restless, until a minute later Kypo returned from his supply stores holding a foot-long steel pin, pointed at the bottom.

Shan took the pin and extended it for all to see, then pushed back the thick hair at the base of Tenzin's neck. "He was sleeping at his new advance camp. There's enough soil and gravel there to use tent stakes like this. Someone came up and sank this one into the back of his neck. It was over instantly—no blood, no pain. Then the killer pulled him from his sleeping bag, dressed him, in his haste putting the boots on the wrong feet, and dropped him over the side." He glanced at Kypo. "Using a frayed rope certain to break to complete the image of someone who had died in a fall." It had seemed so obvious that he had died in a fall no one had bothered to ask any questions. Shan looked back at the small puncture at the base of Tenzin's neck, noticing a speck of soil at the edge of the wound. The pin had probably been taken out of the ground then reinserted after the killer was done.

The villagers reacted as if they had seen Shan himself drive the pin into Tenzin's spinal cord.

"The mountain people don't kill each other," the blacksmith growled. "You outsiders killed him!"

"I didn't kill him," Shan shot back, then gestured toward Yates. "This man didn't kill him." A man stepped forward, an ax in his raised hand. Yates retreated into the shadows. So much for allies, Shan thought. He eased backward to avoid the man's swing but then another villager advanced at his flank, his face dark with anger, his hand clutching a short club.

Suddenly the American was back, brandishing a long hoe, swinging it to clear a radius of several feet around Shan.

"We can finish this here!" the blacksmith snarled. "We will have justice for once! A pyre can hold three as easily as one!" He moved forward, followed by the man with the club and the one with an ax.

Suddenly Ama Apte was at Shan's side, holding out a hand from which hung a necklace with an ivory skull as its pendant. She extended it in an arc, taking in the entire crowd, causing them to step back, then dangled it in front of the blacksmith's face.

"It's enough, Ama Apte," the blacksmith said loudly, though his voice had more pleading than anger in it now.

"It will not end here, nor with Tenzin's pyre. The mountain is still at work," Ama Apte declared, then stepped between Shan and Yates, who had lowered his hoe. She lifted Shan's arm. "This one has been bonded to the dead of the mountain," she declared, then startled Yates by raising his wrist in her other hand, showing the Tibetans his missing fingertip. "And the mountain has marked this one too," she declared. "She has plans for them. My dice have confirmed it, this very night." She kept the arms extended, squeezing them tightly. She smelled of aloe, used by many Tibetans for healing. On the heel of the hand that held Shan was a patch of dried blood. As she moved, there was a soft jingling, from her silver necklaces, and Shan recalled the words of the driver from the ambushed prison bus. When the yeti had gone inside the bus—to steal the prisoner files, Shan now knew—the driver had heard tiny bells.

The astrologer's challenge was not enough for the angry men in the front, but her words were like magic for the others. Their rancor was gone. Some nodded and melted back into the shadows outside. Kypo slipped between his mother and the blacksmith, fixing the smith with challenge in his face until the bigger man muttered and broke away, taking his companions out into the street.

Shan turned to the dead sherpa's sister as the chamber emptied. "We will help you wash him again," he said in an apologetic tone. Kypo turned and soon brought new sticks of incense, his wife basins of water. The sister accepted their help in the preparation but would not let them touch the body again. As Shan and Yates watched from the shadows of the stalls Shan asked the American about the night before Tenzin had died.

"Three sherpas had gone up to scout locations for our staging camps," the American explained, and offered a familiar description of the strenuous work involved in establishing a new line of support camps above the base camp, testing ice ledges, anchoring safety lines along the most difficult rock faces, trying to locate resting points protected from the frigid, incessant winds of the upper slopes. The three had planned to stay together but sudden blizzard conditions had separated the party on their descent after they had pitched a tent for an upper camp and Tenzin had continued down while the others had given up and gone back to the upper tent for the night. The next morning Tenzin, always the tireless worker, had announced on his radio that he would begin setting up a practice climb for the customers who would have to wait at the camp to acclimatize. When the other sherpas finally arrived they could not find him and radioed Megan, their climb captain. A search was begun from above and below. Two hours later Megan spotted his body in her binoculars. "There were over a hundred people at base camp that night," Yates explained, "and since the sky had cleared, leaving a bright moon, any of them could have made the climb to the camp where Tenzin was sleeping."

"The most important question," Shan mused, "isn't who could have made the climb, it is why a sherpa who just arrived from Nepal for the season so threatened someone that he had to be killed."

The bonfire in the square had begun to die as Shan and Yates slipped outside, Shan pointing the way to Ama Apte's house. They had reached the side of the square when Kypo stepped in front of them. "When did you meet my mother?" he demanded of the American in an unsettled tone.

"I never have, until now," Yates replied, with a pointed glance toward Shan that said he had not forgotten the strange encounter with her at the base camp. Shan saw that the American was gazing at the truncated finger Ama Apte had raised to the crowd. "It's nothing," he added hastily. "She noticed my finger and decided to use it to help quiet the mob."

As his two companions stared uneasily at each other, a red

light flickered in the sky along the southern horizon then disappeared behind a peak. The mountain commandos sometimes patrolled with infrared scanners, and outside the Everest zone were known to shoot at anything that moved within a mile of the border, whether man or beast. Shan watched the light absently, nearly overcome with fatigue, following Kypo toward his mother's house, past the center square. Half the villagers still lingered there, listening to a man's harangue about how Religious Affairs had destroyed a farmer's barley stores because the Bureau suspected he had helped the fugitive monks, how the knobs would do the same to all of them when they came.

Another red light appeared momentarily between two ridges to the north.

Shan, now wide awake and frightened to his core, grabbed Kypo's arm. "You have to send them home!" he insisted. "Put out the fire and send them home!"

"What are you talking about?"

"The knobs are coming *tonight*, not tomorrow! They want the village worked up, they want resistance so they can justify detention of every man here."

Kypo raised his lantern close to Shan's face, searching it as if hoping for a sign of deception, then just shook his head despondently. "It's gone too far. Some of them have been drinking. They *want* a fight with the knobs."

"Then your mother—"

"My mother," Kypo shot back, "has put herself in enough jeopardy tonight."

A vise seemed to be tightening around Shan's chest. He knew what Public Security was capable of, but he was probably one of only a few in the village who had seen it firsthand. He stared forlornly at the fire, seeing in his mind's eye how the destruction of Tumkot would become another of the tragic tales told at campfires, another story of Tibetans battered by a century they hadn't chosen to live in.

"Then get Gyalo away."

"What are you talking about?" Kypo protested. "I don't know—"

"There's no more time for games. He is at your mother's house. Get him out, back to Yates's truck, back to the sunken chamber at my stable. And get me four sober men who can be trusted."

MAJOR CAO SAID nothing as Shan opened the door and slid behind the wheel of his utility vehicle parked below the village, did not react when four dark figures took up position around the vehicle. He was used to figures in shadow, and would never for an instant have believed anyone but other knobs would be so bold.

Shan put his hands on the wheel, in plain sight, before speaking. "You're going to call off the raid tonight," he declared.

Cao's head snapped up, his hand went to his holster, then he froze as he took notice of the figures outside the truck.

"You're a dead man, Shan," he hissed.

"Your disadvantage, Major, is that you don't understand investigations for the top ranks in Beijing. But I carried them out for twenty years. Everything is in motion, everything is in play, including the investigator. Especially the investigator. They will turn on you in an instant. The number of antisocial Tibetans you arrest won't matter. Have you asked yourself why they sent you, an investigator from Lhasa, and not someone from Beijing for such an important investigation? You are the failsafe. If things don't go well you become a conspirator. A few adjustments to your investigation file and suddenly you're part of the crime."

"I will start with the bones of your feet," Cao said. "I will keep you alive for a month or two. But after the first hour you will never walk again."

"Do you think Madame Zheng is here for the mountain air? Have you even bothered to ask what her role is?"

"An observer."

"No. She is from the Ministry of Justice. I don't know her but I know her type. She is credentialed as a judge prosecutor, I wager. And for you that makes her the most dangerous person in the county right now."

"Ridiculous. She just sits in meetings and takes notes."

"She will ask for your file. That's when you know they are beginning to doubt your ability, beginning to consider their own version of the crime."

There was just enough moonlight for Shan to see the wince on Cao's face.

"A Public Security bus is ambushed and a state minister killed a stone's throw away. She knows these events must be related, and every hour you lose pretending otherwise puts you that much closer to disgrace." Cao seemed to stop breathing for a moment. Shan's guess about Madame Zheng was right. "You have a few more days at most. Then new reports will be written, your name will go into the file."

"You are delusional. I have fifteen years with the Bureau. That would never happen."

"You have all the proof you need that it does."

Cao's head moved toward Shan.

"I am that proof. Read my file again."

Cao was silent for a long moment. "For all I know, you were Tan's partner in the killing."

"The other element you don't appreciate is that there are foreigners here." As Shan spoke, the right side of the vehicle began to sag. As Shan had instructed, Kypo's men were releasing air from the tires. It was the subtlest act of resistance but enough to cause Cao to hesitate. He had no way of knowing how many of the shadowy figures lurked in the darkness around his car.

"There's nowhere you can hide, Shan," he snarled. "When you attack a Public Security officer your life is forfeit."

"Pay attention to the subtleties, Major," Shan replied in a level voice. "At this point in your career they make all the difference.

This is just an informal conversation. Let's call it career counseling. What you are doing tonight will make headlines in the Western press. Climbers and trekkers from America and Europe are all over this area, most with cameras. By noon tomorrow they will be giving interviews by satellite telephone to reporters in their home countries. The jackbooted oppressor attacks a hamlet of peaceful Tibetans, practically in the shadow of Everest, as a pretext so a Public Security bureaucrat can divert attention from his failed investigation. You may be under tremendous pressure now, yet you still have a chance to come out victorious. But your career is over with the first phone call from an embassy to the Minister of Public Security. They will find you a latrine on the Vietnamese border that needs cleaning for the next ten years."

"My case is finished. I have the murderer. The trial will be next week."

"No. You and I know you wouldn't be here tonight if you were finished. You never had to deal with a prisoner who wouldn't speak. You have to have evidence from some other source. You have to dirty your hands. That's why you're here, to test the market for new witnesses."

"We'll just include you in the sweep," Cao spat. "You'll be lost in the confusion. When you have no papers no one needs to account for you. A nobody can become nothing in an instant."

Shan gave an exaggerated sigh as he lifted the door handle. "I leave you to your witticisms. I think I told you before you are overeducated for your job. Too much wit, not enough judgment. You fail to grasp the most fundamental truth of those you work for. The higher you aspire, the lower must be the denominator on which you base your actions. I fear for you, Major. You may not survive as long as I do."

"I promise I will survive long enough to destroy you."

"You will have to choose. You can destroy me or you can find out the truth of what happened that day on the road to the Base Camp."

As Shan began to open the door Cao spoke again. "I didn't come just looking for hooligans tonight. There is a matter of a body that mysteriously vanished from the experimental hospital. Breach of a highly classified facility, that is an attack on the state. Theft of evidence in a capital case. Now this attack on me. I have enough to shoot you several times over."

"I might understand losing a hand here, a leg there, but a whole body," Shan replied evenly. "That sounds like negligence."

"Imagine my surprise when I found out that you were responsible for taking that same body down from Everest, back to this village. I have learned to study my enemies, before I dissect them. You are a man, like me, of fanatical devotion to his responsibilities."

Shan put one foot out the door, silently surveying the surrounding shadows, for a fleeting, desperate moment telling himself that there were men in the night who, with one word from Shan, would be eager to make a man like Cao disappear. "You are a victim of your own techniques, Major Cao. You need to speak with the doctor who performed the autopsy on that sherpa. Forget the report sent to you for the file. Make him understand that you need the truth. If you had bothered to look at the body even you could have seen that those two bullets were shot into him after he was dead, bullets with a much larger caliber bullet. But he *was* murdered, killed in his sleep on the slopes above the base camp. The foreign expedition leaders have photographs, have the evidence that proves it.

"When those foreigners release the photos of a leading sherpa murdered on Everest and tell how the government hid the body, it will be like an atom bomb detonating in the climbing community. No one will pay to climb on the Chinese side of the mountain, not for years. How many millions was the minister projecting for her new economic model? Fifty million? A hundred? You will be the man who lost it all. You will be the one who shamed China on the global stage. Your star will not fade. It will be extinguished overnight."

These were were terms Cao understood. The major had no reply.

Shan studied his shadowed face, creased with worry now. "I will make you a deal, Major Cao, one that may yet save you."

"You have nothing to offer me," Cao snarled.

"Go to Sarma gompa tonight. Discover the next murder victim."

"What are you talking about?"

"Director Xie is dead."

"Impossible! I saw him a few hours ago."

"You have a satellite phone I believe, as does Xie. Call him."

Cao's eyes seemed to glow as he glared at Shan, but after a long moment he opened the console, pulled out his phone and punched in a number. Shan could hear it ring, five times, ten times, before Cao shut it off and stared at it.

"I found his body at sunset," Shan continued. "No one will have reported it. Seal the site. Call Lhasa. Tell them you believe it should be kept quiet to avoid rumors of civil disorder. Say it to them before they have a chance to say it to you. Tell them you need time to resolve it quietly, for the good of the state. Tell them you are following leads to discover why Xie was alone at the gompa. Then decide what to say to Madame Zheng when she asks about it. Lhasa will call Beijing. Beijing will call her. When you see her next, your head better touch the floor."

The anger on Cao's face was slowly replaced with worry. "Are you certain Xie is dead?"

"He is extremely dead, as you will see."

"Why would you ask for a deal? You just gave me everything."

"Find the body at the back of the gompa ruins. Call your headquarters. Arrange for an ambulance from the yeti factory to secretly take away what's left of the body. All I ask is that you cancel the removal order on Colonel Tan."

"Why would I do that?"

"To save yourself the embarrassment of having to recall him

from prison when the real killer is found. To pay for the favor I am doing you."

"You have already told me what I need to know."

Shan gazed out at the moon rising between two peaks. "Then I will save your career. Keep Tan in town and I will give you the real murderer."

"The antenna attached to the car has been disabled," Shan added as he climbed out. "There will be men hidden in the rocks. If you don't stay in the truck for at least an hour I cannot be responsible for what will happen."

As Cao lit a cigarette Shan saw his hand tremble. "When this is over, Shan," the major spat, "I will have you on your knees begging me to shoot you."

Chapter Eleven

GYALO HAD GONE to another level of existence. He cursed the gods, rattled off the names of the levels of hell as if he were being examined by some ancient guru.

"All the way here," Kypo explained in a pained voice as he sat on a stool in the sunken chapel, "he shouted verses from sutras and tried to get out of the truck. I had to hold him down."

It was no surprise the drunken lama had been left for dead. One arm had been broken, the side of his head had been kicked until it looked like a pulpy, rotten fruit. Two fingers were splinted in place. An eye was swollen shut. Blood trickled from his mouth where a tooth had been knocked out. Whoever had attacked him and thrown him into the pit had thought they were disposing of a dead man.

"I sent Yates away," Kypo explained. "He was very upset. He said he had work to do at the base camp but he acted like it was his fault this had happened."

Shan examined the broken arm. It had been expertly set and splinted. "The American did this?"

"My mother. When we brought him to her, her first words were 'let the old bastard die' and she turned her back on him. But a few minutes later she came back with her first aid kit and worked on him. She said to tell him the gods would look after him despite himself. He woke up and starting shouting like this."

"Saying the same things as now?" Shan asked.

"Mostly." Kypo thought a moment, reconsidering. "He chanted monk's words, charms against demons, in the voice of a terri-fied child. It was as if he were more scared of us than those who attacked him. He reached for me, and said 'just let me die.' She hit him."

Shan looked up, not sure he had heard correctly. "Your mother hit Gyalo?"

Kypo nodded. "With a small club. She knocked him out. She said she couldn't risk having neighbors hear, said he needed to be still so she could set his arm. But she seemed glad for the excuse to strike him." He searched Shan's face, as if hoping for an answer.

"How did she know him? I thought she never came to town."

Kypo shrugged. "And Gyalo never left town. For a while, before she knocked him out, he was trying to crawl to the door." He shrugged again. "He's been crazy for years. An old man. An alcoholic."

"I've known many Tibetans a lot older."

"Old enough to have known another Tibet, I mean."

Shan chewed on the words, sensing the passing, like a leaf on the wind, of a shard of truth. Once all of his investigations had been linear, one fact linking to the next in quick progression leading to the truth. But in Tibet all his puzzles were like giant tangkas, the traditional religious paintings with overlaps of deities, suffering humans, protector demons, even alternate worlds, linked not by events so much as expectation and hope, by relationships in other, earlier Buddhist lives.

"Has your mother always been an astrologer?" Shan asked.

"Of course. It is who she is."

"Was her father an astrologer? Her mother?"

Kypo frowned, bending over the former lama. He was not going to reply.

They washed Gyalo in silence, dressing him in clean clothes from Shan's meager wardrobe. Shan lit more butter lamps. Kypo produced a small cone of incense and lit it by Gyalo's pallet.

"He could still die," Kypo observed in a heavy voice. "I think he wants to die. What will the town do without him? People call him a mascot. But he's something else, something none of us understand."

"I think he is more like a teacher," Shan said. "One who takes on roles to make us understand. Except long ago he lost the ability to go back to himself."

Gyalo stirred, coughing, as Shan held a cup of water to his lips. The old Tibetan ignored it, instead grabbing his arm and studying it, close to his eyes, as if to confirm he was real. There was nothing but bitterness in his eyes when he looked up and recognized Shan. "I know I'm in hell now," he muttered, then drifted into sleep.

Shan sat on a blanket in the corner of the dim chamber, intending to mentally reconstruct his puzzle using its new pieces. But the exhaustion he had been fighting finally overwhelmed him. When he opened his eyes briefly an hour later Kypo was gone. Later when he opened them for a few moments Jomo was there, with a kettle of hot tea, helping his father to drink. Much later, when he fully awoke, Jomo was gone and several fresh momo dumplings were stacked on a low stool between Shan and Gyalo.

The former lama sat upright, gazing with his one good eye at the dim images on the walls. He wore an oddly vacant expression, showing no pain, none of his usual alcoholic haze. He stared at the image of the central demon on the opposite wall. It was Mahakala the protector, in his four armed blue form, holding a skull cup and a sword, draped in a garland of human heads.

"I knew a place like this once," the old Tibetan said in a ragged voice. "but that one was destroyed."

"The tunnels that connected to the temple were filled with debris," Shan explained. "But there was an exit through the stable, probably forgotten long before the gompa was destroyed. I cleaned away enough to be able to enter."

"Why would you do such a thing?"

"All these deities. It felt like they had been buried alive. They needed to be released."

"You were scared of them," Gyalo growled. "They put you under a spell."

"They put me under a spell," Shan readily admitted.

The moist, rattling cackle that came from Gyalo's throat became a groan as the Tibetan clutched his side, doubling over in pain. Blood was seeping into the bandage on the arm that was not broken, but Shan had no fresh one to replace it.

"Who did this to you, Gyalo?"

"I need a drink. A real drink."

"Of the handful of people who know you are here, not one will bring you alcohol."

"Then I may as well die."

"Who did this?" Shan repeated.

When Gyalo finally spoke it was to the demon on the wall, as if he preferred to converse with the old god. "Two strangers in dark sweatshirts, hoods over their heads." His voice was dry as stone. "Big men, built like yaks. They didn't introduce themselves. Someone else stood in the shadows, as if enjoying the show."

"What did they want?"

"They spoke a few words of greeting at first, and gave me a bottle, like maybe they came for a blessing. After I drank some they said more words."

"What words?"

"Questions. Who had spoken with me about the Yama temple that had been up on the mountains. Who had I given a sickle to, with the writing on the blade." A spasm of pain racked his body, and he spat up blood again. He began shivering.

Shan lifted an tattered sheepskin *chuba* coat from a peg by the entry and covered him with it. "So you told them about the American and me."

Gyalo gazed at the demon. "Not at first."

Shan looked up in surprise. Surely the drunken lama had not invited the beating by trying to protect Yates and Shan.

"In the cupboard," the Tibetan said abruptly, and pointed to a little alcove in the dusty stone wall.

"There is no cupboard," Shan said, confused. The small

squared-out space in the wall might well have once held shelves but no trace of them remained.

With what seemed like a great effort Gyalo lifted a finger and pointed insistently at the alcove. Shan stood, carrying a lamp to show that the space was empty. But when the Tibetan grunted and jabbed his finger again he tapped his fingers along the surface of the wall until, on the left side at shoulder height, his drumming reached something hollow. He pressed his fingers into the dust-encrusted stone, scratching until he found the lip of a board and pulled. With a small cloud of dust, a door cracked open. He reached inside and extracted a six-inch painted figure, carved of wood. It was Mahakala, Protector of the Faithful, in his fierce blue skinned form, matching the painting on the wall. Shan blew away the coating of dust from the figure and placed it on the stool beside Gyalo.

The Tibetan seemed to relax as he saw the figure, and for a moment Shan thought he saw the lama of fifty years earlier. But then he began to sway, and he managed only a few words before passing out again. "Look at the old fool," he said, speaking of the little god, "what does he know?"

Shan watched the forlorn lama a long time, working and reworking the puzzle in his mind, before gathering up several musty sacks for a pillow and draping the blanket over the sleeping Tibetan.

HE DID NOT seek the constable's help this time before venturing to the rear of the jail. The cleaning crew arrived exactly on time, saying nothing as he joined them again. The invisible workers who kept Tibet functioning were often invisible to each other as well.

Cao had cancelled the order to transport his prisoner out of the county. Tan lay on the pallet, one filthy blanket covering his body, another rolled up for a pillow. His face was in shadow, but Shan saw Tan's breath momentarily catch as he reached the cell door.

"I need to know how you knew the minister," Shan said. "I need to know why you needed to see her."

Tan stood up, retrieved the tin cup from the sink and, fixing Shan with a steady gaze, urinated in it. When he was finished he hobbled forward, dragging one foot.

"I am encouraged you still have your bodily functions," Shan observed as he retreated several steps.

"Get the hell out of here!" Tan snarled. His face was directly in the light now. Shan could see the way it sagged, could see the bruises and lacerations. Although the eyes still burned with a cool fire, there was no arrogance left in them, only hatred.

"I had thought the killer had somehow stolen your gun. But then I discovered the minister had entertained someone in her room the night before her death. I have struggled to find some theory to explain how the killer got your gun. You would not have surrendered it without a struggle, and if it had been stolen you would have raised the shrillest of alarms with Public Security. I have learned to be suspicious of complicated explanations. I find the simplest one is likely the truth. You were the one she entertained, and *she* took your gun. You were too embarrassed to report that you lost it to a minister of state. A female minister."

Tan, apparently deciding he could not reach Shan, extended his arm through the bars and poured his urine in an arc across the front of the cell, as if casting a charm to ward off an evil spirit. Before he finished his hand started twitching, so that the contents of the cup splattered onto his hand. Tan dropped the cup and clamped the hand under his other arm.

Shan silently retrieved the mop and bucket he had left at the end of the corridor, mopped up the urine, then located another cup in an empty cell and tossed it onto Tan's pallet. He then extracted a sack from his pocket and extended it through the bars. Tan slapped it away, launching it from Shan's hand, spilling the contents onto Tan's feet. Four momos, the last of the dumplings Jomo had left in the underground chapel.

With the reflex of a seasoned prisoner Tan bent and scooped up the momos. He had jammed one into his mouth and was gulping it down when he seemed to remember Shan. With a hint of shame in his eyes he glanced up, then hobbled to his cot and proceeded to eat the rest.

"Tell me about the gun," Shan pressed. "If I can prove she had it Cao's case against you is destroyed, because it is the only connection to you. A sherpa's body was placed beside that of the minister's, substituted for the American woman who died there. He was shot with a different gun. Not yours. A big one, a huge caliber. Not one issued by Public Security or the army."

When Tan did not reply Shan retreated again, stepping into the first of the interrogation rooms that adjoined the corridor, opening drawers in its metal cabinet. When he arrived back at the cell he extended a small brown plastic bottle. Tan's head snapped up. "Painkillers," Shan announced. "Enough to get you through a couple more days."

Tan extended his open palm. Shan tossed the bottle through the bars. Tan stared at the bottle, then clenched it so tightly his knuckles went white. "There was no dead American at the scene," he announced in a thin voice. "Stealing that second body from the hospital was only a ploy to confuse the chief investigator."

"How would you—" Shan began, his brow wrinkled in confusion. Then he understood. Tan was reciting the official version of events.

Tan replied with a bitter grin. "The monk said he saw the American woman running away after helping me commit the crime. The dead sherpa was patriotically trying to stop the murder and was shot."

"What monk?" Shan asked, filled with new dread.

"That one," he said, with a nod down the darkened cell corridor. "It was a busy morning in the interrogation rooms."

Shan found himself halfway down the corridor before he was conscious of his own movement. He paused then followed the faint sound of breathing from a cell in the center of the corridor.

He stepped hesitantly to the cell, discerning a small figure asleep on a pallet in the shadows at the rear. Scratched into the wall were several figures in a line about two feet above the floor, crudely drawn but still recognizable. A lotus blossom. A conch shell. The prisoner had been drawing the *tashi targyel*, the seven sacred symbols. Shan's heart began rising into his throat. He knew before he spotted the shreds of a robe and a dirty prison shirt coat on the floor. Cao had brought back one of the captured monks.

When Shan returned to the colonel's cell, Tan's expression was oddly triumphant. "I don't understand your obsession with rearranging facts, Shan," he said. "When an artist is halfway through his masterwork you can't just run and up and steal his paints. It's unbecoming."

"Cao is no artist. What exactly has he done?"

"He went away for half a day. When he returned he announced he had found the witness he needed to destroy me. He had the monk worked on for a few hours in the back rooms. When it came time for the climax he moved his little opera to this corridor, to the table there in the center so I could hear it all. The Tibetan has confessed to obstructing justice by not coming forward as a witness to the crimes. Cao promised him only a month's imprisonment, and something for some other monk, a lama who will be released so long as he takes off his robe. So he signed a statement that he saw me with the pistol. Otherwise the lama was to get ten years' hard labor."

Shan felt his frail hopes slipping away. Cao had used the old lama from Sarma, the one who had been captured because he insisted on tending to the injured driver.

"Cao made him shout out his confession, like at one of the struggle sessions we used to have, just to be sure I could hear."

Shan, suddenly feeling weak in the knees, gripped the bars in both hands.

Tan opened the bottle, dumped out several pills and swallowed them. "I think," the colonel continued, "that Cao was considering a story of more texture, a more interesting tale for the audience back home. But he seems to have changed course. It is to be a simple trial. A forensic report says the victims died from shots from my gun, a witness says he saw me pull the trigger. He has spunk, that little Tibetan. They raised a baton to strike me when I started laughing and he leaped up to block it, and took the blow on his skull." For a moment Tan hesitated and Shan saw confusion cloud his eyes before derision returned. "The fool."

"He was apologizing for what he had done."

Tan frowned. He had no reply.

"There was another death. Director Xie of Religious Affairs. How will such a report explain that killing?"

Tan shrugged. "The guards told me about it. No doubt it will be recorded as an industrial accident."

"You have to stall him," Shan said in a plaintive voice. "Tell him there was a conspiracy, suggest that Minister Wu was corrupt, that this was about a conspiracy of bribery reaching high into the government. He will have to pause, think about involving others in Beijing. It will buy us a few days. Tell me where you were. Maybe I can help confirm that you were somewhere else that day."

Tan gazed without expression at Shan, then his lips formed a thin grin, made crooked by his swollen lips.

"Do you understand nothing I've said?" Shan asked. "Another day of this and he'll have a confession from you. That is the prize he is after."

Tan turned away to face the wall.

"We don't have religion in China," Shan said to his back. "We have confession. For a zealous Party member it is the moment of consecration. When the bullet enters your skull, some pampered niece of a Party official will watch and realize at that moment that the Party is her god. And that, Colonel Tan, becomes the entire point of your life."

Tan turned back, his lips still curled up in the lightless smile Shan had seen so often in his Lhadrung prison camp.

Realization hit Shan like a sack of stones. He tottered backward, sank onto a nearby bench. "You want to die!" he gasped, burying his head in his hands. "You want the bullet in your head."

Shan looked up once, twice, three times, each time with a new argument on his tongue, each time meeting the colonel's crooked sneer. Finally Tan lay down on his pallet, his back to Shan.

Numb with despair, Shan stared at the floor as he shut the door and walked toward the rear exit. He did not at first notice that the Tibetan cleaners were gone until he nearly collided with a knob guard barring his path, automatic rifle slung forward. A single office was illuminated, cigarette smoke hanging in the air before it.

Shan let himself be herded into the office. The face of the man at the desk was hung in shadow above the metal shade of the goose-neck desk lamp, but the fearful expression of the guard told Shan all he needed to know. He lowered himself into the chair in front of the desk as Major Cao leaned forward and shut off a receiver on the desk. Shan's mouth went dry as he recognized the device. Cao had been listening to his conversation with Tan. "I want the other monks," Cao declared in a venomous tone. "All of them."

"I hear there are a lot of Tibetan monks in India." Shan fought to keep his voice steady. He was in Cao's world now, an automatic rifle aimed at his spine.

"You know where they are, or can find them. You're going to get them. You're going to make sure they give me more witness statements against Tan." Cao rose and walked around the desk, leaning on the front, barely three feet from Shan, as he lit another cigarette. "You won last night," the major declared. "No raid. No detention of those villagers. You were right. It was very old school, what I was doing. A blunt instrument when what is needed is a surgeon's scapel."

Cao let the words hang in the air. Shan's gut began to tie itself in a knot.

The major lifted a small silver and turquoise bracelet. "Director

Xie put up a noble fight with his killers before he was knocked unconscious. He was still holding on to this when the cowards dragged him before the machine. It has been identified as belonging to the American Megan Ross. You were right after all. The American was at Wu's killing. She was there, helping Tan. Now she and the monks roam as a criminal gang in the mountains. You are going to bring them to me."

Cao glanced over his shoulder. For the first time Shan noticed a small figure in a chair in the dim corner of the office. Madame Zheng.

"You know this woman Ross," Cao observed.

Shan gazed woodenly at the major. What Ama Apte had said was true. The American woman kept coming back to life. It was as if she had a truth to speak, a quest to fulfill, and she would not let a little thing like death interfere with its completion.

"The bracelet was planted. Her belongings are still in a tent at the base camp, anyone could have taken it. You need to find out who met with Xie at Sarma gompa. Why was he there alone?"

"He took a radio call, then ordered his deputies away. No doubt a ruse by the American woman."

"I told you I would get the real killers. Give me time."

"A bluff, to persuade me to keep Tan within reach. But you were right about that as well, Comrade Shan. I need him here. With the breakthrough given to us by the martyred Xie we will be able to have our trial in a matter of days." Cao gestured to the receiver connected to Tan's cell. "You heard yourself how well it is going. At this rate I am confident the silent colonel will find his tongue when we put him in the dock."

"You fail to understand him. Letting you shoot him isn't an act of contrition for Tan. For him it will be a redemption."

Cao's eyes flickered with confusion for a moment but he would not be diverted. "The last three monks. I will have them and the American woman. Perhaps all the monks need to say is that they were manipulated by Tan and the American. If so we could be generous, let them avoid the firing squad."

"And serve what? Twenty, thirty years in the gulag?" It was, Shan realized, driven by the new shape of politics in Tibet. The government preferred not to be seen as unduly harsh on Tibetans. And certainly it was more palatable to put them away as common criminals, not for political reasons.

Cao shrugged. "They were accomplices to two murders."

"All they did was get on a bus. I told you before. Look at the bullets from the clinic's autopsy on the sherpa. They destroy your case."

Cao smiled. "The day that sherpa's body was stolen, there was an extraordinary event at the clinic, comrade. A phantom attacked an orderly and stole his identity badge. The badge later showed up on a bus seat. No one recalls much about the phantom. The nurse only remembers another lunatic patient in his underwear. And unfortunately the clinic has not received sufficient funds to install video monitors. It did spend money last year on that new electronic locking system. It tracks every time a security badge is used to open a door. The phantom had the run of the entire clinic. He could have taken drugs, lab equipment, surgical devices. But all he did was enter one room. I went back to the clinic today, to speak with security there. Imagine my surprise when I was shown the names of the inmates in that room." Cao took a long draw on his cigarette and looked down. "I will have that woman and the monks, Shan."

Shan's tongue seemed to have difficulty moving. "He isn't really . . ." he murmured, then desolation froze his tongue.

"Not your son? Of course he is," Cao said in a gloating voice. "The records confirm it. Shan Ko. Not much family resemblance but his file is the spitting image of his father's. A troublemaker, unable to accept authority, too clever for his own good. In desperate need of reform."

"He isn't really sick." The words came in a tiny, hoarse voice. "Tan sent him there for punishment."

Cao laughed.

"I have no idea where the monks are. Do you think they would trust a Chinese?" Shan asked.

Cao leaned across the desk and lifted a small stack of papers. "Experimental surgery is being pioneered by the brave doctors of our clinic." He dropped the top paper onto Shan's lap. "So far it has been extraordinarily effective at curing antisocial behavior."

A black worm seemed to crawl through Shan's heart as he read the memo, a report from the yeti factory to a medical research agency in Beijing. The procedure was called cerebral pasteurization. It consisted of drilling a dozen holes into the skull and inserting red-hot wires to cauterize pockets of brain cells.

"Your son is scheduled for the procedure in forty eight hours," Cao announced. "Bring me the monks," he declared with an icy gaze, "or in the name of socialist progress we will steam his brain."

SHAN WALKED IN the darkness without knowing, without seeing, something inside directing him to his quarters long enough to lift a tattered sack from a peg on the wall then taking him up the half-mile path to the ledge above town where he sometimes meditated. He lowered himself to the ground, facing the south, the massive moonlit peaks of the Himalayas glowing along the horizon.

He was a breathing shell. There was nothing left inside but a black emptiness. Everything he had done had been for his son but all his actions had steadily, inexorably condemned Ko to a living death. He was no closer to the killer, no closer to stopping the killing, no closer to understanding the strange drama the Americans had been involved in. He had stirred up Public Security against the villagers and by encouraging the monks to flee from the bus he might have simply ensured their destruction. He gazed with an unfamiliar sense of fear toward Everest, sensing that he was trapped in some tormenting zone where the wrath of the mountain from above overlapped with the wrath of Public Security from below.

He was not aware of willing his hands to move, only watched as they lit a small fire from the wood he kept stored there, then extract a bundle of worn yarrow sticks from the sack. He stared at the throwing sticks, used by generations of his family for meditation on the verses of the Tao, then tried to will himself to start stacking them in piles, to get lost in the ancient ritual, as his father had taught him, to push away all distraction, all torment. But something kept pushing through, past the Tao. Other verses came into his mind, those of the old Chinese poets, as if his father were reaching out to him with a different lesson.

Su tung-po had been a Sung dynasty official who retreated into poetry and Buddhism after being exiled for offending the emperor. A thousand years earlier Su had written a verse about mountains on a wall at the then-ancient Xilin temple. As Shan looked out to the shimmering peaks of the Himalayas he spoke the words, and then, with a catch in his throat, spoke them again. He could hear his father's voice over his own.

> *Regarded from one side, an entire range*
> *from another, a single peak.*
> *Far, near, high, low, all the peaks*
> *different from the others.*
> *If the true face of the mountain*
> *cannot be known*
> *It is because the one looking at it*
> *is standing in its midst.*

He closed his eyes, repeating the words again, and again, very slowly. Eventually they triggered a memory of a day long ago when his father had begun teaching him about the Tao and the poets with the words "Let us speak about the way of the world," and then another, when they had sat on a rice paddy levee watching winter stars, in violation of the curfew of their reeducation camp. His father had told him of a monk he had known who, in the peculiar blend of Taoism and Buddhism that prevailed in much of China, believed in reincarnation, but both prospectively and retroactively, so that rebirth could be sometime in the past. Shan and his father had lain under the night sky speaking about who in the past they might become, usually settling on hermit scholars or renegade Sung dynasty poets. In prison he had passed many nights lying in the dark, in near starvation, lost in visions of himself and his father in another life.

His father waited for him on the mountainside beside a small comfortable bungalow of wood and stone, completing a painting of intricately detailed bamboo in which a thrush sang. Sipping water from a wooden ladle, the old scholar looked up and gazed expectantly down the misty trail.

Shan reached into his pouch and withdrew a paper and pen.

We are journeying to your Sung house, Father, he wrote. *Ko with fresh brushes and I with a basket of lychee nuts. Not long now, until we slip these chains. Keep the tea warm. Xiao Shan,* he signed it. *Little Shan.*

Shan stared at the letter, fighting his recurring guilt over never having written to his father with the full details of his own imprisonment, for fear he would disappoint the old scholar. He lifted the pen again but instead of writing drew a small simple mandala in the margin then folded another sheet of paper as an envelope around the letter and wrote his father's name. With overlapping sticks he built a small square tower in the fire and laid the letter on it. He watched it burn, watched the glowing ashes rise high up into an oddly gentle breeze and float toward Chomolungma.

After a long time he extracted more paper, this time addressing it with the names of the two Tibetans whose lives he cherished more than his own. He had been sending a letter every week to Gendun and Lokesh, in their hidden hermitage in Lhadrung, and now wrote without thinking, in the Tibetan script they had taught him, of the events of the past ten days, wrote of everything, explaining how first a sherpa, then an American woman, were dead and not dead, playing ongoing roles in the strangest of dramas. He had begun to believe that the mountain goddess was indeed using them, he wrote, though he could not discover her purpose. *I have lost the way of finding the truth*, he finally inscribed. *Teach me again.*

He held the letter in his hands, convinced more than ever that the old Tibetans would be aware that he was sending a message, asking them to help him discover the truth across the hundreds of miles that separated them.

But there was no truth, he could hear his friends say, at least none that could ever be spoken, there was only the particular goodness that resonated inside each man, and each man's form of goodness was as unique as each cloud in the sky.

He sat long after he had burned the second letter, watching the fire dwindle to ashes, driving the world from his mind the way Gendun and Lokesh had taught him. Finally he went to the lip of the high ledge and folded his hands into the diamond of the mind mudra for focus, looking over the sleeping town and the snowcapped sentinels on the horizon. After an hour he found a quiet place within. After another hour he began to let each piece of evidence enter the place, turning it, twisting it, prodding it, looking for and finally finding the one little ember that was smoldering under it all.

SHAN WAS AT the entry to the Tingri County People's Library when it opened, wearing his best clothes, respectfully greeting the Chinese matron who administered the collection, moving to a long row of shelves under the side window. It was a compact, sturdy building, freshly painted and containing a bigger collection than would seem justified by the size of the town, reflecting the largess of the local Party.

The books Shan focused on were all identically bound, all labeled in block gold ideograms *Annual Report of the Tingri County Secretariat of the Communist Party of China*. He picked up the volumes for the early 1960s and began quickly leafing through them. They consisted almost entirely of pronouncements from Beijing, the only local content being commentary on the evolving campaign against the local landlord class, with lists of assets, down to the number of sheep and yaks. It was a familiar saga, in which local cooperatives, formed from what Beijing termed the peasant class, gradually increased their power over the social structure.

"May I be of assistance?" came an aggrieved voice over his shoulder.

Shan turned to the librarian with a smile. "This early period of socialist assimilation fascinates me. When I was younger I spent days and days in the archives in Beijing." That much at least was true. "Each region has its own particular version to tell."

The woman came closer. She smelled of strong soap and peanut oil. "You are supposed to sign in to use the reference materials," she chided, extending a clipboard.

Shan apologized and quickly wrote his name at the bottom of a list of names.

"Beijing?" she asked in a more relaxed tone.

"My home."

The woman's eyes widened. "I am from Tianjin! Practically neighbors."

"Practically neighbors," Shan agreed. He fixed the woman with a meaningful gaze. "Surely there was much drama during this region's transformation. So remote. So close to the border. So many locals mired in the old ways. I used to go to Tianjin," he added. "I used to watch the ships."

The woman gave an exclamation of excitement and Shan listened patiently for several minutes as she recounted tales of walking the docks with her parents when she was a child, of an uncle who used to sail on freighters that traveled all over Asia. At last she stood, retrieved a stool, and searched the shelf over the window, producing a dusty volume that she handed to Shan with a satisfied smile. "So many just want to come in to read about yeti, or all the foreigners who have died on our mountain. And until I arrived last year the collection was so incomplete, it took me months just to understand where she had left off."

"Left off?"

"My predecessor. Poor woman had lived here for fifteen years without ever going up to the base of Chomolungma. And the one day she finally decides to drive up her car fails her."

Shan leaned forward. "Are you saying she died?"

The librarian's eyes widened as she gave a melodramatic sigh. "Brakes failed; off a cliff she flew."

"And books were missing after she died? They were here once, and were stolen?"

The woman shrugged. "Stolen, misplaced. They were part of the overall collection she had been compiling on the local history of the People's Republic. I had to make calls to Shigatse to get these, the only ones in the county I think. I can't imagine why the most important book of all for those interested in local history should be missing."

The book was a limited edition, published by the Party, entitled *Heroes of the Himalayan Revolution*. After passing over several pages of Party platitudes, Shan reached a dry chronicle, written in a clerical style, which opened by stating that the struggle to unlock the grip of the landlord classes in the region required more resources than elsewhere—the Party's way of acknowledging that there had been genuine resistance from the local Tibetans. He passed over pages with more lists of the landlord class, expanded as the fervor of reform spread to include not only the large landowners but smaller and smaller farms. Those who owned fifty sheep, then those who owned ten sheep. Those who owned a yak and a dog. As the reform committees, led by ranking members of the peasant class guided by Chinese, began to redistribute the wealth, "hooligans in the mountains" sought to interfere. A company of infantry was brought in. A brigade. A battalion. It was the closest an official chronicler would come to admitting there was an ongoing armed rebellion against the Chinese. Campaigns to eliminate the hooligans were launched along the border with Nepal, in the hills above Shogo, in the valleys below Tumtok village.

But real reform had not started until Mao had dispatched his youth brigades, the Red Guard. Few members of Shan's generation would speak openly of the Cultural Revolution, Mao's euphemistic caption for the years during which the Red Guard inflicted chaos and terror on the country. Youthful zealots, often no more than teenagers, had set themselves up as de facto rulers in many regions, even taking over units of the army. Only when the Red Guard had established itself in Tibet had the systematic destruction of monasteries and temples begun.

The book switched format to reprints of newspaper articles, complete with photographs. A description of the Red Guard moving against small monasteries came under the headline HEROES DEFEND HOMELAND, with a flowery passage about Mao's Children, one of the Guard's many labels, attacking members of the reactionary Dalai Lama gang in the fortresses they called monasteries. Coarse, grainy photographs followed of lamas being paraded through town wearing the conical dunce caps often placed on the subjects of political struggle sessions. THE LEADERS OF THE EXPLOITER CLASS AT LAST BROUGHT TO SUBMISSION BY THE 117TH YOUTH BRIGADE, read one of the captions. In another photo the flag of Beijing was crossed with another, its insignia blurred by the wind. Others showed mountain gompas in ruin, piles of weapons seized from remnants of the exploiters, smoking remains of the houses of suspected rebels. In one of the pictures members of the Brigade posed with weapons like warriors, wearing bandoliers, waving heavy automatic pistols over their heads. Finally he reached a large photo, carefully staged, of more old Tibetans in conical hats sitting in a struggle session before a raised table of revolutionary inquisitors in the courtyard of the old gompa. Hanging in front of the table was the flag of the youth brigade, consisting of a hammer crossed with a lightning bolt on a dark background. At the center of the table sat an attractive young girl with familiar features. The caption read TIRELESS COMMANDER WU LEADS ANOTHER STRUGGLE SESSION IN SHOGO.

Reports of speeches followed, from National Day ceremonies, visits of Party dignitaries, followed by an article captioned *Final Campaign Against Traitors in Mountains*, a brief description of how the Hammer and Lightning Brigade was finally scouring away the last vestiges of resistance by machine-gunning all herds and leveling most of the villages in the high ranges.

The book abruptly ended with no conclusion, no final chapter celebrating Beijing's victory. Shan closed it and looked at the librarian, who was watching him with a satisfied expression. "The story ends rather suddenly," he observed.

The woman sighed and pointed to a small legend at the base of the spine. Volume One.

"May I see the next?"

"I wish you could. After all the trouble I took to get it last year, it has now gone missing."

Shan chewed on the words. "Missing since when?"

"A week ago, maybe two. Our reference works are not for circulation. Someone," she declared in a pained voice, "stole it."

"Stole it again, you mean."

The woman frowned, then nodded.

"Surely you can determine who could have committed such a crime."

"We are not crowded usually but during the season many people come and go."

"During the season? You mean foreigners?"

"It is why we have fresh paint, a new roof, more funding than any other library our size in the county. When the weather doesn't permit treks to the mountain, tourists need something else to do. We have a display of local artifacts in the adjoining room."

"Would foreigners do research?" Shan asked, working to keep his tone casual.

"A few. Not many can read Chinese."

"Surely you make them sign in? I work for Tsipon," he added quickly in a confiding tone. "I could make inquiries of the foreign climbing parties."

The woman studied him a moment then hurried away to the office at the back of the main chamber. The moment she disappeared he opened the book to the photograph with Commander Wu and, with a shamed glance toward the office, ripped it out and stuffed it inside his shirt. A moment later the woman reappeared, sifting through several sheets of paper as she walked that were identical to the one Shan had signed. The entries for the past four weeks included over three dozen names, several German, some Japanese, another French. Only one person had visited multiple times. Megan Ross had started doing research nearly a month earlier, and had been at the library the day before she died.

Chapter Twelve

As he hurried down the steep ladder stair into the dim old gompa rooms Shan nearly tripped on a limp form at the bottom. Gyalo lay in a heap, more dead than alive. Shan quickly lit more lamps from the one he carried and knelt at the old man's side. The tips of his fingers were scratched and bloody. He had been clawing at the hatch above, Shan realized, like a wild animal trapped in a cage.

The old Tibetan did not acknowledge him, but did not resist as Shan half dragged, half carried him back to his pallet. His breath was harsh and raspy. His shirt clung to his body in patches of red where several wounds had reopened. Shan worked silently, stripping off the shirt, washing the wounds, gently pushing back the hand that now tried to stop him, ignoring the whispered curses in Chinese and Tibetan, gradually becoming aware that the curses had been replaced with a rambling soliloquy made up of snippets of drinking songs, lonely shepherds' ballads, and mantras to the Tibetan gods.

When he finished and Gyalo was wearing one of Shan's old shirts, Shan sat a few feet away on the floor and listened, watching the flame of the nearest lamp, until he himself slipped into a mantra, the prayer for the Compassionate Buddha. He did not know when the cadence of the old man's words changed, but became aware that Gyalo was sitting upright against the wall, chanting in unison with him, staring at the same flame. Shan lowered his voice. Gyalo kept up the chant, pausing several times to look into the shadows and interject louder words of gratitude to Rinpoche. The old Tibetan, Shan realized, was back in a temple of his youth, chanting with the novice monks as they took lessons from a lama.

After several minutes Gyalo's eyes flickered. As he looked up and focused on Shan his words faltered, his face flushed with embarassment and he grew silent.

Shan extended the photo he had taken from the library, holding it a few inches from the Tibetan's face.

Gyalo seemed to take a long time to grasp what he was looking at. Then a shuddering moan rose from his throat. His shoulders sank, his chest sagged.

"They were here," Shan said. "The Hammer and Lightning Brigade lived in your gompa before they destroyed it. But what did they do in the mountains?"

"They died." Gyalo spoke in such a low whisper Shan was not sure he had heard correctly. "They whimpered like children and died." The Tibetan pulled the photo from Shan's hand and held it closer to the lamp, his eyes growing round.

"These were the ones," Shan said, "the ones who—" he painfully searched for words—"who took away your robe."

Before he could react Gyalo began ripping the photo. By the time Shan had seized it he had torn off a long strip, two inches down the left side. The Tibetan jerked free, then slowly turned and set the strip upright in a little chink in the rock wall that had been made to hold a small deity figure. Emotions filled the old man's face as he gazed at the strip, emotions Shan had never seen there, emotions he could not name.

Shan lifted the lamp and held it close, seeing that a single figure was framed in the strip Gyalo had claimed, that of a sturdy, plain looking Chinese girl wearing a military tunic.

It took a moment for Shan to understand, then he looked away in shame. Gyalo had saved the image of the Chinese wife who had been forced upon him to break him as a monk.

CONSTABLE JIN HAD his feet up on his desk, staring so intently at a dog-eared Western travel magazine in his lap that he did not even notice Shan until he put his hand on Jin's telephone. He muttered a quick curse, dropping his legs to the floor.

"I need to make a private call," Shan declared.

"You can't just—"

"Someone tried to kill Gyalo. His son is convinced it was Public Security."

Jin shrugged. "Two officials have been murdered."

"It wasn't the knobs. Whoever did it never asked a question about the killings. They had no interest in detaining him. They left him for dead in the pit, then rifled through his old things. Things from the first uprising."

The constable dropped the magazine onto his desk, opened to a photo of young men and women surfing along a white-sand beach lined with palm trees. "One of those Western climbers read this article to me at base camp," Jin announced, gazing at the photo. "It says some of the experts imagine the water is snow and they are riding down a mountainside. I could do that," Jin declared in an oddly dreamy tone. "I know how to sled."

Shan closed the magazine.

Jin seemed not to notice. "I have a cousin who was able to get across the border without getting shot. He got a job in Thailand, in a restaurant. He says they do this there, this water riding."

"Surfing."

"This surfing. He says he could get me a job too if I ever got permission to leave the country."

Shan covered the magazine with his hand. "Like you said, two officials have been murdered. Why aren't you in the field?"

"I asked Tsipon about getting a visa to live in Thailand, or India maybe," Jin continued in a hollow voice. "He just laughed. He said no one in law enforcement gets permission to emigrate, because we know too many secrets about the government. Tell me it isn't true."

"You collaborated with the American Megan Ross," Shan declared, pushing the tone of a government prosecutor into his words. "You divulged that the mountain road was being closed for the minister, that she was going to drive alone in a car ahead of the prison bus. We could probably find a witness who will recall seeing you give her a ride to the hotel the night before."

The blood seemed to be draining from Jin's face.

"Revealing a secret vital to state security— to a foreigner no less."

"It wasn't exactly . . ." Jin murmured. "I didn't . . ." He looked forlornly at the magazine.

"In this country," Shan continued, "law enforcement officials who breach state security have been executed. When Megan Ross comes down off her mountain you'd better start running." If he couldn't use the American's death to find the truth then maybe he too should start pretending she was alive.

"I can arrest you, Shan. I can ship you away."

Shan smiled and stopped pressing. He didn't want Jin paralyzed, just focused on their mutual problem.

"Gyalo was attacked by two men in black clothes. Hoods over their heads. Strangers. Who were they?"

"Public Security does things differently since the last uprising. They still don't mind hauling off an entire village or gompa. But if they have to deal with an individual Tibetan, they do it in private, in the shadows."

"Why would they want to punish Gyalo?"

Jin seemed to see an offer of hope in Shan's words. "Last week, after Wu was murdered, he got really drunk, stinking drunk. I walked in to see him strutting along the top of the bar like a soldier, pretending to be shot, and dying, again and again as customers tossed coins. I tried to get him to stop, because I knew soldiers were coming into town soon. He laughed when I pulled him down, said he wouldn't want to be a soldier in the mountains now, with all the ghosts coming out."

"Ghosts?"

"He said the only demons that ever frightened the Chinese

were the ones from forty years ago, the ones who had been dead all these years. He said soon they would be swarming down out of the mountains, riding on the backs of yetis."

Shan caught the scent of smoke on Jin, saw for the first time soot stains on the shoulder of his tunic. "You haven't said where you've been."

"There was a fire. Nothing big. That cottage Tsipon loans to foreign climbers. We saved the structure, but most of the gear was lost."

"Whose gear?"

"Tsipon's new American customers used it when they stayed in town."

Shan stepped to the window. He knew the little one-room cottage behind Tsipon's depot, had helped clean it several times. He leaned toward the glass to glimpse the large building at the southern edge of town. There was indeed a thin column of smoke rising behind it.

"Who did it?"

"We are allowed to report only so many crimes, so we're calling it an accident. Those climbers get sloppy, keeping matches and fuel canisters together."

"Who did it?" Shan pressed.

"I told you. No one. But there's one funny thing. When they saw it everyone came running out of the warehouse to help. Except Kypo. He ran to one of the cars and sped away."

"Toward Tumkot?"

"Just being a good son."

"What does this have to do with Ama Apte?"

"Nothing. Like I said, we're calling it an accident."

Shan leaned over the constable. "Why," he said slowly, insistently, "would you connect it to the astrologer?"

"She has a thing about certain foreigners. An American writer was here a couple years ago, researching Western connections to the region over the past century. There are some great stories about the spies the British sent across the border dressed as monks or pilgrims."

"And?"

"I caught her putting dirt in the writer's gas tank."

Shan considered Jin's words a moment. "But you let her go."

"Damned right. She threatened to tell my fortune."

As Shan's gaze fixed on a basket of shiny metallic objects on the desk Jin rose and looked anxiously toward the door. "You said you had a call to make."

Shan lifted a steel carabiner, one of half a dozen in the basket. "What are you finding in the hills?"

"Nothing."

"The snaplinks were supposed to lead you to the monks."

Jin shrugged. "The American woman apparently hands them out to children like candy. Snaplinks with prayer beads attached."

"Beads?"

"Every link she leaves has a bracelet of prayer beads strung through it. Like she's some kind of itinerant nun."

Jin took a hesitant step toward the door.

"Everything's changed, Jin. Publicly they will call it a criminal conspiracy. Behind closed doors, where it counts, it will be termed another uprising. More gompas will be closed. Monks will be considered a threat to border security. You can't suppose they will keep local Tibetans in law enforcement. You'll be sweeping streets in Shogo. That's assuming Cao doesn't find out the entire crime hinged on your leaking a state secret to Ross."

The constable's desolate gaze told Shan that Jin understood perfectly. The Tibetan cast a longing glance toward the glossy image of surfers on the white-sand beach, then he shut the door. "I saw two men in dark sweatshirts that day, coming down the trail, hoods over their heads," he said. "They were running down the trail, toward the murders. Big men, strong, smelling of onions. At first I thought they were Public Security," he said with apology in his voice. "If I had seen them in the marketplace that's what I would have thought."

"But there was no need for undercover guards on the trail."

"I couldn't see their faces."

"And they ran toward the murders. Which means that, if they weren't knobs, they were probably accomplices."

Jin winced, opened the door.

Shan picked up the phone receiver.

Jin's face clouded. "There are other phones."

"I am reasonably certain Public Security isn't listening to this one."

Jin cast Shan a sour look, and fled.

Shan lifted the phone and dialed. The satellite phones used by the trekking companies typically took a long time to connect. But after a few seconds there was a short ringing sound and Yates's voice came through.

"You need to be more careful with your matches," Shan began, speaking in English.

"I wasn't anywhere near that cottage," the American growled. "Now I've got nowhere to sleep but up here. It's like someone wants to drive me away."

"Did Megan Ross keep her gear there?"

"Sure, some of it. It's where she was staying, until she went to the hotel the night before," the American added.

"We need to move those extra porters," Shan said. "Give them some heavy mountain clothes and meet me on the base camp road."

The American took a moment to grasp Shan's meaning. "They're gone. They pushed the boxes out at the back and sneaked away. Like they were suddenly afraid of me. Whoever helped them wants me out of China."

"What do you mean?"

"We're allowed to burn trash in a barrel behind the compound. As I was burning a Public Security officer came up, took pictures."

"What exactly were you burning?"

"Nothing but trash I thought. But in a box I was about to burn they found a monk's robe. They took me inside to search my room here. Under my cot they found a box of carabiners with a strand of prayer beads inside each one. One of the knobs fingered his baton. If there hadn't been a lot of foreign witnesses I'd probably have a broken skull now."

"I need to see you."

"I've got equipment being staged from base camp today. Tomorrow morning I could meet you in town."

"Not tomorrow. Not in town. Tumkot village, in an hour."

SHAN WAS CLIMBING into the old Jiefang truck at Tsipon's depot when two of the warehouse workers rounded the corner, sootstained and carrying buckets. He paused, waited for them to enter the building, then slipped around the corner. Although the cottage was intact, smoke still wafted out of the gap in the open door. He glanced over his shoulder to confirm no one was watching then darted inside. Smoke hung heavy over the ceiling. The acrid scent of burned nylon and plastic mingled with the stench of singed down. The remains of what had been a bed under the window on the wall opposite the door was heaped with smoldering clothes, charred magazines and papers. Tsipon, always wary of strangers on his property, had probably sent away the fire crew prematurely. If given enough oxygen, the bed would probably burst into flame.

Shan found a T-shirt on the floor, pressed it to his mouth and nose, and searched the ruin of the room. A nylon pack, mostly melted into a blue plastic lump. Several novels in English. Three long metal poles, the trekking sticks favored by foreign trekkers. Clothes strewn everywhere, some clearly belonging to a woman. A small chest of drawers under a window on the side wall, the drawers all hanging open. Two empty duffel bags. Four cardboard boxes, sealed, labeled YATES EVEREST EXPEDITION. He returned to the entry and considered the scene. Before the fire someone had been searching, looking for something that belonged to the Americans. He considered where he would hide something in such a simple open space, then moved along the walls looking behind the few pieces of furniture, under the drawers. Nearly gagging on the smoke, he cracked the window on the side wall and studied the ceiling as the smoke was drawn away. He stepped on a chair, then on the chest of drawers by a window on the side wall, studying the angled roof and its beams. Finally he spotted a dark patch in the shadow of the corner nearest the door. He grabbed one of the trekking sticks and probed, feeling resistance, jerking the stick sideways to dislodge a small gray backpack.

Urgently Shan searched the zipped compartments, discovering at last a compact notebook festooned with pencil drawings of flowers, mountains, and birds. He was opening the inside cover as the glass on the back window shattered. Three small metal canisters were thrown in quick succession onto the bed. The sudden rush of oxygen ignited the bed's smoldering contents as the door was slammed shut from the outside.

Shan, still standing on the little chest, kicked out the window as the far side of the room burst into flame. He was halfway through the opening when the first of the fuel canisters exploded.

He found himself on the ground ten feet from the building, face in the dirt, his ears ringing, his fingers aching from their white-knuckled grip on the American's notebook. The bungalow was already a ball of fire. If he had not been at the window, in a position to kick it out, the first explosion would have knocked him out, the second and third would have killed him.

With what seemed to be a great effort he climbed to his feet, stuffed the notebook inside his shirt, and was staggering away as the first of the workers ran around the corner of the warehouse.

"The fool Tsipon ordered the fire crew away," the man groused, and started yelling for buckets of water.

Shan, knowing his hidden assailant would be powerless to act with so many witnesses, could not resist a look inside the notebook.

He scanned the early pages before putting the old truck into gear. The American woman's name was printed in neat letters on the inside cover, which otherwise was covered with a list of mountains flanked by small sketches of monks and prayer wheels. Most pages contained diary-style entries and random technical notes about climbing, some outlined in boxes, some written sideways or even upside down. They were flanked by more images in pencil, mostly of Tibetan scenes or objects though some, like a moose and a cow wearing a large bell, were from other continents. But it was the diary entries that interested Shan. They began with a date three years before, written in Katmandu, then quickly shifted to entries from the southern base camp on the Nepal side of Everest. There were sketches of climbing routes, maps showing advance camps, lines of poetry, transcription of haiku, even names of sherpas with comments on their skills, a single line in large black letters that said, *Wherever there are humans you'll find flies and Buddhas.*

As he pulled out of the parking lot his mind was racing faster than the fire truck rushing toward the warehouse. One of the first names mentioned on Megan Ross's list of sherpas was that of Tenzin Nuru.

SHAN LEFT THE old truck in a clearing half a mile below Tumkot and was picked up by Yates in his red utility vehicle a few minutes before he reached the village. Shan motioned the American to park in the shadow between two sheds at the edge of the village.

"Does this mean anything to you?" he asked as he took a peche sheet removed from his workshop and rolled it, extending it to the American. "A prayer rolled like this?"

Yates took the little cylinder of parchment, unrolled it, repeated the process himself. "Maybe just a way to store a prayer? Or a way to put it in a mani wall, or one of the little statues," he added. He seemed utterly fascinated by the rolled prayer. Shan let him hold on to it as they moved along the dirt street and down the worn stone stairs that led to the main square.

No one was home at Kypo's house. Ama Apte's house was likewise empty. Shan lifted the bench outside the fortuneteller's entry and set it inside, in the shadows just past the pool of light cast through the open door. Yates, restless as ever, wandered around the dimly lit stalls of the lower floor, asking Shan the Tibetan names of some of the implements, the meaning of some of the fortuneteller's signs drawn on the wall inside the door. He stumbled over something lying in the shadows and the goat leaped up with a surprised bleat. Frightened at first, it quieted as the American stroked its back. Shan saw the animal's swollen udder, found the tin bucket the astrologer kept by the door and began milking as Yates sang a song to the goat about a racehorse named Stewball.

There they sat, like two lonely shepherds, when Ama Apte walked in with Kypo and her granddaughter. Though they bore the grime of heavy trekking and looked exhausted, Ama Apte's son advanced on them as if to eject them from the house, resentment in his eyes.

"We are not your enemies, Kypo" Shan stated, putting a restraining hand on Yates as the American began to rise.

"You are not Tibetans." Kypo's voice grew heated as he spoke. "It's always the same. You outsiders dabble in our affairs like it is some game, then leave us to take the punishment."

"Tibet should be for Tibetans," Shan declared. "If my leaving improved the chances of Tibetans achieving their own country again I would pack my bag tomorrow."

The words hung in the air. Kypo stepped in front of his daughter as if to protect her, nervously watching his mother.

"Easy for you to say," Ama Apte replied. "Just words."

Shan returned the woman's steady gaze then looked down at the packed earth floor between his feet, fighting an unexpected feeling of melancholy. "In the yeti factory," he stated, each word like a spasm of pain, "my son is a prisoner. If I cannot find the truth of the killings by the day after tomorrow they will use his brain for a medical experiment."

Not even the goat moved.

"Jesus, Shan," Yates gasped. "You never. . . ." His words drifted away.

Kypo uttered a curse under his breath. His daughter clutched his leg, pressing her head into his hip.

"It is time for the truth," Shan said, gazing pointedly at Ama Apte. "It is time for all the truth. No fortunetelling. No dice. No hiding in the future or behind the fates. You were searching Megan Ross's tent at the base camp. You didn't find what you wanted."

"You don't know that," the woman replied in a brittle voice.

Shan reached inside his shirt, extracted the notebook and dropped it on an empty stool. "This is what you wanted."

Ama Apte sighed, her eyes wide as she stared at Megan Ross's journal. "We shall have tea."

As the astrologer stepped to the doorway to work her churns, Shan scanned the last few entries in the notebook. Anticipation was in the words, even excitement, starting with a visit to a particular curve in the mountain road.

Nathan says it is all too dangerous but he showed me how to rig the site so no one would have to be there. He must think I am some kind of engineer. Began to lay out the new route up the North Col. Nathan wants a private route up, so we won't keep running into the other expeditions. When Tenzin arrives we will start scouting.

Next came a poem about mountains in the moonlight, like silver steps to heaven, then sketches of birds and a hairy seated figure that might have been a meditating yeti. The next day brought a reference to the road, and the reason Ama Apte had been looking for the book.

Ama Apte and I walked the slope today. Bless her, she says I should not worry, that she will do this for me and the mountain, and the monks, that there will be enough moonlight for her to set it up the night before.

Then, after a sketch of a ritual dagger, *Tenzin arrived!* followed by a matter-of-fact entry about the new route above the base camp and calculations of the number of oxygen bottles needed for the first expedition, ending with *Nathan and I are insisting that every bottle be carried back down and that any customer who leaves litter on the top slopes will never climb with us again!*

The last entry was short. *Went up to inspect the first advance camp. I found Tenzin there alone, separated from the others by the heavy blow on the slope above. He agrees with the whole plan, will organize the sherpas to hold up a banner supporting the Compact at the minister's picnic at Rongphu. Had to leave him before dawn to catch an unexpected ride to town. Have to ask Tsipon why we are leaving so much money in the Hong Kong accounts. I told Ama Apte we will rewrite the future of Chomolungma!* They were the last words.

When he looked up, Ama Apte was staring at him, holding the hot water kettle. "She told Tenzin," he explained. "She told him everything. It got him killed."

Ama Apte's eyes filled with moisture. "But he wasn't anywhere close. He wasn't going to do anything but hold up a banner."

It was Yates who explained. "There was another person who knew, an invisible one who couldn't leave Tenzin alive to say he had used Megan's plan as a cover for murder."

The fortuneteller said no more until she had handed her visitors mugs of tea. "Let us go to the yeti factory," she announced. "Let us find a way to rescue your son."

Shan replied with a small, sad smile. "Thank you but no. That is something only I can do."

"They are the new gods, you know," she said into her cup of tea. "What they write down a thousand miles away becomes our truth, like the old lamas who once wrote our sutras. They hung a new slogan on the municipal building. *The Party Is Our Buddha.*"

Kypo bent to his daughter and pointed to the door.

"No," his mother said, putting a hand on the girl's shoulder. "She must hear this. She has no choice but to live with the new gods. There is no going back. The old gods and the old Tibetans, all we can do is to find ways to fade away with dignity."

Kypo's face drained of color. He knelt and tightly embraced his daughter, as if it was his turn to be frightened.

"So is that what this is about, Aunt Ama?" Shan asked in a flat voice as he rose. "It's your way of giving up?"

A tear ran down Ama Apte's strong, handsome face. She bent to the kettle and poured more tea.

"Last summer, at the end of the season," the astrologer said, "Megan came to me, and said she wanted to stay here with me for the winter. It was illegal, I told her. It would endanger Kypo, because the authorities would assume as a local climbing manager he was behind it. She didn't argue, she just asked me to go with her up one of her mountains. A hard climb, but not one needing ropes. We were gone five days. On the last night she watched the stars for hours, like a meditation. She said the universe was different in Tibet. She said she was going to die here again."

"Again?" Yates asked.

Ama Apte offered a sad smile. "That's what I asked. She said she had a sudden realization on her last ascent of Chomolungma, as she stood on the summit, that she had lived here in another life."

"You're trying to make it appear I was involved with her, in the ambush," Yates said after another long silence.

"No. Only I was involved, with a little help from a tarchok ghost," Ama Apte confessed with a glance at the notebook. She did not look at Yates, just stared into one of the flickering lamps by the kettle.

"You tried to get me arrested by Public Security," Yates accused, "by putting a robe in my trash and those snaplinks with beads under my bed."

"Not arrested," Shan said, "only deported."

Ama Apte was biting her lip like an anxious girl.

"I never did anything to hurt you," Yates said to the woman.

"You don't understand," the fortuneteller said, her gaze not shifting from the flame. "You could never understand. Just know it is a killing season on the mountain. Go home. Even if you try the ascent, the mountain will push you back."

"Without the climbers," Kypo said in a near whisper, "I can't put food on my family's table."

Ama Apte replied only with her eyes, which held a sad, soulful expression that Shan saw on old lamas, the look that said the only answers that meant anything were the ones you found for yourself.

As he studied her Shan began to sense that all the mysteries, all the questions about the killings, the strange behavior of so many Tibetans had begun with the mystery of who Ama Apte really was.

"We should eat," she announced in a new, spirited voice, and clapped her hands to rouse everyone from their trance.

The mood quickly shifted as the astrologer returned to the role of mother and grandmother, instructing Kypo to bring a larger brazier, her granddaughter to retrieve water, Shan and Yates to carry trestles and planks outside into the rear courtyard of her house for a makeshift table. They ate thick *thanthuk* noodles and mutton, making quiet, casual conversation, Kypo and Yates at last laying a map of Chomolungma on the table to discuss the always complicated task of staging supplies at advance camps.

Kypo's daughter leaned on the table beside the two men, listening attentively, her eyes wide with a sense of adventure. After a few minutes Yates searched his pockets, producing a metal ballpoint pen that he presented as a gift to the girl, who accepted with blushing thanks.

"Half the oxygen at Camp One for now, and half there," he said, pointing to a mark indicating Camp Two. As he did so, Ama Apte gasped, dropping one of the dishes she was clearing. She stared with a stricken expression at Yates's hand. He was absently holding the rolled-up peche page from his pocket, using it as a pointer. The Tibetan woman abruptly sprang forward, seized the rolled page, and slapped Yates on the cheek.

The stunned American reeled backward. Tears welled in Ama Apte's eyes. She collapsed onto a stool, her head in her hands, sobbing. Kypo, Shan and Yates exchanged dumbfounded looks. Kypo knelt at his mother's side, his hand on her shoulder. As Shan took a step forward, Kypo warned him off with a shake of his head and pointed to the street. Ama Apte began weeping. She seemed unconsolable.

Shan and Yates stood at the American's truck minutes later, the two men gazing back uncertainly toward the fortuneteller's house. "It's like she's having some sort of breakdown," Yates said forlornly. "All the stress. She's going to get herself arrested. She has to stay away from them."

Shan realized the American was talking about the monks, that Yates had reached the same conclusion as Shan. Ama Apte had taken the monks from the base camp, and was hiding them somewhere on the forbidden mountain above the village.

"The fugitive monks are now considered assassins and traitors," Shan said. "Those caught helping them will be treated the same way."

"You're saying it would be the firing squad?"

"And if they try to cross the border there are snipers positioned in the passes. Two years ago nuns trying to flee across to Nepal were killed with high-powered rifles."

"Someone has to tell her."

"She won't listen. I think the astrologer sees her own fate and has decided it cannot be altered."

Yates leaned on the hood of his truck, buried his head in his hands. "I'm finished." He seemed strangely weary, as if he had just returned from an oxygen-deprived climb. "I'm sorry about her. I'm sorry about Megan. I am sorry about your son. But I am done. I won't be involved with more killings. Stay away from me. You and I are on different paths. Stop dragging me onto yours. I'm taking my climbers up the mountain as fast as I can, then going home. It's like she said. It's a killing season."

"Then it is I who apologize to you," Shan replied. He stepped to the window on the driver's door and with his finger began drawing in the caked-on dust.

"What the hell are you talking—" As Yates lifted his head his words died away. He stared without breathing at the sign Shan had drawn. "How could you possibly—" his words drifted away again as his finger traced Shan's crude but accurate drawing of a crossed hammer and lightning bolt.

"I've been trying to make you understand, Yates. You and I are after the same thing. It is all about something that happened decades ago."

Yates cast an uncertain glance at Shan, then his gaze went back to the symbol on the glass. "Kypo says you're like a magnet to knobs. I can't afford any more trouble."

"Just take a walk with me."

"Where?"

"Up to see your father."

THE TWO MEN did not speak as they climbed toward the top of the high ridge that curled around Tumkot. Yates, like Shan, no doubt recalled the last time they had been on the trail, assaulting each other in the moonlight as Yates carried his sack of little gods down the mountain.

The American slowed as they approached the ruined shrine, lingering behind. More than once Shan paused to look back and see Yates stopped, gazingly longingly toward the peak of Everest, visible in the distance. As he reached the shrine Shan halted, kneeling at a crumbling wall of lichen-covered mani stones, restacking and straightening the wall as the American approached with hesitant steps. Yates's countenance held caution, perhaps even fear, but there was also a hint of shame as he glanced at the altar where he had removed the ancient figurines. "I will bring them back," he said of the little gods he had taken. "I was always going to bring them back."

He knelt beside Shan and silently assisted him with the stones, cleaning the faces inscribed with prayers, handing them to Shan for restacking.

After several minutes Shan stood. "I know some Tibetans who have a different way of speaking when they are at these shrines. There are words for addressing old gods that most younger Tibetans don't even know, special prayers, special prostrations. I felt uncomfortable coming to such places at first, like an outsider or worse, like one of those who had caused the destruction. Then a monk took me to a patch of flowers that were bent beneath some stones fallen from a crumbling altar. He told me to remove the stones and replace them in the altar. When the flowers had straightened he said 'Now your reverence is mingled with all the reverence that came before, which makes the shrine as much yours as mine.'" Yates searched Shan's face as if trying to understand, then knelt and restacked a few more mani stones as Shan stepped to the altar under the overhanging ledge.

"This place has nothing to do with my father," Yates declared, challenge in his voice. "If you think you can trick me into—" His complaint faded as he followed the finger Shan pointed toward the end of the altar. The crucifix was still there, in the dust of the altar, where Shan had left it days earlier.

The American's hand shot out to grab the silver cross, then hesitated, lingering in the air. There was no question in Yates's eyes, only a torrent of emotion. When he finally lifted the cross, he cupped it in both hands, as though it might crumble. He brought it out into the sunlight, studying it in silence as he dropped onto the remnants of a stone bench.

"I've seen it in a photograph," he explained in a stunned voice. "That last year he was at home, when I was two years old, there was a photo taken of me in his arms with my hand wrapped around the chain that held this." He looked up with an intense gaze, searching the clearing. "I don't know what it means, finding it here. This could have just been planted here last week."

"No," Shan said. "It's been there for decades. You can see its shape imprinted in the layers of dust. It was there before most of the Yama statues."

"Impossible," Yates muttered. But he was arguing with himself, not Shan. He kept turning the cross over and over in his hand, examining every surface, as if expecting it to somehow divulge its secret. And it did speak to him, for after a moment he pointed to a small set of letters inscribed on the reverse of the cross. "SRY," he declared in a voice that cracked with emotion, pointing the letters out to Shan. "My father's initials. Samuel was his name." He fell silent for a long moment. "*Tuchaychay*," he said, expressing his gratitude in Tibetan. "I owe you."

"What you owe me is the truth."

When Yates did not reply, Shan rose and gestured to the figurines remaining on the altar. "You owe it to them as well. You need to explain to these gods the real reason you came to them as a thief in the night, why one of them was lost over this cliff." He extended his hand toward Yates, palm open. "Only the truth can be spoken in front of them."

The American understood. He dropped the crucifix into Shan's hand, glanced uneasily toward the altar and paced around the clearing in silence, pausing to clean and stack half a dozen more mani stones as Shan waited at the old bench. At last Yates rose and sat before the altar, looking at each of the gods in turn, as if silently greeting them.

"I used to do jigsaw puzzles of medieval paintings with my aunt and uncle who raised me," Yates began. "Hundreds of pieces with shades of gray and brown, with a few patches of brilliant color. They made sense only if you kept the complete picture in mind as you worked. My father was always like that to me. I had only fragments to work with, and never had an image of the man as a whole. My aunt and uncle would speak of him with the same sound bites, never changing. A good, honest man. A great athlete. A lover of freedom. A fantastic aviator."

"Not a scientist," Shan observed.

"Not a scientist," Yates admitted. "Once I heard my aunt and uncle talking about him with an older cousin. They were angry at him, said he could have come back and had a rich career as a pilot with the airlines. None of that made him alive for me. I wanted to know the sound of his laugh, wanted to know what was in his heart, to know the words he would have used to put me to bed if he had ever returned. They kept secrets about him, I knew that. Once when I was nine they were away and I found a shoebox hidden in their bedroom closet filled with letters and photos. There was a cloth pouch with little rolled up papers, only an inch wide, each tied with strips of leather. I had no clue what they were, just some strange adult thing. They frightened me somehow. They had an Eastern scent, incense I learned later. The paper was different, like it was handmade. The letters were tiny, in tiny handwriting.

"The early letters, the normal letters, were mostly to my mother. They looked like they had never been touched by her. I don't think they were ever delivered to her, because she divorced my father a year after I was born and my aunt and uncle never spoke to her. I took a few and kept them under my mattress, reading them over and over. He wrote to her about a place called Camp Hale, hidden in some mountains somewhere.

"Whatever he was doing was a big secret. He kept saying it was very important and someday he would explain everything. What he did speak of made it sound like he was a professor. My students have come along faster than anyone expected, he would say, we are finished with our first round of classes and everyone passed with flying colors. But it was a strange kind of school. Sometimes it sounded like he was a student himself, saying he had finished his course in winter survival and was moving on to navigation and language.

"The more I asked, the less my aunt and uncle wanted to talk about him, as if he was some kind of mistake, which meant I must be some kind of mistake. I began to get angry at them. I took the shoebox out of their room and hid it in the attic. I took the cylinders of paper to a secret place I had up on the mountainside above the house and read them all. In them my father wrote about being in the Himalayas, about the wonderful people he was meeting. He drew little pictures in the margins. Some of strange churches with steeples like upside down ice cream cones. Shaggy cows with long horns. I opened another, and another. He asked about me in every note, kept saying the mission was going well. I couldn't understand any of it. The notes scared me. Finally I got my nerve up and dropped one on the dinner table. My aunt became very angry and wouldn't answer my questions. She said there was no need to drag up that rotten history. My uncle just became sad. Later he told me that his brother, my father, had sent a note mailed by someone else, from a city in India. In it he said he had found a way to send messages back that would be safe, that he would send bronze statues of a god called Yama, that the people who made them used the hollow compartment inside it to hold prayers and things. When the statue came my uncle was to cut open the base or loosen its solder with heat and he would find letters inside, wrapped up like the prayers that usually went inside. My father said that he was sending them because if something happened to him he wanted his son to know of the good work he was doing, of how important it was for the world. He said he would send a statue every couple of months, because he was allowed to send gifts home but letters were always censored.

"I couldn't really understand. It seemed like my father was a prisoner in India. I heard my aunt telling someone that my father had become addicted to the drugs grown there and dropped out, then died in some alley in Calcutta. My uncle got angry at my aunt and said my father was no drug addict, just a good soldier." Yates looked down at the ground for a moment, seeming overwhelmed by his memories. Shan gave the crucifix back to the American, who closed his fist around it and pressed it to his heart.

"So there I was, eleven years old and as confused as ever. My father was an addict, he was a soldier, a pilot, a professor, a prisoner, a mountain climber. I would have dreams about him, but he was always in shadows. No more of the statues ever came after the first, my uncle told me. But he gave me one more thing, a letter from the Army sent to him as next of kin. My father had been killed in the service of his country, it said, and he was being awarded a medal for bravery. The circumstances of his death did not permit recovery of his body. I didn't know what else to do, where else to turn for the truth. I put the letter in the shoebox and didn't open it again until I was years out of college. That's when I noticed something in that letter from the army, a printed line at the top that said Office of Special Operations. I began writing my own letters to the government. It was a slow process. I had my business to worry about, running a sporting goods store first, then my trekking and climbing business. I married and got divorced. But I kept writing letters, to the army, to senators, to the veterans' office. The few responses I received said all the files on the matter were classified, top secret. Eventually I found out Camp Hale was high in the Colorado mountains and I went there, at least to the nearest town. The people there said it had been used for radioactive testing so everyone stayed away from it.

"Then five years ago the files were declassified," Yates continued, "and made available to the public."

"Camp Hale," Shan suggested, "had nothing to do with atomic tests."

"Camp Hale was the only facility in the army that came close to a Himalayan habitat. It had been used as a training ground for mountain commandos in World War Two. The army loaned it to Special Operations, what later became the Central Intelligence Agency. A small group in the American government was formed for the purpose of supporting Tibetan independence. They brought in Tibetan resistance fighters to teach them English, survival training, navigation, radio operation, parachute jumping. It was so secret the Tibetans didn't even know where they were. That's what my father was doing, training the resistance. Eventually a base for the resistance army was set up in Nepal, along the Tibetan border. I finally received my father's service records. They showed that after a year at Hale he asked to be transferred to Nepal, with the fighters he had trained."

Yates stood and paced along the altar. "After that everything gets murky. Officially, Americans never crossed the border, except on air missions at night to drop Tibetans and supplies, sometimes hundreds of miles inside Tibet. Officially, my father was stationed at the base in Nepal the whole time. Officially, he was on a plane that never returned. But eventually I tracked down some of the other Americans involved, old men now, all retired. To a man they insisted no plane was ever lost, and several had known my father, said he was a great climber, that he fervently believed in what they were doing for the Tibetans. Not one would say anything about what happened to him. But when one of them, a pilot who still had a map of Tibet on the wall, discovered I was leading climbing expeditions onto Everest, he opened an old file and wrote down a series of numbers for me."

"Map coordinates," Shan said with a rush of realization. He unconsciously touched his pocket with the paper on which he had transcribed the numbers Yates had hidden in his cot.

"All within a hundred-mile radius of Everest. A preferred location because the Chinese air bases were far removed from this area, and the Chinese planes couldn't handle the wild winds off the mountains." Yates paused, gazed again at the row of silent Yamas as if waiting for them to speak.

"You think he came across, against orders, parachuting in with the Tibetan fighters."

Yates nodded. "I am certain of it. I know it in my heart. And now you proved it with this cross."

"Megan Ross knew about your father."

"We were close friends. More than friends once. She found me with those old letters and we started talking—she loved the intrigue. It became a project for her. She helped me find some of the drop points." He reached into a pocket of his parka and extracted a small handheld device. A cell phone, Shan thought at first, then the American turned its face toward him. "Global positioning. When the right satellites are overhead it tells your exact longitude and latitude."

Shan remembered the pieces of the device he had found at the crime scene. "Megan had one," he suggested. "And you were in a barley field with this one."

Yates flushed with embarrassment. "I didn't mean to damage the crops."

"What did you expect to find at the drop points?"

"I don't know. Anything. Maybe they died jumping, maybe I would find bones. Maybe one of them would be a place where some of my father lingered, left something of himself. It was the only hard evidence I had, that list of coordinates."

"And the sign of the hammer and lightning."

Yates nodded again. "It was drawn on one of those little rolled letters from my father, where he spoke of a new enemy arriving. A couple weeks ago I showed it to Megan, and she drew a copy of it, said she would ask some of the old Tibetans about it."

"Suppose she did ask some old Tibetans about it. Not long after, she stepped into the car with Minister Wu."

"Surely they are not connected."

"You tell me. You knew why she went with the minister that day."

"No. Yes. I don't know. We were going to meet, to wait up the road together and intercept the minister's car so we could have a private conversation about Wu's development plans. But Megan never showed up that morning. I figured she got some other ride."

"What she got was a book," Shan said, "a book she stole from the library in town."

"A book?"

"It had photos of the leaders of the Red Guard unit that had destroyed all the local temples and gompas, and killed the local monks." Shan pulled out the photo he had taken from the library and handed it to the American. Yates gasped as he saw the crossed lightning and hammer; his jaw dropped as Shan pointed to the woman at the center of the table.

"It can't be!"

"Megan was helping you with your project but she had another project that was even more important to her, her Himalayan Compact. This photo, or one like it, provided Megan the pre-emptive strike she needed. The book had long ago been removed from the library, may even have gotten the prior librarian killed. But the new librarian is a fanatic about having a complete collection. She tracked down what may be the only remaining copy this year. Megan was there in the library, reading it, the day before the murder. That's when she discovered that Minister Wu had been the commander of the Hammer and Lightning Brigade."

Yates's face darkened with despair. "The fool. She should have told me."

"Wu is a common name. There is no reason that people would have connected the minister to the Red Guard who used to be in Shogo. If people here knew Wu had been the head of the Brigade she would have been totally discredited in the region, her reputation destroyed in the international community she wants to attract. It was Megan's bargaining chip. But Megan didn't know the minister had a gun. Wu was as relentless today as she was forty years ago. Megan thought she was going to change Wu's mind about her new campaign. But Wu would have known it meant the destruction of her career."

"Surely the minister didn't kill Megan."

"There was no sign of a struggle, by either of them. I think Wu did not protest when Megan was shot, may have done it herself. But someone else was there, who was given the gun by Wu."

"Given?"

"There was no sign of a struggle," Shan said again. "She handed the gun to the third person, who promptly shot her too. I think the photo got both of them killed."

"But what does my father . . ." Yates began in confusion.

"Megan was at the library because of your father, she thought she might learn more about the resistance fighters in the region. She never expected to find that photo. But when she did, it changed everything for her. No doubt she was going to give it to you but first she was going to use it against Wu."

They sat in silence a long time, Yates gazing at the altar, fingering his father's cross, Shan at the outer edge of the clearing, by the cliff. He too had not fully digested the truth. He let the ice-scented wind scour him, peeling away his misconceptions about the murders. There was no mystery in events, his old friend Lokesh had once told him, only mysteries of the people involved. Like many Chinese, every Tibetan he knew had grown a hard, impenetrable shell around memories of the Cultural Revolution, around the years when the Chinese had cleansed the land of all resistance. But Shan knew now that it was in that black, inaccessible place where the truth would be found.

Chapter Thirteen

YATES WOULD NOT leave the shrine without searching every inch of the ground, hoping for some further sign of his father. Shan helped for a few minutes then sat on the stone bench, extracting the notepad from his pocket, and began writing events and dates, one line at a time in English, starting with the *Religious Affairs office burns down, Tenzin murdered at the advance camp, Tan loses pistol, murder of Minister Wu, Director Xie killed, Gyalo attacked in Shogo.* When Yates appeared at his side, finished with his futile search, Shan extended the notebook.

"What's this?" the American asked.

"A wise man once said that if the true face of a mountain cannot be known, it is because the one looking at it is standing in its midst. I want to trade, what I know for what you know. I want you to look at what I know, because I am standing in its midst."

Yates cast a skeptical glance at Shan, shrugged, then went to his backpack and extracted a tattered nylon pouch. He accepted the pad from Shan then emptied the pouch onto the bench. Several old letters, the photos Shan had seen at the base camp, a map, copies of pages from a book, a printed form.

The two men sat in silence for several minutes, Yates flipping pages in Shan's notepad, writing his own notes. Shan read the form, an official copy of the military service record for Captain Samuel Yates, then the letters, which were nothing more than what Yates had already explained. The copied pages contained a description of Camp Hale from some annal of the Cold War, recounting how a small group of elite intelligence operatives and military experts had created a miniature world for Tibetan trainees in the Colorado mountains, teaching them about Western history, introducing them to hot dogs and hamburgers. The pages from the book included photos, showing American men in uniforms without insignia, some with pipes or cigars in their mouths, others with white khata offering scarves around their necks, traditional Tibetan offerings of friendship. There were a few quotes from some of the participants, recorded years later, reflecting deep admiration for the Tibetans. Shan paused over one passage, reading it twice:

> Love of their land and their Buddhist faith burned like an intense fire in many of the trainees. It so moved the American trainers that several requested, and were promptly refused, permission to parachute into Tibet with them when the training was concluded; others requested transfer to the advance base in northern India so they could participate in airdrops and radio support for the missions.

Shan felt a flutter of excitement as he unfolded the map. It was an intricate rendering of the Everest region, in English. He stretched it out with stones on each corner, examining it closely then, noticing Yates's curious gaze, handed the American his own Chinese map.

"I have heard the term political map in English," Shan said. "What does it mean?"

"It means cities and towns and highways, manmade features, are included," Yates explained.

"In China all maps are political," Shan said, and gestured to the map Yates was unfolding. "The government controls all maps. No military bases are shown but also terrain in sensitive areas is obscured."

The American uttered a syllable of surprise and began pointing out discrepancies between the two maps. On the Chinese map large expanses along the border were just fields of white, indicating huge ice fields. Most of the border showed only general topographical lines and nothing else. Shan pointed to the American map. "It's like a different land on your map," he explained, and settled a fingertip on Tumkot. On the Chinese map the area above the settlement, the high plain that could not be seen from below, consisted entirely of an ice field, marked inaccessible, as the villagers insisted. But the American map showed a more narrow glacier above rough, steep, but open terrain.

With a pencil Shan made a mark on the road that led to the base camp. "The site of the murders," he noted.

"What's your point?"

"Ama Apte has admitted she helped Megan Ross with the avalanche that stopped the bus, but she will not explain how she managed such secrecy. No one could have gone up or down the road without being stopped. For someone from Tumkot to be involved they would have had to travel hours by road, and they would have been seen and stopped. But someone who knew these trails could have gone up and over the ridge. A difficult path, judging by the contours, but not impossible for a seasoned trekker." He saw for the first time four different lightly drawn circles spread miles apart, three of them with X's through the center. "You haven't visited this drop zone?" he asked the American, pointing to a circle on the plateau above Tumkot.

"I must have made a mistake when the numbers were written down. There is no way up there. Megan said she tried, and it was impossible. All cliffs and ice along the only possible route."

Shan studied the map again, and after a moment saw a dotted line that crossed into Nepal along a high altitude pass that was marked inaccessible on the Chinese map. He realized he was looking at the route the sherpas used to invisibly cross back and forth across the border. The border guards no doubt knew about it, but the weather would be so hostile at such an altitude that there would be no manned outpost.

"And you?" Shan asked at last, gesturing to his notebook.

"What have I missed?"

"It's all still a puzzle to me," the American admitted. "We can ask the fortuneteller about the hidden meaning of twos when we see her again."

"Twos?"

Yates turned to a page near the front of the pad and pointed to the words, written in English. "Religious Affairs office burns," he read, and drew a line beneath it that extended past the words. "Tenzin killed" he said, and drew another line. "Minister Wu is killed." Another line. "Director Xie is killed, on the same day Gyalo is attacked and left for dead," he finished with another line. With the tip of the pencil he quickly wrote numbers in the spaces between the lines. "Two days, two days, four days. All twos or a combination of two. Ama Apte would probably say the mountain breathes in for a day, then breathes out." He shrugged. "It's nothing. I'm possessed by a math demon. Although," he added in a curious tone, "it's been two days since the last violence."

Shan stood, strangely disturbed by Yates's words, glancing back and forth from the map to the lines and numbers drawn by the American. He stepped to the edge of the cliff, letting the chill wind slam against his face, considering the pattern of life down in the world. Then abruptly he turned and darted over to Yates. "There is a place," he announced as he urgently packed up the items on the bench, "that lives by a pulse of twos. If we hurry we can be there by sundown."

YATES HAD NOT stumbled upon the rhythm of the mountain, Shan explained as they pulled into the dusty truckers' compound in Yates's red utility vehicle, but the pulse of the Friendship Highway. Shogo was strategically situated on the truckers run between the Nepalese border and Lhasa.

"It's the natural break point. Drivers can get food and gas, then they sleep in their trucks or buy a cot in the back of the teashop. At dawn they pull out and reach their destination before nightfall. The regular drivers turn around the next morning and repeat the trip."

"Putting them here every two days," Yates concluded.

"Gyalo said the men who attacked him were strangers. He knows nearly everyone in town. Everyone else seems to think they were Public Security soldiers. But if they weren't knobs," Shan said, "they were transients."

"So now we're looking for murderous truck drivers? How many theories are you allowed before you admit failure?"

"Gyalo said someone watched from the shadows as he was beaten. Wu's killer had help. Two men in black sweatshirts. Most truck drivers would know how to operate a bulldozer, and could arrive at the base camp in a small supply truck without raising suspicion. More than a few are former soldiers."

They watched until dark, studying every truck that entered the compound, watching for those few that had pairs of drivers, then ventured inside after Yates found a hooded windbreaker to cover his features. The American uttered a low choking sound as they opened the door of the cafe to a powerful scent of grease, cabbage, cigarettes, motor oil and burned rice, then followed Shan to a table in the back corner, where they pushed aside dirty dishes and sat with their backs to the wall.

They ordered noodle soup, which was not as bad as Shan expected, and momos, which seemed to be made of cardboard.

"This is your plan?" Yates muttered. "Sit and wait for two drivers to walk up and confess?" He poked at his stale momos. "Of course they might prefer jail to these dumplings."

"The plan," Shan said as he spotted a familiar face exiting the cafe, "is for you to stop speaking English and sit here." Shan grabbed a newspaper from an empty table and tossed it in front of Yates. "Pretend you read Chinese. I'll be back."

Shan stayed in the shadows as he exited the building, following the path that led to the latrine at the rear of the complex then stealing around the parked trucks until he reached the mechanics' workshop at the far side of the complex. The man under the hood of a small truck was too engrossed in his work to notice Shan enter and lean against the workbench behind him.

"Last I saw him," Shan declared, "your father was sleeping. I think he will make it." Jomo's head jerked up so fast it hit the lifted hood of the truck.

"They don't allow visitors in the garage," he groused, pulling an oily cloth from his pocket to wipe his hands.

"When I said it wasn't Public Security who attacked your father you didn't seem surprised."

"I can't afford trouble. I did a year in prison when I was younger. It still could have been the knobs. They hire people sometimes."

"As informers, yes. But not for that kind of work. For sake of argument, let's say it was strangers, like your father said. This is the local market for strangers, you might say, full of Tibet's new nomads. Men looking for a little extra money, who wouldn't be recognized."

"Last spring when an avalanche covered one of the roads they put a sign up here and quickly hired twenty drivers for a couple of days."

Shan nodded. "What was your year away for?"

"A disagreement over the sky."

"The sky?"

"All my life I walked the town at night and watched the stars, would sit right in the town square and count meteors. Then some-one decided to install street lights, those ugly orange vapor lamps. No more stars. I used to spend summers with shepherds when I was a boy. I have always been good at throwing stones."

"Civic pride," Shan suggested, "can take many forms."

Jomo forced a slow, uneasy grin in reply.

"What if I had a special job, no questions asked? What if I

wanted two men in black sweatshirts who weren't afraid of bending the rules?"

The Tibetan turned to the bench, began sorting through a pile of wrenches. "You are the only one in town interested in saving that Chinese colonel."

"That Chinese colonel didn't kill Tenzin or Director Xie."

Jomo shrugged. "Tenzin was from Nepal. And no one cries over Religious Affairs bureaucrats."

"When the real killer finds out your father is still alive those two men will probably be sent again. If they can't find him they will start with you."

The Tibetan lifted a wrench and looked at Shan, as if considering whether to use it on him or the engine. "I have work to do," he complained, then bent over the engine again.

"If you don't choose a side," Shan said, "others will choose it for you." He retreated, though only around the two vehicles in the bays, where he watched Jomo from the shadows.

After several minutes the Tibetan paused and straightened, looking toward the parking lot. He glanced around the garage, then disappeared behind a crude plank door into what no doubt was a tool storage closet. Shan gave him another minute before he followed.

The door of the closet was ajar. Shan hooked a finger around it and silently pulled it open. Jomo stood between two walls on which tools hung, facing a small workbench that had been cleared of all tools. On it sat a small Buddha, a cheap steel casting with streaks of oil on its face. The Tibetan was placing pieces of sweet biscuits in front of the Buddha, as offerings.

"I was still young when the Red Guard became active," Shan said to his back. Jomo's breath caught at the sound of his voice but the Tibetan did not move. "They came to my school and made the students gather up every book in a foreign language. They made us put them in a big pile in the courtyard and said we would have a beautiful cleansing fire the next day. That night

I went back to school. I pulled out twenty books of history and poetry and replaced them with twenty books of the Chairman's essays I took from the classrooms."

"Did they find out?" Jomo asked in a whisper.

"No. But years later, after we returned from reeducation camps in the country, they found my father with Western books he had kept hidden. Some were those I rescued that day. He died from the beating they gave him. He died holding my hand, smiling at me. I always felt somehow responsible."

"It's hard to know the right things to do," Jomo said, speaking toward the Buddha. "It's hard to know how to be."

Shan waited for the rest of the sentence then realized there was no more. "It's hard to know," he agreed.

"An old shepherd knew my father," Jomo said, "before . . . before everything happened. As a boy I used to run away every month or two when my father got really drunk, because he would beat me, and the shepherd gave me shelter. He told me about my father the monk, said he had been a good man who came to the herding camps each spring to bless the new lambs. He would sit at their campfires and recite sutras and the old poems for hours, then sing songs with the herding families. He said no matter what my father did, that was the man I should see in my mind, that he had been a very holy man, probably would have become the abbot when he got older, that the holy man was just lost inside him somewhere."

"I have a friend who is a lama," Shan whispered. "He says the holy things are still everywhere, just harder to see. Consider it a test, he says."

They stared at the little steel Buddha. Shan found a walnut in his pocket and put it with the other offerings.

"It's a green truck," Jomo suddenly declared. "One of the big heavy ones. Some of those with two drivers keep going through the night, switching drivers. But when those two stop for gas they usually park with the rigs that spend the night here. Sometimes they pay for women in the back where the cots are. Sometimes they walk down the road as if to meet someone. Sometimes their rig stays parked for twenty-four hours. They're due tonight."

"How would they know when to go meet someone?"

"Some kind of signal I think. Sometimes just before dusk I see a yellow bucket turned upside down at the side of the road, a hundred yards before the turnoff. They're always angry, often drunk. They'd rather stab you than look at you." He turned back toward his makeshift altar and touched the top of the Buddha as if for a blessing, and said no more.

Yates, restless as ever, did not need to hear Shan's news. As Shan passed the closest truck to the teashop entrance the American pulled him into the shadows and pointed toward the fuel pumps. Two tall, square men clad in black sweatshirts were fueling and cleaning the cab of a large green truck.

"Christ, they're huge," Yates muttered.

"Manchurians," Shan ventured. One of the men paced along the tires, hitting them with a wooden baton.

"So now what?" Yates asked. "Make a citizen's arrest? Stand in front of their truck until they confess?"

"You are going to wait while I go inside," Shan replied. "And when I return you are going to cover your face, walk behind me, and not say a word."

The man with the baton jumped on the running board and the truck began to move, easing into the ranks of vehicles parked for the night.

Yates did not protest, kept his eyes on the men who climbed off of the truck as Shan darted toward the teashop. Inside, he checked through a window that Yates had not moved then asked for a telephone. Five minutes later the American followed Shan in the direction of the green truck. Shan did not aim directly at the truck, but at two strangers who sat at a concrete table at the edge of the gravel parking lot, playing mah-jongg by the light of a lantern. Shan stepped into the circle of light. "We've got good artifacts," he announced in a loud voice. "The real thing. Triple your money in Shigatse or Lhasa."

The men at the table looked up in surprise then cast worried glances toward the green truck. "The real thing," Shan repeated. "We control the artifact trade in this town." He watched the truck, saw movement in its shadows. When he looked back the two men had disappeared, leaving their tiles and lantern still on the table.

A rough, seething voice emerged from the darkness before Shan could make the black shape moving toward him. "You have shit," the man spat. "You have nothing for sale!" Another shape appeared, brandishing a tire baton.

"Everything is for sale," Shan replied, "Opportunity abounds, for one yellow bucket. What's the price of bulldozing a man into a stone wall?"

They sprang like cats, swinging their batons. Shan sidestepped the first assault and Yates charged into the second man with a shoulder to his chest, knocking him to the ground. But the batons moved with determination. A blow to the back of his head knocked Yates to his knees. For every swing Shan dodged, another connected with his arms and back. Yates was on the ground, the second man straddling him, the baton swept back for a bone-crushing blow, when the headlights of a moving truck illuminated the American's head, no longer covered by his hood.

"*Bai ren!*" the man spat. *Foreigner!* The baton froze in midair, the man's partner muttered a curse, and as quickly as they had appeared, they were gone.

Shan and Yates, numb from the encounter, sat on the gravel, blood trickling down the American's cheek as the green truck, its trailer unhitched, revved its engine and began rolling away.

"That went well," Yates observed dryly in English as he rubbed his head.

Shan, looking up as he finished writing the license plate number of the truck on his forearm, wanted to say it had gone as well as could be expected, when he saw the green truck stop. The driver spoke with a man at the fuel pumps. A figure moved in front of Shan, blocking his view. It was Jomo, his face full of fear, his mouth opening and shutting as if he could not find the words he meant to say.

"Christ! No!" Yates shouted and staggered to his feet as the green truck made a U turn and began speeding in reverse toward Yates's utility vehicle. Shan leapt up, grabbing the American's arm as he took a step forward. Yates' resistance lasted only a moment. They stood, transfixed, as the rear of the truck slammed into Yates' vehicle, crumbling the fender, jerking forward and back again, pushing the vehicle into the boulder behind it. Then suddenly it was on fire. The green truck swerved away, steering toward them as it gained speed, blaring its air horn as they leaped to the side. It roared past them, out onto the highway.

The American took a step toward his burning truck.

"Yates, wait!" Shan insisted.

"For what?" the American shot back. "I have things in there. I have got to—" But his protest died away as he heard the sirens coming down the road from town.

"Let bystanders tell them what happened," Shan said.

"What the hell did you do inside?" Yates growled at Shan. "They never could have gotten the alarm this fast."

His question was answered a moment later. Two black utility vehicles with blinking lights sped into the compound, spraying gravel as they slammed on their brakes and Public Security soldiers poured out of the first. From the second stepped Major Cao and the diminutive Madame Zheng. Shan watched as a witness spoke excitedly with Cao, then pointed at Shan and Yates.

"You must have a death wish," Yates muttered as the major marched toward them.

Shan said nothing as Cao erupted, demanding to know what Shan had done, did not react when Cao slapped him. He extended his forearm with the license numbers written on it toward the knob officer. "A green truck left here minutes ago. In it you will find the men who killed Director Xie."

"Idiot!" Cao snarled. "You don't think I see that everything you do is to distract me from the truth?

"Then why do you suppose they destroyed this American's truck?" Shan asked in a level voice.

Madame Zheng was behind Cao now, staring toward the burning vehicle. A soldier ran up to her with a section of the shattered bumper, bearing a bumper sticker, with the words, in English, *Climbing Rocks!* She stared at it, as if it were a vital piece of evidence, and was still staring at it when two knobs appeared from the shadows of the parked trucks dragging a limp body between them.

"Trying to sabotage the fuel pumps as well," one of the soldiers declared.

Shan's heart leaped to his throat as he recognized Jomo, his face battered and bleeding, a dark stain down his shirt. The knobs too had batons.

"Who else is with you?" the knob demanded, raising his stick at Jomo.

Shan sprang forward, covering the Tibetan, taking the blow to his own shoulder as the knob struck.

"It wasn't like that," Jomo cried as the soldiers tried to pry Shan away. "The man at the fuel station shoved me against a pump. I threw a can of oil at him and it burst open." Shan saw now that the stain was indeed oil. "I only wanted to stop him."

"Stop him from what?" Shan asked, dropping to his knees by the Tibetan.

Jomo pulled several sheets of paper from inside his shirt. "He paid me to draw a map of the roads between here and Everest, with the villages and old shrines marked. I thought he wanted to make offerings." He spoke only to Shan, his face contorted not with pain but with shame. "But then I found him selling copies, selling them to some of the truckers. I threw his money back at him, demanded he give me the maps."

Cao took a step forward, then halted as he saw the attentive way Madame Zheng listened.

"Why?" Shan asked. "Who needs maps?"

"It's those monks. The truckers in the dormitory are all excited. Word spreads fast among those kind. Someone is paying a bounty for the escaped monks, or their gaus, those unique ones with lotus flowers from Sarma gompa."

"Why the gaus?"

"Because the monks will never give them up. If someone brings in one of those gaus the monk will be dead. It's the proof, for the bounty."

The fight went out of the knobs. They gazed at Major Cao as Shan pulled Jomo out of their grip. But it was not Major Cao who spoke.

The silent Madame Zheng finally found her voice, the cool, peremptory one of a woman who would brook no discussion of her commands. "The American is bleeding, Major. Get your medical kit."

Cao glared at Shan, seemed about to strike him again, then retreated as Madame Zheng stepped to Shan's side.

Shan spoke matter-of-factly to the woman from Beijing as he watched Cao jog away. "I want to see Colonel Tan," he stated. "Now. I want him to have a meal, a real meal, sitting in one of the front offices with a window onto the street." Zheng gazed at Shan attentively without responding. "I want the major to stand outside the window, under a streetlight, where Tan can see him."

Chapter Fourteen

TAN DID NOT notice Shan at first when they brought him into the office, washed and wearing tattered but clean prisoner denims. Although the guards had removed the chains on his feet, he moved into the room with the half steps of the prisoner accustomed to hobbles. He halted, looking down his feet, then saw Shan. His face flushed and he looked away.

"The barber came today," Tan announced in a flat tone as he reached the window and, as Shan knew he would, as every prisoner did after days in a cell, looked up at the sky. After a moment he gestured to the plate and steaming cartons of food on the desk. "I thought I would be allowed to select my own last meal."

"Consider this a dress rehearsal," Shan said. He studied the colonel. Although he stood almost straight, something in his back was preventing him from reaching his usual ramrod posture. A finger was splinted and taped. The tips of four other fingers were covered with bandages. The left side of his face was gray-green with old bruises.

Tan sat with a ceremonial air, letting Shan dish out the food as his left hand squeezed his right, to stop it from twitching. Shan watched him eat, wary that his words might ignite the colonel's instinctive rancor. After several minutes of ravenously consuming the chicken, noodles, and vegetable rolls Tan paused and, without looking at Shan, pushed the container with the remaining rolls toward him. Shan lifted the container without a word and ate.

When Shan finally found his tongue he spoke into the empty container. "I was only a boy when the Red Guard first appeared," he said in a low voice. "They started with those sound trucks cruising along the streets, shouting out the Chairman's verses or demands for people to assemble for political instruction. Sometimes they ordered everyone to surrender things. Books. Anything made in a foreign country. Any correspondence from abroad. Photos of foreigners. I remember an old man down the hall who had a wooden figure of a horse maybe ten inches high, his pride and joy, sent by a cousin who had gone to live in America. They had a trial for that horse in the street, condemned it as a reactionary and beheaded it with an ax. I kept wanting to laugh but my mother was crying. She put her hand over my mouth. After that whenever the soundtrucks came, my mother burst into tears."

Tan's hand absently went to his shirt pocket and came away empty. Shan stepped to the door, spoke to the guard, and a moment later a package of cigarettes and matches were tossed onto the desk.

"I wasn't supposed to be one of them," the colonel said after he lit a cigarette. "I was just a soldier, a corporal at one of the new nuclear test facilities, at the edge of the desert north of Tibet. They came through in convoys of trucks, with orders from Beijing to go south and construct a new socialist order in the land of the Buddha. It was like they were going on an extended vacation, a party on wheels. They sang songs about the Chairman, held rallies that went on for hours. They scared the hell out of the officers but we were under orders from the Chairman himself to cooperate. They got anything they wanted. Food. Blankets. Weapons, and men who knew how to use them. I was told to escort them to Lhasa. They stopped in towns along the route, organizing processions of old men and women and encouraging their children and grandchildren to throw eggs at them. They forced people into town squares and renamed all their children with Chinese names or conducted struggle sessions with landlords. When I started to turn back in Lhasa their commanders told me the army was for old men, that I could be part of the past or part of the future, that I could be one of the anointed of Mao if I chose."

He turned and faced the window, still speaking in a wooden

voice. "They were more organized by then, with brigades and a command structure. The commander of my brigade demanded the most difficult assignment, so we could prove our love for the Great Helmsman." Tan's hand twitched again, flinging ash against the glass.

"Tingri County."

Tan nodded. "It was a wilderness, a wild frontier. No maps. No real organized government. Vicious yetis and snow leopards that swallowed men whole, if you believed the stories. A reactionary with a gun behind every rock. The town was nothing like this," he said with a gesture toward the street. "It was mostly just the monastery and a few shops. Army patrols came through sometimes, often with wounded men, sometimes with trucks stacked with the dead from an ambush. They wouldn't stay. Our Youth Brigade scared them as much as the reactionaries did.

"We settled in, took over the main halls of the monastery. But we didn't touch the monks, not at first. Our commander was too smart for that. If we had attacked the main monastery first the local people would have wiped us out. She knew we had to do things in stages. Destroy the small fish and the big ones have nothing to feed on, she liked to say. We moved into the ranges." Tan paused, fidgeting with the frayed cuff of his denim shirt. "I thought you said I'd have my uniform in the end."

Shan knew this was the only reason Tan was talking. He was certain he was going to die. "It has to be cleaned."

Tan nodded.

"So Commander Wu began to engage the rebels," Shan suggested.

"I don't recall saying it was Wu."

"I've seen the old records, Colonel."

Tan shrugged. "After the first year we got more equipment, had soldiers assigned to us. No one would say no to her. She had the energy of wildcat, she was smart, she was beautiful. She made me a lieutenant, in charge of her military operations, enticed me into her bed. We would go into the mountains and make the local people dismantle their own religious buildings, every shrine, every little monastery, and organize new cooperatives, hold struggle sessions with all the senior monks and landowners, discipline anyone who resisted. We were gods, she would say to me at night when we lay together."

Tan took a long draw on his cigarette, exhaling slowly. "We were children," he said in a whisper, then looked out the window, his gaze lingering on the figure of Major Cao, who leaned against a car on the opposite side of the street. Shan did not miss the subtle relaxation in the muscles of his jaw, the reaction he expected when Tan saw his interrogator was outside the building. "Who would have thought that she and I would come back after all these years to die here?"

"Were there foreigners in the mountains?" Shan asked.

Tan shrugged again. "Foreign equipment. There were always rumors that Americans were coming, that Americans were being diverted from Vietnam and would parachute onto every mountain. She got film footage of the war in Vietnam and made us watch it, again and again, so we would know the imperialist enemy." He drew deeply on his cigarette, blew the smoke toward Cao outside. "I never saw any foreigners. It was bad enough with just the rebels. They were magnificent. Four Rivers, Six Ranges, they called their army. They were eagles swooping down to engage fields of crows. Disappearing into their secret mountain nests. Climbing like mountain goats. Coming out of snowstorms like ghosts. But we could always call in more troops, always shoot more Tibetans on suspicion of collaboration. An eagle might defeat the first hundred crows, and the next hundred, but when the hundreds keep coming eventually they will be picking eagle bones."

"And you were lord of the crows."

"Deputy lord of the crows," Tan corrected, and lit another cigarette.

"You had a different kind of cigarette back then," Shan observed as Tan exhaled a plume of smoke.

Tan winced. "She called it a symbol of class struggle. At one struggle session with old monks she rolled up prayers and forced them to smoke them like cigars. After a while it became something of a habit. She passed them out to everyone on the tribunals."

"When you arrived at the hotel, she wasn't receiving any visitors, so you found a way to make sure she knew it was you. Why did you want to see her?"

Tan shrugged. "It had been over thirty years."

"You could have had lunch together. Instead you sent her a rolled-up peche page and met in her room."

Tan faced the window. "She sent me a letter last year, saying she had never married, that she and I had been married to the People's Republic. I thought she might have changed, mellowed." He glanced back at Shan. "I seem to recall you were married once."

"My wife started out mellow. Then she married the government." Shan saw the beginning of one of the cold grins he had often seen on Tan's face but it ended in a grimace.

"She had covered her lamp like some teenager. There was a bottle of wine. She always expected tribute. In the last year of the brigade she started demanded payment from villagers to spare their homes from destruction." Tan shrugged again. "As soon as I saw her, she began rattling off statistics, of the number of employees she had in her ministry, her budget, the foreign exchange earnings her work brought in. She began drinking, urging me to join her. I told her I needed to go. She unbuttoned her blouse. She said we should play like the old days, like we had learned to do in this very town. I told her I was tired from the long drive. That's when she took my pistol, to play with. She used to carry one of those heavy American pistols we captured from the rebels, using it as a gavel at the tribunals, and for executions when the Hammer and Lightning Brigade took prisoners. She put it under her pillow and said I would have to come back for it the next night when I was rested."

Tan paused and inhaled deeply on his cigarette. "Why did he

do that, that monk in the cell? Why would he leap out to take the blow meant for me?"

"It was his way of acknowledging the truth. He knew you didn't deserve it. And he doubted if you could take many more blows."

Tan shook his head. "The fool."

"What happened in the end?" Shan asked after a long silence. "How were the rebels finally beaten?"

Tan turned back toward the window, his face clouding. "Damn you! What are you doing to me? I don't talk like this to people."

"We used to talk about death all the time in prison, not with fear but with curiosity. It was among us all the time, it was like an old companion. A herder in our barracks told us that when a man senses death getting close a door opens inside his spirit and releases the most interesting surprises, that old forgotten truths will find their way out. When he lay dying, he kept talking about a white yak he had seen as a boy, said that he could see it flying down from a cloud to take him away. He had half the barracks watching the sky, trying to spot it."

Tan watched Major Cao, who paced along the sidewalk. Cao began yelling at a Tibetan boy approaching on a bicycle, ordering him into the street. When the confused boy did not comply Cao kicked the bike as it passed, catapulting the boy over the handlebars, smashing the bike into a light pole. The boy pulled himself up, glanced at Cao with terror in his eyes and ran into the night.

Tan clenched his jaw. "I don't want him touching my body afterward."

"I don't expect to be invited to the occasion," Shan observed.

"They usually have a cleanup squad," Tan said in a distant voice. "They take a picture before they dispose of the body. It's the last thing that goes in the file."

"I could notify your family. A brother? A cousin? An old neighbor?"

"There is no one. There's you." He glanced at Shan self-consciously. "Not that you're a friend," he hastened to add. "It's just that you're . . . reliable. An honorable enemy."

"What happened in the end?" Shan tried again. "Where the rebels were finally defeated."

"We wore them out. The American government stopped supplying them. If a village supported the rebels we bulldozed it. If a herder gave them food we machine gunned his herd. That Tibetan leader in India summoned them across the border, sending a tape of a speech asking them to lay down their arms."

"You mean the Dalai Lama," Shan said. The name was taboo to officials in Tibet.

"The Dalai Lama," Tan agreed in a whisper, then repeated the name with a perverse, oddly pleased expression. The two men had entered new territory, someplace they had never been. "There was a last group," Tan continued, "the core, the best fighters, maybe twenty or thirty men and women. Wu hated them. She was impatient for her final victory, for the destruction of the big monastery here in town because the monks there continued to hold public ceremonies in defiance of her orders. She kept asking me when I would have their bodies for her to display in the town square. But they always retreated high into the mountains, into their eagle nests. They had hiding places, where they disposed of the bodies of their comrades so we would never know the effects of our bullets. None of the Youth Brigade would join me, they were getting scared. They knew so little of real fighting that they were often killed when they tried to engage the rebels. But by then there were border commandos being deployed here. I was given two companies of real soldiers. Finally we reached the rebels through the back door."

The words hung in the air. "Are you saying," Shan asked, "that there was a traitor?"

"Officially," Tan replied, "someone made a heroic conversion to the socialist cause."

Shan's mind raced. It was, he realized, the link to all the pieces of his puzzle. "Who was it?"

"No idea. Wu brokered the deal. By then she and I were not so close. I had started sleeping in the army barracks when the infantry moved to town. She gave me directions, where we could find them, with a very specific hand-drawn map, showing a secret path. There was a village that was not to be touched. It wasn't easy to find their hiding place. Two of my soldiers died on the climb. But we surprised them as they ate breakfast, killed half right away, and chased most of the others across the border. They officially named me a hero, took me back into the army, made me a real officer."

"A village?"

"Tumkot. We were not to touch it, just march through without a word. The next morning we took truckloads of food up to it, and in the afternoon lined up howitzers and began leveling the gompa here in town."

"As if there had been a trade," Shan suggested after a moment. "The village for the gompa."

"As if there had been a trade," Tan agreed.

"Wu was going to order all the monks inside, to trap them there when the shells fell. But the bastards beat us to it. She was furious."

"You mean," Shan guessed, "that they didn't have to be ordered inside."

"Right. Most of them went inside as soon as they saw us getting the guns ready. Later I realized they had been expecting it for months. They locked the doors from the inside and a monk went up the wall over the gate to throw the key down as the shells starting landing. We probably killed them all in the first half hour but she kept the barrage up for half a day."

They sat in silence, watching the stars over the town.

"A crow picking at the bones of starved, scrawny eagles," Tan said in a near whisper.

"I'm sorry?"

"It's not what I set out to be."

It was the most extraordinary thing Tan had ever said to him. A dozen replies occurred to Shan. It was the opening for the kind of conversation Shan had with lamas, in the night. But then he studied Tan and reconsidered. "Where were you, Colonel, the day the minister died?"

"I came here, to town. I walked around the old barracks and the infirmary building. That was where Wu held her struggle sessions when the weather was cold. I went and sat by that pit we pushed the old gompa into."

"And the bodies of the monks."

Tan did not reply.

Shan rose and piled the empty food cartons on the plate.

"What would you have me do, Colonel, if I am able to retrieve your body?"

"Put me behind the town."

"You mean on the ridge, where you can see Everest?"

"No." Tan's level tone chilled Shan. "You can get out into the pit by climbing up from that old stable at its mouth. I want you to go out there in the middle of the night. I want you to dig in the pit until you strike bones. Then drop me in."

Chapter Fifteen

"YOU AND I both know that no matter what is stated publicly about the murders, you will be expected to return to Beijing with the truth." Shan returned Madame Zheng's unblinking gaze as he spoke. He had watched as the guards took Tan away, his chains reattached, before walking down the corridor. The commissar from Beijing had been waiting for him in the last office in front of a receiver. She had, as Shan had expected, been listening.

"We are beginning to glimpse the truth," he continued. "The minister took Tan's gun. There were not two murders but four."

"Those large bullets fascinate me," Zheng interjected. Though she seldom spoke, it was always in the low precise tone of an accountant. "They are not Chinese." She had taken Shan's advice and obtained the unofficial autopsy report for Tenzin. "If your American friend is involved then you will be the next to die."

"A chance I am willing to take. Give me four days," Shan said. "And I will bring back the proof. I need to have my son protected until then."

Silence was Madame Zheng's medium. She offered a tiny nod then held up two fingers.

GYALO WAS IN the corner of the buried chamber when Shan arrived, picking with a splinter of wood at a dirt-encrusted figurine, a little bronze Buddha. Shan looked at a small pile of fresh earth at the back of the room. The former lama had been digging at the blocked passage.

"I hadn't realized," Shan said abruptly, "that nearly all the monks were killed inside the gompa when the Youth Brigade destroyed it. Why was it different for you?"

Gyalo turned his back on Shan. Shan stepped around him and sat directly in front of him.

The Tibetan frowned but resisted no longer. "By then it was well understood that it was what all of us preferred, dying in the temples. We weren't allowed to resist, we would have no purpose when the temples were gone. With such a death, praying in the temple, at one with the Buddha, reincarnation was nothing to fear."

"But it was for you," Shan said, shamed at his words but knowing he had to press the old man.

Emotion flooded Gyalo's face. It was a long time before he spoke. "Some were singled out for special punishment. By then that Commander Wu understood our ways. For some a quick death wasn't enough. She learned ways to destroy a monk, in this life and the next."

"Singled out because they had offended the Hammer and Lightning Brigade," Shan suggested. When Gyalo did not contradict him he ventured further. "Because they were suspected of being sympathizers with the rebels."

Gyalo began picking at the little statue again. "I need a drink." His hands were shaking, the tremors of an alcoholic in desperate need.

"If you were one of the old rebels it would be reason enough to kill her."

"She was smart enough to keep out of town. If she had ventured into Shogo there's still a handful who might recognize her. I keep an iron pipe behind the bar," Gyalo said without emotion. "If she had walked in I would have gladly beaten her brains out."

"Or shot her?"

Gyalo murmured a mantra to the deity, then looked up distractedly. "You ever see those protector demons in the old tangkas, with human skins draped around their necks? I think they would have used the pipe."

"How many rebels survived?"

"No one ever knew how many made it across the border."

"I mean how many stayed alive, staying here, in the county?"

Gyalo looked as if he bitten something sour. "People moved on, started new lives." He spoke to the Buddha, as if it were listening. "If one happened into my bar we would not acknowledge one another, never say a word about it. We were different people then, with different lives. Everyone finds their own way to survive, eh?"

"As tavernkeepers? As fortunetellers?"

"You don't know how it was. I worked for the abbot, taking messages and sometimes supplies to the hermitages and small gompas in the mountains. I saw what that Youth Brigade did. The Dalai Lama said not to fight. But how could a Tibetan *not* fight, I said to my abbot. He said I had to resist my emotions, he made me do penance, ten thousand mantras at a shrine out in the snow."

"When's the last time you went into the mountains?"

A spasm of pain shook the Tibetan. "I need a drink," Gyalo pleaded to the Buddha.

"Why are you so frightened of leaving town?"

"You don't know her. She was like a tigress, one of the best of the fighters. She vowed she would kill me if she ever saw me again. She told everyone I had betrayed them, to save my life."

"She helped you, grandfather. Ama Apte set your arm."

The former lama gazed in horror at the splint on his broken bones. For a moment he looked as if he would rip it away. Gyalo seemed to be in real agony now, clutching his abdomen, his head bobbing up and down. "Any fool could see who the traitor was. It was my home, my life, that was destroyed. Her village was never touched." He grew very still, his face clenched like a fist.

Shan coaxed the coals in the brazier by the entry back to life, and made black tea. He pushed the hot mug to Gyalo's lips, forcing him to drink. "Did you ever go up to their stronghold, their last hiding place?"

Gyalo took the mug from Shan and nodded. "They had weapons there, many still in their crates as if they had magically appeared. Grenades, machine guns, mortars."

"Where?"

"I don't know. They would take me there in the night, from an old cave hermitage, to help with the wounded, to help with the dead. I remember walking along a cliff face. I remember a hole in the trail, by a high ledge, where they took me by the hand and said if I did not follow exactly in their footsteps I would die. Once you got to the top, it was broad and flat and glowed all white, opened toward the mother mountain. An old place."

"Old?"

"The rebels weren't the first to use it. There were cairns covered with lichen, with shreds of very old prayer flags. It was one of the ancient shrines to the mother mountain, to keep her placated, one of those that helped keep her anchored to our world. No one cares about her anymore." The Tibetan shrugged. "Trash and bodies all over her slopes. No wonder she does these things to us."

"How long was the climb from the hermitage?"

"Two hours, maybe three."

Shan weighed Gyalo's words as he poured him another cup of tea. "What do you mean you helped with the dead? You performed the death rites?"

"They always carried away the bodies of their dead. I would be asked to perform death rites, to call out the spirits, to ask for forgiveness so they would not be offended."

"Offended?"

"The rebels could not risk pyres to burn the bodies, or to go to fleshcutters. They had a place, a deep gully they rolled the bodies into, like a burial at sea."

* * *

YATES WAITED FOR him in the shadows by Tsipon's warehouse.

"We need ropes," Shan said. "We need climbing equipment." He tried the door. It was locked.

"It's the middle of the night, Shan," the American protested.

"There is no time. The answers are all at the last drop zone, at the last hiding place of the rebels," he said, and explained what he had learned from Tan and Gyalo.

When he had finished Yates studied the two-story building. "Is there a maintenance hatch on the roof?"

Shan had barely nodded before the American launched himself onto the wall in front of the building. He found a protruding nail, a narrow lintel, a tiny ledge for footholds as he climbed. He was up and over in less than two minutes, and took even less time to open the door from the inside.

They selected their equipment by the light of the lanterns, nearly filling two backpacks before Shan stopped and ran the beam of his light along the wall shelving. "Look for canvas ground cloths," he said. "Two, with rope to lash them together."

Yates began scanning the shelves then froze and looked at Shan as if reconsidering his words. "God, no. I can't do that. Don't ask me to bring her body back," he said in a haunted voice.

"It's the last chance we have," Shan said. "A real exam, by a real scientist, will show that she died from bullets fired by the same gun as Wu, at the same time. The blood on the shirt I wore that day will match hers. They won't be able to deny the truth."

"I've seen the bodies on the upper slopes. I couldn't look at her. I couldn't touch her."

Shan reached onto an upper shelf and pulled away two ground cloths.

"You'll never find her," Yates said, as if arguing with himself.

"I can't do it alone, Yates," Shan said. "If I don't bring the truth out of the mountains, the monks in this region are finished. An innocent man will be executed."

"And your son . . ." the American whispered.

A tremor of fear shook Shan. He had fought for hours to keep the image of his son on a surgeon's table from his consciousness and now as it returned it seemed to paralyze him. The American pulled the canvas sheets from his hands and began packing them.

A yellow-gray hint of dawn rimmed the eastern horizon by the time they began moving up the mountain road in the battered old Jiefang, starting the long steady climb toward the spine of the Himalayas. They passed the site of the minister's murder, stopping more than once to consult the American map in the light of the rising sun.

"Forget the map," Shan said at last. "Look for a small mound of rocks twenty feet off the road."

"I thought you said the trail to Tumkot was hidden, not marked."

"It isn't. Not exactly." Shan stopped the laboring truck, climbed out, and walked along the road, studying first the terrain to the west, where the massive flank of Tumkot's mountain dominated the skyline, then the road behind them, where a cloud of dust ominously approached. He was about to ask for the American's binoculars when with a low angry mutter Yates darted past him and sprang into the cargo bay of the truck. He leaped onto a pile of canvas cargo covers and cursed as half the pile unfolded itself, and stood.

"Jomo!" Shan called in surprise. The Tibetan mechanic met Shan's gaze with an odd hint of defiance. "What are you—" Shan began then changed his question. "Why are you dressed like that?" Jomo was wearing a tattered ankle-length raincoat.

"They are coming, you know," the Tibetan said. "The knobs. You thought you could make some kind of deal, but they can never be trusted."

"I saw them."

"No," Jomo said. "That group below is all bounty hunters. The knobs are behind them."

"Then they will stop the bounty hunters."

"No. I was working on a truck in the military garage. Cao came in to give his orders personally. He didn't know I was working in the back. They assume I don't understand Chinese. That Cao, he is furious at you. He told them you would be with the monks somewhere high. He said you would help them escape, and that they all knew how to deal with traitors. I think," Jomo added with an uneasy glance at Shan, "he cares more about destroying you than solving his case."

"Surely they wouldn't just shoot Shan," Yates interjected.

"Of course they would," Jomo said impatiently, gesturing them up the road. "They will shoot you both and rejoice to be rid of outsider pests." He seemed eager for Shan and Yates to leave.

Shan let the America pull him away as he studied the Tibetan in confusion. After a long moment he grabbed Yates's binoculars and studied the roadway ahead, spotting the fresh mound of rocks he had piled over the dog's grave less than a hundred yards away. He was looking for a place to hide the truck when a frantic cry from Yates caused him to spin around. Jomo was standing on a ledge above the road. He had taken off his coat. Under it he was wearing a maroon robe, no doubt one of those Shan had found in the old underground chapel. Yates threw off his pack and ran.

Jomo was doing a little jig by the time Yates reached him, first toward the descending road, to get the attention of those below, then toward the American to evade Yates's desperate efforts to pull him down. As Shan reached the Tibetan, shards of rock exploded from boulders at either side.

"The fool!" Yates shouted in English as he grabbed Jomo's arm. "He wants them to think he's one of the monks!" When Jomo squirmed out of the American's grip Yates lowered his shoulder and slammed into the Tibetan, knocking him down, pinning him as Shan lifted the binoculars and ventured a glance over the ledge. Less than half a mile away two of the heavy highway trucks, shed of their trailers, blocked the road. At least two of the men beside them held rifles. Their attention was riveted on the rocks where

Jomo had appeared. They had not noticed the second cloud of dust behind them. Even if the knobs had orders to find Shan, they could not ignore men with illegal firearms.

Shan looked back at Jomo's beloved old Jiefang truck, then studied the straight stretch of roadway before the curve where the heavy trucks sat, above one of the many high cliffs along the road.

He gazed at Jomo, who sat on the ledge, his arms behind him, locked in the American's grip. "They will kill you Jomo. They will kill you with as much thought as swatting a fly. And when they see you don't have the right gau, they will kick your body and move on."

"They'll have to catch me," Jomo shot back.

"Can you outrun a bullet?" Shan asked. He walked along the truck, his hand on its body, then considered the straight road below them, cut through the living rock so that much of it was flanked on both sides by stone. "I'll need your help," he said to Jomo.

Jomo gazed in confusion for a moment, then followed Shan's gaze as he turned back to the truck. "Noooo-oooo!" he cried in a mournful tone. "Not her!"

"Do you want to help the monks?" Shan asked.

As the Tibetan nodded Yates released his grip and the two men listened to hear Shan's plan.

As Jomo stripped off his robe then turned the truck to face downhill, Shan and Yates frantically collected rags, cargo covers, even clumps of heather, then ripped Jomo's robe in three pieces as Jomo began working with a rope around the steering wheel. They quickly produced three dummies seated in the cab, their shoulders wrapped in the maroon of monks' robes, hats pulled low. If Shan's scheme worked no one below would have time for more than a quick glance. They would see what they had come for, three monks making a desperate last stand. With a satisfied nod he turned to Jomo, who was scrubbing tears from his cheeks.

"You said she was a battle junk," Shan reminded him. "This is what they did, ram their enemy to destroy their ships."

"She never failed us," Jomo said in a cracking voice, with a hand on the rusty fender.

"She never failed us," Shan repeated. He rummaged in his pocket and found a cone of incense which he lit and placed on the dashboard. "The spirits will find her," he observed as the smoke curled around the wheel and gearshift.

Jomo insisted on starting the engine himself, which groaned and sputtered one last time before finally coming to life. He wedged a stone on the accelerator and jumped out as the truck began rolling downhill.

As the figures below darted onto the road, guns at the ready to stop the fugitive truck, first one then another spun about. Soldiers had materialized behind them.

The old truck gained speed quickly, the engine's backfire like a battle cry. The bounty hunters and soldiers scattered as they saw it was not slowing down. It smashed into the first semi cab with an explosion of metal and glass, knocking it on its side, sparks flying as the combined vehicles, locked at bumpers, careened into the second truck with a glancing blow that shoved it onto the road below the curve. As it reached the curve, the first truck knocked away the small boulders guarding the cliff below, then disappeared over the edge. Jomo's old Jiefang seemed to hesitate, as if sensing its fate. Then the weight of the first truck, still attached to the bumper, jerked it forward and the old blue junk sailed out into the void.

No one moved, not even at the sound of the explosion, not until a dense column of smoke reached the top of the cliff. The stunned bountyhunters offered no protest as the soldiers relieved them of their guns. Shan studied the short column of men as they were led away. The two tall Manchurians were not among them.

Jomo watched the smoke with a stricken expression as Shan and Yates pulled on their packs.

"She will have a new life," Shan offered to the mechanic. "I think," he added after a moment's thought, "that she will be a jet airplane."

The words shook Jomo out of his melancholy. He nodded slowly and turned to Shan with a sad grin. "You can't go back, Shan," he warned. "Yesterday I saw that Madame Zheng sitting at Tsipon's desk, waiting for him."

"Waiting?"

"He wasn't there. He must have come later. They're planning something against us."

Shan paused to consider Jomo's news. It was hard to believe that Zheng would seek Tsipon's counsel on anything. "I don't want you going back either," Shan replied. "Not until we return. Go up to the base camp."

"In my depot tent," Yates offered, "there is a cot you can use. Take it for the night."

"I'll come up with you," Jomo suggested.

"No," Shan said. "Go to the base. Stay away from the soldiers who will be on the road today."

Yates pulled a T-shirt from his pack, one of those with his expedition company's name. "There. You're one of my sherpas."

"But tomorrow morning," Shan said. "We'll need a ride back to town. Be at the big rocks ahead."

Jomo did not hesitate. "I'll be there before sunrise with one of the company trucks. I'll sleep in it if I need to."

FOR SEVERAL DESPERATE moments Shan thought he must have been wrong in assuming that Dakpo had watched from the hidden trail as he buried the dog, but then he saw a single hoofprint, several days old, then another, and another angling upward. The trail was barely discernible at first, so faint Shan climbed as much by intuition as physical signs. After half an hour of steady ascent they reached a small sheltered plateau where soil had collected, giving life to tufts of grass and heather. They walked slowly about the edge until at last Yates pointed to a large hoof-print, perhaps a week old, made by an animal climbing upward. Shan knelt and recognized it immediately.

"The mule," he said, and without looking back quickly followed a second, and third print into a narrow channel between two high ledges. Soon the trail widened and its packed soil became obvious. They frightened a flock of mountain sheep as they lay on an outcropping, stopping to admire faded paintings of a protector demon on squared boulders that marked what Shan knew must have been the crossing of a pilgrims' path.

After an hour of arduous climbing up steep switchbacks they crested the northern arm of the steep mountain to enter a high plateau with scattered patches of snow. After a quarter mile they rounded the far side and saw Tumkot far below. Shan pointed to a fork in the trail, and gestured Yates toward the higher path, that led into a chill wind from above that smelled of ice.

Half an hour later Shan set his pack down at the entry to a large cave flanked by more faded paintings of deities. With painful foreboding he studied the soil around the entry, compressed with the impressions of so many boots he could not manage a clear count of the number of people who had recently been there.

They advanced with hand lights into the cave, following a vague scent of incense that grew stronger as they walked. When at last they reached the main chamber they had no need for their lights. The cavern in which Dakpo sat was lit by shafts of sunlight slanting in through a long, narrow cleft in the outside wall. The monk was not praying but cleaning, rolling up three worn sleeping pallets. He greeted them with a surprised grin. "I go for months without a visitor," he said, "and now my home is like a town square." He silently accepted Shan's help in rolling and stacking the pallets by a plank that held three pairs of tattered sandals.

"You need to hide all this," Shan warned the old Tibetan. "Men may be coming in search of them." The hermit nodded absently, looking past Shan's shoulder with an amused expression. Shan turned to see Yates standing as if paralyzed before what looked like an altar in a dimly lit corner. But it was not an altar Shan saw as he approached, just a low table made of planks on stones. On it sat a rectangular object under a blanket, with an electric cord wrapped in frayed cloth fiber extending out of it, leading to a strange wooden box with two crank handles jutting out of its sides. Yates shined his light on English words stenciled along the side of the box and gasped. US ARMY, it said in black stenciled letters.

The American pulled the blanket away, revealing a device with several dials and gauges on its front. "It can't be!" he exclaimed in surprise, and kept repeating the words as he knelt, examining it with his light held close.

Dakpo, sitting on a little three legged milking stool, wore an oddly satisfied smile.

"Ama Apte's uncle," Shan said. "This is why he came up here all the time."

The hermit nodded. "Kundu and I were good friends, long before he took that mule shape. We would go outside on a ledge facing south. He had been trained by the Americans to stretch the antenna in a certain way. At first I was too frightened to turn those handles, because of the little lightning bolts they made at the end of the wires, but he taught me how to do it safely, the way the Americans taught him.

"There was a rebel who kept transmitting," Yates recalled in a whisper. His fingers hovered in front of the dials but he seemed reluctant to touch them. "He kept on transmitting for years after the program ended, even though no one answered."

"There was no world afterward," the hermit declared in a thin, haunting voice. "We had to make do."

The words brought Yates out of his trance. "No world?"

"Down below were all those Chinese, destroying everything Tibetan. On the other side of the mountains were all those who had given up fighting, who were becoming new kinds of Tibetans, Tibetans as Indians, Tibetans as Nepalis. If we wanted to stay the way we were, we had to become invisible." Dakpo rose and reverently dusted the top of the radio with a rag.

"The day they . . . the last day of fighting," the hermit continued, "we knew our world was gone. Each of us had to do the best he could. I thought about telling old Kundu that the Americans were gone, never to come back, that he should stop the transmissions."

Yates fingered the worn wooden handles on the portable generator.

"But he didn't?" the American asked.

"Not for years."

"What would he say?" Shan asked after a long silence, "when he transmitted on the radio?"

"The first few years, he stayed on the run, using a sleeping bag from the Americans, saying his mission now was intelligence, whatever that meant. He would watch the highway, watch the Chinese army, then come up and report the movements, like in the days of the fighting. For a while he decided the Americans had changed the codes, or frequencies, and so he would turn the dials and repeat his number, announcing again and again that he was a sergeant in the Tibetan resistance army. In the end he would talk about the weather or read sutras."

"Sutras?" Shan asked.

"Eventually he realized it wasn't the Americans he was trying to reach. He said it was something people didn't always understand about radios, that even if the Americans stopped listening the heavens always heard."

Yates extracted one of his old photos, of Tibetans lined up with parachutes and packs, ready for a jump, and pointed to his father, standing with the aircrew.

Dakpo responded immediately. "He was a good man, your father. Kundu, the two-legged one, was with him in that camp in

America."

Yates seemed to stop breathing for a moment. "How—-how did you know he was my father?"

"The first time you took your hat off in Tibet, the mountain knew," Dakpo said enigmatically. Then with new enthusiasm he took the photo and began pointing to the men, reciting each name in turn. Not until he had finished and looked up did he see the dumbfounded grin on the American's face. "Once, I remember at the end of your year, in our eleventh month, your father taught us some of your festival songs in English and we sang them around a fire eating sweet biscuits he had saved. Songs about snowmen and bells and the birth of his lama on that cross. Jingle bells, jingle bells, we would sing. He laughed a lot, your father. He gave us strength."

"How many of you were there?" Shan asked. "Survivors."

"A few," Dakpo said in a wary tone.

"You said each found his own way to survive. Not everyone became a hermit."

Dakpo nodded. "I had been a novice at one of the little monasteries they burned down in the first campaign. I saved most of the old books, brought them here and tried to concentrate on them the way my teachers had taught me before they died. But eventually I realized I had to fight before I could study."

"Gyalo went to town," Shan said. "Ama Apte went to her village and became a fortuneteller."

"She couldn't very well stay in the mountains. She needed to be with her family."

"Was it one of them who betrayed the rebels?"

"There was always going to be someone. It was the way the Chinese worked."

"You didn't answer my question."

"They each think the other did it. I don't know. All trust was gone after that day. I thought about it, for years I thought about it. There were others who could have helped the Chinese. Shepherds who knew us. Maybe one of our own band who slipped across the border. Who's to know what makes a bird wake up and decide to change its song? It was written that our world would change, and it changed."

Shan pulled away a piece of felt covering a stool by the radio, revealing more military equipment, a compass, a bayonet, a small set of binoculars. He paused, looking back at the stacks of old books at the far side of the cave. Both the equipment and the books were well maintained.

Dakpo saw the query in Shan's face. "The more one understands the world," he declared, "the harder it is to obtain Buddhahood."

Yates began to fire off questions about his father. After a moment Shan held up his hand. "There is no time. The slopes are crawling with people searching for the monks." He turned to the hermit. "Can you take us there, to the hidden place where they are going?"

Dakpo pointed to his sandals. "With these, no. I gave the only boots here to the monks. "But," he added, rising, "I can guide you for the first hour and point the way from there. It is difficult," he warned. "Not even the wild goats can do it."

They paused every quarter hour to scan the slopes with Yates' binoculars. As they rushed up one steep switchback after another, Shan caught Yates looking back with worry toward the smoke of Tumkot's chimneys, visible now over a ridge, the village that had been saved in the deal that had betrayed the rebels. The hermit had not actually denied that Ama Apte was the traitor. And the fortuneteller, while secretly trying to force Yates out of the country, had deliberately hidden the fact that she had known his father.

The hermit led them at a near-frantic pace after the first steep slope, through tight rock passages, under a narrow waterfall, around fields of jagged snow bound scree, through several frigid streams gorged with meltwater. He halted abruptly as they navigated along a glacier-shattered landscape, a fractured wall of granite on one side of the trail, a treacherous vertical drop on the other.

"If you watch carefully, there is an old trail," he announced, "at least the shadow of an old trail. When there is a choice to be made, always go up."

Yates and Shan exchanged confused glances then the hermit stepped aside to reveal a two-foot-wide hole in the ledge they walked on, no different from a dozen others they had passed. Except that this one had a barely perceptible legend painted on a rock above it, a mantra to the mother protector. Shan removed his pack and lowered himself, taking it on faith he would find purchase in the deep shadow below, and in fact discovering slots carved in the wall like a ladder, leading to a flat stone floor eight feet below. A moment later Yates had joined him.

"Lha gyal lo!" Dakpo called as he handed their packs down.

They had dropped into a twisting corridor of stone that soon opened onto a steep sheltered slope dotted with heather and wildflowers. The granite wall they had taken to be the side of the mountain revealed itself to be a massive outcropping that hid the slope and the path above it. They climbed without speaking, spotting fresh boot prints where rare patches of soil showed, at every junction in the path following the hermit's advice to take the more difficult, steeper route, climbing up narrow shelves that had been chiseled into the stone like stairs. Yates moved with increasing urgency, hesitating not a moment when they reached a tall chimney, grabbing the narrow bars of old juniper wood that had been fixed between the stone walls. They climbed another steep slope that glistened with pockets of snow, passing a row of stone columns, then halted at a path through a high wall marked by a crumbling stone cairn.

At the end of the path they emerged onto a broad, nearly flat shelf almost two hundred feet wide and a quarter mile long. Directly to the south a glacier rose toward the horizon. To the southeast was a sweeping view of Everest and her sister peaks Lhotse and Makalu. To the north, in the shadow of the massive granite wall, were several crude structures of dry laid stone. Yates took a step and raised a strange jingling sound. He kicked and loosened several long brass cylinders, bearing the green patina of age. Bullet casings.

There was no sign of anyone, though in several patches of snow Shan saw more fresh imprints of boots. He willed himself not to follow them, to move instead toward the ragged lip of the deep crevasse that ran along the eastern edge of the little plateau.

"We came for evidence," Shan reminded Yates, who insisted on searching each of the crude, crumbling structures before joining Shan at the lip of the crevasse. Lying at the lip, with the American anchoring his legs, Shan searched the fissure with the binoculars, studying the jumble of broken slabs and boulders that lined the bottom nearly two hundred feet below. Much of it was shrouded in shadow, though at its end it curved toward the southeast, where many of the slabs of rock were lit by the sun. The unlikely odds of discovering Megan Ross were compounded by the many gaps between boulders and slabs where a corpse dropped from above could easily have fallen. Seeing nothing, Shan rose and walked slowly along the top, studying the ground. At last, less than fifty feet from where the crevasse opened out onto the side of the mountain, he found older prints in a patch of snow, grown faint with freezing and thawing. There was more, a long indentation where something heavy had been dragged to the edge. He laid down again over the lip and instantly saw a patch of red below, the color of the windbreaker the woman had been wearing when she died.

"You're some kind of wizard, Shan," the American said in a hollow voice over his shoulder. "All these hundreds of miles of wilderness and you come right to her."

Shan eased back from the lip and stood. "From the beginning the killer has tried to make it seem that one of the old rebels committed the crimes. If he ever needed more proof he would see to it that Public Security found this place, would make sure they knew this was where the rebels secretly disposed of bodies, that only one of them would know how to find it."

Yates emptied his pack, dumping out the climbing gear at Shan's feet.

"I can't go down on the ropes," Shan declared. "I've never done it before."

"And I can't do what has to be done at the bottom," Yates countered in a grim tone.

Shan, filled with a new form of dread, lowered his head and listened to the American's instructions as Yates produced two harnesses and began to fasten lines to a huge boulder near the edge.

SHE LAY ON her side as if sleeping, her face nearly as pale as the snow she rested on, one arm jutting at an unnatural angle from under her head. The cold, dry air had kept Megan Ross preserved as it did the dead climbers of Everest, though she had not been there so long as to become affixed to the stone. Shan gripped himself, telling himself not to look into her open eyes, then rolled the body over, straightening the arm along her side. But as he worked he seemed to feel her gaze, and when he finally looked into her face he saw the confusion and longing that had been there when she had died but also something else, an oddly plaintive expression. He glanced at Yates, who sat with his back to Shan, carefully avoiding looking at his dead friend, and was about to begin unwrapping the length of rope he had carried around his waist to fashion a harness for the body when he saw the bloodstains along the buttons of her shirt, faint but unmistakable fingerprints. With a shudder he unfastened the buttons, revealing a small silver gau, Ross's prayer box, also bearing the marks of her bloody fingers at its latch. In his mind Shan replayed the awful moment when Megan Ross had died in his arms. He had almost forgotten that she had pushed her gau toward him, at the moment had simply assumed she had wanted to show him she was

Buddhist. But now the fingerprints told him she had fingered the latch after being shot. She could have told him her killer's name, could have explained everything with her last breath, but instead she had shown him the gau.

Glancing back at Yates, who had retreated further down the long slab that marked the opening of the crevasse, Shan opened the ornate box. There were prayers inside, rolled up in the traditional fashion, a turquoise stone, and a grainy photo torn from a book. He studied the photo with a chill then folded it again and buttoned it inside his shirt pocket.

As he reached Yates, Shan was rethreading the rope around his waist.

"You have to put it around her," the American reminded him. "Make a harness."

"No," Shan said, "I've changed my mind. She doesn't need to go down to the world anymore."

The American searched Shan's face, then shrugged. "If we took her down her body would become the star attraction in an international media circus," Yates observed, obviously grateful he would not have to spend hours carrying the body of his dead friend. "What family she had she wasn't close to," he added, as if trying to persuade himself. "She was always going to die on a mountain."

"In the Himalayas," Shan said, "half those who do are never recovered."

"I will let her friends know she died the way she wanted, doing something someone had never done, making her own rules, at the top of the world." Yates offered a melancholy grin then rose slowly, bracing himself, then turned and walked back with Shan to the dead woman. He produced a wool cap from his pocket and placed it on her head, then cupped her cold cheek in his hand. "I want her to be more comfortable than this," he declared. "I want the mother mountain to know she is here."

They carried her down to a flat slab that faced southeast and rested her back against another rock, her hands in her lap, her legs, stiff from cold, bent under her as best they could. Yates stepped back, returned to straighten her wool cap, and nodded. Megan Ross was facing Everest, meditating, as she often did before a strenuous climb. Shan thought of the strange chain of events that had brought them to the dead woman, of how he had grown close to her after her death. Ama Apte had been right, Shan realized. Ever since the American woman had died, the mother mountain had been using her. The shining light of her death had guided him to the truth he so desperately needed.

HALF AN HOUR later, his arms aching from the climb back up to the plateau, Shan knelt in one of the old rock shelters, coaxing a smoldering pile of dried goat dung into flames to boil tea. He looked up to see Yates bend into the shadows of another of the crumbling structures, probing a pile of debris, extracting several scorched sticks. The American carried them back to Shan, studying them, deep in reflection, until he finally dropped them by the smoky fire. They were not sticks, but charred remnants of a wooden crate. On one, still visible after so many decades, was stenciled the words CAUTION! AMMUNITION! in English..

Yates was already away when Shan looked up, walking the perimeter, eyes on the ground for more evidence. As he watched, the American's head snapped up and he flattened himself against a boulder, warily watching a cleft in the rocks at the far side of the plateau. Shan heard voices as he reached the American's side, then in quick succession three ringing blows that he recognized as a hammer driving a metal piton into rock.

They edged through the cleft to find four figures working hard to erect a leanto of rock and canvas against the rock face. The smaller clearing where Kypo and three men in red and yellow climbing parkas worked was sheltered on three sides by the rock face and high outcroppings, with a shallow pool that caught meltwater as it trickled from the cliff above. Here had been an inner camp, Shan realized, as he saw the ruins of several more rock shelters, imagining the scene decades earlier when it was the hidden head-quarters of the rebels. There were still vestiges of that time, a yak hair rope hanging loose from an iron hook driven into a crack in the rock face, faded paint on a flat boulder in the image of the flag of free Tibet.

Suddenly Kypo stop hammering the pitons being used for support ropes. The Tibetan spun about and advanced on Shan and Yates, the hammer still in his hand. The three men bent low behind one of the old walls, as if hiding. As they did so Shan glimpsed the red robes they wore under their parkas, which bore the logo of Tsipon's climbing company.

"I want to speak with them," Shan said.

"No. She says we must stay away from you. Both of you."

Shan followed Kypo's uneasy gaze toward the edge of the plateau, where it opened to a view of the Himalayas marching along the border to the east. Tumkot's astrologer sat near the edge of the plateau, one hand resting on a low mound of stones and earth, on which a few wildflowers bloomed. There was an odd contentment on the face of Ama Apte as she looked up to acknowledge him. "Once this was the most secret place in all of Tibet," she said. "Now all the world comes here."

Shan was about to quietly settle beside the fortuneteller when he heard the crunch of gravel under running boots behind him.

"Ever since I arrived you've wanted me gone!" came an angry voice. Yates hovered over Ama Apte's back, his face so fierce Shan braced himself lest the American try to strike the woman.

"You found out about what I was doing from Megan! You knew I was trying to find my father and you destroyed the evidence! You sabotaged my equipment, planted evidence so I would be deported. And now I find you here. It's as good as a confession! You betrayed me because you betrayed my father!"

"Your father would have been gone from here, would be alive, but for me," the Tibetan woman agreed in a tight voice, her gaze back on the horizon.

The words seemed to confuse Yates. "Then you admit it," he said in a quieter, though harsh tone.

"It's always felt as though I betrayed him," Ama Apte agreed.

"How can you live with yourself?" Yates snapped.

"I think," Shan said, fighting an unexpected melancholy, "she has only been trying to protect you, to help you." He could see the tears now, flooding down Ama Apte's cheeks. "You came to find your father, didn't you?"

The American glanced in confusion at Shan. "What are you talking about?"

"You haven't listened," Shan said. "The old hermit told us how Ama Apte couldn't flee across the glacier, that she had to be with family in the village. You told me yourself you couldn't understand what force it was that kept your father on this side of the border when he could have fled a hundred times, when his own unit was ordering him, begging him to come back."

Shan turned to Kypo, who now stood with a fearful expression by his mother. "You always wear sunglasses outside, like lots of Tibetans, because the sun in the thin air causes so many cataracts. But inside it's different. Inside you wear contact lenses, one of the only Tibetans I know to do so, lenses that probably cost half a year's income to buy."

"His eyes are too sensitive to the light," Ama Apte said in a wooden tone. "They need special protection or he will get cataracts, because of all his high climbing. So we found a special doctor in Shigatse."

"I think you only wear your sunglasses when the lenses aren't in, Kypo," Shan said. "Take them off."

The Tibetan retreated a step, glancing back toward the passage through the rocks, as if thinking of bolting.

Yates looked from Shan to the tall Tibetan in confusion. "You're not making any sense, Shan," he groused. "Kypo doesn't have anything to do with—" His words died away as Ama Apte nodded and the Tibetan lifted his dark glasses. Yates took an uncertain step toward him, looking him in the eyes, unable to speak for a long moment. "Jesus!" Yates gasped at last. "Oh Christ." He leaned closer to the Tibetan, in disbelief.

Kypo's eyes were blue.

Ama Apte bent over, racked with a sob. She made an effort to rise, seemed sapped of strength. There were no words from any of them, there seemed to be no words to speak.

"We always felt safe here," Ama Apte finally said. "For months our band kept telling ourselves we could always safely escape from here across the border if things went badly. Even when the enemy soldiers became better organized, got better equipment and began climbing higher, this ridge was inaccessible to them. They had no helicopters then, and the resistance moved so quickly, hid so easily that this ridge was ruled out as a possible hiding place because everyone was certain it would take ropes and hours of work to move up its face. Only our friends knew of the secret passage.

"In the end there were less than two dozen of us. The Americans were shutting everything down. Samuel said that if he went back they would send him home to America, said it was only his remaining on this side that kept the Americans connected to us." Ama Apte paused several times to scrub tears from her cheeks. "He would make jokes about how we would build a little house of stone and logs in a valley where no one ever came and invite the yetis for dinner on festival days." She stopped and abruptly pulled a weed from one of the clumps of heather at her side.

"The solders came as we were finishing breakfast. They killed five of our band before we knew what was happening. Some fled up into the ice field. We killed most of those in the first wave but they kept coming, a full company or more. I shouted at Samuel to run to the ice field and hide, and he grabbed my hand and we began to move up the trail. But I was shot in the leg and fell, hitting my head, knocking me unconscious. When I awoke it was late afternoon, and no one was left but the dead. My face was covered with blood. They had left me for dead. Samuel was there beside me, riddled with bullets. He had thrown away his rifle because the magazine was empty. He had an empty pistol in his hand."

"It isn't possible," Yates murmured, his voice still full of disbelief.

Ama Apte slowly unbuttoned the neck of her shirt and pulled out her gau. "In all these years," she said, "only Kypo has seen what my gau has held." But she opened it now, in front of Shan and Yates, cradling it against the wind. There were several rolled up papers, traditional prayers. But on top of them were two yellowed photos. The first was of a young Dalai Lama. The second, tattered from much handling, was of a smiling Samuel Yates, holding a young, beautiful Ama Apte, Mount Everest peering over their shoulders.

Chapter Sixteen

SHAN LOOKED UP at Chomolungma and saw a huge slab of snow and ice career down the side of the mountain. Tectonic plates were crashing together below their feet. This was the place where worlds were shaken.

"It was never supposed to end that way," Ama Apte said, looking up at Yates with wet eyes. "It was my fault that he died."

"I think," Kypo interjected, "it was my fault." He understood that her pregnancy had slowed her down, had made it impossible for her to flee with Samuel Yates.

His mother reached and grabbed his hand. "Never! You were the one good thing that rose out of it."

"My uncle," Yates said, scrubbing at his own eyes now, "told me there was an unusual joy in my father's letters at the end." He turned and embraced Kypo. The Tibetan, embarrassed at first, awkwardly returned the embrace. Yates looked back at Ama Apte. "But where is he?"

"Two others came back from hiding in the ice field," the Tibetan woman explained. "I told them it wouldn't be the way of Samuel's people, to be disposed of like the others. They helped me to scrape a hollow, bring gravel and some soil from the foot of the glacier. I brought heather, though it has always struggled to grow."

Yates acted as if he had just seen the rock-covered mound at his feet for the first time. He sank to his knees, extended his hand to one of the spindly flowers that grew out of it. "He's here?" he said, his voice twisted in confusion. He ran his hands over the grave. "He's here. You knew him," he murmured to the woman. "You knew him better than anyone. But you tried to have me thrown out of Tibet," he added in a confused tone.

"Megan didn't tell me everything, only that you were looking for evidence of the old resistance," the astrologer replied. "I thought you were one of those reporters who came through from time to time to stir things up about the past, write something that just rekindles the anguish. I wanted you away. But then I saw your face at the camp, up close for the first time, and I thought I was looking at your father. Then it became even more important that you go because if you were anything like your father you wouldn't stop until you were confronting the people from the past, and you would never know how dangerous they were until it was too late."

"You put his cross on that altar," Yates said.

Ama Apte nodded. "He and I would go there sometimes on the seventh day, on his Sundays. I would pray my way, and he would pray his."

The American placed his hands, palm down, on the mound. "I never expected it to be like this."

"What did you expect, Na-than?" Ama Apte asked in a tentative voice. She pronounced the name tentatively, with a gap between the two syllables, as if trying it on for size.

Yates shrugged. "I don't know. I wanted to say goodbye, to be able to say I understood him. He was always behind me, looming like a ghost, as if we had unfinished business."

"He took you to the unfinished business," Shan said, gesturing to the two Tibetans.

Yates replied with a small, sad grin. "All these years, if only I had known, I could have—"

The shots came as two quick successive cracks and echoed off the rock face. Kypo grabbed his mother, trying to push her against the mound but she resisted, squirming away, leaping up and running toward the large clearing beyond the outcroppings. Shan was three steps behind her.

The coats of the three monks had been ripped open to expose the robes they had tucked underneath. Constable Jin wore a victorious smile as he paced in front of the monks, who stood in a line flanked by the two truck drivers who had assaulted Shan and Yates. Ama Apte slowed as she approached, then halted and silently complied as Jin aimed his pistol at her and gestured her toward the rock wall behind the monks.

The constable greeted Shan with an enthusiastic nod. "Comrade Shan! Imagine this. A few hours prospecting in the mountains and I strike gold!"

The larger of the Manchurians, with gray strands of hair blowing at the edge of his wool cap, glared at Shan, as his younger companion watched the pistol in Jin's hand with a ravenous expression.

"These men are sought as witnesses to the murder of Minister Wu," Shan ventured. "No doubt you will be commended for bringing them to Major Cao."

Jin acted as if Shan had told a good joke. "My new friends and I are thinking more along commercial lines. We live in a free market economy now, I hear."

"Your new friends," Shan shot back, "killed Director Xie of Religious Affairs."

"The official view," Jin countered, "is that these monks committed that crime."

Shan moved closer to the constable. "It's a remarkable thing, Jin, when the truth starts to come out in a case like this, a little trickle becomes a sudden flood. Everything changes in an instant."

"What are you saying?"

"I am saying that Public Security has all the evidence it needs," Shan lied. "They will soon know the truth about these two truck-drivers. When they're arrested they will sing like birds and you'll be just one more conspirator. Worse, a law enforcement official who turned corrupt." Shan mimicked a pistol with his fingers, pressed it to his head and pulled the trigger.

"Shoot him!" the older Manchurian snapped. "Shoot him and dump him with the other."

"The other?" Shan asked. "So you did help dispose of the American woman."

"Megan Ross is climbing somewhere," Jin said in an uncertain tone.

"She was murdered with the minister. She is in the gully behind you."

Jin took a step backward, aiming the pistol alternately at Shan, then at the monks. For the first time he appeared worried.

"Give me the pistol you fool!" the older trucker barked. As he spoke his companion jerked something shiny out of his pocket, flicking it with his wrist. A long narrow blade, a switchblade, appeared inches from Shan's face.

"All we need are the gaus," grunted the Manchurian with the knife.

"No," Jin said. "They won't give up their gaus."

The oldest of the monks nodded. "We have blessings."

The Manchurians guffawed.

"You are not able to force us," the monk continued.

"We can force you with a bullet in your head," the older man snapped.

"No," the monk said calmly. "I don't think you understand." The youngest monk reached inside his clothes to extract the over-sized lotus covered box Shan had seen at the base camp, opening it inside his coat, out of the wind. He produced a cylinder of paper fastened with a strip of red silk, which he unrolled for all to see. It held a drawing of a scorpion, with sacred words in Tibetan script running along its appendages.

"What the hell is that?" one of the drivers sneered.

"A protector charm," came Ama Apte's voice. She approached Jin again, was only a few feet from his back.

"The night before those police came," the young monk explained in an earnest voice, "our abbot went into his chambers and made this, speaking words of power over it. He only had time to make three. If he had made more, the others would be safe now."

"What the hell are you talking about?" the older driver demanded.

"The charm," Shan said with foreboding, "is against injury from demons." He remembered his first confrontation with the monks in the depot tent, how frightened they had been of him, how they had clutched their gaus.

A frown creased Jin's face as he stared at the charm.

"Fuck your mother!" the young Manchurian spat, and lunged for the constable's gun.

As Jin dodged, Ama Apte leaped at the truck driver, pushing his arm down, causing him to twist about, slamming her shoulder with a fist, knocking her down so she gripped his legs. Then, strangely weakened, she let go. For a moment they all froze, looking at the Tibetan woman in confusion. Then she twisted, her hand to her shoulder, and they could see the knife embedded in her flesh.

Kypo, nearest the man who had stabbed her, crouched, about to spring, but then with a blur of motion Yates was on the man, hammering with his fists, slamming a knee into the man's belly as he doubled over, clenching his fists together and pounding them into his head. As the Manchurian crumpled to the ground Shan prepared to block the attack of his companion. But suddenly Jin's gun was aimed at the older Manchurian.

"I am the constable of this township, damn it!" he shouted in an uncertain tone. "No more!" He swung his gun back toward Shan and Yates. "But we *are* taking these monks with us."

"No," Shan stated. "Your new friends are just leaving. They have less than twenty-four hours left."

"Twenty-four hours?" Jin asked as the older driver pulled his gasping companion to his feet.

"Go down with them and try to collect a bounty and you'll be arrested. Public Security knows about the yellow bucket that summons them, and has the license number of their truck. Law enforcement isn't as efficient as people think. It takes about twenty-four hours for the ownership and drivers of a commercial vehicle to be verified. Major Cao will have sent in the information just after daybreak. By this time tomorrow every border station, every police officer in Tibet will be watching for that truck." He spoke to the Manchurians now. "Your only chance is to leave Tibet before then. That's a lot of hard driving, but you might make it. Get out of Tibet and keep going. Mongolia always needs trucks."

"Not without what we came for!" the older man snarled.

"When they catch you," Shan replied in a level voice, "they will separate you. One of you is guaranteed a bullet in the head."

"One?" the younger driver asked.

"They will work on you both, separately, with wires and blades and mechanics tools, later with chemicals. The one who talks first, providing evidence against the other, will get fifteen or twenty years' hard labor. The other will be executed in less than two weeks. One of you will talk, it's just a matter of which one." Shan fixed the man with a meaningful gaze. "You're still young, you can make a new life after fifteen years."

The two Manchurians glanced at each other uneasily.

Shan looked up at the sun. "Of course by the time you get back to your truck you'll have maybe twenty hours."

"Fuck your mother," the older man spat again.

Shan said nothing, just pointed at the man's companion, who had begun running toward the passageway down the mountain.

As he watched the second man disappear into the rocks a frightened moan rose from beside him. Jin too had been watching the fleeing Manchurians, had ignored Ama Apte, lying on the ground beside him. The Tibetan woman, a long stain of blood spreading down her sleeve, had struggled to her feet. She was suddenly behind Jin, the switchblade at his throat. She grabbed the gun from the terrified constable and tossed it to Kypo. Her son quickly popped out the magazine, walked closer to the gully and tossed it in, then threw the gun into the rocks near the passageway. Jin's face twisted in confusion as Ama Apte released him. He looked at the monks, then at Shan, as if help. "This fortuneteller is crazy!" the constable gasped.

"Before she was a fortuneteller," Shan observed, "she was a soldier for the Dalai Lama."

Ama Apte grinned, then loosened her grip to let Jin slide away.

"We're going to have some food," Shan announced to the crestfallen constable, gesturing his companions to the smoldering fire of goat dung and old crate fragments. Jin cursed and peevishly walked in the opposite direction.

"I can't believe you let the Manchurians run away like that," Yates complained as the others moved to the fire.

"I told them it would take twenty-four hours to track their truck's papers. At most it will take twelve. They might get a few hours' north of Lhasa, that's all."

They ate in an unsteady silence, Kypo tending his mother's wound, which had begun to bleed profusely. "She has to go down to the lower elevation, to the village," Yates said.

Shan nodded agreement, then began silently checking the soles of the monks' boots.

"What are you doing?" the American asked.

"She has to go down," Shan said. "But they cannot."

With a grimace Yates looked up at the rough icebound landscape above them, then glanced at the climbing equipment they had left by the gully. "There's a hundred ways to die up there."

"The trail on your map goes all the way over," Shan pointed out, with an expectant glance at Kypo.

The Tibetan nodded. "It's the route of the sherpas who come across without papers. Tenzin took it last month. There's a cliff on the Nepal side but it has a hidden goat path down it."

"There're border patrols," Yates argued. "Helicopters that drop off snipers."

"And there's also fog and heavy wind and snow squalls. We can deal with the weather better than they can."

"These monks don't know anything about climbing," Yates said, shifting to English.

"They seem to know," Shan replied, "a lot about surviving. They have to go now. More will come for them."

Ama Apte spoke from her seat on a rock, obviously struggling against the pain of her wound. "The mother mountain watches. She will protect you."

Yates stared at the Tibetan woman for a long silent moment then stepped to her, cradled her in both of his arms before turning to Shan. "The mother mountain will protect us," he repeated, then pulled out his map. "But I don't know how far it is. And it's nearly twenty thousand feet at that pass. We have no oxygen."

"I came across that way," the youngest monk declared, "years ago. I was born in Nepal. From here it is maybe four hours, no more."

Shan studied the towering glacier with foreboding. It was a killing field, with crevasses covered with brittle windblown crusts, jagged spires of ice, expanses of treacherous, loose scree. *We should rest first*, he was about to say, when he spotted Jin standing on one of the flat outcroppings near the edge of the little plateau. He had taken out his much reviled radio, and was speaking into it. Jin might not get a bounty for turning in the monks to Public Security, but he would gain enough glory for the promotion and transfer he so desperately wanted.

"Go!" Shan shouted to the monks, pulling the youngest to his feet and pointing toward the distant pass. "He's calling in soldiers!"

By the time Yates and Shan had hurried Kypo and Ama Apte to the passageway and gathered up their equipment the monks were already past the winding gravel path that led to the ice and were on the glacier itself. Shan cast a worried glance at Kypo and his mother, then ran desperately to catch up with the monks, fearful that one would fall and break a bone, ending all chance of escape. He had reached them and was explaining how they must use ropes to connect themselves when the crack of a gunshot split the thin, chill air.

They turned to see Jin at the trailhead, shouting something that was lost in the distance. But there was no mistaking the threatening way he shook his fist at them, or the object he held in his other hand. He had retrieved his pistol and found more ammunition in his pack. As they watched, Jin took off at breakneck speed in pursuit of their little party.

THEY MOVED AT a brutal pace, jogging when they could find purchase in the swales of gravel that sometimes defined the trail, slowing to creep around crevasses that opened unpredictably beside them, pausing to study Yates's map and compass when the young monk, their only guide, hesitated in selecting the route.

Steadily upward they climbed, one foot in front of the other, squinting against the glare, fighting gusts so abrupt they were sometimes caught off balance and pushed backward. The rising spring temperatures had brought a treacherous softening to the ice in spots, exposed swaths of bare gravel elsewhere. For the first hour the monks softly chanted a barely perceptible mantra as they walked. But eventually the lack of oxygen took its toll, and they conserved their breath.

Tiny, sudden snow squalls drove crystals of ice and snow against their unprotected faces. Shan and Yates exchanged agonized glances as the two older monks began to audibly wheeze, knowing that at any moment one of them might clutch his head and burst into the moans of pain that signaled cerebral edema. They stopped often, watching for Jin, consulting Yates' map after the young monk fearfully announced he no longer knew where they were.

Three hours later they stopped, spent, gasping in the thin air, passing around Yates's water bottle, the only one left, scooping handfuls of raisins from a bag the American had stuffed into his pack at the warehouse. Shan's heart thundered as they moved, not only from the altitude but also from the knowledge that they had reached their limit, that they were demanding that their bodies perform beyond endurance, the condition when death took many climbers. They had two pairs of gloves among them, which they alternated wearing, and Shan's fingers were growing stiff from the cold. The hardest, highest part of the climb was still ahead.

They did not speak as they kept ascending, sometimes slipping until a hand reached out to assist, never able to maintain the same gait for more than a few steps, sometimes creeping along the side of ice crevasses with no way of knowing if the lip would crumble under their weight.

As the wind ebbed and the clouds cleared, each man's eyes lingered on the summit of the mother mountain Chomolungma, so close it seemed they could reach out and touch it. They had grown so used to the groaning and cracking of the glacier that only Shan looked back toward a particularly sharp retort to their rear.

Impossibly, Constable Jin was there, less than half a mile away, waving his arms again, not at them but toward the mother mountain, as if he had something to say to her. Then Shan heard the low, metallic ululation that brought terror to so many Tibetans.

"Down!" he shouted reflexively, then he realized the helicopter, rising along the north col of Everest, was too far away to see them. He turned to borrow the American's binoculars but Yates already had them trained on Jin.

"He's lost his pack," Yates reported. "He doesn't have his radio."

"We must go!" Shan urged the monks, "quicker than ever!" When the helicopter crew gave up the wider search they would likely fly to the head of the pass and work a pattern down the glacier. The bright parkas of the monks would be like beacons on the white surface.

They ran, slipping, sliding, falling and scrambling up again. Jin came on relentlessly, jumping recklessly over jagged shards of ice, skidding down low slopes, increasing his speed whenever he saw them pause. Shan stopped looking back, stopped listening for the helicopter, willing himself and the others on, trying with increasing despondency to understand if the next dip in the ice field marked the end of the pass or just another undulation in the glacier.

Suddenly it was over. The oldest of the monks stumbled, then slipped on a patch of ice, wrenching his ankle, crying out in pain. Shan and Yates bent over him, examining the sprain, then Yates handed Shan his pack so he could carry the monk on his back.

"In the name of the People's Republic, I arrest you," came a ragged voice behind them. Jin stood ten feet away, his pistol leveled at them.

Yates lowered the monk to a boulder in a standing patch of gravel.

The shreds of Shan's last hope blew away in the chill wind. Here was the end. With the monks in custody, Cao would create the confessions he needed to execute Tan. Shan had a shuddering vision of himself standing with his hands on the wire fence of the yeti factory, shouting his son's name as Ko gazed blankly out his window.

"A drink," Jin gasped to Yates. "Give me your water." He was shivering from the cold, his heavy uniform coat torn in several places.

Instead the American extracted a pencil stub and a scrap of paper. He braced a leg against another boulder and wrote, then extended the paper to Jin. "What you need is this," he declared. "Give me your gun and you can have it."

"You don't think I'll shoot them?" Jin demanded. He was half delirious with fatigue.

"They do have those charms," Yates observed in a conversational tone. Shan stared at him, beginning to suspect that the American also suffered the effects of the high altitude.

Jin swung the gun toward the monks, wildly firing a shot. A shard exploded off the rock on which the injured monk sat.

"See?" the American said with a shrug. He held the paper up. "I'm offering you a different kind of charm, and I'll throw in my coat. For the gun and your coat."

"My coat?" Jin rubbed his temple, staring at the American in confusion.

"I know them. With my note they will help you. But wearing the uniform of the Chinese government will mean a cold welcome. And by the time you get below these monks better be your best friends."

Jin turned to follow the American's gaze past his shoulder. His jaw dropped. He glanced from the American back to the valley below, to a compound of colorful tents sprouting lines of prayer flags half a mile below them. His face contorted with emotion, then lit with excitement and he began to peel off his coat. They were above the Nepali base camp. They had crossed the Chinese border.

The American's instructions to the monks were quickly pre-empted by loud cries from the youngest monk, who hurriedly explained where they were, that he knew many of the sherpas, how there was a monastery only a day's walk from where they stood. A moment later Jin had exchanged coats with Yates and handed him the gun, which the American tossed away.

Jin paused by Shan after he had helped the injured monk to his feet. "On the trail that day, I saw the Manchurians twice. They came back up the trail after I passed them, demanded that I ride on and find the mule with the body and bring it back, said if I didn't forget what I saw, they would find me and kill me." He glanced at the monks and lowered his voice. "They were the ones who killed the monk that day. He appeared out of the rocks and tried to stop them from taking the body on the mule. I was already moving down the trail by then, there was nothing I could do." The constable offered an apologetic shrug, then marched away to his new life.

"We should go with them," Yates said in a worried voice as

they watched the others descend toward the narrow concealed goat trail that would take them down to the Nepali base camp. Jin was bracing the injured monk on his shoulder. "If we cross now we'll be on the ice in the dark." He studied Shan a moment. "Go down, Shan," Yates urged. "It will mean freedom for you, a chance to start over."

Shan silently tightened the laces of his boots and began jogging back up the treacherous trail.

AN HOUR AFTER sunrise the next morning they reached Jomo, waiting in another of Tsipon's trucks. A grim determination had settled onto their faces. They had passed an uneasy night on pallets in the hermit's cave, having reached it after sundown. Neither man gave voice to their increasing certainty that Tan would have been already tried, that Ama Apte and Kypo would have been seized by the knobs as accomplices and transported to the gulag before they could reach the town.

Yates watched the high ridge as they pulled out onto the road. They had been bone weary by the time they had reached the cave, barely able to stand, but Dakpo had fixed them roasted barley and tea, waking them after they had collapsed onto pallets to make them eat. Then he had presented Yates with a small drawstring pouch.

"When I heard about the Yamas being stolen and returned after being opened up," the hermit said in a hesitant tone, "I knew it had something to do with Samuel. I had been apprenticed to an artisan at the gompa when I was a boy and knew about such statues." The old Tibetan seemed strangely nervous, and poured himself more tea before continuing. "Samuel and I spent many hours sitting on ledges above the highway counting army trucks. He spoke about the problem of getting letters home. That's when we came upon the idea. We had sent one of the statues and had enough letters for another when . . . when the world ended.

"I kept them for a year, then sealed them in an old Yama statue and kept it with me all these years. Then after the murders I took it to the Yama shrine, in case the soldiers searching the mountains found me here. Yesterday I went back for it, and opened up the bottom."

"I am sorry, Dakpo," Yates said, "for what I did to the Yamas."

The hermit smiled. "I have been saying prayers with them. They will heal."

Yates, choked with emotion, upended the pouch. Letters from forty years before tumbled out, thirty or more rolled and folded pages.

Shan watched in silence as the American, wide-eyed, began unrolling letters and reading them. But soon, unable to fight his fatigue, he leaned back on a pallet and accepted the hermit's offer of a thick felt blanket. In his fitful sleep he awakened more than once to hear snippets of conversation between the two men sitting at the brazier. The reticent hermit had been full of words that night, and in the languid warmth of the pallet Shan listened from the shadows to tales of an energetic American teaching Tibetans to dance and sing, of Samuel Yates leading secret missions to recover artifacts from several gompas on the eve of their destruction by the Youth Brigade, of a week during a lull in the fighting when Samuel, Ama Apte, and several others tried to track yetis, of the intense affection between Samuel and Ama Apte that had somehow sustained their little band when they were living on half rations.

As the embers were dying, their faces lit only by a dim butter lamp, the hermit had leaned toward Yates, his voice now that of a wise old uncle. "We sat up all night once guarding a pass as a long line of monks moved past, fleeing to the south with artifacts from their temples, fleeing to freedom. I will never forget it. The moon was full, the ground covered with snow, monks cradling bronze deities in their arms like babies, yaks carrying bigger statues, a long single file of red robes and yaks that stretched across the snow. As the last one disappeared the mother mountain began to glow from the distant sunrise, even though the stars were still overhead. Samuel spoke some words toward her, like a vow to the mountain. He said when it was over, when things were right again in the world, he would bring back his son, because he wanted his son's soul to be filled with the power of this place."

Chapter Seventeen

A SOMBER AIR had settled over Shogo. The residents walked down the newly swept streets with solemn, nervous expressions, staring straight ahead. Three shiny black limousines were parked by the municipal building, a sober reminder of the dignitaries who had come for the trial.

Shan slipped into the hall in the center of the building among the workers who moved tables and chairs inside. A table draped in black with three large wooden chairs behind it sat on a raised platform at one end of the room, with another chair for witnesses at one side, an easel bearing a map of the region at the other. A large portable portrait of Mao on heavy canvas had been unrolled and hung behind the judges' table. As several workers fussed with weights at the bottom to stretch it straight, others brushed it clean. Less than three dozen chairs were arranged in two sections in front of the table. The pageant, as Shan expected, was to be a private affair.

A door opened at the side, admitting several well-dressed officials, led by a strutting Major Cao, who gestured and pointed, playing guide to the visitors. He stopped in midsentence as he saw Shan standing there in his tattered, soiled clothes, his face bearing the grime of hard travel. Shan did not move, did not change expression, though he could feel the heat of Cao's fury from across the room.

The major turned to a lieutenant and was no doubt about to order Shan ejected when a small dapper figure in a plain black suit broke away from the group of dignitaries. Madame Zheng said nothing as she approached, but followed Shan when he turned and stepped out into the corridor.

* * *

THE THREE FIGURES quietly entered the clinic, not waking the receptionist, asleep again at the door. Shan went straight to the bed at the rear of the patient ward, where the driver of the bus still lingered, his layers of gauze now replaced with adhesive plasters, playing his electronic games. Jomo found a broom and swept the floor near the bed of the only other patient, a sleeping middle-aged woman wearing an oxygen mask. Madame Zheng, as Shan had previously cued her, picked up a tray of bandages and medicines by the entry and carried it to a table by the rear wall, then lifted the medical chart on the soldier's bed.

The patient's expression grew uneasy as Shan approached. He stuffed his electronic game under his blanket and pressed back in his pillow as if expecting to be struck.

"About time to be released," Shan observed.

"Tomorrow, or the next day," the corporal eagerly replied. "My barracks knows I'm here. I called them a couple of days ago."

"We were thinking some exercise would do you good. A little ride, a little walk, a little talk."

"Talk?"

"About the dead bodies you saw that day."

"That minister?"

"The other."

"You mean the blond one," the soldier said.

Zheng leaned forward, her head cocked toward the man.

"The Westerner," Shan nodded.

"The one who disappeared. The ghost."

"We are," Shan declared as he handed him the clothes that hung on a peg by his bed, "great believers in ghosts."

A quarter hour later Shan and Madame Zheng stood in the shadows of the garage bay at the rear of Tsipon's warehouse as Jomo eased the long green sedan into the bay and shut the door.

It took less then two minutes before an angry figure in a business suit and tie burst through the side door.

"Idiot!" Tsipon raged. "I need that car! The trial is starting!"

Jomo dangled the keys in his hand, then retreated to the opposite side of the car, the keys dangling in his hand. "You sent men to kill my father."

"Don't be ridiculous. Get in the car. You can drive me."

"They were two truck drivers, outsiders. You paid them to do things, illegal things." Jomo stopped at the trunk of the sedan.

Tsipon looked at his watch. "You're talking nonsense, Jomo. I am your employer. I am your father's landlord."

As Jomo opened the trunk Tsipon's expression darkened. He darted toward his mechanic with a snarl, then halted abruptly when Jomo threw a bulky object at him, hitting him in the chest. A large yellow bucket.

Shan shifted forward in the shadows. Jomo was only supposed to have told Tsipon he knew about the yellow bucket.

"I wondered about the bounties offered for the monks, how they would be paid. The drivers I asked said the manager of the truck stop was to be shown the gaus. The manager and I had a chat late last night, locked in the workshop. I persuaded him to tell me that when he saw the gaus he was supposed to leave a note in a yellow bucket by the road. I didn't have to ask who owned the bucket. My father, then the monks. Trying to kill holy men must be habit forming."

"Your father has been trying to get killed for years," Tsipon said in a brittle voice. "He's unstable. The only reason he stays out of the yeti factory is because I protect him."

Shan took another step forward as Jomo's eyes began to smolder. "I remember when I was young. You retrieved us out of the gutter. You would bring things. Food. Blankets. And he always had money to run the tavern, even when he couldn't pay you rent. I thought it was kindness."

Tsipon seemed to collect himself. He straightened his tie. "I was in a position to help him. You would begrudge a favor? As the senior Tibetan Party member in the county I had an obligation to help with his rehabilitation."

"The help never came from a cooperative or a collective or the county welfare office. It came from you. And every time you made a delivery there was a bottle of alcohol with it."

"He had great pain. A lot of past that needed to be erased."

Jomo gazed into the trunk, reached in to extract a tire iron before shutting it.

"There's work to do, Jomo," Tsipon reminded him. "Drive me to the trial and come back for an inventory."

"People never talk about the members of the resistance. It's as if they were old demons whose names are taboo. I remember paintings of those demons. My father kept some in a chest. All around the big demons were little demons. You were one of the little demons."

"Ridiculous. The rebels were criminals. Worse, traitors."

"You were from a shepherd family in the high ranges, where the pastures have been closed by the border patrols. But what you don't know is that some of those shepherds moved their herds to valleys west of here, past old Tingri town. I drove over there yesterday, while you were at your new hotel. I asked the old ones there about you. I found an old woman who knew your family. They are all in India, like you have said. They all fled when the last rebels were destroyed. Except you stayed. You came to town. You were made the head of the agricultural collective. A teenager, as head of the collective. Who appointed you?"

"You're a fool. I don't have time—"

With a single powerful swing of the iron Jomo smashed the back window of the sedan. "Who appointed you?"

Shan took another uneasy step toward the pool of light by the sedan. Jomo was drifting far from their agreed script.

"I can have you back in the gutter by tonight!" Tsipon snapped.

Jomo inched forward, heaved the iron again and smashed the rear passenger window. "Who appointed you?"

Tsipon backed away toward the door he had come in, seemed about to flee when a long iron rod, one of the scraps Jomo kept for repairs, materialized out of the darkness, pressing against his belly.

"I remember your family," came a raspy voice. Gyalo stepped out of the shadows, using the piece of iron like a staff for support.

The color drained from Tsipon's face. "You were dead!" he gasped.

Shan took another step forward, prepared to leap between Gyalo and Tsipon. Jomo had dropped Shan off at the municipal building, with instructions to meet at the infirmary, but he had obviously sensed Shan's intentions, and taken a detour to the stable. Shan never would have expected Gyalo to have enough strength to reach the warehouse but Jomo's words seemed to have given him new life.

"Good, simple people," the former lama continued, both hands grasping the iron rod. "They tended the wounded, gave us milk and meat when they had some to spare. They had boys, two adolescents and a teenage boy I recall, all of whom helped, even in bringing in the bodies of our dead to the hiding place below the glacier, where I helped prepare them for the next life." The old Tibetan stood tall and straight. He seemed to have lost several years of age.

"You were nothing but a beggar with a baby boy when I found you," Tsipon continued, "both half dead of the cold. I gave you life."

Gyalo's hoarse laugh ended in a hacking cough. "I was a business proposition for you. You needed a floor show, a clown to attract customers to your new tavern."

As Tsipon took another step toward the door the iron rod slammed against his leg, nearly knocking him off his feet. "There was only one person who wielded political power in this county when you were made head of the collective," the former lama observed. "You were doing business even then, even as your own family was fleeing to be with the Dalai Lama. You gave Wu the resistance fighters and she gave you a prestigious appointment."

"I told you it was Ama Apte. She traded her village for—" Tsipon's lie died away as Shan finally stepped out of the shadows.

"It is possible," Shan said, "that a man of your particular talents might have found a way to survive even when the people in this county finally learn who betrayed them that day. You could always find another lie, offer more jobs to quiet them down."

"Exactly," Tsipon said, as if Shan was offering to mediate. "You understand these things, Shan, you're from Beijing. Tell them. The Youth Brigade was always going to win. I had nothing. It was over. Why shouldn't I try to salvage my life? Everyone had to pick up the pieces and move on."

"Everyone else helped their families and the monks," Jomo pointed out. "You helped the Youth Brigade."

Tsipon glanced uncertainly at the mechanic, then turned to Shan as if for help.

"For you it was always about business, like Gyalo said," Shan said. "Back then, and the day Minister Wu died."

Tsipon inched toward the door. "All that is over with. They have their murderer. I'm a witness, you know. Interfering with a witness is a crime."

"What I couldn't understand was how you knew Megan Ross was going to get into that car with the minister, that she was going to reveal her discovery that Minister Wu was also Commander Wu of the Hammer and Lightning Brigade if Wu did not stop her development plan. But then I realized Ross had told you about it herself. You had been with Tenzin and Ross one night at the base camp, and she had told you about her plan. She trusted you, because you had helped with her clandestine climbs. Except Ross didn't know your own connection to the Hammer and Lightning Brigade, didn't know that exposing Wu would most likely mean exposing you. And in any event you recognized that Ross was going to destroy all your own business plans. The international community would never deal with Minister Wu once word leaked out. She would be ruined as Minister of Tourism, she would have to resign. The Compact would have instant credibility. Not only would you lose your protector in Beijing, you would lose the expansion of your hotel, probably lose business because of decreased climbing expeditions.

"Ross must have spoken to Wu at your hotel, maybe gave her a glimpse of one of the old photos that you had tried to keep out of the library, to convince Wu to let her ride up the mountain with her. But the minister didn't get in the car right away, she ran up to her room. Because she had to get the gun she had borrowed the night before, to gibe her old lover Colonel Tan. She was going to kill Ross. But since you were there, she told you to do it."

"Me? Why would I be there?"

"Because you had your own private business with Wu. You had to speak about her secret stake in your guesthouse, about how she was going to block applications for any other new hotels and grant you an exclusive license to supply the trekking parties."

"The high altitude has finally baked your brain, Shan."

"Megan Ross didn't understand that everything you did was a negotiation. You didn't help her because she was a pretty American, you did it because she could help you with your business. She moved money in and out of China for the expeditions she worked on. You asked her to leave some outside of China, in Hong Kong, in a special account. She mentioned it in her journal, the day before she died. She was going to look into the reason for your request. She might have already found out," Shan ventured, "that the account was in the name of Minister Wu. It would have taken one phone call to Hong Kong."

"She never said anything to Wu—"

"So you *were* there. She never had time to say anything because Wu had already decided she had to die, for exposing her role with the Red Guard. But you realized as soon as you pulled the trigger that by forcing you to shoot the American Wu was making you a slave, not a partner. You knew difficult questions would be asked about an American who died in the minister's presence. If the questioning grew too difficult she would have given you up as the killer, would have exposed you as the traitor to the Dalai Lama's fighters."

Tsipon seemed to shrink. He looked at Shan as if he was the only one who could understand. "She always wanted more. First it was ten percent of my new hotel in exchange for the permit, then when she arrived at the hotel she demanded twenty percent of the expanded hotel. She was always the commander and everyone else a lowly soldier. I worked on that hotel for years. But that morning she called it *her* hotel." Tsipon looked forlorn, though not beaten. He looked at his watch. "I'll be missed. The trial is about to start."

"We've already started the trial, Tsipon."

"What are you talking about?"

"For the real murderer of Minister Wu, and the one who arranged the murder of Director Xie of Religious Affairs."

Tsipon took a quick step toward the door and grabbed a large wrench from the workbench, slamming it down on Gyalo's restraining rod. He reached the door, flung it open and froze. Two Public Security soldiers stood in the entry.

He looked back toward Shan, real worry entering his face. "What is your game, Shan? You have no authority."

Shan stepped to the light switch by the garage door and illuminated the bay. The color drained from Tsipon's face as he saw the diminutive woman sitting in a chair by the rear wall.

"I think you know Madame Zheng," Shan observed. "Surely someone in the Party must have told you she is the presiding judge of the tribunal? Did you know she has been visiting your office in your absence, looking at your records?"

Tsipon hesitated a moment, unable to disguise his fear now. "You have no evidence!" he snarled at Shan.

"We have your own words explaining your motive."

"What I said was nothing!" Tsipon glanced uncertainly at Jomo. "Give me the keys! I'll drive myself."

Jomo did not move.

"Shooting Tenzin in the chest, like Ross," Shan continued, "must have seemed like an inspired trick at the time. If you were to substitute the bodies, the new victim would have to be shot, since the soldiers had already reported two dead of bullet wounds. But you had thrown Tan's gun away before you encountered the mule on the trail. The holes you left in Tenzin's chest were huge, no match for any weapon Public Security was familiar with. Forty-five caliber, the Americans call those bullets, big enough to stop a horse. Or a mule. No one here would have such a weapon. It was an impossibility that Cao chose to ignore in order to make his case. But Megan Ross explained it all to me."

Tsipon grew pale. "She's gone. You never spoke with her."

Shan reached into his pocket and produced the folded photo he had taken from Ross' gau. "She had taken this with her to prove you were connected to Wu, as leverage to get both of you to listen and comply with her terms. She didn't know she would be implicating her own murderer." Shan held the photo up for Tsipon to see. The Tibetan reeled backward, as if losing his balance.

Shan tossed the photo on the hood of the car. *The People celebrate the final victory in Shogo*, said the caption. Names were printed below. A much younger Tsipon was there, with Wu and two other officers. Each face was upturned as they fired into the sky. Each held a heavy pistol, a forty-five caliber, captured from the American stockpiles.

"You can't prove I was there with Wu!"

Shan gestured into the shadows and the young patient from the infirmary emerged. "You thought all the soldiers involved that day had been reassigned, unreachable. But one was forgotten, because he was sent for medical treatment. The corporal was the driver of the bus, and bravely walked up to the murder scene despite his wounds. He saw much that day. It was negligent of you not to arrange his transfer too."

Shan had warned the soldier to keep quiet, to let Tsipon assume he could testify not only about Megan Ross being killed, but also that he had seen Tsipon at the scene.

"And we mustn't forget that account you set up for the minister."

"Speculation. You have no idea—"

"You probably weren't aware that there are special anticorruption protocols with all the banks in Hong Kong. You should have chosen Singapore. Madame Zheng will have all the names on the accounts by tomorrow."

"That was business as usual for people like Wu," Tsipon protested. "You know Beijing, everyone—." Tsipon's words died away as he looked at Madame Zheng, Beijing's special emissary.

There was movement behind Tsipon. The two soldiers were at his side now. One glanced at Madame Zheng, who nodded, then began fastening manacles around Tsipon's wrists.

"You killed them," Shan said, "you killed them both and let me be dragged away to take the blame."

"You're nothing but a gulag convict," Tsipon muttered. "Worthless to society. They were always going to take you for something."

Strangely, Tsipon tested the manacles, stretching their short chain tight as if he did not think they could be real. His expression as he looked up at Shan wasn't anger but stunned disbelief. "They can't run the mountain without me," he ventured in a hollow voice.

"Negotiate, Tsipon," Shan offered. "Keep negotiating. The government's priority is to pursue every scent of corruption, especially when high levels are involved. A new murder trial would be messy since Americans would have to be brought into it now. Madame Zheng came here not for the murder, but for the corruption investigation against Minister Wu. Who knows? You may have a chance to escape a bullet if you cooperate on the corruption charge and give evidence against those truck drivers."

"Once every Tibetan in this county wanted her dead," Tsipon said to the floor. "They would have stood in line to pull the trigger."

More officers appeared, guns at the ready, eyeing the Tibetans suspiciously. Madame Zheng snapped a command and they lowered their weapons, then surrounded Tsipon and turned him toward the door. "They can't run the mountain without me," he repeated in a bleak voice as he was led outside. They were the last words Shan heard him speak.

Shan turned to speak with Madame Zheng, but she was gone. He found her in her limousine, the rear door open, waiting for him. "I need a report from you," she declared after he climbed in and the car began to move. "The kind you would have written ten years ago."

"I was sent to the gulag for writing reports like that."

She looked him over. "There's nothing more we can do to you." For the first time Shan saw the trace of a grin on her face.

"Cao will not like it."

"Major Cao will be returning to Lhasa within the hour."

Shan looked out the window and considered her request. "I need doctors, real doctors," he declared. "I want one to be sent to Tumkot village, to care for a woman who was stabbed. I want another one sent to the yeti factory. I will give you the patient's name. And the monks from Sarma gompa. I want them all released."

Madame Zheng extracted a small tablet and began to write.

Chapter Eighteen

THE SUN WAS edging over the mountains when Tan and Shan were met at the entry to the yeti factory by the facility's senior officer on duty, a plump Chinese knob still displaying crumbs from his breakfast on his uniform.

"We're here for one of your inmates," Tan announced.

"I'll need orders."

"His name is Shan Ko," Tan stated impatiently.

"That one?" the officer replied with a sneer. "He's in isolation. I couldn't release him even if I wanted to."

The man's defiance was like a salve to Tan's wounds. Shan watched as a familiar fire rekindled in the colonel's eyes. For a moment Shan almost interjected himself, to save the officer the torment that he knew was to follow but the man cast him a dismissive, arrogant glance and Shan stepped back to give Tan full rein.

Like a bird stretching a wing that had been broken, Tan lifted his arm and with a perverse zeal gestured the officer into a vacant office and closed the door. Shan could not hear many of the words they spoke, but the tones of the knob were unmistakable, shifting quickly from petulance to anger to fear. When Tan emerged from the room, the officer sat at a desk, muttering orders into a phone. He looked as though he had been hit by a truck.

Five minutes later Ko was wheeled toward them on a hospital gurney, his cardboard box of possessions at his feet. With a stab of horror Shan saw that half his scalp had been shaven clean. Then a quick inspection showed no incisions had been made. His son's eyes were shut, his breathing shallow, beads of sweat on his brow. Shan whispered his name and shook his shoulder, with no response.

They stood alone in the entry, Tan's fury having scattered even the security guards. After a moment the colonel gestured toward a sign that said PROCESSING and helped guide the gurney down the corridor. The admissions office adjoined a double glass door leading to the parking lot, where two ambulances sat, their drivers leaning against one, smoking.

Tan found the only uniformed man in the office, a junior officer who seemed to be in charge. "I want an ambulance and driver, now. With a full gas tank."

"It's not permitted to take the ambulance out of the county," the knob protested, stepping into Tan's path.

"You'll get it back when I am finished with it," Tan growled, fixing the man with his icy stare. "I am Colonel Tan, military governor of Lhadrung County. Keep talking and I'll take you back with me."

The man swallowed hard, glancing in confusion at Shan and the gurney, then let Tan pushed him aside.

Minutes later they were on the highway, heading east, Tan in the front passenger seat, Shan on a metal bench beside Ko's narrow bed in the rear compartment. It would be several hours' drive to Lhadrung.

Shan watched the high peaks slipping into the distance, his eyes fixed on the indentation on the horizon that marked the valley where Tumkot lay. He had taken supper there the night before, a peaceful, intimate meal with Ama Apte, Yates, Kypo, and his daughter. As Yates had presented a compass and climbing boots to his new niece, Kypo and Shan had helped Ama Apte, her arm in a sling, serve the meal. When they began to sit Ama Apte had arranged two more plates on the table and as if on cue a figure had appeared in the doorway. Jomo had stepped inside with an anxious expression, his half-hearted protests ignored as Ama Apte silently led him to a seat beside Kypo. Then she had gone to the door and pulled in someone else, a figure who struggled against her at first, then allowed himself to be led, limping, across the floor. Gyalo, washed, freshly bandaged, and looking strangely serene, was wearing the robe of a monk.

"It's time you met Tumkot's new lama," Ama Apte had announced as she settled Gyalo on the bench beside her.

AFTER THE FIRST hour Tan ordered the driver to halt. He motioned Shan out of the compartment to join him on a small knoll by the road. Shan watched in confusion as Tan gathered dried grass and twigs into a pile. Tan lit a cigarette, then with the same match ignited the small fire before reaching into his tunic and producing a familiar dog-eared file. "They took this from my office without my permission," he observed in a flat voice. He ripped off the first page in the bound file, a description of Shan's last disciplinary proceeding in prison, and dropped it into the flames. He extended the rest of the file to Shan like a solemn offering.

Shan accepted the file with a trembling hand and stared at it in silence. "Do you have a pen?" he asked at last.

A question lit Tan's face, but he handed over a pen without a word.

Shan sat on a rock with the file in his lap. He carefully wrote his father's name on the file and folded down the corners like an envelope before lighting a small cone of incense.

Somehow Tan understood. "A message to the dead."

Shan nodded. "I haven't been entirely honest with my father when I send him messages. He thinks I have been on some kind of pilgrimage with old Tibetans these past years. It's time he understood."

Tan did not reply, just gathered more wood to build up the fire before Shan dropped in the file.

"Congratulations," the colonel said as they watched the last ashes float away toward the mountains. "You have officially become nobody."

As they returned to the ambulance, Tan climbed into the back to sit by Shan. The colonel straightened the blanket over Ko, grasping his still-twitching hand when he finished. The colonel would feel the effects of his torture for weeks, Shan knew. They glanced awkwardly at each other then looked out the small window at the peaks of the Himalayas retreating on the horizon.

"On the road crews," Tan ventured after a long time, clearly struggling to get his words out, "allowing the workers to wear their malas and gaus wouldn't interfere with their labor."

Shan pondered the words, taking a minute to piece them together. Tan was speaking of the prisoners in the gulag labor camps he oversaw in Lhadrung, and of the prayer beads and prayer amulets that had always been denied the Tibetan prisoners.

"No," Shan agreed in a tight voice, "it would not interfere."

Tan nodded without expression. "I will issue an order when I return." His gaze drifted back toward Ko. "And I will see he has a place in the prison infirmary."

"No," Shan said. "He needs to be in my old barracks."

"You mean with the old lamas."

"The ones who are left."

The colonel nodded a sober assent.

They grew quiet, and arranged blankets on the bench for cushions, then leaned back. Shan checked on Ko every few minutes, his heart growing heavier as he found no change, no sign that Ko would emerge from his coma. Gradually his fatigue overwhelmed him and he fell into a fitful sleep, punctuated by dreams of Ko spending the rest of his life gazing into the distance with empty eyes. When he woke, the Himalayas were only shadows on the horizon and there was a pile of damp gauze bandages where Tan had been wiping his son's brow.

"Three hours more, maybe four," the colonel observed. "We can stop for tea and—" Tan's words died away.

Shan followed his surprised glance toward the bed and met Ko's weak but steady gaze, lit by a crooked grin. Then, with unspeakable joy, he watched as his son's hand reached out and closed around his own.

Author's Note

In July 1942, in one of the most adventurous missions ever devised by a wartime President, Franklin Roosevelt dispatched the colorful grandson of Leo Tolstoy, Ilya, on a year long journey to Tibet to explore supply routes and initiate a dialogue between the United States and the Dalai Lama. On behalf of Roosevelt, Ilya Tolstoy presented both a gold chronograph—which the Dalai Lama reportedly still uses today—and an offer of support if hostilities were to reach the roof of the world. Geopolitics had undergone a seismic shift by the time the Chinese occupied Tibet ten years later but the offer was not forgotten. The older brothers of the Dalai Lama, Gyalo Thondup and Thubten Norbu, started a new dialogue with Washington which, when the Chinese began open warfare, gave rise to the covert missions that underlie the plot of this novel.

It is not surprising that this American connection to the Tibetan resistance has been absent from our history books—the secrecy that shrouded it was so complete that the Tibetan trainees first arriving at Camp Hale in the Colorado Rockies did not even know what continent they were on. The facts of that mission trickled out over decades, and only recently, as records have at last been declassified, has its full scope become known. Dozens of Tibetans were trained in America to use weapons, codes, radios, and parachutes, then dropped back into their native land from civilian American planes that sometimes flew hundreds of miles inside Tibet. While these airdrops lasted five years, the American support continued for seventeen years, during which secret Tibetan radio teams kept the Americans connected to the Four Rivers Six Ranges resistance army. The final remnants of that army of irregulars, vastly outnumbered and always on the run from Chinese troops, did not lay down their arms until 1971, when the Dalai Lama finally sent a taped message asking them to stop throwing away their lives for a futile cause. For those who wish to more closely follow the path of these freedom fighters and the Westerners who helped them, John Kenneth Knaus' *Orphans of the Cold War: America and the Tibetan Struggle for Survival* does a masterful job of relating their intriguing, tragic, and ultimately inspiring, story.

The Everest region was one of several areas of operations for these resistance fighters, and it is not difficult to imagine some of those who faded into the local population later reconnecting with the new breed of foreigners who came to scale the Himalayas. The slopes of the mountain the Tibetans call Chomolungma and the surrounding peaks hold a drama all their own, poignant not just for the daring of mountaineers amidst the majestic landscape and the grisly remains of climbers that are readily visible below the summit but for the juxtaposition of the wealthy foreigners who annually descend on the mountain with local Tibetans whose annual income would not even pay for one of the foreigners' boots.

Repression by the Red Guard and the Chinese army was particularly brutal in this area due to both the active resistance and the region's special spiritual significance to Tibetans. The poet saint Milarepa, one of Tibet's most revered figures, spent his last years there a millennia ago. It was also on these slopes that some of the most important Buddhist teachings were first offered by the Indian lama Padampa Sangye. For centuries life in the region centered around its many temples, monasteries, and hermitages, nearly all of which have been destroyed.

Like many parts of modern Tibet the Chomolungma region is deeply out of balance. It is no wonder that its native inhabitants are hesitant about the twenty-first century, when their exposure to the global economy and the West consists of foreigners paying massive fees to Beijing for the right to climb their sacred mountain. While the Chinese government has taken a step in the right direction by establishing a refuge below Chomolungma to preserve its wildlife, far greater effort is needed to address the needs of the indigenous human population of the region.

As in all my Shan novels, I have taken great care not to exaggerate the political and social plight of the Tibetans. The systematic destruction of Tibetan culture begun by Beijing fifty years ago has accelerated in the past decade. The inmate population of the hard labor gulag camps is swelling with Tibetan political dissidents and monks; that system also includes hospitals for the treatment of criminal "disorders." Monks are expected to kowtow to political commissars of the Bureau of Religious Affairs, loyalty raids are indeed conducted on monasteries, and Tibetans have learned that the only holy places that are safe are those that remain out of sight of their government. As real life wheelsmashers roamed through Tibet following the most recent outbreak of protests, the future planned for these peaceful, compassionate, and deeply spiritual people was summed up by a senior official of the government that invaded their land two generations ago: "The Tibetan people," he declared, "must accept that the Communist Party is their new Buddha." But as the Tibetans have heroically demonstrated, neither their future nor their spiritual leaders will be determined by government decree.

Eliot Pattison